Not My Type

JAEL

authorHOUSE®

AuthorHouse™
1663 Liberty Drive
Bloomington, IN 47403
www.authorhouse.com
Phone: 1-800-839-8640

First published by AuthorHouse   5/13/2011

ISBN: 978-1-4634-0140-5 (sc)
ISBN: 978-1-4634-0139-9 (hc)
ISBN: 978-1-4634-0138-2 (e)

Library of Congress Control Number: 2011907075

Printed in the United States of America

Any people depicted in stock imagery provided by Thinkstock are models, and such images are being used for illustrative purposes only. Certain stock imagery © Thinkstock.

This book is printed on acid-free paper.

Dedication

This book is dedicated to Juanita Toles and Lucille Walker.

Both women have been instrumental in helping me to become a better wife, mother, and above all, a better woman.

Acknowledgments

WITHOUT THE TRINITY, THIS BOOK WOULD NOT HAVE BEEN POSSIBLE

Thanks to my husband D.W.Sr., your support proved to be invaluable.

Thanks to my son, DWJ 23, your input is greatly cherished. You're going to make some blessed girl a great husband.

I would like to offer up my heartfelt thanks to my editor, Teresa Barton, who sacrificed her time and used her many talents to edit our first book.

Thank you Tina for the many hours of discussion and arguing over the scenes, characters, and the final outcome of the book; you have the patience of a saint.

Thank you to my sister Chantay, and her two Daughters, Shantia and Shannell, my brother Anthony, as well as my good friend Twilla, for allowing me to use them as guinea pigs in the reading of this book.

Thanks to the current Lions of Judah- Derek, Mariah, Vincent, Gina, and Isaiah, the future is yours. Make wise decisions.

JAEL *on facebook*

Prologue

The date was February 11, 2005. Noah Phillips, along with his two sons, watched as the casket holding his wife, Colleen, was slowly lowered to her final resting place. There were no tears falling from his eyes. All hope for Colleen was now gone. He prayed that she had truly accepted Christ, but he secretly had his doubts.

Where did he go from here? He'd made a vow to God that he would not marry again unless she was handpicked by God himself. Right now, he had no desire to remarry. There were more important issues that he had to correct. He needed to be in isolation with God, to become the man God needed him to be. He knew that from this day forward he would teach what God said to teach. He had allowed his wife to make him weak. No more! He would boldly proclaim the Word. He looked at his sons. Adam hadn't cried, but that didn't surprise him. He hadn't been particularly close to his mom. Colleen had always seemed to resent him. Jacob, however, had been grieving for his mother way before the cancer had taken her life. He had always been a momma's boy. He loved his father, but he'd been extremely close to his mother. Noah glanced at Kara. Thank goodness, Jacob had his fiancée to console him. They were to be married in September of this year. Jacob was spoiled, but Kara loved him despite his self-centeredness. He turned and walked steadily away from the grave. He ignored the looks of pity and walked purposefully towards the waiting limo. His two sons followed, one full of grief; the other not knowing what to feel.

☦

Marlena Porter held her sixteen year old son's arm as her husband's silver casket was lowered into the cold, hard February ground. She was still in shock over his brutal unsolved murder. It felt like a dream. No, more like a deep, dark nightmare. She hadn't cried a single tear. She and Shawn, her husband, had been married for nineteen years, but most of that had been in name only. They'd lived in the same house, but he'd been leading dual lives. One she thought she knew, and the other, she knew nothing about. He'd never really participated in their lives. Their only child, Kaod, was a star athlete at the local, public, high school. He'd grown up resenting his father for a variety of reasons. He saw his father daily, but they rarely had conversation. Dad gave him money for school, clothes, sports or whatever he'd needed, but no time or love. Marlena had tried to make up for Shawn's bad parenting skills. Initially, she'd tried to get her husband involved, but to no avail. She'd sacrificed all of her time. Kaod had become her life, after God. Whatever she learned, she taught Kaod. Wherever she'd gone, Kaod was there. Nothing, other than God, was more important than her young son. As a result, Kaod had become well-rounded and respectful of those around him, including his father. If all went well, he was on his way to receiving a full ride scholarship to Ohio State. She glanced at her son. He was in need of a father, but Marlena had no real desire for male companionship. She could do without the nonsense, pain, and aggravation. There was no way she was ever getting married again, unless God instructed her to do otherwise. February 11, 2006 was a day of sorrow and freedom for her. She clutched her son's arm and walked back to the waiting limo.

Chapter One

(April 2, 2009) Noah Phillips glanced around the conference room. He was bored stiff already and the speaker hadn't even started talking. He could tell, just by the man's posture, that he would be one of those dry, monotone speakers who could put an entire audience to sleep in five minutes flat. Why had he signed up to attend this seminar? Noah could feel someone staring at him. He turned and met the eyes of a very attractive redhead. She smiled and he nodded in response. Sorry, not interested he thought. He preferred to do the chasing and she was clearly signaling caught. He avoided any further eye contact hoping she'd get the message. Out of the corner of his eye, he saw someone enter the room just before the speaker shut the door. That was one of his pet peeves, late- comers. "Be early for heaven's sake," he thought to himself. He glanced at the late arrival and smiled. Maybe, late in this case was okay. She was the only black attending the conference. He turned to get a better look. She was pretty, gorgeous was more like it. Noah zeroed in on her fingers. She was not married or engaged. He caught her eye and smiled. The look she gave him clearly stated "not on your life". He grinned. This conference might not be so bad after all.

☦

Noah watched her the entire morning. He was glad that Valerie had come with him to take notes because he hadn't paid attention at all to the boring guest speaker. Watching this woman interact with those around her was more interesting. She'd "denied access" to at least three other men who'd tried unsuccessfully to get her attention. She was definitely more intriguing than "monotone man". When the speaker announced break time, the majority of the attendees charged out of room, no doubt trying to revive themselves. He put his hands behind his head and continued to observe the latecomer. There could only be three reasons why this woman remained impassive toward these would be suitors. She was involved, didn't date white men, or she was a bonafide Christian. He was bound and determined to find out which one.

✝

Finally, the day was over. Noah stood to his feet intent on introducing himself to the late comer, but noticed several others already engaged in conversation with her. He could tell, by the look on her face that she was less than enthused with whatever they were saying. She kept glancing at her watch as though she had to be somewhere. At last, she was alone, but before he could make a move, the redhead stopped him and made it abundantly clear that she was available. Noah, if he hadn't been before, was absolutely not interested now. She was much too bold and aggressive for his taste. In his opinion, it was a weak male that liked this type of woman. They didn't have to do much or take any chances. She did all the work for them. It was like going hunting or fishing and having someone already have the prey set out for you. You didn't have to fire your rifle or throw your line into the water. All you had to do was select which deer or fish you wanted, and go on home. It was already dressed, cleaned, and cooked. It might seem okay; however, in the long run, it made you weaker. You'd eventually lose all the necessary skills needed to hunt or fish for yourself. You'd lose your status as a legitimate hunter or fisherman. Noah, in the same way she'd made herself available to him, made himself unavailable to her. He excused himself, intent on talking to the latecomer, but she was nowhere to be found.

Marlena Porter stepped out into the fresh April spring air. This time of year always seemed to bring out the best in her. She couldn't explain it, but the longer spring days gave her body a vitality that the other seasons didn't. Maybe, it was the additional hours of daylight. Whatever the reason, she thanked God for it. A quick glance at her watch indicated that she had only twenty minutes to meet her best friend, Tina, at their favorite restaurant. "Where in the world were her car keys?" she thought, as she slowly did a thorough search of her small, brown, leather handbag. No keys were there. Feeling mildly frustrated, she headed back inside the hotel and straight to the small, but elegantly furnished conference room. She located her table.

When she didn't find them on the table, she looked underneath. Maybe a good citizen had turned them in at the front desk she reasoned. Marlena turned and nearly collided with someone. She put her hands out to steady herself and they came in contact with a solid muscular chest. She looked up and found herself gazing into light smoke-colored, grey eyes.

She quickly apologized, "I'm sorry."

"Don't be. I like you running into me. Besides, I have a hunch that you're looking for these," a very attractive Caucasian man replied in a husky voice, as he held up a set of keys. "I had a strange feeling that some poor helpless female would be lost without them. So I, being the heroic man that I am, picked them up and waited for the damsel in distress to return."

Marlena bit back the urge to say something less than polite to her self-made hero of the moment; instead, she smiled and expressed her thanks as he dropped the keys into her outstretched hand. Men, she noticed, always felt the need to see themselves as rescuers and women as having to be rescued.

"What made you think that this was a woman's key ring? It could have just as easily been a guy's," she wondered aloud.

"I have the gift of discernment," he teased.

He let out a chuckle of amusement as he watched her beautiful brown eyes roll in disbelief.

"You don't believe me, huh? Well, what if I told you that you have a son who thinks pretty highly of you. Would that make a believer of you?"

Marlena's expressive eyes met his. For one brief moment, he saw what could be described as uncertainty in them, but it quickly disappeared when she realized that he had read the inscription on the back of the small golden cross attached to her key ring. Her son Kaod had given her the key chain as a Mother's Day present the year before. It simply read "Virtuous Woman of God, y Son". There hadn't been enough room on the small cross to inscribe anything else. She'd thought it to be one of the most precious gifts that anyone had ever given her besides the gift of Christ and the birth of her son.

"You've read the back of my cross," Marlena stated in a slightly amused voice. A voice she generally saved for her mischievous students; but, for some reason she found herself caught up in this little game he was playing. "Good heavens," she thought to herself, "this white guy is flirting with me and I can't believe I'm flirting back."

This was so unlike her. She had never been attracted to Caucasian men.

She performed a cursory check of his fingers and spied the plain gold band indicating his marital status. Suddenly, she was annoyed; however, before she could put the little flirt in his place, a soft and very feminine voice interrupted their exchange.

"There you are Pastor Phillips. I see that you've located the owner of the keys," the trendy younger blond noticed as she glided into the room. "Now, if we don't hurry," she continued, "you'll have to reschedule your lunch appointment with the Jaspers."

"Pastor," Marlena gasped in shock.

She wanted to desperately put this pastor in check. He certainly deserved it, but he was God's responsibility not hers. She said a silent prayer thanking God for sending in Barbie, or whatever her name was, before she could say something she might later regret. Grateful for her keys, she darted out of the conference room followed closely by the couple, who she had mockingly dubbed "Ken and Barbie".

Marlena reached her car and was sliding into the driver's seat when "Ken" tapped lightly on the window. What does he want now she thought as she rolled down the window. She didn't bother to hide her impatience.

"Yes?" she asked in a curt voice, pointedly staring at his ringed finger with disdain.

"Ken" didn't seem to notice. With a sheer audacity she had never before encountered, he smiled his most charming smile and said, "This is the first time I've ever done anything like this, but would you do me the honor of having dinner with me? By the way, what is your name?"

For the first time in her adult life, Marlena was rendered speechless. Here was a married man, a pastor no less, asking her out on a date. Was she supposed to feel somehow honored that "His highness" had selected her as his first would be affair? Had she come across as desperate? For sure the "end times" are upon us she reasoned.

The only word she seemed capable of speaking was, "Cinderella." She quickly rolled up her window, slammed the car into drive, and sped out of the parking lot

Pastor Noah Phillips watched in confusion as the gold Jaguar carrying his "Cinderella" swiftly fled the hotel's parking area. He wasn't quite sure what caused the driver's angry reaction. One minute, they were, at least he thought they were, enjoying a very mild flirtation inside the conference room; then, abruptly, he'd sensed a change in her from slight flirtation, to annoyance, and then to obvious anger. He was sure that it had nothing to do with Valerie, his secretary of the last three years. Sure, she was an attractive lady, but it was very apparent that they enjoyed a strict working relationship. He wasn't attracted to her, and to his knowledge, neither was she attracted to him. Well, if it was meant to be, the Lord would direct their paths to cross again. Funny, he thought, he'd never really been attracted to black women or African-American women, or whatever the heck the current politically correct terms were these days. During his college days, he'd dated women from various backgrounds and cultures. He had even kissed a few of them, but nothing had ever become of it. This woman, however, had intrigued him the moment he'd seen her enter the seminar. She'd come late (which he hated) and dressed in casual clothing. She'd worn peach-colored pants with a matching top. The color accented her brown, coffee skin tone. She wasn't overly tall. He guessed about five feet six inches, perfect for his six feet two inch frame. She was slightly plump, but in all the right places. Her face had fascinated him the most. Her mouth was sensual with the whitest, most perfectly aligned teeth he'd ever seen. Her smile lit up the entire room. She had big, beautiful, brown eyes that were framed by the longest, thickest, black eyelashes imaginable. A man could lose himself in those eyes. She seemed to speak with some sort of accent that he couldn't quite figure out. For the first time since the death of Colleen, his wife of twenty-three years, he found himself deeply drawn to another woman. He chuckled when he remembered how she'd systematically dismissed at least three other guys at the conference. There was something about her, and it didn't matter to him that she was black. Noah could imagine his all-white congregation gasping for air at the thought of him even being drawn to a woman of color, let alone him courting her. He chuckled to himself at the picture, but quickly sobered when he realized that courting this woman was exactly what he had been interested in doing.

Valerie's soft voice cut into his train of thought. "Ready to get going?" she asked. He looked up and felt a sudden flash of embarrassing heat at the thought of his secretary witnessing his crash and burn.

Valerie giggled with old-fashioned womanly delight.

"If you're going to ask a woman out, try taking off your old wedding ring. Any woman with a set of decent morals would find your devotion to that ring deeply offensive and a great big turnoff."

Pastor Phillips gave a hoot of laughter. At least, he now understood Cinderella's mood change. Digging in his pocket, he pulled out his car keys and tossed them up in the air whistling. "I'll follow you. Getting back into this courting thing is very invigorating."

As Valerie eased her car onto Interstate 77, she looked in the rearview mirror and saw her boss's sleek red Maxima following her. She had been thoroughly surprised at his obvious interest in "Cinderella". He'd watched her the entire morning. It was fairly obvious that the unknown woman had intrigued her boss; especially, since she'd shown no interest in him or any other guy. It looked as though Pastor Phillips was going to have to "court" someone else.

☦

Valerie glanced at her boss as they headed into the restaurant. "By the way Pastor, no one calls it courting anymore. It's called dating."

A long moment had passed before he gazed at his ringed finger and for the first time ever, took off his wedding ring and slid it in his pocket.

Noah looked at his secretary, smiled, and stated in a deeply serious tone, "I don't date. I court with the intent of marrying."

Valerie wisely kept her opinions to herself, but she quietly prayed for God to send her pastor a "Virtuous Woman of God".

Noah absently rubbed the finger where his wedding ring had been. God was telling him it was time to move on. Colleen had been gone for four years. He finally felt ready to live again. He took a deep breath and smiled to himself. Cinderella had awakened Prince Charming. He no longer needed his wedding ring to symbolize his grief. He was ready to live life again.

Chapter Two

Marlena frowned as she slid into the booth across from her best friend Tina. "You won't believe what just happened to me!" she exclaimed and launched into her story. When Marlena had finished, her best friend declared that this Pastor, whoever he was, should be immediately whipped and thrown out of whatever church he belonged to. The two women laughingly agreed and wondered aloud about what type of woman could love a man with such low morals and what appeared to be no fear whatsoever of God.

Their server, a young attractive man in his early twenties, smiled as he took their order. Tina triumphantly reminded Marlena that she had to pay for the meal again. The women had long ago agreed that whoever arrived late for their monthly luncheons at Chingo's had to pick up the tab. Marlena pled innocent due to extenuating circumstances, but her friend was not buying it. Finally, and with much pretended arguing, Marlena agreed to pick up the tab and then made a beeline directly to the ladies room.

As she washed her hands, "Ken's" face invaded her thoughts. She couldn't seem to put that arrogant man out of her mind and there were still two more days left in the seminar. Maybe, he'd be too embarrassed to show up. Somehow, she doubted the man had any shame. She could skip the last two days, but her job had already paid in full for her to attend and they couldn't afford the loss. The school was run on a tight, shoestring budget as it was. She'd just have to gut it up, Marlena reluctantly decided. She washed her hands, applied more lip gloss, and headed back to their booth.

She heard Tina's animated voice in conversation with someone. Marlena smiled as she turned to enter the booth. The smile froze on her face as she recognized none other than "Ken and Barbie" in friendly conversation with her best friend. Stunned, she could do nothing but stare dumbly at the unwelcome surprise.

Tina, oblivious to her friend's silent plight, and not realizing she was fraternizing with the enemy, began to make polite introductions, "Marlena, meet Noah Phillips and his secretary Valerie. Noah and Valerie, meet my best friend, Marlena Porter."

"Hello, Marlena. Or would you prefer that I call you Cinderella?" Noah laughed with delight.

"Who the heck is Cinderella?" Tina asked. Finally, realization dawned and Tina laughed incredulously. "This is the married pastor you were talking about?"

Marlena was never more thankful to be black then at that moment. She was sure that none of them could see the hot color in her cheeks. She peeked from under her long dark lashes at "what's his name" and felt her face grow warmer when he chuckled knowingly. She made a mental note to choke her best friend at the next available moment.

Tina, in her usual blunt manner, asked Noah if he was still wearing his old wedding ring to ward off the lady buzzards. Then, noticing his newly vacant finger, boldly asked if he had found a new love interest.

Noah's reply surprised even himself, "I think I have a very attractive reason for removing my ring."

Tina was intrigued. "Is it someone I know?" she prodded unashamedly.

The silence was deafening. Marlena refused to look at Noah and instead willed her eyes to stay glued to their server who had thankfully chosen that second to refill their drinks.

Noah favored Tina with a smile before he purposefully stared straight at Marlena. "I think you know her very well."

Everyone's eyes shot to her. Even their server, who was gallantly trying not to listen, stared at Marlena. "Please Jesus, if you truly love me, let the Rapture happen right now!" she silently begged with closed eyes.

But when she opened her eyes, Tina, Noah, and Valerie, and even the server, were still staring at her. She pretended not to notice and narrowed her eyes threateningly when Tina politely asked the dynamic dual to join them.

Noah bit the inside of his jaw to keep from howling with laughter at the not- so-subtle look Marlena directed at her friend. He pretended to consider Tina's invitation and slid into the booth next to Marlena. He casually turned and faced her.

"Sorry, Cinderella, but I already have a lunch date that I've kept waiting for far too long. Will you take a rain check?"

Marlena remained silent and gave Tina a look that dared her to open her mouth. She was not going to give him the satisfaction of a reply.

He chuckled and stood. Noah and Valerie, after what felt like an eternity to Marlena, mercifully excused themselves and went to meet with the Jaspers who had reserved a table on the other side of the crowded restaurant.

Tina barely waited for them to be out of earshot before she announced, in a voice loud enough for the entire restaurant to hear, "Girl, that man has got a serious thing for you. I saw the way he looked at you. It's too bad you don't date white men because he is 'hot'. He won't be on the market long. If I were single, I would definitely make myself available to him."

Marlena tried to hide behind the menu.

"Keep your voice down," she whispered harshly. "You can have him. He's not my type." She hoped her voice sounded more confident then she felt.

Tina's reply was crisp and hit home as only a best friend's could. "Why? Is it the color of his skin? I'm white, and you and I are more like sisters than any white or black women we know. Besides, I think you need to get a new type. You're the one that's always telling me that in Christ, there is no division. Noah is a good man and a strong Christian. Maybe you should be looking for that type. You seem to forget how your husband, who happened to be black, treated you before he died. I'm sorry," Tina quickly apologized when she glimpsed the flash of hurt in her friend's face. "I shouldn't have said that last little bit."

Marlena squeezed her best friend's hand. "You're right though. Maybe I am being a little shallow-minded. But to be honest, I don't think I'm ready to seriously date anyone, black or white."

"Whatever, Marlena, that won't change Noah's mind if he's decided you're the one. He's pretty strong-willed," Tina challenged. Marlena decided it was time to change the subject.

Noah listened absentmindedly to the idle chit chat. He would much rather be spending his time getting to know Marlena. That name suited her to perfection. She looked like a Marlena. He couldn't believe that she'd actually blushed. He couldn't remember the last time he'd seen a woman do that. It was refreshing, to say the least. God must be granting his approval because the likelihood of their paths crossing again was nil. Sure, there were two more days left in the seminar, but he had to be on a flight heading to Atlanta, Georgia in the morning. He would have missed the last two days of the seminar and would not have had the opportunity to find out his Cinderella's real name. He had needed his secretary there to take notes and to complete the last two days. That was the only reason Valerie had accompanied him. He was always careful to never be alone in the company of any woman. He had almost learned that lesson the hard way. Now, he wished he could cancel the trip and reschedule, but it was too late to back out. Besides, his oldest son, Jacob and his daughter-in-law Kara lived in Atlanta and they'd finally get to spend some time together.

Kara was five months pregnant with their first child. Noah smiled at the memory of holding his oldest son for the first time. He had been surprised at how small his son had appeared and frightened at the thought that a tiny life was now solely dependent upon him and Colleen. Funny, how saying her name, or picturing her face didn't hurt any more. When had the hurt disappeared he wondered? Colleen's face was slowly replaced by that of Marlena's. Noah knew within his spirit that God had severed the tie with Colleen and was urging him toward Marlena. What was it about her that made him want to live again? This was strange unchartered territory, but Noah understood that God's strength is made perfect in man's weakness. God did his very best work in him, when his own abilities were rendered useless. He was ready. He had learned to wait on God and to move when God commanded. He smiled a secret smile. He hoped Marlena was ready. If not, he'd have to drag her kicking and screaming beside him.

Chapter Three

Marlena carefully eased the Jaguar in between the SUV and Mustang. This space was the only available spot left in the entire parking area. The owners of the two new vehicles had barely left room for another car to fit. Marlena was sure it had been done on purpose so as to deter anyone from parking next to them. She thanked God for her car, but she certainly didn't worship it or go through extreme measures of protection for something that, in a few years, would lose half of its financial value. She carefully opened the door and squeezed through the narrow gap. Checking her purse to make sure her keys were there, she headed towards the hotel. This was the moment she had been dreading. She hadn't slept a wink last night. She'd kept rehearsing exactly what she was going to say to Noah when she'd see him today.

She walked confidently through the hotel doors and straight toward the conference room. As she stepped inside the room, she immediately saw Valerie who greeted her with a friendly smile. She returned the smile and briefly scanned the room looking for Noah. She breathed a sigh of relief when she didn't see him. She had begun looking for an open seat when Valerie motioned for her to join their table. Over his dead body Marlena thought and pretended not to notice. She continued looking for an empty chair on the opposite side. Where did all these people come from? She was sure it hadn't been this crowded yesterday. Believing that God was humbling her for calling Valerie "Barbie", she realized that the only vacant chair was next to Valerie. Marlena had no choice. She thanked Valerie for saving her a spot, and slid stiffly into the chair.

"Pastor Phillips won't be here today or tomorrow. He's away on business," Valerie informed her.

Marlena let out a deep breath and began to relax. God must have already forgiven her.

Noah arrived in Atlanta right on schedule. If everything worked out, he should be able to finish his meeting by noon, and spend the rest of the day and part of tomorrow with Jacob and Kara. He was really looking forward to a little rest and relaxation.

Jacob and Kara had been married for a little over three years and had desperately wanted to start a family. He was thrilled when he'd been informed that he was to become a grandpa. He knew Jacob and Kara both wanted a boy, but he would be excited to finally have a girl in the Phillips family. He and his older brother John, both had two sons each, and so far, none of their children had produced a girl. Noah grimaced when Adam, his youngest son came to mind. He clearly had no intention of settling down. He claimed there were too many things he wanted to accomplish, and a wife would just get in the way. Adam's exploits constantly kept Noah on his knees and close to God.

Noah adjusted the strap on his overnight bag and headed in the direction of the rental car agency. Stopping briefly to sign the contract, he was soon on his way. He hoped his secretary hadn't forgotten the special instructions he'd left her with. It was exactly half past ten. Valerie should be on break. He punched in her number, and waited with a smile for someone to answer.

When the conference director announced a fifteen minute break, Valerie immediately excused herself to the ladies room. She placed her BlackBerry on the table next to Marlena and in a feigned emergency tone, begged her to answer it if it should ring. Marlena agreed, and with a sigh of relief, Valerie headed towards the restroom. Pastor Phillips had better hope this little plan of his worked. She'd hate to have Marlena angry with her. She was beginning to really like this woman. Although, she still had her doubts about a serious relationship ever developing between Pastor Phillips and Marlena.

The younger generation seemed more adaptable, but she'd still been privy to a lot of racial comments and bigotry, even from them. She didn't even want to think about how the older people in their church would react. Valerie pondered what kind of ugliness would come out of the hearts of his congregation if Pastor Phillips decided to court Marlena. She smiled at his old fashioned use of the word, but had to admit that she wished other men would follow his example.

Marlena jumped slightly when Valerie's BlackBerry began ringing. She glanced toward the open door. Valerie was nowhere in sight. She hesitated, and then reluctantly picked up the phone.

"Valerie's phone," she greeted.

The voice on the other line sent her pulse racing.

"Good morning, Cinderella," a husky voice greeted back.

"Did you wish to speak with Valerie?" Marlena questioned, trying to keep her voice professional.

"No, I have the party on the line that I wished to speak with," Noah responded, imitating her voice.

Marlena laughed in spite of herself.

"This was a total set up," she accused.

He didn't bother to deny it. "Of course it was. Don't be upset with Valerie though, I threatened to fire her if she didn't go along with it."

Marlena couldn't resist laughing. "What do you want Noah?" she finally asked.

There was a slight pause before he said in a clear voice, "You!"

Marlena was glad that he couldn't see her face. This man kept her emotions in a tailspin. She decided the best course of action was silence.

"Well, if I can't have you, may I have your telephone number?" he asked, breaking the silence.

Still, she gave no reply.

"Listen, Marlena, you're making it pretty obvious that you don't want to get to know me, so I'll stop wasting your time and let you enjoy the rest of the seminar, Okay? Tell Valerie to give me a call at Jacob's later on. Goodbye, Cinderella."

Marlena heard the line go dead. In her mind, she could see Tina scowling and saying, "You need to get a new type". She located the recent calls button, took a deep breath and pushed. After the second ring, the voicemail clicked in and Noah's recorded voice said, "You've reached Noah. At the tone leave a message". She quickly left her cell phone number and hung up.

"What am I getting myself into?" she wondered aloud.

Noah sat in the rental car and prayed that he hadn't made the biggest mistake of his life by calling her bluff. He needed her to acknowledge her interest in him. He didn't want to keep playing this little game of cat and mouse. He wanted them to have a mature honest relationship and he was determined to get her to understand that straight from the start.

His phone rang and he smiled when he saw Valerie's number flash on the screen. He reached to answer it, but thought better of it. Let Cinderella have a taste of her own medicine. He clicked to the inbox and listened. Marlena's voice came through loud and clear. She'd just acknowledged her interest by giving him her number. The good Lord tells us to be wise as a serpent, but gentle as a dove. He almost called her right back, but decided to wait. He wanted them to be able to talk without time constraints.

He exited the car and walked casually towards his business meeting. He felt every bit the conquering warrior as he sensed God's pleasure in his pleasure. Spontaneous praise for God rose from deep within him. God had decided to bless him of all people. Noah stepped into the elevator, pushed the button, and began to pray a prayer of thanks.

Valerie returned from the restroom and looked questioningly at Marlena.

"It's alright. He told me that he threatened to fire you if you didn't go along with his little scheme," Marlena teased.

Valerie giggled as she sat down. "Pastor Phillips can be very persuasive when he chooses to be," she acknowledged. Then, looking straight at Marlena admitted, "I've never seen him without his wedding band. There were a lot of women who wanted him to take it off, but he never would. Yesterday, after meeting you, he just slipped it off his finger and put it in his pocket. You're the first woman he's shown interest in since the death of his wife. For him, this is serious, so please don't get involved with him without counting the cost to him. He's a phenomenal man of God and he's going to need a strong woman of God in his corner."

"Thanks for the concern, but we're not discussing marriage. We barely know each other," Marlena responded.

"You don't know Pastor Phillips very well," Valerie suggested with a warning in her voice. "Ask him about his concept of dating."

Before Marlena could reply, the break ended, cutting off any further conversation between them. Marlena pondered the other woman's comments. Again, she questioned the wisdom of giving Noah her number. After all, she was still kind of, sort of, dating Drew.

Chapter Four

Noah finished his meeting ahead of schedule. Everything went smoothly. The Atlanta based publishing firm had agreed to his terms. They were going to express the contracts to his lawyer's office the following day. He now had one more reason to be thankful to God-financial independence.

He had authored a series of popular children's books that had begun to sell so fast that the stores couldn't keep them on their shelves. He owed his success, in part, to Colleen. When she'd died, he'd exerted all of his energy into writing. It was the only thing that had kept him from losing his mind, other than God's strength of course. He had never told a soul about the books and was stunned when they'd become Best sellers. To this day, only he and his attorney knew that he was the best- selling children's author, Noah Flood.

Culver's Publishing Inc., one of the premier publishing companies in the nation, and he, had just agreed to a lucrative contract beneficial to both parties. First' Marlena comes into his life, and now, a contract with Culver's. God had managed to turn his years of weeping into joy, and all in just a couple of days. He served a mighty God indeed.

Glancing at his watch, he decided to call Marlena before heading to Jacob and Kara's. Noah punched in her number and hit the send key. In seconds, he heard the connection go through. She answered the phone on the third ring sounding a little breathless.

"Were you busy? You sound a little out of breath," he queried. "Is now a good time for me to call you?"

Marlena assured him that it was okay. They exchanged pleasantries for several minutes before Noah decided to get right to the point.

"I think you know that I find you very attractive. I'd like us to spend some time together getting to know each other. I thought we could start by going out to dinner tomorrow evening. Are you interested Cinderella?"

Marlena managed to choke out an almost inaudible, "Yes."

Boy, he sure didn't believe in beating around the bush.

"Great. I'll pick you up around 6:00 P.M. By the way Cinderella, what's your address?"

Marlena gave him her address and directions. He thanked her, and laughed off her demand that he stop calling her Cinderella.

"You're the one who told me that was your name, or have you conveniently forgotten?" he challenged. "But, if you ask me in a sweet voice and tell me that you had thoughts of me today, I might be persuaded to stop."

Marlena didn't bother to respond. She simply bid him goodbye and hung up the phone. But not before she heard laughter in the husky voice at the other end of the line.

Why did that man always manage to make her come unglued so easily? Marlena could not understand Noah's affect on her. She wasn't kidding when she said that Caucasian men were not her type. Though she was far from prejudiced, she could admit that there were certain cultural barriers that she had never wanted to explore. She could even admit that she'd never met a white man that had interested her. Come to think of it, not many black men had either.

She blushed and confessed to herself that she found Noah extremely attractive. There was something about those grey eyes of his and his curly jet- black hair. His tall height and solid build added to his appeal. She had been supremely aware of the fact that he'd been watching her yesterday. She'd assumed him to be curious, but not necessarily interested. His constant observation, without saying a word had unnerved her and had been the primary reason she'd forgotten her keys. Still, she didn't know if she was ready to seriously date a white guy. The fact that she'd agreed to go out on a date with him would definitely have her father rolling over in his grave and reaching for his whisky bottle. Not to mention the fact that the "brothers" in the Hood would "trip" for sure; especially, since she hadn't given most of them the time of day. She was aware of the fact that the majority of them already thought her to be stuck up. One date couldn't hurt she convinced herself. He would probably be so boring or one of those deeply religious types that it would be over, even before it began. White guys had a reputation for.... Before the thought was completely formed, she heard the chastisement of the Holy Spirit convicting her of prejudice.

She knew God had rebuked her. Marlena repented and began asking God to forgive her of the sin of prejudice. How could there be fellowship with Christ, if she couldn't get beyond the color of someone's skin? She had been blinded to her own stereotypical beliefs.

"Please, Lord, let me see Noah's heart rather than his skin," she whispered.

She wondered if her beginning attraction to Noah was God revealing the hidden sin that was still present within her heart. As tears escaped from her eyes, she thanked God for revealing the truth to her. Was she open to God's will for her life, or was she just pretending, like a lot of so-called Christians? Marlena understood that it was going to have to be God's way or hers. She decided, even if she didn't understand her path, that she would trust God no matter what. His son was the one true person who had sacrificed everything for her. She would not forsake Him now or ever.

Noah hung up the phone and laughed to himself. So she didn't like him calling her Cinderella, huh. He enjoyed his pet name for her and saw no reason to stop calling her that until she could admit her attraction to him. He could hear it in her voice. He also guessed that she'd been waiting for his call and had probably rushed to answer it before her voicemail could click in. She wasn't nearly as confident as she betrayed either. He'd gotten a brief glimpse of the uncertainty when he had teased her with the key ring. Noah wondered why she was so guarded. Had someone hurt her? Maybe her son's father was the cause. He already found himself becoming protective of her. He instinctively knew in his heart that one day she would become his wife. He was not living in a dream world. He understood race would be an obstacle for her, and others, to overcome. He would leave that part up to the Holy Spirit and not dwell on it. He vowed to show her Christ through righteous living. He wasn't about to back off because he needed certain questions about her answered. Noah was positive it wouldn't be easy for her, but he'd reassure her that he'd be there every step of the way.

First, he had to get his Cinderella to open up and trust him and that involved lots of bonding time. He understood, based on different studies, that females bonded by simple touch. He was definitely going to start working on that tomorrow evening. He would make sure to guide her to the car and into the restaurant with the light touch of his hand on her back. That, he was certain should start them bonding. He felt a supreme sense of peace and joy as he called the airline to reschedule an earlier flight home.

Chapter Five

Noah slowed the rental car down and turned into his son's driveway. Their split-level, Ranch-styled home looked well cared for. Before he could exit the car, Jacob, followed by a pregnant Kara, came out to greet him. Noah embraced them lovingly and complimented his daughter-in-law on how beautiful she looked. Kara thanked him shyly and excused herself to take a much needed nap. Noah and his son decided to surprise her by preparing that evening's meal. During the preparation, he reminisced about Colleen carrying Jacob and how he had pestered her continually. Initially, he would not allow her to do anything. He'd finally realized, after about the fourth month, that it was actually healthier for pregnant women to stay active than to not do anything at all. Jacob smiled at him in understanding.

Father and son resembled each other, but only in some physical ways. Both men were tall and handsome. Both had black curly hair, but Noah's eyes were a light grey while Jacob's were a startling blue. Jacob still had a boyishly slender frame, while Noah's had developed over the years. Their likeness ended there. Jacob's personality was identical to his mother's. He took everything lightly unless it pertained to him and did not tolerate change well. He'd had a terrible time adjusting to Colleen's death and still continued to view her as some kind of super saint. Noah had loved his wife with all his heart, but he had not been blind to her many faults. It was a well-kept secret, but she had strayed early on in their marriage. Noah had struggled through the forgiveness and for the love of his Christ, had never brought it up again. He believed that her desire to be a pastor's wife was ultimately what had kept Colleen married to him. He was far from perfect, and had made many mistakes, but not once had he been unfaithful to her. He fervently hoped Jacob did not have some misguided notion about Kara living up to his unrealistic and outrageous expectations of the ideal wife which were based on the false image he'd created of his mom.

☦

Kara, roused from her nap, smiled gratefully as the enticing smells of dinner drifted throughout the home. Noah held her chair and gave her a fatherly kiss on the cheek. He took his place at the table and waited for Jacob to bless the food. He was in the middle of grabbing a dinner roll, when Jacob noticed his dad's newly vacant finger.

"Dad, where's your ring? Did you lose it?" he asked.

"No, I did not lose it. I thought it was time for me to rejoin the land of the living, so I took it off," Noah calmly replied.

"Good for you!" Kara exclaimed. "I know the ladies will be lined up for miles around," she added with a smile.

Jacob frowned at Kara and turned to confront his father. "You couldn't possibly be thinking about dating. Dad, you're almost fifty years old or have you forgotten?" Jacob complained. When his complaint was met with silence, Jacob stared at Kara angrily. "You talk to him. Maybe, he'll listen to you," he sulked.

Noah had taken enough of his whining. "First of all, almost fifty does not make me old and ready to croak. I still have dreams and desires just like anyone else. Secondly, since you're making a big deal over whether or not I'm dating someone, I should emphasize that it's really none of your business; however, because you are my son and I love you, I will speak honestly. I have every intention of courting, not dating, a very beautiful woman, who happens to be black, the moment I return home." Having dropped his bombshell, Noah picked up his fork and continued eating. Silence permeated the room.

Jacob stared at his father in total disbelief. Had his father truly lost his mind? What happened to his devotion to his wife, their mother? Did he think his congregation would stand for him dating some unknown black woman? "Dad, how could you do this to Mom? You can't be serious? Do you really think people are going to be okay with this? It's insane!"

Noah looked his oldest son squarely in the eye, "Jacob, I loved your mother, but she is dead and I am alive. Whoever I choose to marry, if it comes to that, is my business. I could care less about what other people think."

Jacob stood and spoke enraged, "How could you even think seriously about dating a black woman? Kara and I will not have our child call some n…"

Before Jacob could finish his thought, Noah, with steel in his voice cautioned, "Son, you had better think long and hard about the next words you utter because words like those you cannot take back. I don't know how such hatred got in your heart, but you'd better find a way to allow the Holy Spirit to replace it with love. Now, if you two will excuse me, I think I'll spend the night at a hotel."

Kara spoke up as Noah stood to leave. "Dad, whomever you choose to marry, I will receive with open arms. You have treated me like a daughter. You're one of the finest men I know. I respect your wisdom and I, for one, will support you no matter what." Kara firmly hugged her father-in-law and then turned to look at the man she loved. "I am so ashamed of you Jacob," she proclaimed tearfully as she slowly walked from the room.

Noah stiffly faced his son. "God has blessed you with a strong wife. Go and apologize to her." He picked up his bag, took an envelope out and handed it to him. Silently he left the house and drove to the nearest hotel.

Jacob opened up the envelope and found five hundred dollars along with a handwritten note which simply read "I love you, son". He threw it on the floor and angrily sat down.

✟

As Noah lay across his hotel bed, he thought about his son's bitter response towards Marlena being black. He understood exactly why Jacob had this poisonous attitude. Colleen had felt the same way. He'd failed them both by not holding her accountable for her beliefs. As a result, Jacob was trapped in that same sin. That was how they'd ended up living in a practically all-white, suburban community. During the third year of his ministry, he'd been given the choice of shepherding an inner city church or an all-white suburban church. His wife had pleaded with him to take the position at the all-white church. So to keep her love, that was exactly what he'd done. He'd been weak and unable to properly lead his own home. Neither could he really blame her. It was her fear of people and things that were different which had caused her to be so blind. He should have helped her overcome it, but instead he enabled her by only surrounding her with people and beliefs that were identical to hers. He had been so fearful of losing his wife that he'd given in to her every wish. Even to the point of never confronting her about the open hate in her heart. He had prayed fervently for Jesus to forgive him for not being a stronger husband. As the head of his family, he was responsible for their spiritual welfare. He had grieved so long and so hard for Colleen, not out of his love for her, but his failure to truly husband her. Even today, Noah could not honestly rest in the assurance of her salvation, and for that, he still blamed himself. He'd constantly prayed that God would help Jacob with that same sin. He could see now that God had answered his prayers by giving Kara to his son, but Jacob still had to confront his own sinful heart. He smiled when he thought about the tremendous courage it took for Kara to go against her husband. Noah had sensed that same strength in Marlena, a strength that stays strong in the face of adversity. Her big brown eyes invaded his thoughts as he finally drifted off to sleep.

Chapter Six

Noah's plane touched down at precisely a quarter after four. He had exactly one hour and fifteen minutes to shower, dress, and pick up Marlena at her home. He had chosen a small, comfortable restaurant for their first outing. He'd made sure it wasn't a place where he was well known. He knew Marlena wasn't prepared for that yet and to be perfectly honest, neither was he. They needed some alone time to discover each other without a lot of past pressures or cultural differences interfering. Noah, thankful that he'd only packed the overnight bag, bypassed the baggage terminal and headed straight to his car.

He wasn't unaware of the blatant stares he received from the opposite sex. On occasion, he'd even gotten a couple of cat calls. He could understand, though not sympathize with, why men didn't feel the need to commit themselves to a monogamous marriage relationship. Women were freely offering to fulfill their every physical desire. When had women become so sexually aggressive? He knew it was a snare sent from the pit of hell. Scientific evidence continued to reveal that the more women a man slept with, the less able he was to bond with his partner. The evidence was even more compelling for women. Besides, he thought, he was an old-fashioned kind of guy. He still preferred to do the hunting. Jumping into his car, he realized that he'd have to rely on Christ to help him catch Marlena.

Tina chatted excitedly with Marlena. "I'm glad you came to your senses and decided to give Noah a chance. Once all the single women on the prowl around here get the word that he's dating again, the poor guy will never have a moments rest."

Marlena looked at Tina.

"What was his wife like? I'm not talking about her looks or anything like that. What kind of person was she? I mean, she had to be pretty devoted to him if it's taken him this long to go out again."

Tina hesitated before answering, "I really didn't know her that well."

Marlena looked closely at Tina, "What is it that you're not telling me?"

Tina shrugged her shoulders and said, "To be honest, I didn't care for her too much. I hate to speak evil of the dead, but I personally think she was a racist. You know, just by some of the things she said. That's partly why Charles and I stopped going to church. If we wanted to be around that kind of crap, we could have gone out to the local bars and had a better time."

Marlena had known Tina long enough to know there was more to the story. "What else?" she prodded.

"I probably shouldn't be the one to tell you this," Tina started, "Charles will kill me if he finds out I told you, but you're my girl. Anyway, I know that Colleen cheated on Noah."

Marlena stared wide-mouthed at Tina.

"And how do you know this?"

"Charles and I saw her with a certain guy, and they weren't exactly holding hands," Tina finally confided.

"Are you absolutely sure it was Colleen?" Marlena stammered.

"Yes, you think just cause she was married to a pastor that she wouldn't fool around? Girl, sometimes you can be so naïve. Most of these women wanting to be the next Mrs. Noah Phillips, just want the title and prestige. Colleen was one of them. I think she liked being the 'Pastor's wife' more than she ever liked being a Christian. And yes, I am positive we saw her getting her groove on, and from the sounds of it, they must have been having a good old time," Tina added.

Marlena shook her head in disbelief. Tina was full of drama, but she wasn't a liar.

Tina suddenly remarked to Marlena, "You know, I do think Noah found out. He left town for a couple of weeks, supposedly to attend some school or another, came back, preached a damn good sermon on adultery, and I never heard another thing about it. I think he scared her straight."

Both women began to laugh hysterically.

"Seriously, Marlena," Tina said. "Noah is a good man. You two were made for each other. By the way, how does Drew feel about you going out with another man?"

Marlena pretended not to hear.

"So now you don't hear me talking. You sure heard me when I was telling all Noah's business. What are you going to do about Drew, Cinderella?"

That got Marlena's attention.

"Don't call me that. Drew and I are not really dating. And, for goodness sakes, Noah and I are only having dinner, not getting married. I see no reason why I should say anything about Drew."

Tina snorted, "Suit yourself."

✝

Noah pulled up in front of Marlena's older two-story home. He could tell that she lived in one of the better neighborhoods of the inner city. He looked around and smiled at the older African-American couple sitting on the porch next door. They were openly curious about him. He chatted with them for several minutes. Before he could knock, the door opened and Marlena appeared. She waved at her neighbors and politely invited Noah inside.

"You have very nice neighbors," He said.

"They're the Kingleys. They've lived in that house forever," she responded.

He complimented her on her home and its décor. On the mantel, he noticed several pictures of her with a smiling child. He assumed it to be her son. There was a large frame which displayed pictures of the same boy during the various stages of his life. The young man looked very familiar to him. He was sure that he'd seen him around town. He noticed that there was only one picture of her with a very handsome brown-skinned, muscularly built man. The man had his arms around her waist and his cheek pressed close to hers. She looked radiant and they were both smiling. They made an extremely handsome pair. It was fairly obvious that he was the boy's father. The resemblance was uncanny. He wondered if this man was still a part of her life. The thought of an ex-husband or ex-boyfriend lurking around in the background was not something he could take lightly. He heard her respond to his comment about her home.

"It's getting to be a bit much for me to keep up ever since…"

Noah noticed how she suddenly cut off what she'd been about to say. He wasn't going to let her get away with that. He mentally stored the information away. She was going to finish that statement as soon as they were comfortably seated at the restaurant.

"Ready to go?" he asked.

She nodded and reached for her sweater. He smoothly placed his hand on her lower back and felt her stiffen and then relax as he courteously escorted her out of the house and into his car.

Waving goodbye to the Kingleys, Noah headed off to Sophia's, a quiet, cozy, little restaurant about thirty minutes north of the city.

"You look a little nervous Cinderella," he teased. "Don't worry. I'll try to have you home by midnight."

"My name is not Cinderella," she quipped.

"Did you think about me today?" he shot back, determined to make her acknowledge her attraction to him.

"Yes, Noah, I thought about you, a lot," she admitted honestly.

He smiled at her and secretly thought he'd gotten a bonus when she'd added the "a lot" part. "Good, because I thought a lot about you too Marlena," he said, honoring his word to call her by her name.

She glanced at him, but said nothing else. Her silence didn't bother him. There'd be plenty of time to talk at Sophia's.

A few minutes later, she surprised him by asking, "Why did you take your wedding band off?"

"Because it was time, and because of a very powerful attraction I feel for you," he answered. "Listen, Marlena, I have every intention of spending a lot of time with you. I guess what I'm saying is that I'd like to court you. Are the feelings mutual?"

She hadn't heard the term "courting" in years. It was absolutely archaic, but she understood its meaning. She too, was tired of all the guessing and game playing of dating. At least now, she knew the rules. She smiled to herself and said in a teasing voice, "Yes, Mr. Phillips, I would like to be courted by you."

"Good!" was his only reply.

Marlena sat back. What in the world had she just agreed to? She couldn't believe that she'd actually told him that she would date him only. They hadn't even finished an actual date, and they were already exclusive. This was happening way too fast. She could always tell him that she'd changed her mind if this evening didn't go well she reasoned to herself. Why had she allowed Tina to influence her to go on a date with him? This was definitely all Tina's fault.

Minutes later, Noah escorted Marlena into the charming little restaurant. He'd requested a booth because it afforded them more privacy. He had bragged on the food and the service earlier. He was proven right.

Both were excellent. Marlena had allowed Noah to order their dinner. He had chosen rib eye steaks, California blend vegetables, and oven-roasted potatoes with some sort of creamy cheese sauce. They'd both declined dessert.

Noah was enjoying a glass of wine, while Marlena had soda water.

"Dinner was magnificent," she expressed as she wiped her mouth. "How did you manage to find this place?"

Noah took another sip of his wine and shrugged, "Colleen and I were going through a pretty rough time in our marriage. We'd separated for about two weeks or so. I came up here and stayed with an old seminary professor of mine. We came here to eat one day, and I've been coming here ever since. You're the first woman that I've ever brought here. I usually dine here when I need some alone time."

Her friend Tina had been right. Noah had known about Colleen's affair. Not wanting to pry, she kept quiet. That was deeply personal, and if he wanted to share it, then it would have to be his choice. She understood his pain though. Her deceased husband had cheated on her, more than once.

Noah's voice cut into her thoughts, "So, tell me why your home is a bit much to keep up. Who used to help you out? Was it your boyfriend, son or ex-husband, and is he the one that's pictured with you on the mantel?"

Noah saw the pain in her eyes as she looked away. He had known it was going to be difficult. He almost relented, but he was a lot wiser now. Caring about someone meant you didn't let them stay in their comfort zone. It meant helping them get to the next level so they could stay strong. Allowing them to stay too long in the same place caused them to fall asleep and become defenseless. That's how life destroys so many people. He wasn't about to allow what happened to Colleen, to happen to Marlena. Yes, the two women's fears were different, but the end results would be the same. Marlena would never move forward and fear would always keep her from growing.

"I can see that it's hard for you to talk about yourself; but, I've trusted you with some pretty personal stuff. Now, you're going to have to trust me. Just think of me as a pastor," he said sardonically. When she still hadn't looked at him, he reached over and gently turned her head toward him. "Come on, Cinderella. You can trust me," Noah promised solemnly.

Marlena blinked back her tears and smiled faintly at his use of that silly nickname, took a deep breath, and told him things she'd never ever told anyone else, not even Tina, her best friend in the world. By the time she'd finished, he had learned that she was an only child and both her parents had passed. She had a son, and that she taught at a small Christian school. He also learned that the man in the picture was her deceased husband. She'd been a widow for three years, but she and her husband Shawn had been married for nineteen. The early years had been fair; both had been trying to live for Christ. Then, Shawn had decided that living a life for Christ was too boring. He no longer felt attracted to his wife. He became easily angered and eventually they had stopped communicating altogether. She'd stayed with her husband for the sake of their young son and because of the covenant she had made before God. She confided that Shawn had not only been unfaithful, but he'd been living a secret life which had surfaced after he had been brutally murdered. His death still remained unsolved even today. She told Noah about Kaod playing football at Ohio State University and even about her relationship with Drew, one of Kaod's coaches.

Noah had listened without interrupting, but he had to ask her one more question. "Marlena, have you and Drew been intimate?"

He held his breath and waited for the answer.

Marlena held his gaze and answered honestly, "No, we haven't."

Noah felt like leaping in the air or doing some ridiculous touchdown dance, instead, he sat calmly and smiled.

Marlena fidgeted with her napkin and wondered, "Would it have made a difference if we had been?"

"It would have made a very big difference Cinderella," he said with deadly seriousness.

"Then I'm very glad we weren't," she responded in an equally serious tone.

Marlena felt as though a weight had been lifted. Why hadn't she been able to cast her burdens at the foot of the cross? She had become so comfortable in her fears that it just seemed easier to keep them. In fact, it had been easier. She didn't have to risk rejection or failure. She could just put on a fake smile and walk around pretending. No wonder the Bible tells us to confess our sins one to another. She looked at Noah. She no longer saw him as white or black. He was simply a Christian. She thanked God, for only in Christ was there no division.

She had known that Tina was right when she'd suggested telling Noah about Drew. Honesty was crucial in any relationship and so far, Noah had shown himself to be a man of integrity. She was also so thankful to God for keeping her sexually pure. There was no doubt in her mind that sexual purity was of the utmost importance to Noah Phillips. He had been deadly serious about her relationship with Drew affecting the outcome of any relationship they might establish. She recalled the countless times that Drew had suggested becoming intimate. Prayer, her friend Tina, and a lot of bad memories had prevented her from giving in.

Noah couldn't help but be pleased with the way things were progressing. He'd been thoroughly shocked when she'd announced who her son was. He should have recognized him from the pictures on her mantel. He wasn't just a football player; he was one of the best in the nation. She hadn't even made a big deal about it. Most people would have been shouting it from the rooftops, but she hadn't. She seemed a bit on the shy side, but he liked it. In fact, he liked her. He'd enjoyed her conversation and the way she laughed. This woman was going to be his wife and he knew it.

Chapter Seven

On the drive home, Noah shared his life with Marlena. She laughed hilariously when he talked about events from his childhood and college days. He treated her to stories of his two sons. How the younger, Adam, was more like him, but looked like his mother. While Jacob, the eldest, resembled him, but was more like Colleen. Both boys were grown and living on their own. Adam, a freelance writer, was always getting the church to donate to some cause or another. He told her about Kara expecting her first child, and the baby being his first grandchild. He talked about his church, the deacons and their wives, and his desire to form a ministry that would help inner-city youth. She learned that he was the younger of two children. He had an older brother John, who was set to retire from the local police department in a couple of years. John had practically raised Noah when they'd lost their parents in a freak automobile accident years ago.

Before she knew it, they were in front of her home. Neither one wanted the evening to end so Noah suggested a walk. Marlena disappeared into the house while he sat on her porch and watched children playing without a care in the world. He observed a group of teenagers on the corner. The guys were involved in roughhousing, while the girls giggled in amusement. One of them shouted if he was five-O. He knew the boy was wondering if he was undercover. He shook his head no and stood as Marlena reappeared in a pair of baggy jogging pants and some Nike sports shoes. She looked adorable he thought.

She smiled and said, "I thought I'd take Beauty with us." She vanished around the back and returned with the largest dog he'd ever encountered.

Noah eyed the huge black monster of a dog warily.

"This is Beauty. Beauty, greet your dinner," she joked.

Noah roared with laughter.

"She won't hurt you. She has a great temperament. She's only aggressive in the house or in the fence," Marlena explained. "Come on," she coaxed.

When he hesitated she grabbed his arm and pulled him along. True to her word, Beauty never even so much as looked in his direction. Noah relaxed as they headed off down the street. He watched as she spoke with various neighbors and waved at others. He could tell that she was well liked and extremely comfortable in her environment. He wondered if that would change when he introduced her to his. He'd just have to move slowly. "Wait on God, be patient," he reminded himself. Noah glanced down at her dog. It was well-behaved and listened to her every command. He'd bet all of her students were as equally well-behaved.

They headed up a steep hill. Noah's longer legs easily kept pace with her shorter ones. The walk was exhilarating. The fresh air felt good in his lungs. Up ahead, he noticed a crowd of men milling about. They were casting admiring looks in her direction. She didn't seem aware of them until one called out a greeting and asked how her son was doing. Soon all the men were casting opinions on the approaching football season and Kaod's stats. Noah found himself in a spirited debate on which school had the best all around team. Suddenly, the conversation ceased. All eyes were on Marlena, as one bold gentleman asked when the two of them were going out. Noah watched as she blushed from embarrassment; he was enjoying every minute of it. Finally, taking pity on her, he stepped in and informed the would-be suitor that she was already spoken for. In good natured fun, the man asked by whom.

Noah responded by pulling her to him and asking her in an overly loud dramatic voice, "Tell him who's your daddy."

The group of men erupted with wild delighted laughter, giving each other high fives and slapping Noah on the back. Speechless, Marlena felt her face flaming and wondered where he'd learned that kind of slang. After a last pat on the back, Noah bid the men goodbye.

He whispered in her ear as they walked away, "What would you do without me, Cinderella?"

Marlena rolled her eyes and walked faster.

They reached the house in record breaking speed with Noah laughing and teasing her all the way.

Marlena released Beauty, and the big dog began to roll around in the grass.

"You've got her trained pretty well," he noticed.

Noah turned to face her and became aware of the sudden change in her demeanor. He watched her shift from side to side. What was she expecting him to do? Pounce on her.

"I'm not going to bite you. Come here, Cinderella," he said softly holding out his arms.

She slowly walked towards him. She reminded him of a cornered animal. What was she afraid of?

"I had a good time this evening."

"Thank you, so did I," she responded shyly.

Noah took her in his arms and hugged her warmly. He kissed her tenderly on the forehead, turned her towards her door, opened it, and pushed her gently inside.

"Call your pony in and lock the door," he ordered gently.

Waiting for the dog to get inside and the door to shut and lock, Noah jogged down the stairs and jumped into his car. With a beep of the horn, he drove off down the street.

Marlena sat on the sofa and exhaled the breath she'd been holding. Her mind recalled the evening's events. Noah was an enigma. She'd never met a man who carried himself in such a manner. He was confident but not pushy; attractive but not egotistical; and he seemed comfortable no, matter the environment. She had watched, in shocked silence, as he'd ordered a glass of wine at Sophia's. Most pastors that she knew, would be sooner cast into hell than to let someone see them drink alcohol of any sort.

She'd heard arguments on both sides of the spectrum concerning drinking. Personally, she believed that God was more concerned with the hidden sins that lie deep within a person's heart than with them enjoying a glass of wine. Alcoholism, she clearly understood, has been a plague on society, beginning before the flood, and should never be taken lightly; however, the sin exists in the heart of the person drinking, rather than the substance. Her father had been an alcoholic and had desired the bottle above everything, including his wife and daughter. He'd never cultivated a relationship with Jesus. His dependency was solely on alcohol. In short, alcohol had become his god. Marlena knew that most people had some form of dependency on something other than God. Maybe it was their ability to make money, or their own intellect, or even something as subtle as the government or their church. Whatever it was, they'd allowed it to replace a reliance and faith that should only be entrusted to God. Noah had managed, in one night, to begin a resurrection of something that had slowly died in her. Respect! It hit her like a bolt of lightning. She had never, after watching her father drink himself to death, really respected any man. She thought about Shawn. He was the closest she'd ever come. She had loved her husband, but had never fully come to respect him. He had loved the world more than God, and as a result, never completely earned that honor. It must have been hard for him to live with that knowledge. In all of her forty-three years, the only man she'd ever come to love and respect was the person of Jesus the Christ. He, she was beginning to comprehend, was what she saw reflected in Noah. Marlena picked up the phone and called her best friend's number. Tina would be impatiently waiting to hear the details of Noah's and her first date.

Noah pulled into his driveway, pressed the remote and waited for the garage door to open. He eased the car inside, put it in park, and turned the ignition off. Not bothering to exit, he revisited the events of his first date with Marlena. He thanked God for setting the foundation so early. It was clear that she fellowshipped with Christ. She'd never once cast the blame of her unhappy marriage on her husband alone. She'd accepted the fact that some of the problems had come as a result of her trying, in her own power, to fix things. She had stayed in the marriage because she had made a covenant with God, and had above all, desired to please Him by doing all she could to honor her vow to both God and man. She had remained faithful, in body and spirit, through times of great strife and turmoil and had, by the grace of God alone, managed to raise a son who had excelled despite the adversity in his life. Noah hadn't mentioned it to her, but he'd frequently watched her son play on TV. He had himself commented on how well-spoken and humble Kaod was. This, before he had any personal knowledge of Marlena or her son. In truth, he'd heard many others replicate those same thoughts. He admired this woman. He intuitively knew that it would be a challenge to capture this woman's love and respect. He'd have to go through Jesus to capture her heart.

Although Noah discerned God at work, he understood the protocol of going to a father and seeking his permission to wed his daughter. He'd done exactly that with Colleen's earthly father. Marlena's earthly father was no longer alive, so he did what he should have done with Colleen, sought approval from the Heavenly Father. He prayed that God would find him a worthy husbandman. Tomorrow, he would, God willing, assemble his deacons and inform them of his intentions towards Marlena. As much as he loved and trusted these men, he had no clue what their reactions would be. He had not planned to attend the seminar and find a woman he'd want to court. He'd been caught by surprise, but his mighty men of valor (that's what he had dubbed them) knew him well enough to know that he was not impulsive or careless in his decision-making abilities. Noah's choice had already been made, but he hoped that his deacons would support him, even if they could not understand. He also wanted to talk to Adam, his youngest son, about Marlena. He felt confident that Adam would stand by him. None the less, God had known beforehand the path he'd take. God, himself, would remove all obstacles. Noah bowed his head in prayer and left it all in the hands of his heavenly Father.

Chapter Eight

Valerie had been surprised when Pastor Phillips had phoned her late last night. He had instructed her to call all of the deacons for an impromptu meeting on Saturday. It was set for 10 A.M., with all of the men in attendance. There was not a one of them that hadn't been curious. After all, this was Saturday, and very seldom had a deacon's meeting ever been called on a weekend. They'd all come in asking if she could clue them in. She couldn't, but she had a wild hunch, and believed its name was Marlena.

As Noah walked into the meeting, he could tell that curiosity was getting the better of his deacons. There was no talking, all eyes were on him. He almost thought it comical, but managed to rein in his humor. He greeted the men, said the opening prayer, seated himself, and began to explain why he had assembled them together. When he had finished, the room was absolutely quiet. His trusted friend, Hal Lindstrom, finally broke the silence by asking if the Pastor had any more deep dark secrets. Everyone began laughing. They hammered Noah with question after question until they were satisfied that he was still sane. Then, with the biggest vote of confidence he'd ever needed, unanimously pledged their support. They all seemed eager to meet Marlena and suggested that he bring her to church the next day and then to the special volleyball games that evening. Noah promised to extend the invitation.

Noah hadn't seen Marlena since the Thursday of their date, although they had spoken in length several times on the phone. He'd wanted to see her on Friday, but she had been attending the last day of the seminar, and he'd had a meeting in Cleveland and had spent the rest of the day with Adam in Akron. Besides, he'd wanted her to have a little time to absorb all that had taken place between them. They'd made plans to spend the majority of Saturday together. He was looking forward to seeing her again. He could sense that she felt the same way. He picked up his cell, pushed her name and waited to hear her voice.

Marlena picked up the phone on the third ring.

"Hello, Cinderella," a warm voice greeted her.

She smiled at the phone. "Hello, Noah."

"What, no complaint about me calling you Cinderella?" he teased.

"I've gotten used to it, besides, complaining hasn't done me any good," she pouted.

"You little storyteller, I think you like my little pet name for you. Anyway, I've missed you," he confessed. "Are you ready for me to pick you up, or do you need a little more time?" he asked.

"No, I'm ready now," she answered.

"Then, I'm on my way, sweetheart." The endearment just came out naturally.

Marlena said goodbye and replaced the receiver. She had missed him too. She wasn't brave enough to admit it though. She liked being around him and enjoyed his company tremendously. His knowledge of God's word kept her wanting to ply him with questions. She'd never met any man quite like him. She could talk to him for hours and never get bored. They shared many bonds, but the bond that was the most significant, was that of Jesus Christ. They both considered Him to be their Lord.

✞

Noah greeted Marlena with a tender hug and kiss on the forehead. He was dressed in denim jeans with a lightweight grayish-blue sweater that enhanced the color of his eyes. She found herself staring at him and thinking how comfortable he made her feel. She shook her head as if to clear it from a thick fog of some sort.

He glanced curiously at her. "Is there something wrong?" he asked.

"No. No. You just look so different. I mean there's nothing wrong," she sputtered.

"Well, if you're up to it, I thought we could ride out to the local flea markets and browse around. Are you game? Do you like flea markets?" he enquired.

"I love them, and yes, that would be great," Marlena said as she picked up her purse.

✞

The flea markets were crowded as usual. They took their time walking up and down the aisles, stopping frequently to look at the various wares each vender supplied. Noah used the crowd as an excuse to hold her hand. He tightened his hold just slightly when she tried to pull away and held her glance. "Are you embarrassed or uncomfortable with me, wanting to hold your hand?" he asked.

She wasn't either. She was nervous, and told him so. "I want to be honest with you. It's not you, it's me. It's a trust issue, and this is happening very fast," she explained.

He nodded his head in understanding, but kept hold of her hand as they walked. For the next two hours, they walked hand and hand, viewing every single booth at every local market. Soon, her hand relaxed in his. By the end of their exploration, she was feeling quite comfortable. Even when they left the crowded markets and headed towards his car, he did not let go of her hand.

Noah looked across at her as he drove. She was beautifully unaware of how attractive she was. It pleased him that she didn't seek out approval from other men concerning her outward appearance. Women that desired to have the attention of every man they encountered, did not appeal to him.

He also understood her concerns about them. He too, was very much aware of how swiftly this courtship was moving, but they weren't young pups either. It wasn't a physical thing. Sure, she was attractive, but he'd been around other women that he'd found equally attractive, and in a more physical way. This was vastly different. She was meant for him. He'd known it from the first moment she'd stepped in that seminar. Something in him had resurrected. She was his Eve. She was his soul mate. Instinctively, he reached over and grabbed her hand. To his pleasure, she smiled at him. He winked at her, and laughed happily when she blushed, but did not pull her hand from his.

✟

They stopped for lunch at a little Chinese restaurant. After finishing lunch, Noah, who had been waiting for the right moment, asked her to attend his church's service with him. He explained that his assistant pastor would be bringing the message, and about the volleyball games later on that evening. They would be playing against a sister church. Matches would be held between the various age groups. Their age group would be last and hopefully playing to regain the trophy. His church had lost the event the past two years, so the elusive trophy remained elsewhere.

Whichever church lost the contest would have to host the end of the summer picnic.

He also informed her that his youngest son would be there. Noah watched her face closely. She avoided looking at him. He could tell she was mulling this around in her head. Everything in him wanted to tell her she didn't have to come, but the truth was that she did. It was necessary for him to observe her in his environment. They could never move to the next level without her becoming a part of his church family or meeting his children. In fact, this was a crucial decision, not just for her, but for them. Noah remained silent. He was feeling a little unsure at the moment. Maybe he should have waited.

Marlena turned and met his eyes straight on.

"I guess if we're going to give this thing a try, I really don't have a choice. I'd love to attend your church's service," she said.

"And the games afterward?" he pushed.

"Are you any good?" she tossed back.

"Good enough. What about you? Do you play?" he replied. This was the first time he'd encountered this confident side of her, but he liked it.

"I play well enough. You just concentrate on holding your own if you want to win that silly little trophy back," she stated in a sure voice.

Noah stared at her as if she'd grown another head. Where did this cocky woman come from? He continued staring. She stared back, and then did something that caught him totally off guard. She winked at him. Noah threw back his head and roared with laughter. He laughed so long and so hard that people began to stare. Finally, he'd settled down enough to ask in a teasingly serious tone, "Who are you Browneyes, and what have you done with Cinderella?"

That comment, drew a corresponding laugh from Marlena.

✝

Noah watched as Marlena fed the big dog. She talked to the animal as if it were a child. This woman was thoroughly enchanting. There were many facets to her. Each one was like a piece of a puzzle, that when finished, would give you the complete picture of her. One minute she appeared vulnerable, the next very capable. He knew that she was extremely intelligent. He also noticed how she had calculated the risk of not going to church with him. Their bonding time had helped her to make the choice. Her actions spoke a lot louder than she did. And that wink- she'd been flirting with him. That only came out when she felt confident in her abilities he perceived.

He followed her into the house and took a seat on the large paisley patterned sofa. She tossed him the remote and contemplated where to sit. Noah made the choice for her by reaching out and grabbing her hand and tugging her down beside him. She laughed aloud as he pulled her next to him and began flicking through the channels. He settled on a Western and she nodded her approval.

Marlena felt her body relax as she sat next to Noah. He smelled good she thought. She liked the way he sometimes simply made the decision. She didn't always have to be the one in control with him, the person responsible for everything. It took a lot pressure off. It afforded her the opportunity to just relax and be a woman, and not always have her guard up. She let out a yawn, sighed contentedly, and promptly fell asleep.

An hour and half later, she stirred and started to move when a firm arm around her waist pulled her tight. Marlena slowly awakened. She had been using Noah's chest as a pillow and her feet were curled up on the sofa. She could hear the beating of his heart and feel his breath on her hair. She lie there not quite sure what to do.

"I could hold you like this forever," he whispered softly.

Marlena smiled against his chest, content to lie there.

"Are you worried about visiting our church or meeting Adam?" Noah asked.

"Not really. Should I be?" she responded.

"No, everything will be fine. Adam's a good kid. I've talked to him about you. He's kind of excited to meet you. What about your son? Have you told Kaod about me?"

She lifted her head slightly and met his glance, "Yes. He doesn't have a problem with you, but he'd always hoped that I'd marry Drew."

"Were you hoping for that also?" Noah asked, experiencing a pang of jealousy.

Marlena sat up. "To be honest, Drew's been like a father figure to Kaod. That's kind of how we started dating in the first place. It seemed like the right thing to do at the time."

"And Drew, does he know about me?" he asked casually.

She could feel her face grow warm as she explained to Noah that she and Drew had discussed him; however, Drew hadn't said anything about it, nor could he. It was he who had set the tone by going out with other women.

The conversation had been extremely awkward, and Marlena had known by Drew's tone of voice that he was less than pleased with the idea. She was embarrassed by the whole dating concept that Drew had. He claimed a belief in Christ, but had continually pressed the issue of them being a little more intimate, whatever that had meant. When she hadn't agreed to it, he had started this occasional dating of other women, trying to force her hand; nevertheless, she had tried to make it clear to Drew that she and Noah were exclusive.

Noah nodded his satisfaction as he stood and stretched. "I guess I'd better get going. We have a long day ahead of us tomorrow. I'll pick you up early, and we can stop and eat breakfast before heading to the service," he said, grabbing her hand and pulling her behind him as he headed towards the door. "I'll be here around eight or so. Don't forget to bring your volleyball gear, Browneyes," he added.

He hugged her and planted an exaggerated kiss on her forehead. He reminded her to bring the pony in and lock the doors as he went down the steps to his car. She stood in the doorway watching as his car disappeared from sight.

✞

After leaving Marlena's, Noah drove directly to Hal Lindstrom's home. He and Hal talked privately, and in more detail, about his courtship of Marlena.

"So, is she coming to the service tomorrow, or are we going to have to wait to meet the little lady who's thrown our Pastor into a tailspin?" he joked.

Noah grinned in response to Hal's teasing. "She's coming. I'm praying she can handle all the busybodies. She's a strong woman of God, but she'll be coming into a vastly different environment. People still have a certain amount of loyalty to Colleen, and you and I know, very well, how she felt about the black community," Noah confessed.

Hal sat thinking for a moment. "Noah, I believe God is in this thing with you and her, but I think it's more than that. I have the feeling God's going to shake up an entire community. Those that are hiding sin in their hearts, are either going to have to deal with it, or walk away from the faith. You two are the tools to get the job done. I have a notion that your little "Cinderella" aint gonna be running from this ball, not if she's falling for Prince Charming," he remarked humorously.

The two men's conversation turned to Hal's desire to court Valerie.

Hal reminded Noah that she was almost sixteen years his junior. Noah smugly reminded him that when you snooze you lose, and that if he and Marlena could overcome the race issue, then overcoming age should be relatively easy.

"Besides," Noah said, "we are more that conquerors through Christ who strengthens us."

The two men lifted their bottles of water and drank a toast to each other.

Chapter Nine

Marlena inspected her appearance in the mirror. She'd chosen to wear a long navy blue skirt with a matching blazer and matching slightly heeled open-toed sandals. The clothes were both dressy and comfortable. She'd decided to curl her hair rather than wear it braided. The black curls framed her face and brought to notice her Indian ancestry. Marlena applied her chocolate colored lip gloss, grabbed her purse and sports bag, and headed down the staircase.

Beauty sat waiting with the leash in her mouth. "Not right now girl," she laughed as she took the leash and hung it on the hook next to the door. "I promise to take you for a walk when I get back. In the mean time, let's get you settled out back," Marlena coaxed.

She'd just finished locking the back door when Noah knocked at the front.

"Come in!" she called. "The door is open."

"I could have been anyone…" he stopped right in the middle of chastising her when he caught sight of her.

She was gorgeous. He'd never seen her with her hair down in curls. He couldn't take his eyes off of her. "You look beautiful," he finally managed to say.

"Thank you. You look very handsome," she returned.

He'd worn a dark blue suit with a matching shirt. His tie was a combination of various colors which complimented his suit. On his feet, he wore a pair of black oxford dress shoes. Their outfits matched perfectly.

She suddenly became acutely aware of the fact that they looked like a couple who had intentionally dressed the same so that there would be no mistaking that they were together.

The twinkle in Noah's eyes told her he was thinking the same thing. For once, he didn't say a word.

Marlena was tempted to believe that this was a coincidence, but she knew better. God was beginning to speak loud and clear.

Noah couldn't have been happier as he escorted her to the car. Not a soul could look at them and think they hadn't deliberately dressed alike. He'd pretended not to notice for fear that she'd run upstairs and change. It was amazing how God could send a message in the simplest of ways. He began humming a tune of praise as he drove. He reached over and grabbed her hand. She glanced at him from beneath her dark lashes. She was feeling unsure of herself he realized. Noah squeezed her hand. Browneyes was gone and Cinderella was back.

"What's wrong?" he asked as he eased the car into a vacant spot at the local diner.

She didn't know how to quite explain it. "We look like a couple," she blurted out. There, she'd said it. It was out in the open.

"Exactly how do you want us to appear to others, as friends, or acquaintances, or what? Wasn't that your confusion with Drew? I'm not interested in a platonic friendship with you. If other people look at us and think we are a couple, why is that a problem?" he said, feeling mildly irritated with her way of thinking.

When she didn't respond, he got out of the car, walked around to the passenger side, and roughly opened the door. Reaching in, he firmly grabbed her arm and helped her out of the car. Instead of letting her arm go, he pulled her towards him, lifted her face, and kissed her on the lips in front of anyone who cared to notice. "There," he said after the brief kiss. "You think a kiss magically moves us from the platonic to the couple stage of this relationship? Does that make you feel better?" Without waiting for an answer, he ushered her into the busy diner.

Seated at their booth for more than five minutes, Noah still hadn't said a word. Marlena felt terrible. He was right. She had contradicted herself. They were a couple. What message was she sending to him? They couldn't be a couple because he hadn't tried to seduce her? Whose standards had she been using? She realized that she was falling for Noah in a big way. Why should it embarrass her if others saw them as a couple? She was the one that was confused, not Noah.

Marlena peered at him, then reached across the booth and took his hand. "I'm sorry, Noah. Please, forgive me," she pleaded sincerely.

Noah gazed at her hand on his. "You need to understand that for me, we are a couple. There is no magic standard of physical intimacy that establishes us as more than friends. I'm not embarrassed by my beliefs and if you are, that's something you are going to have to come to grips with. What do you want me to do? Demand that we become more intimate?" he asked quietly.

She shook her head no.

He reached for her hand and gave it a squeeze.

Her respect for this man was growing by leaps and bounds.

They arrived at the church thirty minutes before the service was to begin. With his hand resting gently on the center of her back, they walked inside the church. All eyes seemed to rest on them. She looked up at Noah and he encouraged her with a smile. One of the senior deacons, Hal Lindstrom, introduced himself, and soon the others followed suit. Marlena smiled politely as they, one by one, were introduced to her. She made a mental note of something unique about each of them so that she could recall their names later. It was a trick she'd learned when she'd first started teaching.

Noah glanced around and grinned when he spotted the person he had been trying to find. Excusing Marlena and himself from the group, he led her in the direction of his youngest son, Adam.

Adam had watched from afar as his father had escorted Marlena into the sanctuary. Word had spread fast concerning their courtship. Apparently the Deacons and their wives didn't have gag orders placed on their mouths, and had exercised their right to free speech. So far, he'd counted at least eleven people who had asked him how he felt about it. This wasn't a shock to him. His father didn't see others by the color of their skin. He only looked at the character of the person. When Jacob had called him ranting and raving about it, he'd told his older brother that it was their dad's choice with whom he chose to spend time. If he wanted to marry a purple woman, that was fine by him. Adam just wanted to see his dad happy. It had been at least four years since his mom had died. His dad deserved some happiness, and if this woman made him happy, he'd love her for that alone.

They actually made a good looking couple he mused. She was quite beautiful he noted. He could see why his dad was drawn to her. Adam heard the whispering as the different people became aware that their pastor was now dating a stranger, a black woman no less. He knew that some of the single women had expected him to date one of them. He thought how vicious women could be and suddenly felt the need to ally the underdog in this situation. He straightened to his feet, and with a sure steady stride went to meet his father and possibly, his future stepmother.

Marlena watched as father and son embraced. They were nearly the same height, but their coloring was completely opposite. Noah had dark curly hair, while Adam's was blond and straight. She noted that Adam's eyes were the color of a clear blue sky. She assumed his physical characteristics resembled that of his mother's.

Noah slid his hand in hers and pulled her forward to meet Adam.

With the entire church looking on, Adam, when she'd extended her hand to shake his, instead pulled her into a warm embrace and whispered for her ears alone, "Thank you for making my father smile again."

Marlena heard the softly spoken words and genuinely returned his warm embrace.

The trio talked while all eyes watched. Adam couldn't help commenting on their twin outfits. "You do know Dad, that this means you're officially a couple?" he remarked.

Noah and Marlena exchanged a knowing look. She blushed and turned away, while he roared with laughter. Adam looked on in bemusement. Was she blushing? He stared back and forth between the two of them as they shared some sort of secret joke. It hit Adam like a ton of bricks. They were in love, and there was no doubt about it.

With the service coming to a close, Marlena prayed that the Assistant Pastor had the good grace not to ask all visitors to stand. By now, you'd have to be blind or absent not to know who she was. During the earlier part of the service, when it had been time to go and shake hands with others, she had felt sure that the whole city had been present and gawking.

She slid a sideways glance at Noah and then at Adam. The younger Phillips was desperately attempting to control his laughter as he caught her gaze. He knew what she was thinking and was barely suppressing his mirth. Suddenly, she saw the humor in the situation and began to shake with laughter. She put her head down and hoped that no one could tell. This caused Adam to lose control and he began to laugh even harder and soon she followed suit.

Noah glanced at the two of them and tried his best to look stern. This just added fuel to the fire. Noah fought hard not to give in to their laughter.

Mercifully, the Assistant Pastor, didn't call for visitors to stand, but instead, asked everyone to prepare for dismissal.

Marlena asked the Lord to forgive her for not being able to recount a word of the message. She'd been too keenly aware of her surroundings and hadn't been able to concentrate. She could still feel all the curious eyes. Some of them had been pretty hostile. She sensed that his congregation was very protective of him and made another mental note not to sit in the front row unless she came as his personal guest. She reined in her negative thoughts and allowed the Holy Spirit to give her peace. Marlena eased her hand into Noah's and felt his reassuring squeeze. Finally, prayer was concluded and the congregation dismissed.

Adam looked at the two of them and smiled, "One down, the rest of your lives to go."

Noah grinned and began guiding Marlena toward the exit. They were stopped every two or three feet by people wanting to be introduced. At last, they made it outside. Noah took out a set of keys from his pocket, opened an adjacent door, quickly tugged her in behind him, and shut the door.

He pulled her in his arms and held her tightly. "Are you all right?" he asked.

Marlena was content to rest in his arms.

"I'm okay, Noah," she said after a long moment. She became aware of a sudden tension in him.

He looked into her eyes, and spoke uncertainly, "This is my life. They are my congregation, my responsibility. God has called me to shepherd them."

She met his glance, "What are you trying to say? Do you want me to walk away? Do you think we are a bad idea? What?" She didn't understand his sudden change of mood.

Noah turned away from her and strode over to glance out the window.

"Everyone is just about gone. Let's make a run for it." He reached for her hand, but she pulled back.

"I don't want to make a run for it. I didn't ask to come in here, Noah. I was okay with their curiosity. Yes, it was a bit challenging, but I'm not some silly little woman in love with the idea of being Noah Phillips' wife. You asked me to be here today, and I came because of you, not them. I'm here to see if you and I are worth it. If you are feeling torn, Noah, it's because you think I'll ask you to make a choice, them or me. Don't try

45

to make me be Colleen. Now, if you want, we can sneak out of here, and you can take me home."

She turned her back so that he couldn't see her angry tears. Time seemed to stand still.

Noah came to her and gently turned her to face him. "I'm sorry. I don't want to take you home. I'd like you to stay here, with me. I was so wrong. I thought you wanted to leave. Will you forgive me for hurting your feelings?"

That started a bucket of tears flowing from her eyes.

"I forgive you," she managed to say as his arms came around her.

Noah began to pray. He asked God for guidance and strength. He asked God to forgive him for hurting her and for courage in the face of adversity. He prayed for the ability to overcome hate with love, and finally to walk in faith knowing that God guided their steps. He held her until she'd finished crying. He felt like a heel. He'd tried to handle things his way and had done more harm than good.

"I'm ready now," she whispered.

He opened up the door, and they walked hand and hand to the car. Starting the engine, he headed to his home. By now, he was sure that Adam would be there.

Noah pulled into the open garage. Adam was sitting in the kitchen when they walked in. He'd wisely said nothing about her tear-stained face. Noah showed Marlena where she could change clothes and freshen up. When he returned to the kitchen, Adam demanded to know who was responsible for her tears. Noah sat down, and feeling like an idiot, explained what had happened.

"Dad, how could you think she'd ask you to choose? I can't even imagine how hard today was, but she handled it like a trooper," Adam defended her.

"I know son. I guess, in a crazy sort of way, I was trying to protect her," Noah reasoned.

"She's a lot stronger than you think, Dad. I'd be willing to guess that she came today for you, which proves how important you are to her," Adam asserted.

Noah nodded in agreement and excused himself to go and check on her. He tapped lightly on his bedroom door and when there was no response, he eased the door open. There, in the middle of the bed, was

Marlena curled up and fast asleep. He chuckled softly and shut the door. He went back into the kitchen.

Adam clucked his teeth in mock sternness. "Wait until your congregation finds out that she's slept in your bed already," he teased. Adam ducked as his father threw a dish cloth at him.

✝

Marlena awoke and looked at her watch. She'd only meant to close her eyes for a moment. She'd slept for nearly an hour. Marlena slid off of the bed and eased into her gym shoes. She could hear male voices coming from down the hallway. As she entered the kitchen, Noah, Hal, and Adam stood in greeting. She flushed, wondering what they thought of her sleeping in his bed, and returned the greeting.

"Are you hungry?" Adam asked before Noah could say anything.

"Ravenous," she supplied, still embarrassed by her untimely nap in Noah's bed.

Adam opened up the refrigerator, grabbed a tray, and motioned for Marlena to follow him. Stepping outside, she saw a table already set and the grill hot and ready. He began putting selected portions of meat on the fire. She sat down and watched as he cooked. Marlena could tell that he was at ease grilling. She wondered who'd taught him to cook.

Noah observed them from the window. He was glad to see the two of them getting along. He'd been aware of the fact that she had been blushing profusely. He glanced at Hal who was smiling.

"You are quite taken with her aren't you?" Hal stated knowingly.

Noah didn't bother denying it.

Marlena laughed when Adam's curiosity got the better of him as he began to ask her questions about her son. He stared at her when he realized who her son actually was. Her son was Kaod "The Pittbull" Porter. He was huge in the football world. He started on both sides of the ball. He played linebacker on defense, as well as fullback on offense. Barring some kind of injury, this kid was definitely going pro. Adam couldn't believe it. He'd read somewhere, that she and Kaod's coach, Big Drew Clarence, were dating. He tried unsuccessfully to conceal his excitement. His dad, Mr. straight-laced, courting not dating, old fashioned kind of guy, had just carried off the biggest upset in dating history.

Bursting with barely contained excitement, he excused himself, and dashed into the kitchen. As soon as the screen door closed behind him, he raced over to his dad, and as Hal looked on in confusion, began to pay mock homage to him.

Adam then turned to Hal and in slow precise words said, "My father, the supreme square, has managed to single handedly score, Kaod 'The Pittbull' Porter's mom. And, if I know my dad, 'he could go all the way'," he mimicked in his best football announcer's voice.

It slowly dawned on Hal what Adam was going on about. The two looked at each other and went wild. They were chest bumping and high fiving each other when Marlena walked in.

"Why all the excitement?" she asked innocently.

While Adam and Hal looked sheepish, Noah, casually put his arm around her waist, and calmly stated, "They're celebrating the fact that I'm courting Kaod 'The Pittbull' Porter's mother."

"Oh, is that all," she said smiling.

Noah gave the two men a conspiratorial wink over his shoulder as the couple headed outdoors. Hal and Adam waited for the door to shut, and continued their victory celebration.

✠

Noah and Marlena cheered as Adam's team easily defeated their opponent; however, Noah's congregation lost the next match. Each age group had to win two of the three games played and the pressure was now on Noah's team. If they won, the trophy came back to his church. If they lost, their sister church would keep the coveted trophy for the third consecutive year.

Noah looked at Marlena. "Are you still willing to play?"

"Sure, if you need me to" she replied casually, keeping her voice neutral. She looked around and noticed a full gym. This must be quite the big deal she thought.

Noah counted his players. He had eight, but really only four of them could be considered true players. The rest were persuaded volunteers. He wondered how well she could play. The other team had good athletes who loved to spike it down his team's throat. Not to mention Caroline who happened to be an ace player, both during high school, as well as during college. Determining his options, he motioned for her to follow him. Noah had decided that he'd let her play a little of the second game if they were losing. What harm could be done, he reasoned to himself as he positioned his six players on the court.

From the first serve, he knew they were in trouble. Caroline was serving, and she definitely wasn't feeling merciful in the least. The ball was coming close and hard over the net. She deliberately kept hitting it to the weakest link on their team. The poor guy didn't stand a chance. With the score seven to zero, Noah called time and tried to rally the troops. Simon, the weakest link, looked ready to bolt. He kept apologizing to no one in particular. Noah wondered if Simon was in volleyball shock. He looked at the other players sitting on the bench. Henry was sweating buckets of water, and he hadn't even played yet. Marlena looked slightly bored, but cute he thought. He glanced up and saw Adam wildly motioning for him to put Marlena in the game. Was he nuts? He was positive that angry gleam in Caroline's eyes was directed at him. There was no doubting that she'd probably heard about him and Marlena. It wasn't like she couldn't figure out exactly which woman was her, Noah thought ruefully. He glanced up at his son again. Again, Adam motioned for him to put Marlena in.

Noah bent down and looked her in the eye. "Have you noticed how hard her serve is coming? Are you sure you want to play?" he asked, almost begging her not to.

Marlena smiled as she stood and removed her jogging pants to reveal cute little girly pink kneepads.

Noah groaned when he saw them and held her back as the others took the court. "Are you sure?" he asked again.

"What do I get if I help you win your trophy back?" she asked.

He stared blankly at her. Browneyes was back, but he had no clue what she wanted.

"What do you want?" he challenged hesitantly.

She leaned in close and, in a voice only he could hear, said, "How about you explain to me why your lady friend on the other side is so angry with you."

Noah flushed slightly and pushed her gently onto the court, "I was going to anyway you little flirt," he scolded lightly.

Chapter Ten

Marlena took her place on the court. She knew that the ball was going to come at her with a vengeance. She set her stance and waited.

Noah cast a furtive glance in her direction, and headed towards the net. He heard the whistle blow and saw the ball fly low and hard directly at Marlena. He closed his eyes. The crowd was silent. Suddenly, his congregation erupted into wild cheers. He turned to see a perfectly dug ball coming straight to him. He whirled and positioned himself to set for Hal. Hal, waiting for the set, slammed home a perfect spike.

Noah looked at Marlena who was looking at Adam and smiling. Noah swung around and looked at Adam. He was smiling an, I-told-you-so kind of smile. He glanced back at her, she was now pointing to her girly pink kneepads which had his whole congregation in stitches. He looked at her and rolled his eyes. Hal looked at him and erupted with laughter.

He watched Marlena with amazement. She was quite the athlete. Nothing got passed her. She wasn't showy, nor did she try to humiliate the other team. She was a very gracious player, and quick to praise others. Even when the other team, in particularly Caroline, would slam home a spike at the weakest players, she'd encourage them to get it the next time.

By the time the match was concluding, every guy on the team was in love with her. He watched as she served the final point to win the match game and calmly walk over to take a sip from the water fountain. Adam joined her, followed by Hal and the rest of the team. A pouty female voice interrupted his observation of Marlena.

Noah turned to face the tall and model slender Caroline Rivers. She stood with her hand perched on her hip and a slight tilt to her head. Her dark brown hair was pulled back into a ponytail and she wore a scowl on her otherwise attractive face.

"So that's your new friend. I'd heard that you were dating again. You must be serious about her, or temporarily insane to bring her here, or are you using her to get my attention?" Caroline mused.

Noah fixed her with an angry stare. "Only in your mind Caroline could you have a reason to be so vain. Now, if you'll excuse me, I must rejoin my fiancée, I mean Marlena and the team," he responded.

Noah walked towards the team. He'd intentionally stumbled over his words, hoping Caroline would get the hint.

Noah watched with amusement as his players fawned all over Marlena. He managed to finally get their attention and reminded them to shake hands with the other team. They gathered their composure and headed over to shake hands.

All went well until Caroline reared her ugly head. She deliberately attempted to provoke Marlena as they were shaking hands. "Enjoy him while you can, honey. Sooner or later reality will intrude on your little dream world," she taunted.

Marlena ignored her, but threw a glance at Noah who was busily shaking hands. She was the only minority present and she began to wonder whether or not she and Noah were indeed living in a fantasy world. Marlena didn't particularly care for Caroline, but her words begged closer scrutiny.

With spite in her heart, Caroline also began to whine about Marlena playing and how it shouldn't be allowed since she was not a member. A few of the others nodded their heads in agreement. All eyes focused on Noah and Pastor Wade as they stepped to the side, away from everyone, to discuss the issue privately. Noah said something to Jim Wade who turned and looked back at Marlena with a smile. The two men shook hands and returned. It was agreed that the trophy would be given to Noah's church. Amid the loud cheers, everyone shook hands and patted Marlena on the back. Marlena privately thought that Caroline had held on to Noah's hand longer than necessary, especially since she'd made such a fuss about the trophy in the first place.

Marlena walked away and sat down on the bench. A seed of doubt had been planted. Did she really belong in Noah's world? She looked up as Adam sat down beside her and laughed as he began to chatter excitedly. He reminded her so much of Kaod. He was only a couple of years older than her son. He smiled at her, told her to wait a moment, and headed towards his dad. Whatever he said to his dad caused Noah to turn and walk towards her.

"Ready to go?" he asked casually.

She smiled and nodded.

Adam returned, picked up her bag and walked with her out of the gym, and back to the car. They practically ignored Noah altogether as Adam heaped praise upon Marlena. The two of them even made plans to get together with Kaod. Several minutes had passed before Adam spoke to his father. "You can drop me of at the house before you take Marlena home. Good game, Marlena. If it wasn't for you, oh yeah, and you too Dad, we wouldn't have stood a chance," Adam expressed with unconcealed admiration.

✟

The ride home was accomplished in silence. Both of them were engrossed in their own private thoughts.

Noah bypassed her street and instead, headed to the local park. He located a secluded spot and turned the ignition off. "Let's take a seat over there," he suggested, pointing at a bench near the waterfalls.

He helped her out of the car, and they walked silently to the bench. He sat studying the water for a while, before speaking. He told her that he'd taken her to church today because he knew he wasn't bringing the message and that would afford him the opportunity to sit with her. By now, everyone knew their status, and if they didn't, it would probably be the hot topic at the dinner table. He wanted his congregation, in a small way, to be a part of their courtship, so as he got to know her, so would they. He was their shepherd, and this involved being in the public eye more than she may be accustomed to. People, not just his congregation, would be watching them to see how they conducted themselves. He believed that too many of God's children had bought into the world's idea of dating. Usually, that meant multiple dating partners with the luxury of flitting from person to person, leaving everyone involved to continually guess where the relationship was heading. As the head, he had to lead by example. He explained that the next few months would keep him extremely busy. They would have to grab time together whenever they could and that she would be sitting apart from him during the services. He'd be the one bringing the messages and that required a lot of studying and focus. He gently brushed a stray curl away from her face. "You made me so proud of you today. God's grace and mercy was evident in your every action. Even through Caroline attempting to goad you, Christ prevailed," he acknowledged softly.

Noah chuckled heartily at the flash of jealousy that glinted in her eyes. "I promised to tell you about her. It's something that I'm not proud of, something that should have never happened. Caroline used to be my secretary. It was about six months after Colleen had died and I was still grieving and feeling very lonely. She started staying later and later at the office. She encouraged me to talk about my feelings and soon she began bringing me lunch and dinner. Then the hugs and kisses on the cheek started. One day, Hal came over to the house and told me a rumor he had heard, a rumor about Caroline and me. I had no idea who'd spread such a lie, but it woke me up out of the stupor I'd been in. I began to slowly back away from her. I'd leave the office on time, refuse lunch and dinner, and avoid any type of physical touch. She started to come on a lot stronger and in a lot more obvious ways. Eventually, she showed up at my house one night and made some very sexual suggestions, all of which I turned down. I asked her to leave and she did, but not before she made vows of undying love and devotion. To sum it all up, I spoke with some people and arranged somewhat of a secretary swap. I ended up with Valerie, who is very professional, and in return, they got my headache which happened to be Caroline," Noah finished.

"So Caroline still has you in her sights? It was fairly obvious that she was not a happy camper this afternoon," Marlena noted wryly.

"Are you jealous, Cinderella?"

Noah grinned, when she rolled her eyes.

"Do I need to be?" she countered.

He slowly lowered his head toward hers. Stopping just short of his lips touching hers, he whispered, "Never!"

Marlena could feel her heart pounding in her chest. "Never?" she whispered back breathlessly.

"Never," Noah promised, just before his lips gently claimed hers.

The kiss was gentle, but filled with a firm promise of faithfulness. It was a kiss that held no hint of seduction but spoke of a lifelong journey together; a journey that only soul mates, bonded by the word of God could understand. Noah slowly eased his mouth from hers. His eyes smiled at her and spoke a secret message which caused her spirit to leap in acknowledgement. "Now, you fully understand my intentions. There should be no more confusion," he spoke softly.

Marlena lay in her bed thinking about the events of that day. She thought about Adam, and how much like his father he was. She knew that he and Kaod would get along tremendously. They had a lot in common. She hadn't met Jacob yet, but she hoped he was like Adam. She would call Kaod tomorrow and express her desire to have him meet Noah and Adam. She hoped that he still wasn't holding on to the dream of her and Drew getting married. That was definitely not a possibility now. Noah had changed her whole concept of what a relationship was. She'd never felt like she could ever trust a man so completely, but if that man was thoroughly in Christ, it was as though she was trusting Jesus who made it clear that He would never leave or forsake her. Marlena prayed for wisdom, and that she would be obedient and allow God to have his way in her life. She prayed for Kaod, Noah and his sons, and for his church family. Finally, she prayed that Christ would continue to be reflected in Noah and that God would strengthen her to put away those thoughts of doubt concerning the cultural differences of their backgrounds.

Noah sat in his study thinking about Marlena and all that had transpired that day. She had a strength that shocked him, yet she carried herself with such humbleness. He'd never known a woman with as much wisdom concerning the things of the Lord. The more he conversed with her, the more her love for Christ was revealed.

She was also extremely athletic, but not showy. He'd seen her son play football the same way. He wondered what her son was like. He'd definitely have to meet him soon. Things were moving very quickly and he wanted to spend time with him as well.

Noah knew that he was captivated by her spirit. He was not going to pretend that he wasn't. He was also aware that there were some in the church that didn't approve of him courting Marlena. He clearly understood that it wasn't because of the content of her character, but the color of her skin. His own son Jacob fit into that category. He would pray for them and hoped God would change them from the inside out. Yet, a nagging question remained. What if he had to choose? Noah pushed the thought out of his mind. He preferred instead, to think of his upcoming Bible study and then the sermon on Sunday. He dropped to his knees in prayer and afterward, picked up his pencil and began to outline his lesson plans.

Chapter Eleven

Time had passed so swiftly. It was already the second week in June. Noah had been courting Marlena for almost two months and they'd settled into somewhat of a weekly routine. She would, on most days, meet him for lunch, since school was now out for summer recess. They usually lunched near his church.

Initially, there had been a lot of raised eyebrows, but eventually all who were acquainted with Noah accepted her as part of his life. During the evenings, he would drive to her home, where they'd prepare dinner together and take Beauty for her evening walk. There was never an evening in which they didn't pray together, or discuss the topic of his Bible lesson. Marlena was thrilled to have a pastor at her disposal and he was equally excited with her interest in his study of the Word. Sometimes they would watch TV, sometimes they would sit on her porch and watch the children play or talk with various neighbors, or sometimes they would meet Adam for dinner in Akron.

On Wednesdays, he taught Bible study and she went with him. On Saturdays, he would take hours cross referencing and reviewing the Sunday sermon. On Sunday, she attended the services, but never sat up front with the deacons. She always had someone inviting her to sit with them. Wherever she would sit, Noah would always locate her (which wasn't too difficult) and smile at her in acknowledgement. Then he'd become the no-nonsense Pastor Phillips. She never tired of hearing him teach the Word. He spoke frequently of issues that other pastors seemed too afraid to broach and he constantly reminded all to examine what was in the secret recesses of their hearts. This week, however, would be a little different. Kaod had come home from college.

Marlena sighed as the phone rang again for the fourth time in twenty minutes. She loved her son, but it became hectic whenever he came home. It was though everyone wanted a piece of her son, and he could get no peace. She looked at Kaod and smiled resignedly. Marlena walked over to him and gave him a motherly hug. He was as handsome as they came. He stood about six foot tall and had hair that was unusual for the black culture. It was a unique combination of red and brown, with streaks of gold jetting through it. His face was honey colored with kisses of freckles on his cheeks and nose. He had the same smile and the same big brown eyes as his mother, but the stature of his father. Kaod had the thick muscular build of an athlete. It would have been hard to confuse him for anything other than a football player.

Kaod hugged his mom back. She knew he was always happy to be home with her. They were extremely close and a day never passed without them talking on the phone when he was away. Marlena knew that he worried about her living alone. His dream was to one day buy her a home anywhere she wanted in a better area.

She reached up and kissed him on his freckled nose. "Don't forget, Ka using her nickname for him, we're eating dinner with Noah and Adam this evening," she reminded him.

"Oh, you can believe I haven't forgotten that. I'm anxious to meet the man who thinks he's courting my mom. I leave you for a minute, and you get all exclusive with some guy I've never even heard of; and a white guy to boot. What am I going to tell my boys?" he teased laughingly.

"Half your 'boys' are white. Somehow, I don't think they'll have a problem with it," she responded smiling.

Kaod's expression turned serious. "Coach said to tell you hello and that he still thinks about you a lot. He asks me about you all the time. Why don't you call him? He really does care," he said persuasively.

"Stop it, Kaod! Drew likes Drew. He's the one who insisted on dating other women. We had our chance and it wasn't meant to be. I know you love him like a dad, but let's just leave it like that," she added, sounding mildly frustrated as the phone rang.

It was Noah informing her that he was on his way to pick her up for lunch.

✢

Noah pulled up to the house and saw an older model, candyapple red Mustang parked in the driveway. He rightly assumed that it belong to Marlena's son, Kaod. The kid had good taste in cars. If he were twenty years old and single, that would probably be the car he'd select. Noah jogged the stairs and rapped lightly on the screen door. He was met at the door by a ruggedly handsome young man who he assumed was Kaod.

The kid was all muscle and oddly enough, reminded him of a pit-bull. His exterior commanded admiration, but the look in his eyes kept you in a ready posture.

The two males shook hands and exchanged greetings. Noah knew that he was being sized up. He had to give Marlena credit; her son was as polite as any person he'd ever met. Every answer was prefixed with 'yes or no sir', and he even addressed Noah as Mr. Phillips. The two of them sat on the porch and chatted until she came outside.

She greeted Noah in a more cordial manner due to Kaod's presence. With raised eyebrows, he stepped politely around Kaod, grabbed her hand, and pulled her to his side. He gave her his customary kiss on the forehead and grinned knowingly when she tried to ease her hand out of his grasp. Marlena's eyes flew to his and she felt her face flush when his grip tightened on her hand and he pulled her even closer to him.

He bent his head and whispered in her ear, "Not on your life, Cinderella." He turned and looked Kaod in the eyes and simply said, "See you later, 'Pittbull'."

Kaod at first glance appeared confused, but then waved goodbye. He watched as his mom was helped into the car. He didn't quite know what to make of this Noah guy.

✝

"Why did my grabbing your hand in front of Kaod make you uncomfortable?" Noah asked as they sat eating lunch.

Marlena stopped in the middle of taking a bite of her sandwich and gazed at him, trying to find the right words to use. "It's always been me and Kaod. He's never seen me with a man in any other capacity than as friends. Even with Drew, there was never a kiss, holding hands, or anything like that in front of Kaod. His father is the only man that he's ever known to have been a part of my life in an intimate way. I hope you can understand why I feel a little awkward," she said bashfully.

Noah leaned over and brushed her cheek with the back of his hand. "I think you're forgetting we're in the same boat. What you've said, applies to me also, but how my children deal with it though is up to them. They're adults, not children. Kaod's a little different, but he's still a big boy. Sooner or later, he'll have to realize that he's going to have to share his mother. He didn't do too badly this afternoon. You, however, behaved as though we were doing something illegal," Noah joked.

Marlena picked up her napkin, crumpled it, and threw it at him laughingly. He smiled as he artfully dodged the napkin and continued to tease her.

✢

Kaod was absorbed in his own thoughts as his mom seasoned the meat for grilling. She and Mr. Phillips had opted to prepare this evenings meal rather than dine out. He loved his mom's cooking, and had missed it while he was away at school. This suited him much better than eating out anyway. Kaod wondered what Mr. Phillips' intentions were towards his mom. He'd observed how he held her hand. She'd looked a little uncomfortable, but he kind of got the feeling that she'd felt that way because he'd been there. He'd never seen his mom interact in more than a platonic way with any guy other than his father. She'd always teased Kaod about being her only love. He couldn't recall her and Coach Drew ever holding hands or anything like that.

He looked out of the window and saw Mr. Phillips putting the charcoal in the grill. He felt resentment ease to the surface. That had always been his job. He was the man of the house. He wondered exactly how much time his mom had been spending with this guy. Why hadn't it bothered him when she been sort of dating Coach? He knew in his heart that it was because his mom would never marry someone like Coach Drew. Coach wasn't a strong believer in Christ, if he truly believed at all. His mom loved the Lord and always emphasized to him that you should not be unevenly yoked.

He looked at his mom and then at Mr. Phillips. They had to be nuts. He's a pastor at a predominately Caucasian church dating an African-American woman.

"He'll be lucky to keep his membership if things get any hotter," Kaod reasoned.

And what was his mom thinking? Of all the black Christian men that he'd seen looking at her, she dates a white guy? This wasn't a regular "Joe Blow" walking around town either. No one would really care if it was, but this guy was in the public eye. Kaod couldn't fathom Pastor Phillips committing to be with his black mom over his sons and congregation. That was the reality of it. He made up his mind. He wouldn't just stand by and watch his mother get hurt. By the end of this evening's dinner, Pastor Noah Phillips was going to understand Kaod's position, and then he and his mom could go back to the way things were.

Adam arrived and introductions were made. He and Kaod seemed to hit it off immediately. Adam plied Kaod with questions about the upcoming football season. He then changed the topic to Kaod's field of study. Adam and Noah were both surprised to learn that Kaod was majoring in veterinary medicine. They were further amazed that he kept a 3.8 grade point average. Kaod explained that he had somewhat of a bossy mother who still, even though he was in college, would not let him play football if he didn't keep his grades up. Waiting for the laughter to subside, Marlena excused herself to go inside.

Taking this opportunity, Kaod broached the topic most on his mind. "Adam, how do you feel about your dad dating my mom? Please, be honest with me," Kaod questioned bluntly.

Noah carefully stilled his expression and glanced sideways at his son.

Adam, took a moment to sort out his thoughts and said, "If your mother makes my father happy, than I am all for it. Neither one of them is delusional about the possible consequences of this relationship. I'm fine with having a black stepmother if that's what you're asking. My dad has never made a difference between the races. I think they are perfect for each other. Do you have a problem with my dad dating your mom?" Adam threw the question back at Kaod.

"That depends entirely on his intentions. If he wasn't a pastor, the situation would be a whole lot easier. And, since I've brought up your intentions, I'd like to know what they are, Sir?" Kaod boldly turned and asked Noah.

Speaking with complete honesty, Noah looked from Kaod to Adam and back again, and simply said, "My intentions are to make Marlena my wife."

You could hear a pin drop, but Kaod, wanting to be perfectly clear, retorted, "Even if it means losing your congregation or your sons?"

Noah responded with firm conviction, "If it is God's will, then so be it."

Adam looked at his father and smiled. Kaod gave a reluctant smile and offered Noah his hand as a conciliatory gesture.

As the two men shook hands, Kaod declared in a firm tone, "Don't give my mother any reason to cry. She's cried enough tears over my father."

Noah clasped Kaod's hand more firmly and promised that he wouldn't.

✝

Adam and Kaod stood in the kitchen washing the dishes. The two looked at each other and simultaneously burst into laughter.

"I feel like a kid. What next, be home by midnight?" Kaod complained good-naturedly.

That caused another round of laughter.

"They just want some alone time." Adam paused, searching for the best words. "You know that you asked my dad some pretty tough questions. What if he hadn't answered them the way he did?" Adam asked in a serious tone.

Kaod stopped washing the plate in his hand and replied, "I'd have done everything within my power to convince my mom to break off the friendship."

Adam grinned, "I've got news for you bro. They are way beyond the friendship stage. My dad was never interested in just being your mom's friend. I think he made that pretty clear from the beginning. I'm sure they've built a friendship of sorts, but I don't look at my friends the way Dad looks at your mom. You'd better start picking out a tuxedo little brother."

Kaod looked pensive. "I don't think there will be a marriage anytime soon. My mom dated Coach and he never got past first base. They went out for at least a year and a half. She's really slow when it comes to relationships."

"Get real little brother. My father is not about to wait years. He's been on first, rounded second, and is on his way to third. My guess is that your mom will be a June bride next year."

"You're crazy. And stop calling me little brother. I know my mom, and she's not irrational," Kaod defended.

Adam leaned against the counter and stared at Kaod. "I know my dad and he's very level headed too, but if you watch the two of them, they act like they're married already. Take a good look at them. Twenty bucks says my dad gets your mom to kiss him in front of us before the night is over. If that happens, it's a done deal. I'm betting neither one of us has ever seen our parents kiss anyone else. Am I right?"

Kaod reached in his pocket pulled out a twenty dollar bill and slapped it on the counter.

"You're on," he smiled confidently.

Noah sat near Marlena with his arm thrown comfortably around her shoulders. She had just begun to relax her head on his shoulders when Kaod and Adam came out of the house. Immediately he felt her tense and shift slightly away. He easily shifted his body with hers and then squeezed her shoulder in encouragement. Adam and Kaod plopped down across from the pair smiling.

"You two look as though you're up to something," Noah commented.

"Nope, we're just getting to know each other. We were talking about our parents and how well we know them," Adam supplied, with a wink at Kaod.

"Right now, Mom looks like she's about to do her usual get comfortable and fall asleep. I've never seen anyone fall asleep so quickly. You can be having a conversation and think she's listening, but she's not. She's asleep. Has she fallen asleep on you yet, Mr. Phillips?" Kaod teased.

Noah didn't have to look at Marlena to know she was blushing. He also guessed that Kaod was trying to figure out just how close he and Marlena really were.

Before he could speak, Marlena covered his mouth with her hand and said, "As his attorney, I advise him to plead the fifth."

Kaod looked at his mother, who deliberately kept her eyes averted. The conversation soon turned back to football. Marlena felt herself relaxing as she eased her head onto Noah's shoulder. Kaod gazed at his mother and had a sinking feeling that he was going to lose the bet.

Noah stood to his feet and stretched. He extended his hand towards Marlena and assisted her to her feet. "I guess it's time for me to head home. I've got a ton of studying to do tomorrow. Come on sweetheart, walk with me a minute," Noah coaxed.

Adam glanced at Kaod and gave him that, I-told-you-so look. They continued to watch as the couple walked hand and hand, a short distance away, and paused.

Noah looked down into her eyes and pulled her close. He knew she was expecting his usual kiss on the forehead, but instead, he lifted her face and gave her a questioning look.

She understood that he was leaving the decision up to her. She glanced behind her and saw both sons watching.

"Pretend like they're not there," he advised gently.

Marlena smiled and reached up to caress his cheeks softly. Standing on her tiptoes and pulling his head down, she pressed her mouth to his. As soon as her mouth touched his, she really did forget about the others.

Noah stood absolutely still. He let her kiss him and smiled at her when she pulled back. He glanced over her shoulder and chuckled to himself at the expressions on Adam's and Kaod's faces. They both turned and went back into the house debating something. Noah watched the door close and looked down into Marlena's brown eyes.

"Thank you for trusting me. Do you think you can trust me again?" hc askcd with a twinkle in his eye.

She reached up and pulled his head down and they shared a tender good night kiss. Somewhere from within the house, they heard Adam's shout of triumph and Kaod's groan of defeat, but neither one of them cared.

Chapter Twelve

"So tell me, how things are going between you and Noah," Tina declared.

Marlena smiled and filled her friend in on everything that had been happening.

"So Kaod and Adam are both okay with your and Noah's relationship. What about Noah's other son? Have you met him yet? How does he feel?" Tina questioned.

"I don't know. I've never met him. I know that Noah talks to him every day and that his wife is due to have a child in about two months," Marlena admitted.

"Honey, if you haven't met him or talked to him, then there's a problem. I don't think that Noah would allow it to interfere with the two of you, but would you be okay with that? This kid may not want a new stepmom. I think you understand what I'm saying," Tina responded.

Marlena nodded her head absentmindedly. She made a mental note to question Noah about his oldest son.

Tina sat across from her and looked directly into her eyes. "You've told me everything except whether or not he's finally kissed you." When Marlena didn't respond, Tina squealed with delight. "You kissed him and you were going to keep that little tidbit to yourself. Give up the goods, girl. Was it a peck kiss, a he's so sweet kiss, or the bombshell kiss?"

"What's the difference?" Marlena laughed.

"You're forty-three years old and you don't know the difference," Tina cracked.

"Maybe, Noah is so good that all three feel the same," Marlena slyly countered.

Tina, for once, was speechless.

Noah sat thoughtfully at his desk. In an hour or so, he and Kaod would be having lunch. He'd watched Adam and Kaod yesterday. They were a lot alike. He shook his head in amusement when Adam had revealed the bet he'd made with Kaod. Both young men, he knew, were straight forward and honest. He'd sensed that Kaod was also very protective of his mother. Noah thought how proud he'd been of Kaod for questioning him concerning his intentions toward Marlena. It was pretty astonishing for such a young man. He wanted to build a friendship with him and wondered how close he was to this Drew character. He wanted them to get to know each other and establish their own relationship outside of Marlena. Kaod was probably inundated with people wanting to be in his life for selfish reasons, not to mention the women. Noah wanted to be there for him, to help him through difficult decisions that were sure to come. He pulled the window curtain aside when he heard the unmistakable roar of a Mustang engine arriving. Kaod was early. Somehow that didn't come as a surprise. Noah clicked the intercom button and told Valerie to allow Kaod to come right in.

Kaod strode into the office and shook Noah's hand. They conversed about common topics before Noah broached the more difficult subjects. He asked Kaod about college and the possibility of him going pro. They talked about the temptation of the opposite sex. Noah was surprised when Kaod admitted to still being a virgin. He told Noah about some of the things that had happened to him, the teasing from the other players, and even about Drew encouraging him to sow his wild oats. He explained how his mom had always taught him about abstinence and only being intimate with one woman. He believed that God wanted him to have one wife and one family, unless, of course he found himself in the same situation that Noah was in. Noah was impressed, to say the least, at how well adapted Kaod was. He confided in Kaod about some of the situations he'd found himself in with the opposite sex. Kaod's eyes went wide with amazement. They were enjoying their time together so much that they decided to order in rather than go out.

Kaod, himself, brought up Drew. He told Noah about how he and his mom had met Drew and how Drew had become like a father figure to him. He didn't agree with some of his ideas, but that was to be expected. Noah found the opening he'd been waiting for.

"Do you think your friendship with Drew could affect my relationship with your mother? I certainly couldn't tolerate him being in your mother's life on a personal level. I know that the two of you are pretty close. At one time, it seemed as though your mom and he could become serious," Noah spoke solemnly.

Kaod pondered Noah's words and after several moments spoke earnestly.

"I love my mom and I'd never do anything to get in the way of her happiness. You can't possibly know all that she's been through. I thought Coach Drew would be the guy in her life. Obviously, that may not happen now. If she cares about you and you care about her, then I'm satisfied. It's not a personal issue with you, but you're the pastor of an all white church and I wonder how your members are going to respond when they realize your desire to marry my mom. Can you stand the pressure? Will you defend her at all cost? I mean, the idea of someone saying something racial to my mom kind of makes me crazy just thinking about it. So I guess, in a way, my mom marrying Coach Drew seems less chaotic, but it's still her choice."

"Son, let me tell you something. I would defend your mom with my life. I know it's difficult for not just you, but for most everyone, to understand my courtship of your mother. From the moment I saw her, I knew she was the one. I've prayed to God and there is no doubt that she was given to me. She is to be my bride and God himself will make room for his gift unto me. You are her son and my desire is to graft you into my family as well. That, however, is a choice you will have to make," Noah replied confidently.

Kaod nodded his understanding as the two finished their lunch in idle conversation.

✠

Sunday morning dawned and Noah took his time dressing. There was a lot on his mind. He had to pick up Marlena. He knew it was probably easier for her to meet him at the church, but he liked the time spent with her. It relaxed him and put his mind at ease. He wished she'd sit up front during the service where he could know where she was, but for some reason, known only to her, she wouldn't. He always had to take several seconds to locate her in the congregation before beginning his sermon. He hadn't told her that he loved her, but he could no longer deny it. He was pretty sure she felt the same way. He wondered, to himself, if it was too soon for him to pop the question. He was ready to let the world know his feelings. Was she prepared to commit to him and only him? For the first time in his life, he was nervous about someone else's feelings for him. He said a silent prayer for trust in the Lord. He hadn't told a soul, but he'd been looking at rings and already had one picked out.

Why was he so nervous? Maybe because Kaod had told him that Drew was coming up to speak with her sometime this week about his junior year and the fact that there were plenty of NFL scouts wanting him to skip his senior year and turn pro. Was he nervous about her possible emotional reactions toward Drew? He'd never been a jealous person; however, he didn't at all like the idea of Marlena spending alone time with this guy. He knew she'd kissed the guy previously, but that was way before she'd ever met him. Noah looked in the mirror and adjusted his tie. He'd just have to deal with it. He'd have to wait and see. He smiled ruefully to himself and thought how God was jealous for the affections of his children. He wanted nothing to take His place in their lives. "Boy! Was he made in the image of God," Noah acknowledged.

Marlena smiled hello at Noah as she opened the front door. He grabbed her hand and pulled her towards him. She loved the feel of his strong arms around her. He was always so gentle and kind. She hugged him back and waited for the usual kiss on the forehead. She tilted her head back, and with a questioning look in her eyes glanced at him when there was no kiss. When he still didn't kiss her, she did the next best thing and pouted. That brought a chuckle and the customary kiss on the forehead.

Waiting for her to lock her door, they walked hand and hand to the car. Marlena gave Noah a questioning look, but said nothing. He was in a strange mood. He'd held her hand all the way to the church, but his mind seemed to be elsewhere. Marlena was puzzled. She'd never witnessed this part of Noah. She wasn't uncomfortable with his silence, simply unfamiliar with it. Once again she glanced at him. "Is there something wrong?" she asked.

Noah patted her hand and leaned across the armrest to kiss her on the cheek. "No, sweetheart, everything is fine," he said, giving her a tender smile.

As he helped her out of the car and escorted her into the church, Marlena relaxed. She felt his familiar hand firmly resting on the small of her back.

Marlena stood beside Noah and half listened to the conversation between him and Hal. Kaod said that he would be here, but he hadn't arrived yet. She hoped he didn't walk in during the middle of Noah's sermon. It wasn't that she was a stickler for being on time, but once he walked in, the buzz would begin about "The Pittbull" being at their service. He would become a huge distraction. Ironically enough, Kaod was usually early to anything he attended, whereas she had the tendency to arrive with only moments to spare. She frowned to herself. Noah hated her time schedules, while she didn't particularly care for his need to be a day early to every event he attended. He would definitely display an attitude if they were going somewhere together and she wasn't moving according to "Noah Time". In this instance though, it would definitely be better for everyone if Ka' arrived before the service started. That would allow the congregation the chance to get over the excitement of him being in attendance.

She was sure that, with the exception of Noah, Hal, and Adam, no one else had a clue that Kaod Porter was her son. She liked it that way. She valued her privacy and did not enjoy at all being in the spotlight. It was bad enough constantly being scrutinized as Noah's new "girlfriend". She really was going to be in a fix when Kaod arrived. He always made it a point to let others know who his mom was. She loved her son, but she could do without the hype.

Marlena's nervousness increased until the door finally opened. Tina and her husband Charles, followed by Adam and Kaod walked casually through the door. The entire building watched in total silence as all four walked in the direction of Noah and Marlena. Finally, the whispers began as people began to recognize Kaod. Charles smiled as Tina hugged a surprised Marlena, while Adam and Kaod, hugged Noah. Had she missed something? She stared at Kaod and Noah in wonder. When had they established a blossoming friendship?

After greeting Noah, Kaod ignored the crowd and stood protectively beside his mother. Marlena was grateful when she heard Hal announce that the service was to begin in ten minutes. She turned to find a seat, but Noah placed his hand on her back and began to guide her forward. She had no choice but to allow him to lead her to where he wanted her to sit. There was no doubt in her mind that it would be the front row. She knew Noah well enough to understand that he was definitely making a statement to anyone who cared to notice and that included her. She was contemplating not going until she caught the hard glint in his eye. Marlena was becoming very familiar with that look. It was an unspoken command, not a request. She was learning to pick her battles and this was one not worth the fight.

She allowed him to seat her and watched as he took his place on stage. She was going to have a long talk with "Mr. Bossy Pants" a little later on. As for the moment, she was content to hear him bring God's word.

✝

"Noah preached a heck of a sermon. Don't you think so?" Tina asked Marlena after the service. "He must have some serious inspiration," she joked.

Marlena smiled and gazed around the room. The people were torn between talking to their pastor and meeting Kaod who was standing right beside him. She was relieved to see that the attention was not on her. Kaod appeared to be at ease in the company of Noah and Adam. It was almost as if he had allowed Noah to assume some of the burden. She was stunned. Kaod was a momma's boy. He usually hovered around her as though she needed protection. She glanced around and then it became clear. Noah had understood Kaod's concern for her safety and had steered the crowd away from her onto them. He could relax knowing that his mom was safe. Marlena caught Noah's eye and smiled brightly, a smile that was only meant for him. He returned the smile and gave her a conspiratorial wink.

Tina, catching this little exchange proclaimed, "You love that man and he loves you. I can see it in both your eyes. He watches over you like a hawk. He even has Kaod's admiration. I've known Kaod since he was a baby and I've never seen him gravitate so quickly towards anyone."

Marlena didn't know how to respond.

Tina spoke again, but this time there was seriousness to her voice. "Noah called me a couple of days ago and asked me to come today. He said that you'd be more comfortable with a true friend to sit with. You know that he apologized to Charles and me for not being a better pastor. Can you believe it? He wasn't the reason we left, but he said he'd let us down by not confronting the problems in the church. He begged us not to allow his past mistakes to keep us from honest fellowship with Christ. He even asked us for forgiveness. Charles and I both decided to start attending church again."

Marlena hugged her friend joyously. This was a minor miracle and something she had been praying for endlessly. God had used Noah to answer her prayer. She felt elated. She even repented for calling Noah "Mr. Bossy Pants".

Tina hugged her goodbye and waved at the others as she and Charles departed. Marlena walked slowly towards Noah. Without looking at her, he slid his hand around her waist and eased her by his side. No one seemed to pay any attention to the gesture. It was as though it was the most normal thing in the world.

The last of the congregation had blessedly left. She listened as Noah instructed several of the remaining deacons to lock up before he and Marlena departed. He turned to her and spoke, "We have some important things to discuss, my place or yours Browneyes?"

She completely ignored the question and asked one of her own, "Why do you keep calling me different names? My name is Marlena."

Noah grinned and said arrogantly, "One day, when you get to know yourself better, you'll figure it out Browneyes."

Marlena could feel herself becoming a little irritated as he opened the car door. "Browneyes, Cinderella, Browneyes, Cinderella, you're going to make me schizophrenic. One minute I'm Cinderella, the next, I'm Browneyes. Pretty soon, I'll need you with me just to help me keep my names straight." Marlena retorted, not bothering to get in the car.

She knew that she was being defiant, but it felt good. He was getting too bossy, too big for his shoes. It was about time for him to understand that, she noted to herself.

He didn't say a word, but simply spun her around and planted a firm swat on her bottom, and then chuckled and said, "Get in Browneyes."

It didn't hurt, but it shocked her into action. She looked around the parking lot, relieved to see that no one was around, and obediently slid into the car. "They really were going to have to talk," she thought to herself.

Noah slid into the driver's side and gave her an amused look. "That was for being cheeky."

When she didn't respond, he asked with a smile, "What, nothing to say?"

Marlena cast him a sulky look and cheekily said, "I'm waiting for you to tell me who I am, that way I'll know what to say."

Noah chuckled heartily, "Okay, Browneyes, your home or mine?" he asked.

"Let's go to mine," she answered swiftly.

"Why yours?" he couldn't resist asking.

"That way I can put you out. Could you imagine me walking home from here if I don't like the topic?" she replied with sarcasm in her voice.

Laughing uproariously, he started the car and headed in the direction of her home.

Noah watched as Marlena played with Beauty. The huge beast galloped back and forth across the yard, barking in ecstasy. He couldn't help smiling as Beauty loped towards him and put her head on his lap. She nuzzled his hand until he finally gave in and began to stroke her head. Marlena rolled her eyes when, instead of calling the dog by her name, he called her his "little pony".

"Her name is Beauty," Marlena complained, aggravated at his random attachment of silly nicknames.

Noah deliberately ignored her and continued to sweet talk the big dog which absolutely loved the attention.

Marlena plopped down next to Noah. She wondered what he wanted to talk about.

Noah continued to pet Beauty until he gently eased her away. He faced Marlena and took a deep breath. He started to say something then changed his mind. He stared deep into her eyes and slowly moved closer. He lowered his head and, just before his lips touched hers, whispered, "I love you."

Noah's words didn't surprise her because she felt the same way, but his kiss did. It was different from his previous two kisses. This kiss conveyed his feelings in a way that words could not. It was no longer tentative, but exploring. It searched for a mutual response, a response that clearly reciprocated her love for him.

Her reaction to him made his heart leap with joy. She hadn't said a word, but she didn't need to. Noah knew when he slipped his mouth away from hers that she loved him. Her love for him was written in the depths of her eyes as she gazed wide eyed at him. She opened her mouth to say something, but Beauty began barking frantically and emitting low throaty growls. Both Noah and Marlena looked around trying to determine why the huge dog was so disturbed.

Marlena opened the gate and headed towards the front before Noah could stop her. He reached for her arm and managed to grab it just as they rounded the front corner of her home.

A large crowd of teenage boys and girls was gathered in the street. An argument between two separate groups of girls had turned into a full blown brawl. Suddenly, Noah glimpsed a flash of silver. He threw Marlena to the ground and barely had time to cover her with his body before the shots began. He heard screams and the frightened sounds of gym shoed feet scattering in every direction. Then more pops as someone fired rounds a second time. He prayed for God's protection as bullets whizzed by dangerously close to them.

Chapter Thirteen

Still shielding Marlena with his body, Noah looked around and saw that the street had emptied. He commanded her to stay down as he slowly came to his feet. Verifying that it was safe, he reached down and pulled her up quickly and ordered her into the house. When she didn't immediately move, he grabbed her hand, dragged her towards the back of the house, opened the gate, pushed her inside, then repeated his order for her to take Beauty, go inside, and to call Kaod. Satisfied that she was going to listen this time, he pulled out his cell phone and dialed 911, before racing back up front.

He was sure that someone was down on the opposite side of his car. He had a good view of a body as he lay covering Marlena. He began praying as he rounded the front of his car and to his horror, realized that it was the slender frame of a teenage girl. She looked to be no more than thirteen or fourteen. He knelt over her body and checked for a pulse. She had one, but it was irregular. She was painfully gasping for air. Noah quickly dialed 911 again and notified them of the situation.

It wasn't long before he heard sirens in the distance. The small body began to struggle in pain and fear gripped her eyes. He took off his shirt and gently placed it under the girls head. "Hey sweetheart, you're going to be fine," he told her in a soft calming voice. He could see where a bullet had pierced her body just below her heart.

"I'm scared," she whispered back.

"What's your name, honey?" he asked as he sat near her, holding her hand.

"Chandra, my name is Chandra," she managed to utter. "You're that white pastor that's dating Ka's mom. I'm scared…, scared that I'm going to die. I don't wanna die and go to hell," she gasped fearfully.

Noah gripped her hand tightly and began to tell her about Christ. A crowd had started to gather, but he paid no attention to them and continued to minister to her about Jesus.

The medics arrived, but Chandra would not let go of Noah's hand. They finally gave up and worked around him. Noah kept his focus on the tiny girl. When they loaded her unto the gurney, and attempted to move her into the waiting ambulance, she still determinedly held onto his hand. She told the medics that he was her pastor. Noah flipped open his wallet and showed the medics his pastoral license and they finally agreed to allow him to ride in the back with her. He jumped into the ambulance, and with sirens blaring, it raced off to the nearest hospital.

Noah held onto the tiny hand and said a final prayer of thanks. Her grip on his hand had slackened, then had lost its hold altogether. He didn't need the medic to tell him that Chandra's battle was over. He fought back the tears, and gathered strength from the knowledge that God had granted her time to claim Christ as her Lord and Savior. Nevertheless, he was angered at Chandra's senseless death.

Noah watched as they rushed her lifeless body into the emergency room. He sat down and waited for her family to arrive. That tiny slip of a girl had claimed him as her pastor. A faint smile creased his mouth at that thought.

Marlena and Kaod stepped into the emergency room and hurriedly glanced around. They spotted Noah holding his head in his hands. He looked tired. Marlena slowly walked towards him and called his name. He looked up and sadly shook his head in answer to the question in her eyes. Tears clouded her eyes as she went into his arms. Oblivious to all, he held her tightly and thanked God for sparing her life.

When they returned home, the street was still crowded with police and residents. Kaod had to park on the next block. Noah gripped Marlena's hand possessively as the three of them walked to her home. As they approached, one of the detectives called out his name. Noah, still gripping her hand, greeted the officer as he hustled towards them. Marlena and Kaod grimaced as they recognized Officer Littner. He had attempted to date her for several months before he'd finally given up. He was a very pompous and arrogant man.

"Hey, Noah, what are you doing in this neck of the woods?" Littner asked, glancing from Noah to Marlena.

Not in the mood to converse, Noah ignored his question and filled the detective in on what happened.

"If you need us to write statements, we'll gladly do it tomorrow. Right now, we are all pretty worn out. If you don't mind, we'll be on our way."

Detective Littner nodded his okay and stepped aside to allow them access to the house. Noah could feel the detective's eyes on them as they walked to the back of the home.

The trio went inside and sat tiredly on the sofa. Noah had his arm around her shoulder. He was exhausted, yet concern for Marlena was forefront in his mind. He could have lost her today. That had been a very real possibility. He'd heard the bullets flying past their heads. He shook his head as though to clear his thoughts. Noah reflexively tightened his arms around her and felt her snuggle closer to him. She had fallen asleep, safe in his arms. He closed his eyes to relax and soon drifted off too.

Kaod sat observing the couple. If he'd had doubts concerning this man's love for his mother, they had definitely been dispelled today. He picked up his cell phone and dialed Adam's number and quickly explained the circumstances. He bowed his head and thanked God for his protection over his mom and Noah. He gave thanks to Him for bringing a strong man of God into his mother's life. He knew that Noah had saved his mom's life at the risk of losing his own. Kaod had seen the evidence produced by the bullets. It was only inches above the ground upon which Noah had sheltered his mother. His respect for Noah had been growing over the past weeks, but today, it had soared to new heights. He gazed once again at the sleeping couple. His mom was cradled safely against Noah's chest, while Noah looked every inch the conquering warrior protecting her from the world. Kaod picked up his phone and snapped a picture. He replaced his previous wallpaper on his phone with this new photo.

Noah awakened to find Marlena still curled on his chest. It took several seconds before his mind cleared. He wondered what time it was. Gently easing her head off of his chest, he slid off the sofa and wandered into the kitchen. It was almost one o'clock in the morning. He stretched and spied his overnight bag on the kitchen table. Kaod must have gotten Adam to bring it from the house. He picked up the bag and scurried up the stairs to find the bathroom. Minutes later, he exited feeling refreshed and headed back down the stairs. Marlena was still asleep when he eased himself back onto the couch. She stirred, but didn't fully awake. Noah laid there listening to her breathe and feeling her heart beat against his. His last thought before he drifted off was that he needed to convince her it was time to move.

✞

The scent of fresh coffee brewing and breakfast cooking drifted throughout the house. Marlena smiled as she heard Kaod moving around upstairs. The smell of food was like an alarm clock to that boy. She peeked in the living room, Noah was still asleep. She padded over to the sofa where he lay sleeping. Maybe, she should just let him rest. She turned to walk away when his hand snaked out and grasped her arm. With a swift tug, he pulled her across his chest.

"Good morning, Marly," he grinned.

Not another nickname she grimaced. She noticed the teasing gleam in his eye and refused to respond to the bait. Instead, she leaned forward and kissed him. His initial response was surprise, but quickly changed to pleasure. That, she thought with satisfaction, ought to teach him a lesson. She broke off the kiss and stared smugly at him. Without warning, the atmosphere between them changed. It was no longer teasing, but deadly serious.

Noah held her eyes with his. "I love you, Marly. I was so afraid for you yesterday. I could have lost you," he whispered honestly.

Marlena smiled timidly, "I love you too, Noah Phillips, and thank you for saving my life." She bent down and kissed him once more. Hearing Kaod coming down the stairs, she tried to straighten, but Noah cupped the back of her head and would not let her escape. She gave in and returned the kiss. They both ignored Kaod whistling nonchalantly as he passed.

Marlena and Noah were finishing the dishes as Kaod watched TV. "Oh man, the shooting made the news. Hey, Mom! Our house is on the television!" he announced.

Marlena stopped washing the dishes and followed Noah into the living room. There, on the screen, clear as day, was her home, then a picture of Chandra, and finally Chandra's mother and sister. Marlena's heart broke as she listened to the family beg for the violence to stop. Chandra's mother went on to thank Noah for all he'd done to make her daughter's last moments on earth peaceful. She thanked him for transcending racial barriers and being a true man of God.

Marlena spontaneously embraced Noah. He looked surprised. He couldn't understand what was so spectacular about what he'd done. Kaod and Marlena tried to explain it to him.

They told him that many people felt as though they had no hope. They couldn't see Christ in the churches. There was no reason for them to believe, not when the average person saw no difference in their lifestyle and that of a supposed Christian's.

Marlena looked Noah straight in the eye and said, "There is a church on every corner, yet not one ministry is relevant to these kids. They see no strong presence of God. Pastors show up after the fact. How can anyone respect that? Don't you get it? Chandra spent her entire young life in this community. She knew dozens of pastors, but she chose you. She believed you. She could see Christ in you. You led her to Christ."

Noah sat motionless. A knock on the door, interrupted their conversation. Kaod rose from the sofa and headed to the door. He came back followed by Chandra's mother and older sister, Mia.

"She wants to speak to you, Noah," he informed him.

Noah looked surprised as he stood and shook hands with the mother.

Chandra's mother hesitated, then spoke softly, "Pastor Noah, I was wondering if you would speak at Chandra's funeral. You were the only pastor she trusted. Everybody said she wouldn't let go of your hand before she died. I was just wondering if you'd hold her hand just once more, but this time it would be for her family."

He was silent for a moment. Then he spoke in a voice humbled by this woman's petition, "I would be honored to speak at Chandra's going home service."

The woman released the breath she'd been holding and instinctively hugged Noah. "Thank you! Thank you!" she repeated over and over again.

Noah smiled, thanking God that out of a dark tragedy could shine bright rays of happiness.

The tranquility at the Porter house was soon shattered when Noah's cell began ringing endlessly. Family, friends, fellow pastors, and reporters all wanted to be enlightened on yesterday's tragic events. This ensued Detective Littner's subsequent arrival, and the mega surprise of the day, Noah's older brother, Police Captain Phillips.

Noah dealt swiftly with the phone calls by disregarding most of them, and rerouting some to Valerie; however, Littner and the dynamic Captain Phillips were unavoidable. The Detective was his usual arrogant self. He appeared more interested in Noah and Marlena's relationship than executing any relevant investigatory work. His chief questions pertained to Noah, and his reasons for being at the scene of the crime. His sloppy attempt to disguise it as authentic and necessary police business would have been hilarious, but for the thunderous expression in Noah's eyes.

After listening to Marlena's attempts to avoid his personal questions, and watching him stare lewdly at her, Noah interrupted and spoke softly, "Come here, Marly."

The deceptively calm tone of his voice belayed his anger. Marlena, without hesitation, walked to his side. Noah's gaze never left Detective Littner's face.

"If you want to ask her questions about us, then you should start addressing them to me. Otherwise Detective, stick to questions that pertain only to your investigation."

Littner's face turned a crimson shade of red, but instead of deviating from his personal agenda, he added insult to injury by declaring to Noah in a flippant tone, "Who you bed, 'Pastor', is your business."

Before anyone could stop him, Noah had taken Littner by the shirt collar and slammed him against the nearest wall. He spoke with barely controlled fury, "I'm a big boy and can take whatever sleaze you want to dish out, but make no mistake about Marly. You will treat her with the utmost respect, and if I ever hear you imply something like that about her again, I will take you apart and your badge, and my being a pastor won't stop me."

Captain Phillips and Kaod, both, tried to break Noah's hold on Littner, but to no avail. Ultimately, the Detective broke the hold by glancing at Marlena and extending an apology to her. Noah reluctantly released the disheveled Detective. He walked to Marlena, grasped her by the hand, and headed outside via the back door, leaving a stunned audience in the living room.

Noah was still simmering as he paced back and forth across the patio. Marlena reached out and took his hand. He stopped, looked at her, and hugged her to him.

"I'm sorry, Marly. I'm really angrier with myself, than anyone. I should have exercised better judgment and not put you in a situation that leaves room for guessing," he confided.

Marlena stared at him in disbelief. Caroline's comment to her during the volleyball matches came to the forefront of her mind. Reality had crashed into their world. "Do you really think that he said those things because he thinks you and I are intimate or because you're a pastor? You can't be that naïve. Look at me Noah! Tell me what you see," she prompted.

"I see a very beautiful, godly, and intelligent woman who I happen to love. That's what I see," he stated honestly.

In a voice devoid of emotion, she asked a similar question, "Now tell me what the Littners of the world see."

When he remained silent, she supplied the answer.

"They see a black woman, and that's putting it nicely, involved with a prominent white pastor. That is what Littner sees, and probably so do a lot of other people. Noah, I love you. I really do, but maybe we need to rethink this relationship. It seems to me that God has some serious plans for you. I don't want to be the stumbling block in your life." She turned and started to walk back into the house. Before she'd even taken a step, he grabbed her arm and whirled her back around to face him.

"You want to know what I think Littner sees. You want to know the truth. I think, to put it bluntly, he sees a woman that he desires sexually and he thinks that I've beat him to the punch. All that aside, maybe, it's you who can't let go of the racial aspect of this relationship. Don't pretend it has anything to do with God. God will use whoever He chooses. We can't limit Him by our expectations. If you want to walk away, then be honest and say that you can't handle me being white."

"Maybe I can't handle it. Maybe, you'd be better off with a white woman," she admitted candidly.

"Is that what you want Marly? You really want me to be with another woman?" Noah raked his hand through his curly black hair in frustration. He lifted her chin and looked in her eyes. "You need to do some thinking about us and decide whether we are worth it or not. I'll give you some time to sort thru your convictions. You come to me when you're ready to deal with the fact that every couple faces adversity and we are no different. Trials and tribulation should bond us closer together, not rip us apart. You can either let go and let God, or you can choose to throw us away. I love you, Marly, but I won't wait around forever, and don't make me wait too long, or I may take your advice."

Their conversation was interrupted by Captain Phillips' presence as he came out the back door. "Have you calmed down yet, baby brother?

I thought Littner was going to wet his pants," he chuckled as he recalled the scene.

When Noah and Marlena both remained quiet, he took inventory of the situation and deduced that something was wrong. Captain Phillips observed his younger brother's somber demeanor and watched as Marlena fidgeted with the string on her jacket.

She spoke first.

"I'll let you two have some privacy. I'm sure the Captain would like to speak to you alone."

Noah's gaze followed her as she went into the house.

"All right, baby brother. What's going on with you and your damsel in distress, and is she the one you damned near got yourself killed for yesterday?" John Phillips asked bluntly.

"Nothing to your first question and yes, to your second," Noah supplied grudgingly.

"Listen Noah, what the heck are you doing on this side of town anyway? You could have gotten yourself killed. Then you fly off the handle because of some silly comment Littner makes. What the hell is going on between you and her?"

Noah stared at the back door and remained quiet.

"Come on, Noah. Talk to me," he pleaded after encountering silence.

Noah sat down tiredly and began recounting everything that had transpired between Marlena and him. He told of how they'd become acquainted, Jacob's and Adam's reactions, her unofficial introduction to his congregation, and the events that led up to Chandra's death.

John sat quietly listening. He loved his baby brother and knew that he didn't make rash decisions. Noah was as levelheaded as they came. That is why he'd been so surprised, and Littner had been as well, when Noah had flown off the handle. There was no doubt, in John's mind, that his brother loved this woman. To be honest, he thought to himself, he had never seen Noah react in anger. Not even when their parents had unexpectedly been killed by a drunk driver, or when he'd found out that Colleen had cheated on him. Noah was probably the most self-disciplined man he knew. It was one of the innumerable traits that made him a great pastor. His ability to be the voice of reason during a crisis placed him a notch above most men.

John was proud of his younger brother. He not only preached the word of God, but he seemed to genuinely try to live by it. "So, you're going to marry this woman. What does she have to say about the matter?" he inquired.

"Nothing, but she doesn't know that," Noah grinned.

John laughed heartily. "I've taught you well," he teasingly bragged, "but, on a more serious note, tell me what I interrupted a few minutes ago."

Noah concluded his explanation with the fact that he believed she was genuinely afraid that he would let her down and that she was fearful of the unknown, dating someone who's not from the same racial background. She seemed to see everything in black or white, literally. Noah acknowledged that there were people who were definitely prejudiced, even in his own congregation, but that was their problem.

"How are you going to get her to come around to your way of thinking?" John wondered aloud.

"I'm going to sit back, relax, and allow God to do all the work," Noah shrugged.

"How long are you willing to wait?" John asked with a twinkle in his eye.

Noah sat back and put his hands behind his head. "I'll give her a week," he confessed laughingly.

Captain Phillips roared with laughter as he patted his younger brother on the back.

John spent some time bringing Noah up to date concerning Chandra's case. Noah was left astounded when he found out that the shooter was a fourteen-year-old female, and the dispute had been over a sixteen-year-old boy. Chandra had been hit by a bullet intended for one of her friends. Noah was still mulling this senseless tragedy around in his head as he walked with his brother to the front of the house. He thanked God for His divine protection when he was shown the actual holes the indiscriminate bullets had made. They were no more than seven or eight inches above the location where he had used his body to shield Marly. God had been merciful to them.

Chapter Fourteen

Marlena watched from behind the curtains in her bedroom window as Noah embraced his brother goodbye. She sat on the full sized bed and waited for him to come inside. Instead, Kaod knocked on the door and informed her that he was taking Noah to pick up a rental car since his car had been damaged and was still needed for evidence. He'd return in an hour. Kaod kissed his mom goodbye and hastened back down the stairs to collect Noah. She decided to do some badly needed dusting of the upstairs rooms to keep her runaway thoughts under control.

An hour later, she recognized the sound of Kaod's car pulling into the driveway. A few minutes later, she heard the familiar sound of his light-footed steps on the stairs. She was baffled when he did not come looking for her. She stepped out of the spare bedroom and looked expectantly at Kaod. "Did Noah get the rental?" she inquired in a blank tone.

"Yes, he rented one of those new 2010 Mustangs. Those cars draw women like magnets. Noah said that a Mustang makes him feel young again. They must make him look younger too because there was a little "cutie" in the office giving him the once over," Kaod supplied smiling broadly.

Marlena tried hard to quell the jealousy that invaded her thoughts. She'd like to know just how he'd responded to that little "cutie". She looked away. What was wrong with her? Hadn't she been the one to want to end the relationship? Why was she so afraid of being with Noah? Honesty called for her to admit that it was because God was requiring her to let go of everything that she was comfortable with, to leave her comfort zone and enter the realm of the unknown. She was being rebellious, not in a defiant way, but because she was fearful. She enjoyed her nice quiet life in contrast to constantly being in the limelight. Noah's position and standing in the community required more of her than she was willing to give. To complicate things further, throw in their cultural differences and it became way too much for her to handle. She truly didn't want Noah having to defend her the way he had this morning. She didn't want him risking his reputation for her. All she'd ever wanted was a nice quiet life with a strong godly "black" husband. Noah was definitely strong and godly, but he was also white. Marlena had a hunch that life with him would be anything but quiet.

She had to be honest with herself. She wasn't up to the challenge. Besides that, Noah was becoming too bossy and he was constantly pulling her from her nice relaxing world with those irritating nicknames, Cinderella, Browneyes, and now, Marly. She would have never allowed anyone else to get away with calling her anything other than her name. She had to admit that when he used them, it did make her feel special. It impressed upon her that he'd taken the time to get to know the various traits of her personality. He had discovered things about her that no other man had ever taken the time to explore.

"Did you hear me, Mom?" Kaod's voice broke through her musings.

"What did you say, sweetheart?" she asked.

"I said that Coach Drew called and rescheduled the meeting for next Monday," he repeated, sounding slightly impatient, "and, I said that I invited Noah to come and give his input," Kaod added.

"Why? I thought you valued Drew's advice. By the way, when did you start calling him Noah?" she wanted to know.

"He insisted that I call him Noah. Why does it sound like you prefer Coach Drew all of a sudden? Did something happen between you and Noah?" he asked curiously.

"No, I don't prefer Drew and I don't want to talk about Noah right now," she answered, dodging the question as she headed down the stairs.

Noah sat in his office at the church. Valerie had been surprised to see him. She hadn't expected him to be in at all today. Truthfully, he had intended on working from Marly's home. He still didn't feel comfortable leaving her there alone. He'd had a long talk with Kaod on the way to the rental agency and asked him to stick around the house for the next couple of days. He'd also asked John to have the officers on patrol in that area, pay a little extra attention to the kids on the corners near her home. She seemed oblivious to the dangers. He cringed as he remembered how she'd carelessly walked towards the fighting teens. He'd thanked God again and again for protecting her and he'd prayed for a continuous hedge to envelope her.

Noah smiled reluctantly, thinking about how stubborn she could be. He'd chuckled at some of the stories Kaod had told him about her stubbornness. He hoped she didn't keep him waiting for more than a week. He was ready to officially claim her as his own, but he needed her to accept him without condition. In fact, he wanted her to claim him as her own. He had deliberately not returned to her home today. His plan was to have no intentional contact with her. He'd probably encounter her at Chandra's funeral, but he was not going to seek her out. This would take all of the self-discipline he had, especially since he knew she'd be in need of comfort. He wanted her to miss his fellowship, to miss him enough to come to the knowledge that they belonged together. He was depending on God to keep him strong. He desired that she, as well as her son, would become a permanent part of his life. Noah looked at the time and forced himself to push Marly out of his mind. He picked up his pencil and began writing Chandra's eulogy.

Saturday dawned, and Noah was up early giving thanks to God. For an entire week, God had kept Noah so busy that when he'd arrived home, he'd been too exhausted to do anything but grab a small bite to eat, shower, and go straight to bed. He hadn't had a lot of time to think too much about Marlena. He'd made good on his promise to help Hal. It had taken two evenings, but he and Hal had finally finished Hal's new deck. Then, he'd spent Wednesday evening teaching Bible study. Afterward, he'd spoken with Jacob and had gone to visit Adam. Everyone, including Adam and Hal, had assumed that Marlena was not with him due to Chandra's death. He preferred to allow them to think that was the reason. Noah had been a little surprised when Marlena hadn't attended the weekly Bible study, but he had also felt a little relieved. He missed her tremendously and didn't want her to catch him at a weak moment. He was determined to wait her out. On Thursday, Noah had met with the pastor of their sister church, Jim Wade. They had ironed out the details of their annual end of summer picnic. Later, he'd driven up to Cleveland to meet his attorney and to sign the final contract in reference to his childrens novels. Finally, on Friday, he'd devoted the entire day to drafting and completing his Sunday sermon since he wouldn't be able to do it on Saturday, due to the funeral. Afterwards, he'd gone straight to bed.

Noah told the Lord of his love for Him and how God had always shown Himself to be faithful. He offered up sincere and passionate praise. He then prayed that God would use the words He'd given Noah to convict people's spirit at the funeral. He wanted Chandra's death to give life to someone, and for God to get all the glory. He prayed that the Lord would claim Marlena's neighborhood as His own. Noah also prayed that the Lord would intervene on behalf of his and Marlena's courtship. Feeling a sense of peace, Noah arose and began preparing for the long day that lay ahead.

Marlena stretched and rolled out of bed. She dropped to her knees and began praying. She thanked God for his divine protection and for Him being a faithful and just God. She asked for His guidance in her life and for her to be obedient to His will for her. She prayed for Noah to be used mightily of God today and for his forgiveness if she'd hurt him. She told the Lord of her love for Noah and how much she missed him. Marlena prayed for the courage and strength that only God could give her. She prayed for Kaod, that God would keep him safe and strong in the face of adversity, and that he would make the right decision concerning his future. Finally, she asked God to bring His light to her community, a community that seemed to be covered in darkness, and that Chandra's death would not be in vain.

Marlena turned and sat on the floor. She wondered what would happen when she saw Noah today. She hadn't heard from him all week. Would he still be angry with her? She wasn't quite sure where she stood with him now. After all, she had suggested they break up. Maybe he had moved on with his life already. Noah was the kind of guy who meant what he said and there were plenty of women waiting in line. With that thought upper most in her mind, she headed towards the bathroom.

✟

Noah saw Marlena way before she even realized he was there, but made no effort to greet her. She was escorted by Kaod who appeared very relaxed. Mother and son presented a handsome picture. Kaod was wearing a double breasted black suit with the customary white shirt and black tie which matched her very feminine version of the same suit, but without the tie. She had her hair pulled back and held in place by some type of black scarf. Even at a funeral, she looked beautiful Noah thought. She, as well as Kaod, was receiving a lot of attention. The women, both old and young were almost salivating over him. He handled the attention masterfully Noah thought as Kaod acknowledged him with a wave and immediately headed in his direction, guiding his mother ahead of him. Noah pretended not to notice the men staring at her. When they had finally made their way over to him, he embraced Kaod and gave her a very polite kiss on the cheek. Hal, who had accompanied Noah, looked on in surprise. He slid Noah a questioning glance which Noah ignored.

Marlena stayed silent as the three men carried on a conversation. She wanted to talk to Noah, but after that obviously impersonal kiss on the cheek, she didn't think there was anything left to say. She decided to step outside for a breath of fresh air, but first she paid her respects to Chandra's family. She glanced back and noticed that Noah and Kaod were surrounded by a lively group of women and appeared to be engulfed in conversation. She'd only taken a couple steps outdoors, when she heard someone call her name. She turned to see Tina approaching her.

"Girl, what are you doing out here, when Noah is in there?" she inquired.

"I just need some fresh air before the service starts. Right now, everybody is mixing and mingling and there's not a lot of room to move around," Marlena explained, trying to sound convincing.

"Don't you think Noah needs your support in there? Come on, let's go inside and get a seat before there aren't any left," Tina persuaded.

"Somehow, I don't think he needs my support anymore," Marlena mumbled to herself as she followed her friend back inside.

One hour later, people began streaming out of the exits. Noah had eulogized Chandra in such a beautiful way. Everyone in attendance had been touched in one way or another. He'd retold her last moments and how she had accepted the gift of eternal life. He'd spoken as though he'd known Chandra all of her life, not just for those short moments. He'd explained faith and works and how the two must go hand and hand. His message carried rays of hope for those that were living in darkness. He'd emphasized that although Chandra's earthly life had been taken, the Lord had replaced it with an eternal life. Noah had confessed to all that the church had not been living according to God's standards and before it could call others to account for their actions, it must first bring to task its own members. He emphasized the church's obligation to begin tackling the problems of its communities. People began standing and clapping so loudly that he had to wait several minutes before he could continue. How could the church speak on the actions of those living in darkness when it had failed to be the beacon of light, even within its own family? He hoped that Chandra's death would be the catalyst that awakened God's church. The clapping had begun again. In conclusion, Noah hadn't asked for people to come forward and accept Christ. He directed them to take the time and fully examine their own lives over the next few days. If, after their emotions had calmed down, they wanted to truly commit their lives to Christ, then he and his deacons would be available to any and all.

Marlena was extremely proud of Noah. She hadn't the chance to tell him because he'd left with the funeral procession, while she had opted to go home. She wondered what his plans were for the rest of the day. She wasn't about to call him. He hadn't so much as looked in her direction the entire service and that meant only one thing. He'd lost interest in her. A deep unexplainable loneliness engulfed her.

Noah felt bone-tired as he finally kicked his shoes off and dropped down onto his sofa. What a day! He was glad it was over. He almost wished he didn't have to preach tomorrow. He knew that a lot of the people at the funeral had been filled with emotion. He prayed that some were genuine in their convictions. He would know next week. Either they would call or they wouldn't. Inadvertently, his mind went to Marly. She'd looked so hurt when he'd simply kissed her on the cheek. He'd almost given in and followed her outside, but he'd sent Tina out after her instead. He wondered if she knew that she wore her feelings on her sleeve. She was like an open book. There was no doubt in his mind that she loved him. Her gaze had followed him the entire time. She hadn't even glanced at another man and there had been plenty of them making themselves available. She was going to have to trust him. He missed her company and the smell of her. He'd give her until Monday evening, at the latest. He hoped she'd missed him as much as he'd missed her. Tiredly, he closed his eyes and drifted off to sleep.

Chapter Fifteen

Noah arrived at the restaurant fifteen minutes early. He looked around and saw that Kaod was already there. He wondered if Marlena had ridden with her son. She hadn't come to the Sunday service yesterday and he'd shrugged off questions concerning her absence, but his patience was beginning to wear thin. He slid easily out of the car, pressed the lock button, and headed towards the entrance of the restaurant.

Marlena hurriedly located an empty space and quickly parked the Jaguar. She had made it, and with five minutes to spare. Exiting her car, she took a deep breath and walked steadily into the restaurant. She had no trouble spotting Noah, Kaod, and Drew. All three men stood as she approached the table. Drew wrapped her in a bear hug and bent down to give her his customary kiss. At the last minute, she turned her head slightly and the kiss landed on her cheek rather than her mouth which had been the intended target. Marlena was aware of Kaod's hurried glance in Noah's direction and pretended not to notice Noah's penetrating stare. She frowned when she noticed the empty chair between Drew and Kaod. This meant she had to look directly across at Noah. She wondered who'd come up with the seating arrangements. Her guess would be Noah, judging by the amused expression on his face. She could tell that he knew exactly what she was thinking. Marlena purposefully avoided making eye contact with him.

"You look lovely," Drew complimented.

She smiled her thanks at him. "I take it that you've met Noah?" Marlena asked Drew, still avoiding Noah's stare.

"Yes, Mom, everybody's been introduced," Kaod laughed. "We were just waiting on you to arrive."

Drew smiled his usual charming smile and tried to engage her in idle conversation. After several minutes, he turned towards the others and began explaining what Kaod would encounter during the upcoming football season. He had no doubt that Kaod would more than likely be selected in the first round of the draft if he opted not to finish his junior or senior year. He had brought with him a list of the most respected and honest agents; however, he advised Kaod that if he signed with any agent, then his college football career would be terminated on the date of that contract. Drew went on to explain the different types of contracts that Kaod's agent could obtain for him and the dollar amounts that could be expected. Marly and Kaod both gasped when they heard the dollar amounts. What would anyone do with that kind of money? After hearing the rest of the pertinent information, everyone faced Kaod who sat silently. He looked at his mom, and then at Noah, and finally at Drew.

After several seconds, he grinned and winked at Noah. "What color Mustang would you like?"

Noah grinned back. "Do you mean after you graduate?"

Kaod frowned and glanced from his mom back to Noah. "I believe there's a conspiracy against me."

Noah chastised Kaod gently. "God blessed you with a scholarship. Honor Him, and your mother, by completing it. Trust in Him. If it's meant to be, two years won't make a difference, son."

Kaod nodded in understanding, but then openly confessed, "I really need to get my mom out of that house and into a better neighborhood. Every time I pull up, I picture Chandra lying there. If it wasn't for you, Noah, my mom might not be alive today. I'll be honest with you; it bothers me to think of her alone in that house. I'll be returning to school in a couple of weeks. If I left school early, then I'd have the money to move her into a new home in a better area, and I could relax."

Noah sat back and nodded his head in understanding. How could he get this kid to comprehend that he needn't shoulder this burden? God willing, she would soon be his responsibility.

Marlena cut in and tried to explain to Kaod that it wasn't his job to take care of her.

Noah could see that Kaod wasn't listening to her, and she couldn't see that her little boy was now a man. He felt that it was his duty, and rightly so, to take care of his mom. Hadn't Noah, himself, felt that same desire to protect her the night of Chandra's death? Noah gazed at Kaod.

"Why don't you take a quick walk with me?" he suggested. Kaod nodded in agreement and the two of them excused themselves and headed towards the exit.

Drew immediately turned towards Marlena with a questioning glance.

"So that's your new friend? Come on Marlena, he's white. You shoot down all the brothers for him. You can't be serious."

She looked at Drew. He was a tall, very handsome, and a distinctly built man. Every inch of his body was sculpted. He didn't have an ounce of fat anywhere. His black hair was cut low in a fade, and his deep brown skin was flawless. He had light brown eyes and when he smiled, women melted like butter. Yet, she had never been, in any way, really drawn to him. She had dated him because he'd befriended her son. She was aware of the fact that most football fans had expected them to announce their engagement in the near future, but it had never gotten that far. Drew assumed that she'd be so happy to be seen on his arm that she'd cave in to his demands concerning their level of intimacy. She'd never allowed him more than a chaste kiss and he claimed her actions, or lack of actions, had led to him dating other women. He'd accused her of being frigid on numerous occasions, but the truth was that they were unevenly yoked and she'd always known it. She doubted that he knew the Old Testament from the New, and she'd never seen Christ reflected in him. She listened to him rant and suddenly felt herself becoming slightly defensive about Noah.

"He's the best thing that's ever happened to me. I love him and it doesn't matter to me if he's white," she admitted shyly.

"How in the world could you, Miss.-Hands-off-until-we're-married, be in love with a guy you've known for less than three months? What could you possibly have in common? I barely got to touch your hand without you freezing up, but here he is giving input concerning your son's future. Have you lost your mind? Tell me you haven't slept with him," Drew spat out accusingly.

"How is that any of your business? Did I ever once ask you about any of your dates? Let's just stick to the topic, and leave personal lives out of this and for your information, Ka' invited him here, not me," Marlena asserted.

"Are you doing this to get back at me? You know that I care for you. What about Kaod? He's like a son to me," Drew persisted.

She was prevented from answering when Noah and Kaod returned.

Noah took one look at her face and asked, "Is there something wrong, Marly?"

Marlena saw Drew's expression turn accusatory at Noah's use of his nickname for her. She had never allowed Drew that privilege. She diffused the situation by making Kaod the focus of the conversation. Noah sat down, but kept staring at her. She refused to look at him, but instead looked at her son, and waited for him to declare his decision.

When Kaod announced that he was going to finish school, Marlena threw a grateful glance at Noah. His gaze had still not left her face. After what seemed like an eternity, he turned to Kaod and congratulated him.

Noah stood, and made his apologies to all for not being able to stay for lunch. He had no valid reason for leaving except that there was no way he was going to put on a happy face as he watched "The Hulk" flirt with his future wife. He and Marly were officially not a couple so that left him without the right to say anything. This Drew guy was crossing boundaries and practically claiming Marly as his. He'd liked to know exactly what they'd been discussing as he and Kaod had returned. Judging from her expression, it hadn't been an enjoyable conversation.

He shook Drew's hand, gave Kaod a pat on the back, and leaned down and whispered for her ears alone, "I'll be at my office if you need me." He sensed Marlena's eyes following him as he left the restaurant.

Noah looked out the window and saw the gold Jaguar as it pulled into the slot next to his. He breathed a sigh of relief and sent up a prayer of thanks to God. He watched as she entered the building. Valerie pressed the intercom and announced Marlena's arrival.

"Send her in," Noah instructed.

Marlena hesitated and then walked in.

"Have a seat," Noah invited as he walked over and closed his door, something he'd never done with any other female. Retracing his steps, he sat down on the front of his desk, folded his arms, and waited for her to speak.

Marlena looked nervously around his office and then back at him. "I'm sorry, Noah. I came here to tell you that I'm sorry and to ask your forgiveness," she spoke softly.

"I forgive you. Is that all you wanted?" he asked, deliberately keeping his voice neutral.

"No," she answered truthfully.

When she didn't immediately respond, Noah asked, "What is it that you want from me?"

Before she could say anything, the phone rang and Valerie had buzzed him on the intercom.

"There's a Suzette on line one. She says it's important."

Noah almost moaned in frustration, but then an idea came to mind. Suzette had made no attempt to disguise her attraction to Noah. He'd ignored her phone calls up until now. "Put her through, Valerie," he ordered.

"You want me to put her through?" Valerie questioned, sounding confused.

"I want you to put her through," Noah informed her patiently.

Valerie did as she was told and put the call through.

Noah stared at Marlena and put the phone on speaker. A seductive female voice asked, "Are you available for dinner this evening?"

Noah told the voice to hold, stared straight at Marlena, and pushed the mute button.

"Am I free for dinner tonight, Marlena?" he asked her.

Marlena knew exactly what he was asking and there would be no turning back if she answered yes. She blushed to the roots of her head, but managed to answer, "No."

Noah depressed the mute button and told the voice that he was not free for dinner. The female voice doggedly asked if he was free for lunch the following day. Noah told the voice to hold, pressed the mute button, and not looking away, asked Marlena if he would be free for lunch.

Marlena, realizing that he needed her to claim him as hers, with sprouting confidence declared, "No."

Noah depressed the mute button and told the voice that he was not free for lunch either. With frustration straining her tone, the voice asked, when would he be available?

Noah repeated the process and waited for Marlena's answer. Boldly looking Noah in his eyes, she assured him he would never be available. Noah smiled with untold pleasure as he told the voice on the phone that he belonged to someone, and therefore, would never be available. With a decisive click, Suzette hung up the phone. He stood and held his arms wide in an invitation to Marlena. She wasted no time and was across the room in a flash and into his arms.

They held each other tightly, as though they'd spent a lifetime apart. After several minutes, he pulled back and kissed her on the forehead, then tilted her head up to meet his eyes.

"I love you, sweetheart, and I've missed you so much. Don't ever push me away again," Noah uttered with a slight warning to his voice.

"I'm sorry, Noah, and I've missed you, too. I love you very much," she whispered sincerely, understanding that he had deliberately allowed himself to be vulnerable to whatever decision she'd make. He had made himself weak in order for her to become strong. If it were possible, she loved him even more and vowed to dedicate her life to making him happy.

He reached in his pocket and removed a velvet red box. He opened it to reveal a solid gold ring with two heart shaped diamonds that appeared to be interlaced. It was the most beautiful ring she had ever seen. Noah's voice cracked with emotion as he asked her to become his wife. Without hesitation, she accepted tearfully and watched as he slid the ring on her finger. It fit perfectly. He brushed her ringed hand gently with his mouth.

Tilting her head back, Noah captured her mouth in the same manner he had captured her heart. His kiss branded her as his and connected their souls with an unbreakable bond. It sealed their engagement in the same manner as the Holy Spirit seals believers into the family of Christ. When, at last, he lifted his mouth, they were both aware that there was no reversing course. From this point on, the ultimate goal was to achieve oneness in each other and as a couple in Christ.

✠

Noah wrapped his arms around her and pulled her tighter. He kissed the top of her head and began to thank God for His love and protection. He asked God to bless the covenant they'd both made. He expressed their love for Him and their desire to have their engagement and, when the moment arrived, their marriage to mirror that of Christ's engagement and eventual marriage to the church. God, alone had ordained this. Noah was sure of it. This woman had been given to him. God had given him his heart's desire, a virtuous woman of God. As if to confirm his belief, God brought back to Noah's remembrance, the inscription on her key chain.

Noah watched as Marlena parked her car in the garage. He had quit work early and had given Valerie the rest of the afternoon off. After a week of not seeing Marly, he'd wanted to spend some time with her. He felt like a kid with his first love. He smiled at her as he opened the door for her. "What would you like to do today? I am at your disposal."

"Let's go and tell Tina. If she isn't one of the first to know, she'll kill me," she told him.

He pulled off and headed towards Tina's house.

"Marly, what happened between you and Drew this afternoon?" he asked, glancing sideways at her.

"He was a little upset at me because of you," Marlena hedged.

"He wants you back. Is that what you're trying to say?" Noah questioned.

"No, he wanted to know if I'd slept with you yet," she quickly blurted out. "I don't understand men. Not everything is sexual. You've never given me that impression. You're different, Noah. We've kissed, but I've never felt like you were pushing me in that direction. It's nice," she admitted.

Noah looked at her with wry amusement and pulled into the next vacant parking lot. He turned off the car and faced her. Now is as good a time as ever to talk about intimate things he thought.

"Marly, don't think for one moment that because I'm a pastor, you don't arouse those types of feelings in me. Do you really think that when we're married, I won't want to make passionate love with you? We'll just hold hands and exchange gentle nonthreatening kisses and be content. Everything has it's time and place. I'm a man that just happens to believe our God means what he says when he commands us to wait until we marry."

He could tell that she was embarrassed by this frank conversation, and he was sure that she'd never been with anyone but her husband, but she needed to understand him and not put him on some type of pedestal.

"Sweetheart, I'm no different than other guys in the fact that I find you very sensual, but that's not all I see or want. I desire the whole package and I want it for the rest of our lives; however, I'm not willing to risk God's blessings for our marital bed, because I can't control my desire to make love with you." Noah reached over and turned her chin so that she had to look at him. "When the time comes for me to make you my wife in every sense of the word, I don't want you looking at me as a pastor, but as your husband. And, I hope that you'll want to make love with me every bit as much as I want to make love with you."

She spoke in a barely audible tone, "I already do."

Her softly spoken admission caused an involuntary moan to escape from his throat. "Sweetheart, you'd better hurry up and set a date," he advised as he started up the car and pulled out of the vacant lot. He laughed huskily and squeezed her hand when she quickly turned her head away shyly.

Tina was sitting outside when the Mustang pulled in front of her home. She smiled in recognition as Noah opened the passenger door for Marlena.

"Hi. What are you two doing here and why are both of you smiling like the cat that ate the canary? Did Kaod decide to finish college?" she quizzed.

Tina couldn't figure out what was going on until the sun glinted of the ring on Marlena's finger. She screamed for Charles, who came running out of the house in his bare feet looking confused. She reached for his hand and pointed to Marlena's ringed finger. Tina hugged Marlena and began laughing and crying at the same time. "I'm so happy for the both of you. Have you set a date? Does Kaod know?" she rushed out.

Noah looked at Marlena and chuckled. "Is she going to allow us to answer?"

Charles, finally understanding what his wife was going on about, hugged Marlena and shook Noah's hand.

"Excuse us, gentlemen," Tina said as she grabbed Marlena's hand and nearly dragged her into the house. Once inside, she let go with a barrage of questions that had Marlena giggling like a teenage girl.

Marlena explained the when and the where's of the engagement. She even told her friend about Suzette which had Tina in stitches.

"I think you've finally met your match. What does Kaod think about your engagement?" Tina asked.

"He doesn't know yet. I think he's still at lunch with Drew," Marlena furnished.

"Drew! Has he met Noah, yet?" Tina wondered.

Marlena filled her in on all that happened with Drew.

"I can't believe that he had the nerve to ask you that. He had his chance. He's going to be really angry when he finds out that you're engaged to Noah. He expected you to wait on him," Tina said.

Marlena didn't respond as they headed back outside.

"Where are we going now?" Marlena asked, as Noah turned down an unfamiliar road.

He had suddenly remembered seeing something that might interest the both of them.

"I'm not quite sure, but I'll let you know when I see it. I hope it's still there," he said, smiling in a way that aroused her curiosity.

She sat back and enjoyed the ride. Minutes later, he pulled into the driveway of a beautiful log cabin home. Marlena stared at the house. She had always dreamed of living in a home like this. She looked at Noah and wondered if someone he knew lived here. He walked around the car and opened her door. He put his arm around her waist and stood viewing the house and its surroundings. Finally, he nudged her forward.

She looked at him quizzically and asked, "Who lives here?"

He shrugged his shoulders, took her hand, and pulled her across the well manicured lawn to a patch of tall grass that hid a metal real estate sign. It was lying flat, and had concealed the fact that the house was for sale. Marlena's eyes grew as large as saucers as she realized why he had stopped. She was speechless. Her feet refused to move. "Would you like to look around, or are you just going to stand here and gawk?" he teased.

She nodded yes.

"Yes, you'd like to look around, or yes, you're going to just stand here and gawk?" he laughed.

She gave him the most beautiful smile he'd ever seen, grabbed his hand, and pulled him toward the house. It was pretty obvious that the house was vacant, so they spent the next thirty minutes walking around the grounds. Behind the house, as far as you could see, were woods and a stream which seemed to act as a natural boundary for the property. The house had a wrap-around porch with the back portion enclosed. Noah noticed a path which lead from the house into the woods and wondered if it traveled in a complete circle back to the house. Near the stream, were two swinging benches directly underneath a huge weeping willow tree. The scenery was absolutely breathtaking.

They both tried to imagine what it would look like during the other three seasons. Noah hugged her from behind and lightly rested his chin on top of her head. "So what do you think?" he asked softly.

"I love it," she admitted.

"How can you love it when you haven't even seen the inside, yet? I guess we'll have to make an offer without seeing the inside," he joked.

She laughed aloud. Marly turned in his arms and asked in a serious tone, "Are you really interested in buying a new home?"

"We have to live somewhere. Somehow, I don't think that either one of us would be comfortable living in our deceased spouses' home. Unless of course, you don't mind living in a home that Colleen lived in. I sure as heck don't want to live in Shawn's," Noah reasoned.

"You've got a point. How much do you think this house cost? Can we afford it?" Marlena thought with a frown.

"We haven't even gotten married yet, and you're already trying to figure out what's in my pocket," he teased mercilessly.

She buried her head in his chest to hide her flaming face. He hugged her to him, enjoying how easily she succumbed to his teasing. "What next Cinderella? You'll want to see my bank statements and then use my charge cards," he couldn't resist adding.

She groaned and tried to escape, but he held her imprisoned in his arms. She could feel his body shaking with laughter. Marlena took her fingers and began poking him in his sides. He easily captured her wrist and pulled her close.

"Somehow, I think we'll be able to manage it. I have some money put aside and very little debt. What about you? Where do you stand financially?" he asked, walking her towards the front of the home.

She situated herself in the car and waited for him to get in. She explained to him that she didn't have any debt, nor did she like to use charge cards. When her husband had passed away, he'd had life insurance. She'd paid off the home, purchased her and Kaod's vehicles, and the rest of the money still remained in the bank. She and Kaod had lived off of her income and since he'd received a full ride scholarship, she hadn't needed to spend the money on his education. It was still in the bank for future necessities. Currently, there was a little over one hundred forty-five thousand dollars.

Noah stared at her with his mouth wide open. "Are you telling me that, other than your cars and the house, you haven't touched the money from Shawn's death?" he asked with incredulity in his voice.

"I know the Jaguar seems a bit much, but I always dreamed of owning one," she confessed as though she'd done something wrong.

"This woman was unbelievable," he thought to himself.

He couldn't believe she felt guilty about her car, and hadn't so much as spent a dime on anything else. Most of the women he knew, would be either so far in debt, or flat broke by now, and she's worried about what he thought of her because she'd bought a car. He started to say something, but thought better of it. From what Kaod had told him about his father, she deserved a heck of a lot more than a car. Her husband's lifestyle had hurt her tremendously.

"What are you saving the rest of the money for?" he asked casually.

"I thought Kaod might need it after he finished school, but the way things are going, he'll be able to take care of himself. I really don't know," she responded. "Maybe we could use some to put down on the house if we like the interior," she suggested.

Noah couldn't help but smile.

"I think I can manage to finance our house. In the mean time, if you really want to help, you could move into an apartment when Kaod goes back to school. I'm no longer comfortable with you being in that house all alone and neither is Kaod," he entreated firmly.

She casually dismissed his worry.

"I don't feel the need to move. Beauty and I will be fine. Besides that, what would I do with Beauty? There aren't too many places that permit dogs her size, and I don't want her cramped in some small apartment for the next year or two," she complained.

Noah's mind completely left the subject of Beauty and honed in on the length of time she imagined she'd be in an apartment.

"What do you mean by a year or two? Just how long are you planning on being engaged?" he inquired.

"The normal engagement lasts about twenty-four months. Which, (she brought the topic back to Beauty) is why I don't want to move into an apartment."

Noah allowed her to debate her point all the way back to her home. He had tuned out after hearing twenty-four months. Was she nuts or did she not comprehend his little talk earlier? Wait for two years. He could care less about the effects of an apartment on Beauty right now. Noah was more concerned with the "effects" of a two year engagement on him. Desperate situations called for desperate measures he thought. He waited patiently as she unlocked the door and stepped inside. She continued her defense of why she didn't feel the need to move. Yada, yada, yada …. Noah calmly shut the door, walked towards her, and pulled her into his arms. His last thought was for the Lord to be with him as his lips met hers and silenced her words.

Instead of being tender, the kiss was meant to awaken and elicit a mutual response. This wasn't his usual brief kiss, this kiss hinted of something still as of yet, unknown between them. He sensed her initial surprise turn to familiarity. But unlike previous times, he deepened the kiss until her arms slid up and around his neck and her hands entangled themselves in his hair.

He released her mouth and kissed his way to her ear, where he whispered, "Let's get married in June."

Before she could respond, his mouth had found hers again. He leisurely explored her mouth before returning to her ear and whispering the same suggestion. Noah heard the shift in her breathing as she nodded yes.

Maybe he should kill two birds with one stone he thought as he kissed her ear again and asked, "Move into an apartment for me?"

She shook her head yes again and tugged on his hair as an indication that she was impatient for his kiss. He obliged her and once again found her mouth with his. This time however, he was the one caught off guard when she eagerly accepted his kiss. It quickly erupted from teasing to passionate. Noah's entire body responded as she pressed forward. He had ignited something in her that had previously been dormant. With a superhuman effort and help from God, he tore his mouth away from hers and pushed himself away.

Her expression showed confusion, and then shock, finally embarrassment. She managed to stammer out, "I'm sorry."

He combed his fingers through his hair and attempted to rein in his desire. After several minutes, his breathing calmed and his racing pulse slowed. She looked mortified and as though she was trying to find some place to hide. Noah grabbed her hand before she could escape.

He ever so gently hugged her to him and simply said, "No, Marly, I'm the one who should apologize. I was wrong. I took advantage of you, trying to make a point and I allowed it to get out of control. You didn't do anything wrong, I did. Will you forgive me?"

She lowered her head, feeling deeply ashamed, but shook her head yes. He held her for a moment, and then leaned back and looked at her. He prayed that he hadn't broken her trust in him. He attempted to lighten the mood.

"Now that both our heads have cleared, when would you like to get married?" he asked, leaving the decision up to her.

She hid her face in his chest and mumbled, "Tomorrow."

Noah laughed softly, "Me too, but I think we can hold off until June."

"What about the apartment?" she brought up.

"Will you move for Kaod's and my peace of mind? I'll keep the pony at my house, if we can't find a place that allows horses," he pledged.

She giggled at his reference to Beauty.

"Okay," she finally complied.

He swung her around in a circle and gave her one of his goofy kisses on the forehead. She laughed uncontrollably until he finally stopped. Noah smiled and hugged her to him. He felt relieved that despite everything, she'd agreed to move.

✟

Noah lay in his bed thinking about the day's events. He knew that God loved him, despite the foolish thing he had done to Marly. He told God how sorry he was again. He took full responsibility for what had almost gotten out of control. It was his own vanity that had wanted to see if he could seduce her into doing things his way. Now, they would have to suffer the consequences of aroused passions for the next eleven months.

He already knew enough about Marly to know that she liked to cuddle and she'd grown accustomed to him touching her in a nonsexual way. She was a woman, and that was how she bonded. But, what was once innocent, may be a serious challenge for him now. Having experienced how responsive she could be, he knew his body had reached a level of heightened awareness that was going to be hard to overcome. She, on the other hand, might feel rejected or as though she'd done something wrong if he didn't touch her in his usual way. He was going to have to suffer through the next months due to his own selfish vanity. He'd rather pay the price, than to have Marly feel hurt.

He thought about men, and how they'd thrown the responsibility of sex and pregnancy onto the woman. It was a sign of weakness for any man to expect a woman (whom God made to respond to the man) to be able to control the outcome of ignited passion. Noah had known the minute he'd kissed her that third time, she'd allow him to go as far as he wanted. She had trusted him and he had almost betrayed that trust.

He wanted to live a life pleasing to God and knew that he had a greater accountability because he was a preacher of God's Word; however, he was as sinful as the next guy. It was the Holy Spirit that was responsible for all the good he'd ever done. If not for the Holy Spirit that dwelled in him, he'd probably be in her bed right this very moment. Living for Christ was difficult. People assumed that you were perfect with no flaws, they didn't understand that you were exactly like them, except forgiven. You still have the same struggles, but Christ fights your battles and he never loses. He is the reason you battle against the sins that others are content to commit.

God's authority and love over a believer is supreme. The sooner mankind understood that, the better off the world would be. He closed his eyes and thanked God for chastising him and for giving him the power to pull back this evening. He groaned out loud when he remembered the embarrassing look on Marly's face. He apologized to God for almost shaming His daughter. Noah fell asleep at peace, knowing that even in this, God had forgiven him.

Marlena sat on her bed reviewing today's events. She was now an engaged woman. Adam and Kaod had received the news of their parents' engagement with gladness. Jacob had been less than thrilled, but that didn't come as a surprise. As Noah had said, "Jacob would have to learn how to deal with the life and family God had given him". She wasn't too thrilled about moving, but if it made the men in her life feel at peace, she'd make the sacrifice.

She tried not to think about what had happened between her and Noah. She didn't know why she'd lost control. She had never in her life responded to anyone as though she were some infatuated teenager. Her body had suddenly fought against her mind. She clearly knew God's Word, but if Noah had not stopped, she groaned in shame knowing how far she would have gone. Still, a part of her felt rejected. The memory of her husband not finding her attractive was very much lodged in the back of her mind. She had pushed those thoughts away and had pretended throughout the rest of the evening that it was over and forgotten. She had no clue how she would respond when she saw him tomorrow. Marlena asked God to forgive her and prayed that he would help them stay pure until their wedding night. For obvious reasons, June now seemed like an awful long time away.

Chapter Sixteen

Marlena sat at her kitchen counter and looked around. Why had she agreed to move? She was perfectly safe. No one had ever bothered her. A knock on her door startled her out of her musings. She looked up to find Drew standing on her front porch. She unlatched the door and invited him in.

"Kaod isn't here, he went to work out," she informed him casually.

"I didn't come to see Kaod. I came to talk to you. I hear congratulations are in order," Drew commented offhandedly.

Marlena smiled her thanks, but kept quiet. She excused herself for a second and went into the kitchen to turn off the faucet. Beauty, who was lying beside the table, watched Drew as he entered the house.

"Is that protection against me?" he laughed half jokingly.

She gave him a lopsided smile and asked, "Do I need protected from you?"

Drew took a couple steps toward her. Beauty's hair stood up on her back as she gave a warning growl. Marlena hooked her hand underneath the dog's collar and tried to calm her down.

She looked at Drew and asked, "Have you come here to insult me some more?"

"No, I'm leaving, and I thought I'd drop by to get one last goodbye kiss," he said mockingly.

Beauty lunged forward. It was all Marlena could do to hold on to her.

From behind her a voice chuckled, "My sentiments exactly, Beauty." Noah opened the back door and came in. Beauty immediately settled down and began wagging her tail. He reached down and took hold of the dog and stroked her head. Standing, he nodded to Drew and kissed Marlena on her forehead.

"I'll be out back with Beauty," he said, taking the huge dog outside.

The storm door closed behind him.

Drew acknowledged quietly, "Noah is a good man."

"Yes, he is," she agreed.

An awkward silence ensued until Drew finally spoke, "You're a unique woman, Marlena and you've raised a great kid. I shouldn't have spoken to you that way yesterday. You didn't deserve that. I was feeling jealous. I suppose I thought you'd always be mine. When you and I talked about Noah, I didn't think you were serious. I guess what I'm trying to say is that I really blew it and I wish you two the best."

Marlena walked to him and gave him a hug. "Thanks. Drew."

He gave her his usual bear hug and told her that he'd always be there for her and Kaod. He kissed her on the cheek, hugged her once more, and headed out the back door.

Noah glanced up as he heard the door swing closed. Instructing Beauty to stay, he opened the gate and met Drew as he dismounted the stairs. Drew extended his hand and Noah clasped it in a firm handshake. Beauty raced towards the gate growling protectively.

"What is up with that dog?" Drew questioned laughingly.

Noah grinned proudly, "She loves me."

Drew's expression became serious, "So does Marlena. You take good care of her. Keep her happy or else I may have to steal her back."

Noah chuckled and gripped his hand tighter, "If it makes things any easier, I love her more than life itself, and I'm willing to spend the rest of my life keeping her happy."

Drew nodded his satisfaction and walked towards his vehicle. Watching Drew drive away, Noah realized that he wasn't the only man in love with Marlena.

Marlena glanced at Noah as he came in the back door, "Thanks for giving us some time. That was very gallant of you."

"I can tell you're a schoolteacher. Who else would use a world like gallant? Most people, ordinary people that is, would use a common word like 'thoughtful' or 'sensitive'. Gallant," he repeated in a proper tone.

Marlena couldn't resist laughing as he pulled her into his arms.

✝

Marlena sat in the middle, with Tina and Charles on one side, and Adam and Kaod on the other, as Noah began the conclusion of his Sunday sermon.

He had preached on the book of Ruth. He'd explained the relationship between Boaz (the hero in the story) and Christ. How it was necessary for Ruth (the damsel in dire straits) to claim Boaz as her redeemer, and how those, that were still unbelievers, must claim Jesus as their redeemer. He told of how Boaz could not force Ruth to accept him. She had to take the first bold step of claiming him; likewise, all nonbelievers must claim Christ as their redeemer.

Marlena knew the story well, but the way Noah presented it moved her to want to be closer to Jesus. She imagined Jesus walking beside nonbelievers every day, patiently waiting for them to realize that saving grace was theirs. All they had to do was ask. She bowed her head and thanked God for sending His son as Redeemer of the world.

Concluding his sermon, Noah asked everyone to remain seated for an important announcement. Gazing at Marlena, he asked Hal to escort her up to the pulpit. She sent Noah a questioning look as Hal helped her from her seat and escorted her towards the pulpit.

"Don't worry sweetheart, I'm not going to bite you," he teased as she made her way up the steps.

The congregation laughed in delighted amusement. Noah grabbed her hand and pulled her gently to his side.

Standing in front of the microphone, he announced in a pleased tone, "I proudly introduce to you, friends and church family, my fiancée, the future Mrs. Noah Phillips, Ms. Marlena Porter."

Applause erupted from within the sanctuary. Most of the deacons were grinning from ear to ear. Marlena was blushing profusely as she looked at Noah and then at the congregation. She shyly put her arm around his waist and smiled. Noah reached down and kissed her briefly on the lips. Their church family clapped their approval. Waiting for the applause to die down, Noah led them in a closing prayer and dismissed the congregation.

Forty-five minutes later, they were still being congratulated. Marlena leaned against Noah and debated on whether or not to slip her shoes off. She had no idea what the protocol was. She didn't want to do anything that would embarrass him, but had she known she'd be standing for what seemed like an eternity, she would have worn pillows on her feet. And they say women talk a lot. Whoever said that must not have ever been around a pastor and his deacons after a service. She glanced at Noah again, used his arm to hold steady, and removed her shoes. Wriggling her toes, she met his smiling eyes. That, she decided, was much better.

✞

Time sped by. Noah took time to show her the ins and outs of his ministry and what he required of her, and her role as a pastor's wife. She learned that he had a prison ministry which accounted for his knowledge of slang. They discussed various meetings, boards, personal finances, and the merging of their accounts. Both homes, they decided, would be placed on the market, unless Adam or Kaod wanted them. They went apartment hunting and arranged to view the logged cabin home. They learned more about each other's likes and dislikes. The two of them knew enough to be open and honest about past hurts and failures. He learned more about her school, the subjects she taught, the children and their families, and the daily struggles of teaching. Noah and Marlena discovered that merging two lives together was not an easy task, especially lives that involved different cultures and existing children. The fact that Christ was their foundation and the center of both their lives made the transition much smoother. They hadn't encountered a problem that Christ had no answer for. She was more than willing to allow Noah to lead and to have the final say over points they couldn't agree on. So far, that had never occurred, and she respected him enough to believe that he'd always have their best interest in mind if it should come to that.

✞

Noah and Marlena had viewed at least four apartments over the past two weeks and she hadn't found any to her liking. She wouldn't say exactly what the problem was, but he was beginning to wonder whether Marlena was just being picky or suffering from moving anxiety. Quite frankly, his patience was wearing thin. They had an appointment this afternoon to look at another apartment. He hoped she'd like this one, regardless of whether they allowed pets or not. Besides, he thought, this particular apartment was only five minutes away from his home.

An hour later, they arrived to view the apartment. Noah sensed a change in the manager's attitude when he saw that Marlena was not white, but he ignored it.

Marlena glanced around the apartment with no interest whatsoever. The apartment was quite nice. It had two bedrooms a decent sized kitchen and bathroom, with a reasonably sized living room. She could even open the doors and sit outside on a spacious balcony. Noah pulled her aside and asked her if she liked it. Marlena shrugged and looked around the apartment blankly. He could tell that this wasn't a change she wanted to make. There was nothing wrong with the apartment. She just didn't want to move. He sighed, and asked the manager if they could have some time alone. Noah watched the manager leave, and turned to faced Marlena.

"What's wrong Marly?" he asked tiredly.

She turned her back and didn't answer. He was beginning to recognize this mood. It conveyed that she didn't want to talk about it because she didn't think he would understand. "Talk to me Marly. I promise I'll try to understand," Noah pleaded, trying desperately to keep the frustration out of his voice.

Suddenly, she blurted out, "I don't want to move. I like my house, in my neighborhood, where I feel very comfortable. How would you like to live in a place, where it's pretty obvious, that you're not wanted? Nothing's changing for you. You still get to live in your house, in your familiar neighborhood. To top it all off, I can't even bring my dog. The one thing in the world besides Jesus that I know loves me."

So, she had noticed the manager's attitude. He could understand how that would make her angry, but that silly comment about the dog pushed him beyond his limit. "Don't blow this out of proportion or make irrational comments. You know that I love you very much, so don't say things you really don't mean. I understand this is a huge change, but cut me a little slack here."

She whirled to face him with eyes flashing full of angry fire.

Noah cut her off before she could say a word, "Oh, no you don't. You're not going to start a fight so that we can forget about renting this apartment."

He walked to the door and yanked it open. She heard him saying something to the manager. Fifteen minutes later, he returned with paperwork in hand and a receipt for the deposit, and, the first and last month's rent.

"I've decided that you like this apartment very much because it's right down the street from your loving fiancé," he declared sarcastically.

Fuming, she marched ahead of him out to the car. She went to yank open the door, but he hadn't unlocked it. She stood waiting by the door while he proceeded to take his time. When he reached the door, he calmly unlocked and opened it, then waited for her to get in. She turned to face him with a sharp retort.

He was standing so close to her that they were almost touching.

"Rule number one, Marly: if we are going to argue, we do it in the privacy of our own home, and rule number two: because you're angry, doesn't mean you stop allowing me the privilege of treating you like a lady. Now, you can get in the car Browneyes."

Marlena opened her mouth to speak, but saw the apartment manager staring at them and the unmistakable warning in Noah's eyes. She angrily plopped down into the car.

Noah fought to maintain a calm exterior as he shut her door and went around to the other side and climbed in. Without looking at her, he drove off.

Not a word was spoken, even when he headed in the opposite direction of her home. Still smoldering with pent-up anger, Marlena refused to ask him where they were going. Eventually, he left the highway and turned down a familiar road. She finally looked at him as the car pulled into the parking lot at Sophia's. All of her pent-up-anger began to deflate and she felt slightly foolish.

They sat without speaking until Noah faced her and asked gently, "What's really bothering you, Marly? I know you can't possibly think that I don't love you. Why are you so angry?"

She tried to fight back the tears. "When did I become a crybaby?" she wondered. She'd never been a crier, not even when Shawn had said the vilest of things to her. Now, here she was with Noah, and it seemed as though she was constantly crying. She felt weak and helpless. Marlena turned her head to keep him from seeing her tears. They were streaming down her face, and she couldn't get them under control.

Instinctively, Noah knew she was crying. He climbed out and walked around to the passenger side. Opening the door, he reached in and gently pulled her out and into his arms.

"Please don't cry, Marly," he pleaded tenderly. "Tell me what's wrong, sweetheart. I'm not going to guess, you're going to have to trust me enough to share."

He bent his head and tenderly touched his mouth to hers. He tasted her salty tears, but kept his mouth pressed to hers.

She tilted her head back and looked at him through a wet blur.

"Let's go home," he said as he helped her back into the car.

Noah held her hand the entire way back, but did not say a word. He drove to his home and pulled into the garage. They had a lot of talking to do and he figured no one would interrupt them at his place.

Seated on the sofa, Noah waited patiently for her to speak. Instead the tears began to flow again. He took her in his arms and spoke soothingly to her. He didn't push the issue, he just allowed her to cry. He felt totally inadequate to help her. He couldn't understand unless she confided in him. He prayed to God for wisdom on how to deal with the situation. When there was no answer, he gave it completely to God. Marlena had become so still that he knew she had cried herself to sleep. He replayed her conversation at the apartment in his mind. "Nothing is changing for you" she had said. He exhaled a deep breath. She was moving away from everything that was familiar to her: her only child was leaving the nest with a future that was financially secure to the point that he was no longer dependent on her, she wouldn't have the constant adoration or companionship of her pet, and to top it off, according to God's word, she would soon be submitting to the authority of her husband after years of independence from any man.

Noah was shocked anew at the depths of this woman's love for him. She was willing to give up everything to become his wife. No one, save the Lord, had ever sacrificed so much for him. Colleen had been his first crush, but even she had loved him for what he could do for her. He kissed the top of her head and vowed that nothing but death would separate him from this woman. He would try to love her as Christ loves his church.

Marlena awakened to the smell of food cooking. She lay still trying to comprehend her surroundings. Sitting up, she eased from beneath the comforter. Noah she thought. She was in his home, asleep on his couch. She rubbed her eyes. They felt swollen from all the tears. What was she going to say to him? There were so many emotions that she was feeling. She loved him with everything she had. She wanted to be his wife, of that she was positive. It was the change from the familiar to the unfamiliar. Kaod wasn't her little boy any longer, she was moving out of her home, and submitting herself to a man's authority, all these things were happening so fast and all at once. She stood up and slowly walked into the kitchen. There, lying on the floor was Beauty happily chewing on a huge, roasted rawhide bone. She greeted Marlena happily before returning to her prized bone. She turned to face Noah, not knowing what to say.

He spoke before she could say anything, "Let's have dinner, and then take our pony for a walk."

Marlena threw herself in his arms, grateful for his understanding.

Noah held Beauty's leash in one hand and Marlena's hand in the other. He'd decided to try and gradually acclimate both to the changes that were going to inevitably take place. He believed Marlena was feeling overwhelmed by the swiftness of the changes. He hadn't asked her another word about it. She'd open up when she was ready to talk.

They walked in silence until they reached a nearby park. Noah unleashed the big dog, which stood looking confused.

Marlena giggled, "She's trained to stay near you because people are naturally afraid of big dogs. She'll fetch if you throw a stick or ball."

Noah smiled and pulled a ball out of his pocket. He showed Beauty the ball and tossed it a ways out. The big dog took off after the ball, retrieved it, and brought it back to Noah. He kept the dog retrieving for the next ten minutes until she appeared tired.

Marlena sat down on the bench and observed Noah. She owed him an explanation for the tears. Noah sat down beside her and casually dropped his arm around her shoulder. She played with the ring on her finger and watched Beauty roll around on the grass.

At last, she spoke, "I'm feeling like everything that is familiar to me is disappearing, as though I have no identity, no home, no anything. I don't know if you can understand any of it, but it's not you. I love you so much. I want to be your wife, share everything with you. I wish we were married right now so I wouldn't have to look at that apartment and feel lonely. I'll miss all that's been my life. It sounds silly, but when you leave my home in the evenings, I still have familiar sounds and people. What happens when I move into that apartment? It's all gone, everything will become strange."

She glanced at him and then looked away.

"What do you want me to say Marly? That you can stay in your home until we are married? I know it's your neighborhood, but things are changing. You've got kids carrying guns, young girls dying. You could have been killed. I lie awake at night thinking of you being there all by yourself. Kaod has his own life and he has to meet his obligations to his team. It's unfair to him. He's confided in me that he's afraid for you also. Tell me, what you want us to do," Noah stated earnestly.

He realized that she wanted to stay in the home she'd known for years, but he was not about to give her his approval. If she decided to stay in her home, things wouldn't change between them; however, she'd do so with the understanding that it didn't please him in the least. Her life was more important than her comfort.

She looked at him sadly, "I want to make you happy and at peace."

He gave her an appreciative, but no nonsense look, "Then you'll move, and I promise to be there with you every step of the way."

She nodded okay.

He grabbed her chin and looked deep into her eyes, "You are the love of my life. I couldn't bear it if something happened to you."

Chapter Seventeen

Noah looked around Marlena's home. Everything was neatly packed up and arranged in various order. Kaod had returned to Ohio State, and she was to complete the move by the end of this week. Certain boxes were going into a storage facility, while others were going to the apartment.

Time had flown by. It was already the end of July. He'd received a call from Jacob saying that Kara was due to have the baby in a week or so. Noah was excited for the both of them. He'd already talked to them and had let them know that he, Adam, and Marlena would be there when the baby was born. It was time for them to meet her. He didn't anticipate any problems and he had made that clear to Jacob. Jacob didn't have to love her, but he would respect her.

Noah glanced up as she came down the stairs. He met her at the foot and pulled her into his arms.

"Have I told you how much I love you?" he teased gently.

"Are you trying to take my mind off all these boxes?" she smiled knowingly.

"Yes! Is it working?" he laughed.

With a twinkle in her eye, she shook her head no.

He leaned in closer and whispered, "Will a kiss take your mind off them?"

Laughing him off, she pushed away and walked toward the kitchen.

Noah watched with a frown on his face. She'd been a little standoffish ever since that night when things had gotten a little out of control. He knew it wasn't the impending move. He was feeling the ramifications from his foolishness. He followed her into the kitchen and watched as she pretended to busy herself.

"You never answered my question," he continued.

She turned and faced him, "What question was that?"

He put a hand on either side of her and asked, "Will a kiss from me take your mind off the boxes?"

She blushed and admitted, "I think you know the answer to that."

Noah looked thoughtfully at her and confessed, "I'm feeling a little rejected here. Are you pushing me away for yourself or because of me?"

Marlena put her hands on his chest as though trying to ward him off, "Stop teasing me Noah."

He leaned in closer, and said in his most boyish voice, "If I promise to be very, very nice, and a very, very good boy, will you kiss me?"

She giggled and nodded yes.

Noah waited for her kiss, but she quickly brushed her mouth across his and laughed.

"That wasn't a kiss, that was a peck," he complained.

She laughed loudly when he pretended to pout. Marlena wrapped her arms around his neck and kissed him tenderly. When she lifted her head, they both began to laugh like silly children. Noah hugged her to him.

✝

They were sitting on her front porch when Marlena looked expectantly at Noah as the ice cream truck approached her street. She stood to her feet and tugged at his arm.

"Let's get some ice cream," she suggested sweetly.

Noah frowned. "I dislike those guys. I remember as a kid how they'd always pretend not to see you, just to make you chase them an extra block. That way, you are even more hot and bothered and are willing to spend extra money on treats that are already overpriced."

Marlena laughed and said, "You're not serious. Everybody loves the ice cream man."

"Watch," he grimaced, pointing to a group of young boys, "You see those little boys?"

Marlena observed the small boys down the street, waving frantically for the ice cream man to stop. The driver seemed not to notice, and turned in the opposite direction, causing the young boys to run behind the truck screaming for it to stop.

Noah looked at Marlena with an, I-told-you- so kind of look.

She fell into a fit of laughter.

"If I go down those stairs in that hot sun, and that truck does not stop,

I will not run a single foot," he stated in such a serious voice, that it caused her to fall into another fit of laughter.

Tears began to roll down her eyes. He stopped and looked at her, clueless as to why she thought it so funny. Finally, he grabbed her hand and tugged her with him.

"You'd better hope that truck stops, or there will be no ice cream for you, missy."

They made it to the corner (no thanks to Marlena's tummy ache from laughing) just in time for the truck to stop. Noah grudgingly whipped out his wallet and paid for her snow cone and, feeling a kinship to the sweating young boys exhausted from their mad sprint after the truck, for theirs as well. He smiled as the boys, breathing heavily, thanked him. He patted their heads and watched as they crossed the street safely. Giving the driver an angry glare, he walked a giggling Marlena back to the house.

As they sat sharing her snow cone, a group of teenagers, mostly girls, approached the house and asked Noah if they could talk to him. Noah recognized the majority of them from Chandra's funeral. The teenagers filed up the stairs and sat in various places on the porch. They began to ask different questions about Jesus, heaven, and eventually, Noah and Marlena.

Marlena sat quietly as Noah explained why he believed the only way to heaven was through Christ, and why Christ had been willing to give his life for all. He explained Christianity was different in the sense that it was the only religion whose God gave his son as a sacrifice. All other religions call for mankind to sacrifice to them. Marlena was amazed to see them sit still in rapt attention as someone explained Christ to them. He didn't use any other method to capture their interest except the Word of God.

Eventually the subject changed to Noah's and her relationship. One bold young lady asked Noah if he loved Marlena. Without hesitation, he looked at Marlena and replied that he loved her more than life itself. That sent the girls into fits of girlish giggles. One of the boys asked him if he was going to marry her. Noah grinned and told him that he'd like to marry her that instant, but they'd set a date for June. That same kid asked bluntly it Noah had already hit it. Everyone grew silent with anticipation. Noah looked the boy straight in the eye and answered with a firm no, not because he didn't want to, but, because God has commanded his children to wait until marriage. Some of the girls clapped their approval, while the boys stared at Noah in stunned disbelief.

"You mean to tell me that you're going to wait until you get married in June to get busy. What's wrong with you? Aint no way I'm waiting that long for no girl," he declared with obvious annoyance.

"Then you really don't love her. All you want is to get in bed with her. Right, Pastor Noah?" one young girl argued.

Undaunted, Noah smiled and began the long explanation of why God commands couples to wait until they are married. He started with the commandments, and expanded the explanation to cover the topics of sexually transmitted diseases, bonding issues, step families, and self-control.

"When you decide to marry someone you really love, how many partners do you want your future wife or husband to have had before you? How many people are you willing to share them with or be compared to?" he questioned looking pointedly at each of them.

Still not satisfied, the boy who seemed to be the spokesman of the group, challenged with a gleam in his eye, "How you supposed to know what you're doing if you don't get plenty of practice? How you gonna please your girl, if you ain't had some practice? You know what they say, 'practice makes perfect'. "

The guys on the porch smiled in triumph at each other, while the girls waited for Noah's response.

"As far as practicing goes," he looked purposefully at Marlena, "I think the night we are married; we are going to enjoy practicing with each other until we get it right."

The teenagers went crazy, while Marlena felt her face heat up. Noah waited for them to settle down, and then asked if any of them wanted to accept Christ as their Savior. Several of them looked as though they wanted to, but peer pressure seemed to hold them back. Not deterred by this, he asked if he could pray for them. All of them eagerly nodded yes. Noah prayed for their safety, a boldness to believe in the written Word, and a life filled with blessings, purity, obedience, and self-discipline. Before they departed, the unofficial leader of the group asked if they could come and talk to him again. Noah gave his approval and the group left, still discussing that evening's issues.

Noah watched the group disappear. If he was a betting man, he'd bet that the leader was still a virgin and he was trying to persuade the boldest girl in the bunch to sleep with him. Noah pondered that for a minute and then turned to Marlena and grinned. He imitated the slang they'd used, "I can't wait until we can get busy. I'm going to need a lot of practice."

Marlena stood and escaped into the house, but not before she heard his delighted chuckling.

Noah glanced at his watch. He was in no hurry to leave his position on the sofa, but it was time for him to get home. Marlena was snuggled up against his side sleeping soundly. He was proud of how she'd conducted herself earlier. She hadn't become offended when those kids had spoken so boldly about things that were generally viewed as private. Today's inner-city youth were tougher, smarter, and bolder. If you weren't living what you were preaching, they weren't buying what you were selling. He'd known for quite some time that they'd been watching him and Marlena. Whether she realized it or not, they had a lot of respect for her because she'd never carried herself loosely and because of the way she'd raised Kaod. He was their local hero. He wondered if she knew that Kaod had once cared a lot about Chandra's sister, Mia. Anyway, Marlena would be the perfect mate to have when God established Noah's inner-city ministry. She wasn't afraid, and she already had a rapport with the community.

Noah thanked God again for giving them the strength and the desire to wait until they were married. He couldn't imagine the counter effect that it would have had on those teens if he and Marly had already been intimate. Christians didn't realize that hypocrisy caused more damage to the faith than just about anything else. How could you convince someone else to believe in Jesus, when your very actions contradicted His Word? Noah sighed heavily, not one believer in Christ was perfect, but our lifestyles should definitely not influence others to turn away from God. He gazed at Marlena and wished that they were already married so he'd never have to leave her side. Noah glanced at his watch again. Maybe, he'd stay just a little longer. He felt her beginning to stir.

She opened her eyes and smiled up at him. "What time is it?" she asked sleepily.

"Almost eleven o'clock. It's time for me to be going home, sweetheart. Come on, get up, sleepyhead," he told her gently.

Marlena eased off the sofa and stretched. She went to the back door, opened it, and waited for Beauty to trot in. Locking the door, she followed Noah to the front. She waited while he performed his customary check of all the windows. He embraced her, kissed her on the forehead, and instructed her to lock up behind him.

Marlena turned off the porch light after watching Noah drive away. She loved that bossy man. Never in a million years would she have imagined allowing herself to willingly submit to the authority of another man. Things were different. She now found herself in a relationship with a man she fully respected. That alone, opened up boundless levels of trust and love that she'd never before known. She smiled to herself as she remembered how he'd gone on about not liking the ice- cream man. Yet, he'd gotten up and pulled her with him to buy her a snow cone. She recalled how frustrated he'd become with her when they'd gone to look at the apartment near his home. She was ashamed of herself now, but at the time, she'd wanted him to feel as frustrated as she'd felt. Still, he'd put his foot down and hadn't given in to her desire. He loved her enough to do what he thought was best for her safety. She would never forget how he'd shielded her with his body the day of Chandra's death or how he'd nearly beat the stuffing out of Littner on her behalf. He had earned her love and respect. His actions spoke more to her than most men's words ever had. For the first time in her life, she understood why Sarah had called Abraham her lord. God had given her a man that, in the most human way imaginable, reflected His love for the church. Noah was not perfect, but he was perfect for her. He was her soul mate. The one man she'd willingly submitted to. Hadn't she not said a single word back to him on the several occasions she'd seen that warning glint in his eyes. Everything in her had wanted to buck against his authority, but she hadn't. Instead she'd bit back her tongue and remained silent. Most, who were acquainted with her, would be shocked at how docile she'd become. She giggled to herself as she thought how God had used Noah to perform a minor miracle in her.

As she prepared for bed, she offered up thanks to God. He had given her the freedom to just sit back, relax, and finally be a woman. It wasn't a freedom that most women had the luxury of experiencing these days. Be it either by their hand, or the hand of the men in their lives. She'd learned that through her relationship with Shawn. He'd initially given her the impression of strength, that she could drop her guard and depend on him to be the spiritual head of the family, but when the newness of her had worn off and the tediousness of life had set in, things had begun to slowly slide downhill. Initially, Shawn had stopped reading the Word. Next, he'd begun to find fault in every little thing she'd done. No matter the situation, it was always her fault. When Kaod had come along, he had used his son's birth to further distance himself. Truthfully, Shawn had been more interested in excitement, than in being a family man. Marlena had thrown herself into raising Kaod. She'd become both mother and father; But, the more she had tried to do what was right, the more Shawn seemed to dislike her. He'd begun to be verbally abusive. At one point her self esteem had been so low that she could have been an easy target for any sweet talking man that came along. Marlena had called out to God and he had responded. He'd taught her his Word and had shown her how much he loved her. She had held on to His hand and had never let go. It hadn't been easy, but it had been worth it. God knew the desire of her heart. She'd never prayed for wealth or anything like that. All she'd ever asked God for was knowledge, and wisdom of His Word and a husband who loved God with all his heart. God had brought Noah into her life. Suddenly, moving from the old to the new didn't seem so bad. She smiled as she pulled the covers back and waited for Noah to call and tell her how much he loved her. Exactly like God did every night.

Chapter Eighteen

Marlena had spent the morning unpacking boxes and putting things away. She hadn't chosen to bring much, just the basic things. The apartment had come furnished with a stove and refrigerator, so hers had gone into storage. She looked around and realized that her things made the place feel more familiar. She sat on her sofa and began to unpack the last boxes which contained miscellaneous pictures. She smiled as she looked at the different poses of her son during the various stages of his life. Where had the time gone? She placed them on the mantel above the electric fire place. She had opted not to display the photo of her and Shawn. She had, instead, given that photo to Kaod. It was now sitting in his dorm room. Noah had never mentioned the picture, but Marlena had noticed his pensive expression whenever he looked at it. She realized within herself, that it was time to move on. She wished she had a picture of Noah. Maybe she'd get one from him. The doorbell rang, jolting her from her thoughts. She wondered who it could be. Noah had a key, so she didn't think he'd ring the bell. She looked through the peephole and didn't recognize the face outside. With the door chain securely in place, she opened the door.

"Yes?"

"Hi, I'm Josh from down the hall. I see that you're new to the building. I'm the building representative. I thought you'd like to see where the laundry room and the bulletin boards are."

Marlena studied him from behind the door. He was an attractive Caucasian man who looked to be in his middle thirties. He was about six feet with brown eyes and sandy brown hair.

He smiled engagingly at her, "I promise that I'm not a serial killer or anything like that."

Marlena didn't smile back, but she unlocked the door and stepped into the hall shutting the door behind her. She introduced herself and the two shook hands. Josh seemed nice enough, but she got the feeling that he was used to women falling all over him. He kept being somewhat flirty with her. After becoming familiar with the location of various rooms, she smiled her thanks and headed back to her apartment.

Marlena twisted the knob, but it wouldn't turn. The door was locked. She reached into her pockets, but they were empty. Her cell phone and keys were sitting on the mantel. Feeling frustrated and blaming Josh for his untimely interruption, she stomped towards his apartment. Knocking on his door, she stepped back in surprise when the door quickly opened.

"Do you have a phone I can use? I've locked myself out of my apartment."

Josh reached behind him, grabbed his cell phone and handed it to her.

"I'd invite you in, but I get the feeling that you'd refuse."

Marlena smiled, but didn't say a word. She punched in Noah's number and waited. When he picked up, she began explaining the situation. He laughed and told her to look up. Noah was standing in front of her apartment smiling. She ended the call, thanked Josh, and met Noah halfway.

"Noah, to the rescue! Admit it, Marly. You need me," he teased.

She blushed and lifted her face for his kiss. He looked surprised, but obliged her. Noah looked over her shoulder and noticed her audience. He immediately understood why she was behaving oddly. The glint in this guy's eyes said that he viewed Marly as a challenge. Unknowingly, she'd just thrown down the gauntlet. That little kiss had wetted junior's appetite.

He stepped around her and greeted her new neighbor. Noah shook hands with Josh, introduced himself, and then thanked him for helping Marlena. As he put his arm around her waist, he heard Josh's door click shut. He hoped, for Marly's sake, she could handle, this would-be Casanova.

Noah unlocked the door and let her in. She'd gotten a lot accomplished. He looked around and spotted the box marked pictures. Kaod had said that there was a surprise in there for the both of them. He dug inside and found a wrapped silver gift box. He handed the box to Marly and told her it was from Kaod to the both of them.

She quickly opened the gift and gasped in amazement. There, encased in a silver frame, was an eight by ten photograph of her and Noah. She was curled up, with her head on his chest, fast asleep. While Noah, although sleeping, had his arms wrapped around her protectively as though he were guarding her. Noah read the simple note attached to the frame.

"Mom and Noah, You have each other now. To love, cherish, and protect. Love, K." Noah took the frame and placed it on the mantel beside the pictures of Kaod. He was selfishly pleased to see that the picture of her and Shawn was nowhere in sight.

She came to him and wrapped her arms around his waist. He hugged her to him and smiled.

"I have something for you, too," he told her, with a mysterious grin. "Actually, I have a couple of things," he corrected as he led her to the sofa.

She gazed at him not quite knowing what to say. Noah stood up and walked over and grabbed her key chain off the shelf and sat back down.

"The first item on the list is this," he said dramatically as he held up a key and put it on her key ring, explaining that it was the key to his house. He held up his hand when she would have objected. "You'll need it to check on Beauty, and me," he added mischievously. "The next item is this." He handed her a small grey jewelry gift box. Marlena opened the box and admired the roped gold necklace with a tiny solid gold key attached to it.

"This is the key to my heart. Only you have it. There are no duplicates, so don't ever lose it," Noah proclaimed solemnly as he took it out of her hands and placed it around her neck.

She reached out and gently caressed his face. In a tender voice, she told him how much she loved him and how she would always take good care of his heart. Their mouths met tenderly in an unspoken vow to love only each other. He had exposed his vulnerability to her and she understood that. She took the lead and gently explored his mouth, trying to convey a message that words couldn't express. Her kiss gave him the assurance that, if need be, she would be strong, but always mindful of the power he had given her over him.

"I love you," she whispered as she brought the kiss to an end.

Noah sat quiet for awhile.

"You are coming with me to Atlanta when Kara has the baby right?"

She hesitated for a moment.

"We start preparing for school next week, but I should be able to," Marlena told him.

He plucked a pillow from the sofa, placed it on her lap, and stretched his long frame out with his head resting on the pillow. She smiled at him. He must be tired she thought absentmindedly. Her fingers strayed to his hair where she timidly began to massage the grey at his temples. He closed his eyes and sighed with pleasure. Marlena studied his strong features as she felt him relax. He really was quite handsome.

Noah startled her out of her observation when he asked her to tell him why Josh's obvious attraction to her bothered her. "You don't miss a thing, do you?" she replied, amazed that he'd picked up on Josh.

"Not when it comes to you," he said as he took her hand and placed it back in his hair, an indication that he wanted her to continue.

She explained that it was a matter of respect. Josh knew that she was engaged, but it didn't matter to him. She felt as though he was making Noah irrelevant, and that made her angry.

Noah chuckled, "Sweetheart, your anger at him is what makes you so attractive to him. He views it as a challenge. The girl that doesn't want him is the girl that's the most attractive to him."

Marlena grew irritated with his logic.

"That doesn't make a bit of sense. Are you telling me that if I'd thrown myself at him, then he would have responded differently toward me?" A thought suddenly occurred to her. "Is that why you were drawn to me?"

Fighting hard not to grin, he stated in a matter of fact voice, "No, I knew all along you were trying to get me to marry you. You practically threw yourself at me."

She blushed and stammered, "Noah Phillips, you know…"

Marlena stopped when she heard him laugh loudly.

He grabbed her hands and placed them back on his head.

"You're so easy to tease. I knew the moment I met you that you were the one. I even picked up your keys and waited, just so that you'd have to come back in, and I'd have a chance to talk to you. So, to answer your question, having to chase you definitely fueled my interest."

She pretended to contemplate a solution. "Then, maybe I should let Josh catch me," she grinned saucily.

He reached up and grasped her hands. Pulling her down so that she could see his eyes, Noah stated in a serious voice, "The only one that will be catching you is me and I hope you get that point across to Junior, or I will."

Marlena, still refusing to take Noah's reaction seriously, teased Noah further. "Are you jealous?"

"Are you trying to make me jealous?" he countered.

Marly suddenly remembered the little golden key and Colleen's affair. "No," she answered honestly.

He placed her hands back on his head, closed his eyes, and said, "Good, because you wouldn't like it if I had reason to be."

✚

Marlena sat alone in her apartment. It was Saturday, and Noah typically spent most of the day on his sermon. She decided to stop by his house and headed out the door. Trotting down the stairs, she heard someone call her name. Marlena turned and realized too late, that it was Josh. She waved and shouted to him that she was in a hurry. Josh didn't let that deter him as he jogged to catch up to her.

"How's the apartment coming?" he asked.

She turned to face him. Marlena thought about Noah's words and chose to take the direct approach. "Are you hitting on me?"

He seemed a bit taken aback, but quickly recovered. "What would you do if I said yes?" he questioned.

"Are you?" she asked again, demanding an answer.

"You have the prettiest eyes," he said as he avoided answering her question again.

Tired of playing this game, she turned back around, and headed toward Noah's home. He hurriedly caught up with her.

"Can I walk you to wherever you're going, or would your fiancé have a problem with that?"

She stopped and looked him directly in the eyes. "Even if Noah doesn't have a problem with it, I do," she stated calmly and walked away, leaving him standing alone.

By the time she reached Noah's home, her irritation had abated and she was feeling much better. Key in hand, she cautiously unlocked the door and softly whistled for Beauty. The big dog, followed by Noah, trotted happily out of the kitchen to greet her. Noah leaned against the frame and smiled at her.

"I wondered if you'd get up enough courage to use that key."

She walked over and stood near him. She'd never seen him in such a personal way. He was dressed in an old pair of cut off jeans and wearing a sleeveless t-shirt. His feet were bare and she could tell that he hadn't shaved. She was supremely aware that they had breached another level in their quest to know each other. For some reason she felt shy, in a way she couldn't quite explain. She'd seen bear arms and feet before, but this was different. This was more intimate, as though she were getting a glimpse into what life with Noah would be like, life without the public expectations of a pastor. She alone, would have the privilege of seeing the naked man, his inner soul, his vulnerability, his anguish and disappointments, everything that made him a man.

Now she understood the significance of the keys and what he was telling her. He had trustingly gifted her with knowledge of him that no other human would ever have. Marlena completely comprehended that the Joshes of the world could never become a distraction to him again. She touched his unshaven face and laughed when he intentionally rubbed it against her cheek. "I was coming to take Beauty for a walk. Did I interrupt you?" she asked.

He hugged her and kissed her on the forehead.

"I've already taken her and no, you did not interrupt me."

He invited her into his study and asked, "Would you like to help me finish preparing tomorrow's sermon?"

"Really?" she asked incredulously.

"Come on. Let me show you what I'm working on. You can help me cross reference the different scriptures."

For the next three hours they worked on his sermon. He taught her how to translate from the Greek or Hebrew into English and explained why it was important to know literal meanings of certain words. He showed her books on historical cultures and traditions. He'd already had most of the work done, but he took great pleasure in teaching her. She had an above average grasp of the meaning of scripture and the backgrounds of the different books. She listened intently and then asked very intelligent questions. They were in tune with each other and with the spirit. Noah enjoyed every minute of it. He watched as she delighted in something new she found out and it delighted him. He finally pulled her out of his study laughing. "That's enough for today. You've worn me out," he told her with a smile.

He led her into the living room, turned on the television, and gently pushed her onto the sofa. "I'm going to take a shower. If the phone rings, answer it. It may be Hal."

Before she could respond, he had disappeared into the bathroom and she heard the water running. She began looking at the different pictures that were scattered throughout the room. One picture, in particular, captured her eyes. It was an eight by ten photo of Noah holding hands with a woman. She was tall and willowy with those long legs that white men seemed to love. Her shoulder length blond hair was cut in stylish layers. She had sparkling blue eyes which hinted at seductive secrets. Her provocative pose was a shock to Marlena. It was strategically alluring, as though she were seducing the photographer. Marlena thought it strange since the woman was with Noah and was holding his hand. Marlena wasn't jealous, but it did cause her to wonder why Noah was now attracted to a five-feet-six-inch black woman; especially, since there were no obvious similarities between her and Colleen. She was the complete opposite of Colleen in physical looks. Marlena had a body type that seemed to be more appealing to black men. Her full hips and alluring backside were what had caught Shawn's initial attention. She kicked her feet up beneath her and looked at the photo again. Noah appeared happy and at ease. He and Colleen had made a striking couple.

"Okay," she mumbled to herself, "I am a little jealous." She didn't like the idea of having to stare at that picture every time she came over. She suddenly jumped when the phone rang. She listened to see if he was still in the shower.

"Get the phone, Marly!" Noah called out from the bathroom.

She wanted to shout for him to pick up his own phone, instead she reached over and picked up the receiver.

"Hello, Phillips' residence," she answered politely

A familiar voice on the other end responded.

"Marly, is that you?" Adam enquired.

He politely asked how she was doing. After several minutes, he requested to speak with his dad. Marlena informed him that Noah was in the shower, and suddenly thought how that might sound.

"Don't worry, Marly, I won't tell anyone. This will be our little secret. You know, something I can blackmail Dad over," he joked.

Marlena was grateful that the conversation was taking place over the phone. He had no way of knowing that she was embarrassed.

"Who's on the phone and why are you blushing?" Noah asked her, observing her face.

Adam gave a hoot of laughter from the other end and Marlena quickly handed Noah the phone. Noah looked at her and grinned when he recognized the voice on the other end. She tried to sneak away, but he held onto her wrist. He deliberately responded aloud to Adam.

"No, I didn't ask her to wash my back."

She knew her face was becoming warmer by the minute and she also knew that both of them were enjoying it. The conversation finally turned to Adam's reason for calling. Noah let go of her wrist as she pulled away. He frowned as he watched her wander into the kitchen. Minutes later, he followed her.

"Is something wrong, sweetheart?" he questioned, observing her facial expression.

She lowered her eyelashes to conceal her thoughts. "Nothing that I want to discuss," she replied truthfully. He might think it silly, but that picture had made her feel slightly uncomfortable.

He didn't push the issue, but instead asked, "Are you up to going out for dinner? I kind of told Hal we'd double date with him tonight."

Marlena looked confused.

"I don't mind going out, but why does he need you to go with him and who is he taking out on a date?"

Noah explained that Hal had finally gotten up the nerve to ask Valerie out and Hal was a bit nervous, so Noah had agreed to a double date. He'd planned to drop her off at the apartment, take Beauty for a quick walk, and then pick her up and head to the restaurant.

She smiled her okay, kissed him on the cheek, gathered her keys and cell phone, and waited for him to back the car out. She was pleasantly surprised to see Beauty sitting happily in the rear seat.

Noah jumped out, opened the door for her, and returned to the other side. He dropped her off at the apartment and waited for her to go inside.

Marlena put down her purse and rushed to the shower. She was in and out in record time. Wrapping a towel around her, she stood in her bedroom trying to decide what to wear. She finally decided on a casual outfit. She slipped on a jean skirt with a deep green trimmed in white shirt. She hurriedly found her matching sandals and slipped them on. She had just finished curling her hair and putting on her earrings when Noah walked in. He didn't say a word, but simply pulled her into his arms and kissed her.

She was a little dazed when he let go and said, "Thank you, for looking gorgeous, and for agreeing to go on this double date."

She smiled with pleasure, picked up her purse and followed him out the door.

Noah and Marlena arrived at the Steak House before Hal and Valerie. A few minutes later, Hal's midnight blue F150 truck pulled up. Noah glanced at her with a gleam in his eye. She wondered what he was up to. He purposely sat in the car and waited for Hal and Valerie to get out first. Hal walked around and helped Valerie out. He placed his hand on her back and escorted her towards the restaurant. Noah laughed happily, jumped out of the car and assisted Marlena. They walked hand and hand toward Hal and Valerie. Greetings were exchanged between the two couples as they entered the restaurant.

Noah intentionally requested a booth and they were soon seated. The booth was large enough to provide adequate room for both couples. Noah sat comfortably close to Marly with his arm casually thrown around her shoulders. Hal, however, sat with a considerable amount of distance between him and Valerie.

Noah started a casual conversation and soon everyone joined in. The conversation was steered towards the date of their upcoming wedding. He gave her a masked look of pleasure when she announced that the wedding would definitely be taking place in May, not June. Noah joked about her rushing him to the altar, but it was very evident to all that he adored her.

They were enjoying a leisurely dinner when Noah's phone rang. He excitedly identified the number as Jacob's, excused himself as well as Marly, and speedily guided her outside with him. She listened as he eagerly talked with his eldest son. When the call ended, he embraced her and proudly announced that Kara had given birth to a baby boy. His grandson weighed eight pounds, seven ounces and his name was Collin Michael Phillips. Immediately, he called his travel agent and had her book three seats to Atlanta for Friday evening, with return tickets reserved for Sunday evening. He even had her reserve their hotel rooms.

Marlena was genuinely happy for him, but she was beginning to be a little nervous about accompanying him on the trip. Noah grinned when his phone signaled incoming pictures. He shared the first photos of his grandson with Marlena. She knew he wanted her to be a part of every aspect of his life, but she wasn't so sure that Jacob wanted it that way. They went back inside to share the happy news with Hal and Valerie.

The two women had gone to the restroom, when Hal brought up the trip to Atlanta. "How is Jacob going to take Marly being there with you? I know he practically worshipped Colleen. He even named his son after her, and it's no secret that Colleen was prejudiced. Jacob took on a lot of her personal beliefs. Are you willing to risk Marly getting hurt? There is no doubt that you two are perfect for each other, and I understand that you want to share everything with her, but Noah are you sure this is the right time to take her to meet Jacob?" he asked earnestly.

"Do you really think that now or later will make a difference to Jacob? Hate is hate. He's going to have to deal with the fact that Marly will be my wife. Jacob is a grown man with a wife, and now a son. He'll have to answer to them as to why I will either be a part of their life or why I won't. God knows that I love my son, but God also commands us to cleave to our spouses, not our children. Jacob will either honor my right to marry Marly and respect her, or he can choose to hate her and force me out of his life. Quite frankly, those are his only two choices, love or hate, and he's going to have to choose one of them this weekend. I've already informed him that Marly will be with me and he clearly understands how I feel about her and how I expect him to conduct himself around her. God has restored my life to me. I can't let anyone, not even my son, stand between God and his blessing." Noah expressed fervently.

Hal nodded in understanding, hoping that all went well during their trip. He really liked Marly and didn't want to see her hurt.

"How are things going between you and Valerie?" Noah asked, changing the subject.

"I've been speaking with her on the phone and swinging by the church to see her. She agreed to come out with me tonight, but I'm not sure what she feels," Hal said honestly.

"She agreed, or did she want to? That's the question you need to find out the answer to," Noah suggested firmly.

✠

Noah reclined on the sofa in Marly's apartment. She was in the middle of an intense conversation with Kaod. She had thanked him for the picture and assured him that she was doing okay. She told him about the upcoming trip to Atlanta. Noah watched her carefully as she tried to keep her voice level. Kaod must have expressed his uncertainty because she stood and began to pace back and forth. He turned away and smiled when she informed Kaod that she was the mother, and he the son. Becoming exasperated, she simply handed him the phone and walked away. Noah sat up and took the phone from her and watched as she headed towards her room.

She needed a minute to think. She wasn't some helpless child who needed the men in her life to decide what was right and what was wrong for her. When had she become so weak? Kaod didn't want her to go to

Atlanta, but Noah did. Kaod obviously knew about Jacob's feelings and didn't trust that Noah could handle his oldest son. She sat on the bed tiredly and prayed that God would give her the answer.

Marlena felt, rather than heard Noah's presence as he entered the room. He gazed at her, trying to decide what to say. She held up her hand to halt his words.

"Please, let me speak first and then you can tell me what is on your mind. Since I've known you Noah, my world has changed drastically. You've made me face a lot of things that I really didn't want to face. I had no intention of dating, let alone marrying a white man. You've changed that. Moving to this apartment was something I didn't want to do, but you convinced me it was for the best, and it was. You asked me to trust you and put my well being in your hands and then you saved my life. I haven't submitted to you because I'm weak or fragile, it's quite the opposite. It's because I'm strong enough to let you lead and I need, very much, for you to understand that. I have no reason to oppose this trip to Atlanta. You've proven yourself to me time and time again. I'm wearing your ring and the key to your heart. I trust you, Noah. With everything that's in me, I trust you. If you say let's go to Atlanta, then that's where I'm going. I'll follow you as you follow Christ. I love you, because you first proved your love for me."

Noah stood still, at a loss for words. She was voluntarily giving him authority over her. She had put aside her son's wishes and chosen to follow him. He didn't quite know what to say, so he uttered what was in his heart.

"You will be my true wife in every sense of the word."

"I know," Marlena said as she stepped into his arms.

Noah lay on his face before God. He was at a loss for words. He was feeling overwhelmed with joy. There were no words that could express his thanks. He lay there knowing that the spirit would say what human words could not. Who was he that the Lord would bless him so? Joyous praise began to burst forth. He had spent twenty-three years faithfully married to a woman who he had fought to love. He'd thought they'd had a decent marriage at one point, despite the ups and downs.

Now, he knew better. God had blessed him with a true woman of faith. One that was strong enough to allow her husband to lead. He understood that this would not be possible if he were not in his rightful place with

God. He'd had to go through Christ to find Marly's heart, and once there, he knew there was nothing that this woman wouldn't do for him.

His mind revisited life with Colleen. He had seen her flaws, as she had seen his, but she'd never given herself fully to him or to Christ. He'd always known that she hadn't truly been his. Colleen had loved receiving admiring looks from other men, even flirting with them. She'd wanted other women to envy her position and stature in the church. She hadn't earned any of it. Noah doubted that she could have coherently explained the death, burial, resurrection, or the ascension of the Lord Jesus. She'd never shown interest in his sermons, but loved to stand on stage with him. Even still, he'd tried to love her. When she had become ill, he'd thought that it would change her. Noah had sat with her and read the Word to her, but to no avail. Instead, she had obsessed over wanting him to promise that he'd never marry again, and that no other woman would be mother to her children. At the time, his ego had attributed it to her love for him, but in retrospect, he realized it was her vanity. Women would think that they could never compare to Colleen.

He thanked God for giving him the strength to not make that promise, even to his dying wife. He prayed for God to break her stronghold on Jacob. Noah was sure that she'd maneuvered Jacob into some kind of loyalty vow to her. She'd always said that Jacob was her son and Adam was his. Noah knew that it was because she could control Jacob by holding his love for her captive; Adam, however, had a stronger foundation in Christ, and was less enamored of his mother. In any case, it was abundantly clear that Colleen had never been Noah's soul mate. She had been the partner he had chosen out of lust. God, however, had chosen Marly for him. The Holy Spirit had gently persuaded him to slip his wedding ring off his finger, to sever the vow between him and Colleen, and to pursue Marly. He had never sought after any woman as quickly or as completely as he had Marly.

Noah remembered how her eyes had lit up as she'd helped him prepare the sermon. She'd received joy and he, pleasure at her joy in fellowshipping with Christ. Her questions to him concerning the Word had provoked a deeper desire in him. This woman, he thought again, had first given her heart to Christ and he'd had to go through Him to capture it.

Her words tonight had shaken him to his core. He prayed that he would always honor her trust in him and that God would strengthen him to be a worthy husband. Noah finally crawled into bed still humbled by her words and God's hand upon his life.

Marlena sat staring at the pictures on her mantel. Kaod was now a man. He had his own life to live, but he was still playing the leading man in her life, her protector, her hero. She'd thought it was cute, but now that role needed to change. Noah was her leading man, her hero. He had selected her and had proven himself worthy. Why had she believed herself weak when she'd allowed him to make decisions? It was because she had been rebelling against God. She didn't want a man in authority over her. She was afraid that he'd abuse it in the same way that Shawn had abused his role as the man in her life. He had made selfish decision after selfish decision. Marlena hadn't wanted to repeat that mistake. She had gone to the Lord in prayer before marrying Shawn, and knew that God had given her in marriage to Shawn. She'd never understood why until years later when she'd begun studying the book of James. She had thought that God had been punishing her, but James had given her an understanding that God was proving to her that she belonged to Him. No matter what Shawn had done, she had stayed strong in the faith. God, through trials and tribulations, had shown her that she was a true believer. He'd strengthened her.

She felt sorry for those professing Christians who'd never gone through anything. Trials had forced her to dig into the Word and firmly grasp the hand of Christ. She'd gotten to know him intimately and developed an unshakable dependence on him. He was her rock, her refuge. God had used Shawn to securely ground her in the faith. Her bad marriage hadn't been a curse, but a blessing.

She turned her attention to the picture of Noah and her. It brought a smile to her face. Noah would die for her, of that, she was positive. He was her blessing from God, yet it had been harder for her to accept him than to accept Shawn. Her hard fought independence now had to be put aside in order to become one with her future husband. She had to have the strength to trust God yet again. She must let go of her fears and give them over to God. In essence, her trust in Noah was based first on her trust in Christ to always know what was best for her. God had handpicked Noah to be her husband. Initially, she couldn't see through her own prejudices, but now, she understood and was truly thankful for him. She loved Noah more than she had loved any man.

Marlena bowed her head and prayed for obedience and a willingness to follow her husband. She prayed for Noah and their three sons, and for God to cleanse their newly forming family of all racial prejudice.

Chapter Nineteen

Their plane touched down in Atlanta at exactly a quarter 'til seven, Friday evening. Noah, Marlena, and Adam looked at each other and smiled as they walked through the busy airport. All three had packed lightly and hadn't needed to stop at the baggage terminal. Noah suggested that they stop at their hotel first to get settled, and then head over to Jacob and Kara's.

As they walked through the hotel, Adam noted the large Olympic sized indoor swimming pool. Noah glanced at Marlena and casually asked if she liked swimming.

"Not really, it's okay if I'm hot, but it's not my cup of tea. Besides, I'm not that great a swimmer," she admitted shrugging her shoulders.

Adam swung around to face his dad in mock disappointment.

"I knew we'd find something wrong with her. How could a true Phillips even contemplate marrying someone who does not absolutely, unconditionally love swimming? You're setting a bad example for me, Dad."

Noah joined in on the fun by adding, "You're right, son. I am faced with two choices. Remain a horrible dad, or kiss her until she agrees to change her wicked and scandalous ways."

He proceeded to pull her towards him and cover her face with silly wet kisses until, after much laughter she gave in and agreed to let him teach her to become a better swimmer.

Adam grinned and watched his dad with happiness. He seemed so happy and carefree. He couldn't recall his dad ever being this way with his mom.

Adam's grin broadened when Noah pulled Marly into his arms and looking at Adam, declared, "I don't think she means it," a second before his mouth found hers in a persuasive kiss.

Adam tapped his dad on the shoulder and whispered loudly, "Okay Dad, I think she means it."

Noah lifted his head and asked her in a husky voice, "Do you mean it?"

Marly looked from Adam to Noah and with a knowing grin shook her head no. The Phillips men roared with laughter.

Marly's room was adjacent to Noah and Adam's. Noah wished they were already married so he could share a room with her. He was happy that she'd moved their wedding date to the third Saturday of May, but was still undecided as to where he should take her on their honeymoon. Out of curiosity, he asked Adam his opinion. Adam grinned and said a place where there would be no interruptions or distractions. An Idea began forming in his mind as he knocked on Marly's door.

Noah could tell that Marly was nervous about meeting Jacob. She'd been fidgeting with the decorative string on her shirt since they'd left the hotel. He reached across and found her hand and gave it a squeeze as they pulled into the driveway. As Noah was opening the door for her, Jacob, followed by Kara, who was holding little Collin, came out to greet them. Marlena tried to hold back while all the greeting and fawning over little Collin took place, but Noah grabbed her hand and pulled her forward. He made the introductions to Jacob and Kara. Jacob nodded his hello, while Kara hugged her with her free arm and presented little Collin. Marlena returned the hug warmly and sincerely complimented Kara on how handsome their baby was. Kara turned and promptly placed Collin in Noah's arms. Then she linked arms with Marlena, and ushered her into the house.

"I don't know if I like this trade. My future wife, for my grandson," he called after them teasingly.

Adam was glad that their father had missed the angry expression on Jacob's face.

"You can do without her for a little while," Kara threw back laughingly as she and Marlena disappeared into the house.

Kara pulled Marlena into a little sitting room. After the two women had seated themselves, Kara, with girlish delight, demanded to know how

Marlena and Noah had fallen in love. Marlena laughed with amusement and proceeded to tell their story from the beginning until the present.

Kara sat back and sighed, "I'm so happy for Dad. I've never seen him so full of joy. Not even when Jake's mom was still alive. I'm happy for the two of you."

"What about you and Jacob? How did you meet?" Marlena asked curiously.

Kara explained that they'd met four and a half years ago. The two of them had been attending the same local university. She'd been working at a campus bookstore when Jacob had walked in. He'd returned everyday for the next three days until she'd agreed to go out with him. Kara giggled as she revealed that they'd only had two small problems, her boyfriend and his girlfriend. Kara finished her story and laughed softly.

Marlena observed Kara silently for a moment before asking, "What is your ethnicity, if you don't mind me asking?"

Kara had dark brown hair with dark eyes to match. Her skin tone was darker than the average Caucasian's which hinted at her being something other than white.

Kara looked away, appearing slightly uncomfortable.

Marlena quickly interjected, "I'm sorry, it's really none of my business."

"No, no, it's okay. My grandfather was black and my grandmother was white," she confessed quietly.

With raised eyebrows, Marlena asked if Jacob knew about her ancestry. Kara quickly shook her head no.

Marlena wanted to ask why, but instead, hugged her and said, "Then it will be our little secret, until you decide otherwise."

Noah poked his head in the room and jokingly asked whether or not it was safe to come in. Marlena laughed and patted the place beside her. Noah sat next to her and smiled. He asked Kara how things were going with the new baby and they soon fell into easy conversation. Adam joined them, and the four passed the time away talking about Collin's birth and Noah and Marly's upcoming wedding.

Jacob was conspicuously absent which, truthfully, didn't bother Marlena in the least. He'd eventually join the family when he realized that no one was going to cater to his rudeness. Marlena likened Jacob to a spoiled child who was intent on having his way. Once he truly realized that she wasn't going anywhere, he'd have to accept her or face being alone, without the support of his own family. She intuitively knew that Jacob would not risk rejection from those whom he loved. His personality type couldn't handle the isolation nor could it handle any type of perceived rejection. From what she had learned through Kara, Jacob truly loved his father and brother, but his loyalty to his mother was a formidable opponent, even in matters pertaining to his own marriage. Nevertheless, Marly knew that sooner or later, Jacob's deep personal prejudices would be exposed and his wife and child would suffer the consequences.

True to form, Jacob joined the group minutes later. He seated himself on the arm of Kara's chair. He loved his wife. It was evident in the way he looked at, and responded to her. She wondered if Noah looked at her like that. She felt Noah's hand slide around her shoulder and pull her close. Marlena, without thinking, rested her head against his chest and looked up at him. He was enjoying this time with his sons. She was glad that she'd decided to accompany him.

✞

Noah waited for Marly to unlock the door to her room. Adam had bid her goodnight already and had discreetly disappeared into his and Noah's room. Marly pushed the door open and entered. "Aren't you coming in for a little while?" she asked.

Noah eyed the bed warily and shook his head no. "Was she crazy or what? He thought he'd gotten her over that pastor on a pedestal hump," he said to himself. He put his hands on her shoulders and turned her so that she was facing the bed. He bent down and whispered in her ear, "That's why I'm not coming in for a while."

"Oh!" was all Marly could manage to say.

He turned her to face him again. "Good night, Sweetheart." He groaned when he saw the look of expectation on her face. Even after he'd shown her that huge, invitingly, seductive bed, she stood there, with the audacity, to expect him to kiss her goodnight. This woman, he decided, was intentionally trying to drive him insane. If she wanted a good night kiss, then he'd give her one to remember. He grabbed her hand, opened the door, and yanked her into the hallway. Holding on to her hands, he bent his head and kissed her hungrily. He deliberately would not allow her arms free or their bodies to touch. After several seconds, he broke off the kiss, opened her door, and pushed her inside. He saw the look of frustration on her face and smiled with supreme satisfaction. He told her good night, closed her door, waited to hear the chain lock slide in place, and promptly went into his room.

133

"That ought to fix that little problem," he thought with a smile as he went into the bathroom to take the first of many cold showers.

The month of May was too far away he complained to God, but Noah knew he was reaping the folly he had sown.

Marlena understood Noah's frustration, but she hadn't asked that they jump in bed. All she'd expected was a simple good night kiss; however, she hadn't minded that last kiss in the least. Noah's kisses always made her feel cherished and close to him. Well, all except tonight's kiss and that one other time, they'd made her feel something completely different. She pushed those thoughts far from her mind, said her prayers, and fell soundly asleep.

Noah came out of the shower expecting Adam to be fast asleep. Adam grinned knowingly at his father and easily averted the pillow thrown in his direction.

"How do you do it Dad? How do you wait until you're married?" he wondered aloud. "I mean, it's pretty obvious that you and Marly haven't, you know."

Noah was pleasantly surprised by Adam's line of questioning. "We haven't what? Made love to each other?"

Adam nodded, a little embarrassed to be talking with his dad about such an intimate topic.

"You want to know how we've done it so far, or are you talking about in general?" Noah asked, wanting Adam to be more specific.

Adam sat up, "Both, I guess. Were you a virgin when you and Mom were married?"

"Yep," Noah admitted smiling.

"Was Mom a virgin?" Adam asked, hoping his dad would be honest.

Noah wanted to be open with his son, "No, no she wasn't."

Adam thought for a moment and said, "Then I guess the question would be how come you waited, and what helped you to wait?

Noah sat on the bed and faced his son.

"I wanted to wait because God commanded us to wait and I desired to be pleasing to God. Through my walk with Christ, I understood it was necessary to avoid looking at ungodly images, listening to others recount their sexual experiences, ungodly and seductive women, and I read the Word daily. Was it an easy thing to do? No, it was extremely difficult, to say the least."

Noah went on to explain some of the challenging situations he'd found himself in. Adam could only stare at his dad with a new-found respect and admiration.

Noah chuckled and shared experiences he'd had while married to Adam's mother and, after she had passed.

Adam couldn't believe it. Why had he thought his dad could never understand what he was going through; probably, because his dad always seemed so much more disciplined than the average man. He realized now, that his dad's self-restraint was a direct result of him actively pursuing God, who in return, strengthened him. Abstinence wasn't something that happened by accident. It was a deliberate course of action taken by those who desired to show their love for God through obedience to his commandments.

"What about with Marly, is it less difficult?" Adam wanted to know.

Noah smiled ruefully and confessed, "She, by far has been the most difficult challenge I have ever come across. The fact that she's a woman of God and my future wife makes it so much harder. It's like, knowing you're getting this fantastic present on a certain day, but you want to play with it right now. Only the Word keeps me from justifying being intimate with her. The other temptations, I already understood were not mine. Plus, she completely trusts, that I, being a man of God, will not let things get out of hand. It is my responsibility, so all the pressure falls on me. In addition, she's a cuddle bug that loves to snuggle up to me. It's purely innocent in her mind, and I understand that it's how she shows her trust in me."

Adam's interest was evident, "How do you deal with it Dad?"

"Every man handles things differently. I pray, a lot, and I try to do things that keep my mind focused. I've never touched her inappropriately, which keeps her hands still and I set the boundary of each kiss. Marly needs to bond so I always try to hold her hand or put my arm around her shoulders or waist and that fills that emotional bonding need that women desire and it gives her the security of knowing that I find her attractive. Lastly, I take plenty of cold showers," Noah declared sincerely.

Adam laughed and nodded his head in understanding. He looked at his father, hesitated, and then asked quietly, "Did it bother you that Mom wasn't a virgin; that you weren't the only man she'd been with?"

Noah sat down, and searched for the right way to word his answer without revealing facts about Colleen that Adam didn't need to know. He faced his son and confessed that initially, it hadn't bothered him. He'd thought that she'd just been young and foolish; however, later on he'd been disturbed by her knowledge of carnal pleasures which ultimately affected their level of intimacy.

Noah stared at his youngest son.

"Tell me what you really think of Marly?"

Adam smiled at his father. "I think that she is everything that Mom wasn't. She is the gift that God has hand-picked just for you."

"I think that you're right," Noah agreed as he closed his eyes and reclined on the bed.

✝

The next morning, Marlena eyed Noah, trying to determine his mood. He usually greeted her with a hug and a kiss on the forehead, but after last night, who knew what to expect. She watched him lock the door and approach her with a light-hearted step. He smiled as he hugged her to him and kissed her on the forehead.

"In a much better mood this morning, are we?" she mumbled.

He leaned down and whispered for her ears only.

"Yes, I am, but I won't be for long if you keep inviting me into your bed," he warned adamantly.

"I did not invite you into my bed," she denied indignantly.

"Don't be naïve, Marly. There's me, you, and a big bed. How do you think my body is going to react?" he corrected.

"And that's my fault? How do we usually say good night? We hug and kiss. You should have told me the rules had changed. Don't take your sexual frustration out on me. If you can't handle a good night kiss, then be a big boy and say so, but don't throw the blame on me," she advised him sternly.

He looked at her strangely. He opened his mouth to speak, but was forced to admit to himself that she was right. He had changed the rules in the middle of the game. He reached for the hand that had been poking him squarely in the chest and covered it with his.

"I'm sorry, Browneyes. You're right. I took my frustration out on you. Will you forgive me?"

She smiled sweetly and said, "Always." She looked around. "Where's Adam?"

"He's waiting for us downstairs. I think he's itching to try out the pool."

They rode the elevator down to the lobby and made their way to the swimming pool. Adam sat gazing longingly at the crystal blue water.

Marlena glanced at Noah whose expression mirrored the look in Adam's eyes.

"Why don't you two take a swim before we go to Jacob's? The hotel has a little shop where you can buy trunks if you don't have any."

Noah and Adam smiled at each other.

"I'll call Jacob and tell him we're going to take a swim before we head over to his place. Why don't you join us?" Noah suggested.

"No thanks, you two enjoy yourselves. I'll sit right here and read or something."

Noah and Adam went to purchase swim trunks, while she decided to check out the bookstore she'd spotted yesterday. It was humid outside, but the store was closer than she'd expected.

Not finding anything interesting, she decided to start journaling about her life with Noah. Fifteen minutes later, she was back in the air conditioned hotel sitting by the pool. She immediately caught sight of Noah and Adam. They were swimming in the deep end of the pool. She watched as Noah climbed out of the water and onto the diving board. She was mesmerized by how graceful he was. He executed dive after dive perfectly and seemingly with little or no effort. She forgot all about her journal and sat entranced. Adam was good also, but there was no comparison between the two, even though Noah was twice his son's age. Marlena had never been a fan of swimming, but after witnessing Noah, she decided the sport may have some merit after all. She looked around and noticed she wasn't the only one. Quite a few people had gathered to watch, including a group of very attractive scantily clad young ladies. Noah, realizing that there was a crowd, declined to execute any more dives. Marlena giggled when he appeared a bit embarrassed by all the female attention. She watched as he disappeared from view and resurfaced near her. He swam to the side of the pool and smiled at her.

"How long have you been sitting there?"

"Long enough to be impressed by your diving ability, where did you learn to dive like that?"

"School, but I've been a swimmer all of my life. My parents loved the water, so I spent a lot of time in it. Eventually, it earned me a full ride scholarship."

"Why'd you stop?"

"Got a call from the big guy upstairs and that took precedence over everything else." Noah heaved himself out of the pool and walked over and took the seat beside her.

Marlena glanced away, feeling a little shy.

Noah chuckled softly, "Do me a favor Cinderella. Will you grab my towel, shoes, and shirt from the table at the far end of the pool?"

Marlena turned to face him and smiled knowingly as she stood to go and retrieve his things. She picked up Noah's things and glanced at Adam. He seemed as embarrassed as his father had been by the overly aggressive, near naked females. Only, he lacked the wisdom and the knowhow to extricate himself from the potentially harmful situation.

He looked at her helplessly.

She rolled her eyes, grabbed his things too, then hooked her arm through his, and boldly stated, "Sorry, ladies, he's not your type."

Relieved that she'd rescued him, he allowed her to lead him away.

Noah watched Marlena practically drag Adam away from the group of girls. Instead of Adam appearing embarrassed, he actually looked relieved. Maybe Adam wasn't as knowledgeable as he put on. He made a mental note to check on his younger son more often.

Hours later, Marlena rocked little Collin as Noah and Adam competed against Jacob and Kara in a game of badminton. Jacob was athletic, but poor Kara was out of her league. She giggled helplessly every time she attempted to hit the birdie. The game was quickly over with Jacob and Kara unsuccessful at scoring a single point. Jacob demanded a rematch, but Kara declined to play again. She pleaded fatigue and volunteered Marlena to take her place. Marlena handed Collin to Kara and calmly kneeled down to tighten her shoe laces.

Noah recognized that look and smiled.

Jacob, desiring vindication, selected Adam for his teammate and teased his father about payback.

"Are you ready, Browneyes?" Noah teased.

"You just handle your side, Phillips," she teased back.

Jacob tossed the birdie to his dad, indicating he wanted them to serve first. The game began with Marlena serving a deep high serve to Adam. The score was fifteen to ten, in favor of Noah and Marlena, when the game ended. Jacob looked from Marlena to his dad in disbelief. Adam patted his older brother on the back.

"Don't worry, Jacob. Next time, you'll know what you're up against."

Noah observed Jacob's countenance and attitude change. He kissed Marly on the forehead and watched as she sat near Kara and the baby. He casually approached Jacob and Adam and grinned.

"Good game, boys. Let's go eat. Your old man will pick up the tab."

"I'm game," Adam speedily agreed.

"She's incredibly athletic," Jacob commented, ignoring his father's offer.

"Yes, she is, among other things."

"Okay, Dad, did you tell Jacob the secret about Marly, something that could possibly affect the happiness of our entire family?" Adam asked, attempting to keep the peace.

Before he could finish, Jacob supplied in a flat voice, "Besides her being black you mean?"

Noah's eyes narrowed into angry slits.

Jacob, seeing his father's threatening look, backed down and asked Adam in a joking tone, "What's this big secret?"

Adam leaned in close and said in a stage whisper, "She can't swim very well."

Noah smiled at Adam. "I guess that means we'll have to do something about that, because she's a keeper."

Adam stared at Jacob and spoke directly to him, "Marly is definitely a keeper. Get used to it big brother." He marched away, leaving Jacob tongue tied at his younger brother's obvious loyalty to Marlena.

Noah faced Jacob, "Are you coming to dinner with the rest of the family or are you staying home?"

Jacob understood exactly what his father was asking, and it didn't really pertain to dinner. "I'm coming."

"Good," Noah replied as he turned to rejoin the others.

Jacob also comprehended that "good", spoken by his father, meant that the discussion deciding whether Marly was a member of the family was officially over.

Chapter Twenty

Marlena sat behind the large wooden desk trying to decide which posters to display on the classroom walls. School was to begin in a few short days and she still hadn't finished decorating her room yet. She'd finished everything else, but couldn't decide on this year's theme. Her mind went back to Noah. He had started a youth ministry of sorts at her old home. He would leave the church and head back to the inner city and assemble with the youth from the neighborhood there on her front porch. He'd been meeting with them for the last two weeks or so. She was going with him tonight for the first time since she'd moved. She wondered why he hadn't asked her to go with him before. In a way, she felt as though she were a traitor, someone who had turned her back on the community, someone who had taken the easy way out and escaped, never to lend a helping hand again. She knew it was ridiculous to think that way, but she couldn't seem to help it. She glanced at the clock and began putting things away. She'd told Noah that she'd meet him at the apartment. She'd better get a move on or else she'd be late and she was not in the mood for his "Noahtudes".

Noah thought about the group of kids that consistently met with him at Marlena's old place. They would always ask him, "Where's your girl at? How come she don't come with you?" He'd told them yesterday that he'd bring her along with him today. He hadn't asked her to come before because he'd thought it might make her homesick for her old house. He had the feeling that they were going to ask her some difficult questions. Maybe he should prepare her. Noah knew that they were curious about her leaving. He'd explained to them that it was his idea, but they weren't buying it. It was as though they felt betrayed by her departure. He was trying to understand their logic, but it was foreign to him. He prayed that she could.

Marlena smiled when Noah parked the car in the driveway of her home. She laughed aloud at Beauty's antics as she ran around the fenced in yard, stopping to sniff at something she'd found. Everything seemed so different, yet it was the same. She closed her eyes and listened to the familiar sounds. She got out of the car and walked to the front. The Kingleys were sitting on their porch. She greeted them warmly and chatted for several minutes, before climbing the stairs to sit on, what used to be her front porch.

Noah sat beside her and placed his arm around her shoulders. He couldn't get a read on what she was feeling. She hadn't said a word nor had she looked directly at him. She was absorbed in her own thoughts and emotions, while he thought on how this evening's events might affect their relationship. He had a sense of impending change, something that would be a new experience for him, the quiet before the storm. He closed his eyes and prayed silently that God would gift him with the wisdom, knowledge, and desire to handle whatever situation would arise this evening. He didn't have long to wait. The teenagers began arriving in groups of twos and threes. They all, guys and girls, seemed genuinely happy to see Marlena. The mostly teenage group fired off questions immediately. Where do you live? How is it? Do you like it better? Marlena laughed and tried her best to answer. Malcolm (Noah had become familiar with him), the unofficial leader of the group, predictably, was the responsible party who started the ball rolling.

He stared directly at Marlena and stated in an accusatory tone, "We all know Kaod is blowin' up in football and probably won't come back. Then you decide to marry a white man. Pastor Noah is cool an' all, but he's still white. Is that why you moved out to the white suburbs? We thought ya'll was gonna be different. What I see is that you an' Ka' aint no different than everybody else that made it big. Soon as you get the chance, you leave."

Noah wisely kept quiet. Marlena looked from Malcolm to every kid present.

"You know what Malcolm? Sometimes I feel as though I've abandoned you guys, as though I've left for something that appears better; however, I refuse to let you make me feel guilty about decisions that were mine to make. It's very easy for you to rationalize away my actions or stand in judgment, but let me give you my take. It was never in my mind to leave

141

here, because it wasn't in my mind to marry, let alone marry a white guy as you characterized Noah. You and every kid on this porch, understands the implications of that. It's as though I've told every black man in the world that they weren't good enough for me. I'm engaged to marry the one thing they could never be, 'white'. I didn't deliberately search for Noah, nor did he intentionally look for a black woman. God put the two of us together. He's a fellow believer in Christ, and in Christ, there is no division. He's a godly man and Christ calls for us to be evenly yoked. Therefore, I'm at peace with marrying him. Now, what about me leaving my home and moving away? Have you forgotten Chandra so quickly? It's Noah's responsibility to ensure that I'm in the safest environment possible. He made a decision and I agreed with it for reasons that are my business. You don't approve, but if you want to keep productive families in this community, then it's up to the members of this community to pitch in and make it safe. You know what I'm saying, Malcolm? Stop selling drugs, shooting up homes and at each other. Why would anyone want their loved ones to stay in a location that may put them in danger? If it hadn't been for Noah, you know, this 'white' guy sitting beside me, I might not be here right now," Marlena declared firmly.

When they all remained quiet, she hammered home her declaration by stating in simple terms, "The day your fathers, mothers, brothers, sisters, and you begin to accept his and her responsibility for the condition of this community, is the day you'll begin to see people returning to their roots."

Malcolm looked away in shame, knowing he was guilty of some of the offenses she'd listed.

"What do you mean by our mothers and fathers? They aint out here sellin' drugs or shootin' up people's homes," one girl responded angrily.

"Maybe not, but do they know about it? Are they living off of the drug money? How many of your parents know where you're at right now? How many of you actually live with both your father and mother?"

"My mom has to work two jobs to pay the bills," another girl challenged.

"And, how do you thank her, by hanging out with the wrong crowd? Let's not forget that your mom has to work those two jobs because she chose to ignore God's way and to do it her own. Doesn't God command us to be married before having sex? No matter the excuse you come up with, God's Word has an answer for it."

Noah, himself, flinched at that last statement, but recognized the inherent truth in it. She was boldly proclaiming God's Word in a way that would have branded him a racist. He was beginning to understand why God had her here with him. He also acknowledged that God was telling him that he could not do this ministry without his helpmate.

Marlena continued, "Most of you think that somehow or another I've got it made now. It may be physically safer, but the people are still locked in bigotry. A lot of them have simply tried to outrun their own prejudices. They have no desire to change or overcome them. They're in a comfort zone, which makes it harder for them to accept their inner faults, and even more difficult for them to accept Christ and enter into the Kingdom of Heaven. They've become blinded by the need to keep up with their neighbors. They view money as a way out of having to deal with the troublesome facts of life and the wide variance of cultures. Meanwhile, they set up their inner city social missions that hand out food and school supplies to 'underprivileged' children. In their minds, they can clearly see that the problem is the lack of Christ in these poverty, crime infested neighborhoods. They've completely forgotten that same 'lack of Christ' exist at the top of the social ladder as well as at the bottom. Money has just white-washed it. Divorce, premarital sex, adultery, lying, covetousness, just to name a few, are all just as prevalent in suburban America, and the last time I checked, God still considered them sins. All the man-initiated social programs in the world will never be able to come up with a solution, nor will it give you bonus points towards heaven. Until we begin to face the fact that sin is the root of the problem, and that it exist in the heart of every person, in every neighborhood, nothing will change. Social programs or living in better neighborhoods aren't the answer. God is, and every individual will one day stand before God and give an account. God does not care about your social status, but he does care about the status of your sin. Kaod and I have lived in this neighborhood for most of your lives. The only thing that we have of value to offer you is Christ, and although we left this community, God never will. You want a hero? Try worshipping God, and stop looking for man to solve your problems.

It was Noah's turn to feel the sting of the truth. How many times had the desired to initiate some sort of social program as a way to solve the problems of the inner city entered his mind? She was right, those same problems exists everywhere. The living conditions, on the surface, just appear better. God is the only answer.

"Boy, when she gets rolling, she doesn't care who's in the way," he thought to himself. He had the crazy feeling that this was going to be a long night for him.

✠

That will be the last time those kids ask for her, he thought with amusement as he watched the road ahead.

She'd left them with a lot to think about and she hadn't minced words either. His amusement rapidly faded when he noticed that she hadn't said a word all the way back. This wasn't the usual "he's not going to understand" silence either. Her jaw was tight as though she were having difficulty holding back her words. He recalled the day, trying to remember if he'd done something wrong. He was at a loss, but there was no mistaking her expression.

Cautiously, he probed, "Anything on your mind, sweetheart?"

She looked directly at him, eyes blazing, "Remember, rule number one, Noah? If we are going to argue, and we are about to argue, we will argue in the privacy of our own home. Yours or mine sweetheart?" she fired at him.

Noah was flabbergasted. He had no clue what was wrong, but in her current mood, he had enough presence of mind to keep quiet and drive to his home, rather than the apartment.

They had barely gotten inside the kitchen door, when she whirled around and stood face to face with Noah.

"What am I to you Noah?" she asked calmly.

He tried ineffectively to figure out what the correct answer could be. "I'm not exactly sure what it is your asking me," Noah responded, looking somewhat confused.

"Well, let me supply you with several possible answers. Am I your little porcelain doll, your super spiritual fiancée, your little playmate that you're eager to show off, or maybe Colleen's new replacement?" she asked unflinchingly.

It was his turn to become angry. "What the heck is that comment supposed to mean? You can't possibly think that I want you to be like Colleen," he declared in an angry voice.

"Answer the question Noah. What am I to you? You seem to have this little idea stuck in your brain that I can't handle anything. You need to hide the truth from me. You know, keep your little doll put away until you decide it's time to play. You deliberately didn't tell me about your trips back to the house. Those kids thought I abandoned them, that I didn't care a thing about what happened in my community. And, no matter what you think, that is still my community. You can take me out of it, but you can't take it out of me. I'm black and I will always have black roots. If you wanted a woman that would be content with 'playing' the role of your wife, then you should have picked someone else."

Angry tears had begun to form in her eyes.

"If you want to fight Marly, then we can, but I've never for one moment wanted you to be Colleen. That's below the belt."

"Is that what you're fixed on? Of all the things I've said so far, is that all you have to say? Noah, I am not about to exist entirely in your world, with your friends. You can pick another queen to reign if that's the case. I have a different cultural identity from you and it's about time you acknowledged it. You can't keep me solely in your environment. I love those kids and they need to understand that I haven't abandoned them," she stated firmly.

"Are you trying to break off this engagement?" he questioned, holding his breath.

Brown eyes met grey eyes, neither willing to turn away.

"Will you force me to?" she questioned, not backing down from his stare.

"If you take that ring off Marly, I will break your pretty little neck."

Ignoring his silly threat, she asked again, "What am I to you Noah?"

"Tell me what you want to be to me," he countered.

She sighed with frustration and turned to find her purse and keys. Noah watched her walk out the front door, satisfied that she hadn't taken his ring off. He didn't bother trying to give her a ride. She was too angry to accept a ride from him. Besides, she needed time to cool down. He knew that she loved him and she wasn't willing to throw in the towel, but he honestly had no clue why she was so angry. He picked up the phone and dialed McGhee's number.

✝

Layman McGhee laughed heartily as Noah explained the problem.

"You couldn't find a good white woman in your neck of the woods, so you come way over here to steal one of our black women, and she's giving you fits already," he teased good-naturedly.

Layman McGhee was a very good friend of Noah's. He also happened to be a fellow pastor and black. If anybody could explain what the heck Marly was upset about, Layman could.

Noah grinned, "Don't hate on me now. I'm trying to figure out what's got her so riled up."

Layman was enjoying having Noah at his mercy for once. He'd never seen Noah at a loss as to how to handle a particular problem. He was looking forward to meeting the woman that could shake the unshakable Noah Phillips. Layman hadn't been the least bit surprised when Noah had informed him of his courtship, even as he revealed that the lady of interest was black. He was one of the least prejudiced men Layman had ever encountered. Layman wanted to tease Noah mercilessly, but he took pity on his friend and brought in the expert on black women, his wife of twenty-six years, Marcella. Noah had to suffer through another twenty minutes of good natured teasing from her before she explained the problem.

"How much time have you spent in her community, around her friends?" Marcella asked candidly.

Noah thought for a moment. "Hardly any since she moved into the apartment," he admitted.

"So you're expecting her to be a trophy wife? You know, like Colleen. Her only asset is her beauty?" Marcella asked bluntly. She softened her words when she saw the look of surprised hurt in Noah's eyes.

"Those had almost been Marly's exact words to him," Noah thought to himself.

"Noah, try reversing the roles. She's trying hard to be submissive, but you're practically shutting her off from everything familiar to her. She lives in your community and associates mostly with your friends. You have to remember, she's an African-American woman and the people you're trying to reach are her friends and neighbors. She's lived among them all of her adult life. If you are going to minister to them, don't you think she should be by your side? She has gifts other than her looks. She's expecting to be your help mate, especially, if you're attempting to reach the black community. Do you want to take that away from her too? She has every right to wonder what kind of wife you're looking for," Marcella finished in a loving voice.

Noah sat in a thoughtful silence. He was beginning to understand how Marly felt. From her perspective, it could seem as though he wanted her to only be around his friends. He hadn't meant it that way at all. In Noah's mind however, the most important blunder he'd made was overlooking her God-given gifts, thus giving her the impression that she was of no value to God's ministry. Marly was beautiful, but more than that, she was a dedicated woman of God and he needed to affirm that aspect of her. "I guess I have some apologizing to do," he admitted with a deep sigh, glancing at the older couple.

Layman couldn't resist adding one more teasing remark, "You sure you don't want to trade her in for one of those easier, more passive models from your neck of the woods?"

"Leave him alone, McGhee," Marcella chastised with a soft laugh. "Any man that goes to this extreme, trying to figure out his woman, is a man that's in love." She turned to Noah and smiled. "I hope she knows how blessed she is."

Noah, without hesitation, corrected Marcella, "Thank you, but I'm the one that's blessed." Thanking the both of them tremendously, he jumped back into his car and drove straight to Marly's apartment.

Noah turned the key and opened the door. Marly was asleep on the couch. He knew she had waited up for him because she wasn't dressed for bed. He bent down and kissed her on the cheek. "Hey, sleepyhead, wake up."

She opened her eyes and smiled, "I knew you'd come to tell me good night."

He sat down and pulled her into his arms and said tenderly, "You want to know what you are to me? You're my Cinderella, Browneyes, and Marly all rolled into one. You're the other half of my life, my best friend and my soul mate. I need you, Marly. Not just for show, but to help me be a better man. I don't want you to be white or like Colleen or any other woman. I need you to be you. I trust you to be my representative and to carry my name. I understand there are differences between the cultures and I need you to teach me about them, if that's okay with you. I'm also very sorry that I didn't trust that God gave you to me as a helper in the ministering of His Word. You should have been by my side from the first time I went back to your community. Will you forgive me?"

"You are one incredible man, Noah Phillips," she complimented sincerely.

"Does that mean you're not angry with me anymore?" He laughed when she hid her face against his chest. He reached down and lifted her face and looked deep into her eyes. "You've definitely got more spunk then you let on. I've never had the luxury of my wife truly being my helper. It's something that I'm going to have to get used to. Forgive me for being blind to your gifts and strengths. The last thing I ever want you to feel is that you're irrelevant to me or to God's ministry. Okay?"

She nodded her understanding and snuggled deeper into his arms.

✞

Marlena recalled today's events. She really had been angry with Noah. She wanted him to need her and to love her unconditionally. She didn't want to be a sideline wife. She desired to be a complete part of his life, for him to look at her and know that she could add value to his ministry. It was also necessary for him to understand that, although he wasn't prejudiced, there existed differences between the cultures, differences such as perceptions, social habits, and even entertainment. She wanted him to be willing to experience and accept her culture in the same manner that she had responded to his. Most interracial couples, either fully assimilated to one culture or the other, as though one was more beneficial than the next. It's what had allowed her to fully understand the betrayal that Malcolm had expressed. She wasn't ashamed of her ethnicity neither was she trying to escape the color of her skin. She fully comprehended that Noah had been trying to protect her, but the goal had now changed. They needed to get busy doing the work of their Father. There were lost souls and hurting people that knew nothing of God's love and grace. The mission had changed and Noah hadn't trusted her enough to take her with him to the battlefield. She understood her role was to be that of his helpmate. Hopefully, he now understood it too.

Her mind shifted to Malcolm. He was kidding himself, if he claimed that he wouldn't prefer to live in a nicer home or in a better neighbor. She perceived that God was going to use Noah to help those kids, in particular Malcolm. Malcolm watched Noah like a hawk. He was blunt and to the point and rough around the edges, but that was his way of keeping people at a distance. She knew that Malcolm's father had abandoned him years ago and that he didn't trust anyone. He was trying to see if Noah lived what he taught. She wouldn't be a bit surprised to see Malcolm hanging out with Noah one day. Maybe, she'd ask Noah about taking him to the church picnic on Saturday.

Noah considered Marly's reactions toward today's events. She'd felt left out of his life and pulled from her culture. He hadn't intentionally tried to separate her; he'd just wanted her to become a part of his life so much, that he'd forgot to share her life with her. Today had been the first time she hadn't backed down. He tucked that away in his memory bank. If she felt strongly about something, she'd stand her ground. That is what made her a solid Christian. There were lots of believers who frequently backed away from the truth when confronted with opposition. He'd take her in his corner any day. He had decided to ask Marly if she'd like to visit Layman McGhee's Sunday service in the near future. From personal experience, he realized that Sunday services in an African-American church were vastly different from services conducted in a Caucasian church. Layman was a more boisterous pastor. Noah knew that it was important that he not cast aside her heritage. Noah prayed to God for guidance and protection. He prayed for the youth in his church and in the inner city. He asked God to raise up strong godly leaders among them. He prayed a special prayer for Malcolm, whom God was beginning to bring to Noah's thoughts more and more.

Chapter Twenty-one

Marlena walked over to the sofa with her pink and white Nike sports shoes in her hand. She sat next to Noah and eyed him cautiously. "Why are you looking at me like that?"

"Like what?" he asked, feigning ignorance.

"As though you're trying to figure something out, are you?"

Noah ignored her question and asked one of his own. "What other sports do you know how to play?"

"Getting a little nervous about today's picnic, Phillips?" she taunted impishly.

Noah grinned, "I'd just like to know what I'm getting myself into beforehand."

"What sports do they typically play at these picnics?" she asked.

"Basketball, softball, flag football, and volleyball," he supplied.

"Yes, to all the above," she answered nonchalantly.

He stared intently at her. "You can play all of those sports?"

She nodded, slightly embarrassed.

"As well as you play volleyball?"

Once again, she nodded yes.

"Do me a favor, sweetheart…"

She cut him off before he could finish, "I know. I know. You don't want me to participate."

He looked at her strangely as she bent down to lace her shoes. Noah gently grabbed her arm and forced her to turn and face him. There was no mistaking the obvious hurt in her eyes. He couldn't even begin to grasp why she would think that he'd not want her to participate.

"What I was going to say was this, 'Do me a favor, sweetheart. Make sure you're always on my team.' Why would you think that I wouldn't want you to participate?"

When she didn't respond, he asked again.

"Shawn always had a problem with me playing sports, especially around guys. He said it made them feel as though I was showing off and that no guy wanted to play against a woman who was better than he was."

Marlena had spoken so softly that he'd barely heard her.

Noah was furious. Why would a man knock his wife, a woman who had born him a child, so low that she would feel embarrassed about the gifts that God had given her? It took every ounce of strength he had not to speak ill of her dead husband.

"Tell me what else he said about you," Noah demanded quietly.

Marly became so embarrassed that she groaned. "Can we talk about this later?"

"No, later won't make it any easier. We've got all the time in the world right now. What else did he say to you?"

She began to fidget with a loose string on her shirt.

"Marly, we are not leaving this apartment until you tell me what else he said to you."

"He told me that I was incapable of pleasing him or any other man in bed. He said I was, you know."

Noah looked at her and suddenly smiled, "He thought you preferred women?"

He laughed aloud when she turned away in embarrassment. Noah turned her around to face him and stated in a matter of fact voice, "We'll debunk that little theory on our wedding night, won't we Browneyes?"

She blushed, but nodded her head in agreement. He laughed heartily and hugged her to him.

✠

The park was quickly filling up with members from both churches. Noah eased his car into a spot under a huge maple tree. He glanced at Marly and told her to just be herself and have fun. After opening her door, he ushered her towards the shelter where Pastor Jim Wade and his staff were seated. Once there, he introduced her to all. Pastor Wade smiled brightly and offered his congratulations on their engagement. Marlena sensed a genuine warmth emanating from him. His wife, on the other hand, was stiff and cold. She hardly glanced at Marlena and never offered her hand.

Marlena pretended not to notice, but she felt Noah's hand tighten on her waist. She smiled up at him to let him know that it was okay.

As Noah escorted her towards his congregation, he whispered in her ear, "It's not over yet. We have to eat lunch at the same table."

She struggled to control her laughter.

✟

Noah pretended to listen to the conversations of the men all around him, but he was really watching Marly as she played with the younger children. She was very good with them and they seemed to love her already. They followed her around as though she was the pied piper. When she sat, they sat. When she played, they played. He was impressed with her patience. He looked at his watch and realized that it was time to call everyone in for lunch which meant the food had to be blessed. He gave the order and soon the pavilions were filled to capacity. The blessing was pronounced, and as was the tradition, both pastors, and their spouses or guest, were given the honor of being served first. Noah gripped her hand and pulled her directly in front of him. He groaned to himself when he saw that Caroline was one of the servers.

Marlena was conscious of the fact that she and Noah were drawing their unfair share of the attention. Most of the servers were very polite and greeted her warmly. Some even extended congratulations on her and Noah's engagement. Caroline and her cohorts were quite the opposite. They practically threw the food on Marlena's plate, while they ever so delicately placed Noah's on his plate. Marlena looked from her plate to his and politely swapped him plates. She then held her new plate out for Caroline to place food on. With a red face, Caroline, with impeccable manners, served her.

Marlena deliberately faced Noah and spoke with a dramatic tone, "I told you, Noah, that the problem was with my plate, and not me. You silly man, you actually thought that they would be so rude as to embarrass their pastor."

Marlena thanked Caroline and continued through the line, gushing about how nice and polite Pastor Wade's congregation was.

Noah had to bite the inside of his mouth to keep from laughing. He could hear snickering all around him. He escorted Marlena to the table and turned to face Jim Wade who was red-faced from embarrassment. Noah waited until Jim's wife was seated before sitting next to Marly. It was no surprise to see a noticeable change in her manners toward Marly.

Noah glanced at Marly, who was in turn peeping at him. He knew that she was trying to gage his reaction to the stunt she had just pulled. She had the nerve to attempt to appear contrite. He gave her a stern look. Doing his level best not to smile, he told her that she needed to apologize for embarrassing Pastor Wade's staff. Obediently, Marly apologized, and for good measure, swapped plates with Noah again. That little swap, brought chuckles from all around the pavilion. Noah looked over at Hal and the rest of his staff. They all had their heads bowed as though praying, but Noah knew better. Jim Wade assured Marlena that her apology was not necessary, since his congregation had initiated the affront. Noah watched as Marly escaped to get drinks for the two of them.

Marly was contemplating what to drink when two small girls asked her if she was going to continue to play with them after lunch. She smiled and teasingly told them that she had been a bad girl and Pastor Noah had put her in time out beside him. The two girls stared wide eyed at Marly and ran to inform Noah's entire congregation of poor Marly's sad plight. Word spread like wildfire and an eruption of laughing soon ensued. Marly pretended not to notice until Valerie approached her giggling. Marly looked at the younger woman and smiled slyly.

"Can you give me that salt shaker off the table over there?" Marly asked.

Valerie complied and stood in amazement as she watched Marly pour half the contents into one of the cups of lemonade.

"Thanks. That ought to awaken your pastor's senses."

Valerie stood motionless and then rushed to tell Hal and the rest of the staff. Marly calmly picked up both cups and, with a cheery smile, walked back to where she and Noah were seated.

Noah accepted the cup from Marly and placed it on the table in front of him. He continued eating as he conversed with Jim and his wife. He picked up the cup to take a drink, but was interrupted by a group of young children from both congregations. Their little faces were serious.

One little girl came boldly forward and asked in the sweetest voice imaginable, "Pastor Noah, can Marly please get out of time-out and come and play with us?"

Noah's head shot to Marly who was smiling at the children. All around the pavilion, people were shushing each other in order to hear his response. Before Noah could say a word, one of Marly's little self appointed protectors, stepped forward and volunteered to help keep her out of trouble. Once again amused laughter could be heard. Noah cleared his throat noisily and declared that Marly was released from time out, but if she got into any more trouble, he was going to personally come and find her.

Marly jumped to her feet and quickly ushered the overjoyed children from under the pavilion and towards the play area. Noah glanced over his shoulder at his staff. All of them were smiling as though they knew something he didn't. He shrugged, turned, and took a huge gulp of his drink. As soon as it hit his taste buds, he knew what they had been smiling about.

He stood and faced his congregation, all of which were doubled over with laughter, swallowed the contents in his mouth, and with a knowing gleam in his eye asked, "Who?"

Not one of them would tell, but he already knew the culprit. No small wonder, she'd hightailed it out of there so quickly. He excused himself and headed out to get Marly with the entire pavilion watching in anticipation.

Marly had her back turned, playing with the children, when she heard a female voice shout, "Run, Marly!"

She whirled in time to see Noah headed towards her, walking at a lightning fast pace. She screamed and took off running. The children ran alongside her, thinking it to be a new game she'd invented. The chase was on. She heard the women cheering her on, while the traitorous men were yelling for him to catch her. She looked behind her to see where he was, but he had disappeared. She stopped, but reasoned that Noah had not given up. She retraced her steps and cautiously peeped around the corner of the building she had rounded just as he had started the chase. She saw Noah making sure that all the children were safe with their parents.

Noah stooped down and tightened his laces. He was reasonably sure he could catch her if she ran again. He heard all the chatter behind him. The men were throwing in with him, while the women were with Marly. He stood to his feet and walked in her direction. He wasn't going to expend any unnecessary energy until he absolutely had to. She was standing near the building, resembling a deer caught in the headlights.

"What are you going to do, Noah?" she asked warily.

He narrowed his eyes and responded, "Come here and find out."

From behind him, a man shouted for him to go and catch her. That started the cheering from both sides. Noah saw a clump of trees directly behind her. With any luck, he could get her to head towards them. He'd definitely catch her in those trees. He began walking towards her and talking at the same time. Suddenly, without warning, he took off in a surprise sprint towards her. He increased his speed when she screamed and turned to take off running. As hoped, she headed straight for the trees. He focused on catching his prey and tuned out the cheering coming from behind him. He rounded the building just as she entered the clump of trees. Noah slowed his pace enough to steadily gain on her. She turned to find his location and shrieked when she realized how close he was. She turned to run again, but directly in front of her was a wide stream. Noah smiled and slowed to a walk.

"Come here, Browneyes!" he commanded softly.

Marly looked behind her as though contemplating whether or not to cross the stream.

"Don't even think about it," he ordered sternly.

Marly sighed and nervously walked to Noah. He stretched out his hand and snatched hers.

"Now, what kind of punishment can I give you?" he whispered huskily as he pulled her to him. He kissed her gently. "I've wanted to do that all day," he admitted. He looked at her and smiled, "I love you, Marly."

"I love you, too," she responded.

He edged her closer and kissed her once more, his lips clinging longingly to hers. Noah released her reluctantly and grasped her hand. "Let's make this look good, Browneyes," he said as he pulled her gently behind him.

The men began to cheer wildly as Noah emerged from out of the woods, pulling Marly behind him. He brought her to the table where the cup of salted lemonade still sat. He stood her in front of him, reached for the cup, handed it to her, and announced loudly, "Drink."

Marlena seized the cup, and without batting an eye, took a huge gulp, and swallowed it down. The women began clapping and cheering. She grinned cheekily and proceeded to bow. Noah frowned and grabbed the drink from her hand. Placing the cup to his mouth, he sipped cautiously. This was not the same cup of lemonade, someone had exchanged the cups. He scrutinized the faces of the smiling women and stopped on Valerie's. She flushed and glanced at Marly. Noah laughed loudly and called Valerie a traitor.

Valerie giggled and replied, "We women have to stick together,"

✠

With the excitement over, the various games were announced. People began to scatter in the direction of their interests. Noah watched as young Stephen tugged Marly in the direction of the football matches. He observed the boys face as she allowed herself to be led away. The little guy was definitely in love.

Pastor Wade watched also. "You've got your hands full with that one," he commented half-wistfully.

"I wouldn't have her any other way," Noah admitted.

"She'll make you a heck of a wife, Noah. I'm not just saying words either. She brings out the life in you. You know, something to really live for, that keeps you alert and on your toes. A man's wife should make him feel like a hero. I'd like to chase after my wife like that, but the problem is, she just won't run," he added insightfully.

Noah nodded thoughtfully.

Marlena smiled down at the dark haired boy. He had just informed her that he was going to marry her. She nodded absentmindedly as she tried to locate Noah. Out of the corner of her eye, she spotted Caroline walking with someone. Marlena did a double take, and realized with a jolt, that it was Noah. She tried not to stare, but her eyes seemed fixed, unable to move. As if in a dream, a very bad dream, she watched as Caroline threw her arms around Noah and hugged him. A jealousy so fierce engulfed her. Was he out of his mind? Allowing that woman to touch him, let alone hug him. She wished fervently that Mr. Noah Phillips could read her mind at this very moment. He'd get an earful. He must have heard her thoughts, because he looked right at her and smiled. Marlena decided he couldn't have heard her thoughts after all, because if he had, he most definitely wouldn't be smiling. She felt a tug on her hand and looked down. Little Stephen was informing her that he had to go because his parents were calling him. Marlena watched the boy dash off to his parents and was a little startled when a strange voice spoke to her from behind.

She turned to see who was speaking. It was a tall, very attractive blond-haired, middle aged man. Marly looked surprised. He'd called her name as though she should know him.

"I'm sorry, do I know you?" she asked sincerely.

He smiled and apologized, "Excuse me. That was kind of presumptuous of me. I figured that you must be Noah's fiancée. You are the infamous Marly, right?"

"I don't know about the infamous part, but, yes, I am Marlena, and you are?" she replied, waiting for an answer.

He introduced himself as Levi Jamison. Marlena decided he seemed nice enough and the two were soon chatting easily.

Noah observed Marly and Levi from a distance. Memories of hurt and betrayal flooded his mind. Colleen and Levi, that guy had a lot of nerve. He'd never confronted him about Colleen, but had always wished he had. She had been unnaturally protective of the guy, as though he was her husband and Noah, the lover. She had begged him over and over again not to confront Levi. Once again, he'd given in to her tears. She'd promised never to see him again and Noah had vowed to divorce her if she did.

He glanced at Marly. Noah forced himself to remember that Marly was innocent. She had no idea who Levi was, or the role he'd played in Noah and Colleen's marriage; however, he was sure that Levi knew exactly who Marly was. He prayed that Levi was not up to his old tricks. The word around town was that he loved unavailable women. Noah made up his mind that he would make it clear that Marly was off limits. He started towards the pair, but before he could reach them, Hal appeared at their side.

Marly smiled at Hal as he joined them. He grinned and told her that Noah was looking for her and she needed to find her lovesick fiancé. Marly glanced around and saw Noah walking across the field. She forgot her jealousy and happily went to meet him.

Noah took one look at her smiling eyes and grinned as she threw herself into his arms. He twirled her around until she giggled and begged him to stop. Then, entwining his fingers with hers, suggested they take a walk. The two of them walked hand and hand for a while before either of them spoke. They stopped under an oak tree, enjoying the shade.

"Tell me why you were hugging Caroline," she blurted out.

"First of all, I was not hugging her, she hugged me. I told Caroline, in no uncertain terms, what would happen to her, should she choose to publicly disrespect my fiancée again. She also understands that you are the only woman who is at liberty to hug me at will."

Marly wrapped her arms around him and hugged him tightly. Noah rested his head on top of hers and hugged her back.

"I was jealous," she confessed unashamedly.

"You don't have reason to be. Marly, listen to me for a moment, okay."

She shook her head yes, not ready to leave the circle of his arms.

He continued, "Stay as far away from Levi Jamison as you can. He has a reputation that you don't want to be associated with."

"Then why is he here?" she wondered.

Noah shrugged, "Because he attends Jim Wade's church. Stay away from him, all right."

Marly nodded in understanding.

✝

The day was finally over and Marly sat in the car waiting for Noah. He was talking to Hal, but he kept glancing at her. Whatever they were talking about, it must involve her and it was making her extremely nervous. Finally, the two finished their conversation and Noah made his way to the car and sat down. He twisted in his seat to face her.

"Did you enjoy yourself today?" he asked casually.

She got the impression that he was trying to make light of an issue that was very serious to him. She faced him and asked him directly, "Is there something wrong, Noah?"

"What did you think about Levi?" he queried lightly.

Marlena held his gaze and inwardly tossed about an answer. This was a loaded question to be sure. She decided to take the offensive rather than the defensive. She didn't know where this line of questioning was headed, but she wasn't at all comfortable with answering, unless he would be more specific. Levi was very attractive. To be absolutely honest, attractive was an understatement. He was "fine" in every sense of the slang word. How in the world do you tell your fiancée that another man was gorgeous, and you had actually been flattered that the guy had been a little flirty? Levi had seemed boyishly cute about it, unlike the Josh type, which was completely obnoxious. No way was she going to say more than she needed to.

"In what way are you talking about?"

Noah narrowed his gaze. Marlena hoped beyond hope that the shade of the tree, and her skin tone, hid the fact that she was blushing.

"Did you find him attractive?" he asked in an irritated voice.

"In what way?" she replied, still trying to avoid answering. She could definitely detect a hint of iron in his tone. It was the same tone he'd used when she had teased him about Josh.

Noah was becoming increasingly frustrated. Marly was usually a very direct and to the point person. Why was she beating around the bush? Then it came to him. She was attracted to Levi. Levelheaded, no-nonsense Marly had fallen for that boyish charm of Levi's. He fought the sense of betrayal he felt. She hadn't done anything wrong. He knew that he was allowing an old ghost to invade a new relationship. He tried to be rational, but anger filled his voice when he spoke.

"You're attracted to him. How could you be attracted to a guy you've just met?" he accused irrationally.

"That's silly, Noah. Attraction is what draws people in the first place. I was attracted to you the first time I met you. It's what happens after that, what people do after the initial attraction," she rationalized.

"And what are you planning on doing?" Noah threw at her.

She resisted the urge to be sarcastic. He was behaving as though she was contemplating having an affair or something. What was wrong with him?

"I'll tell you what I'm planning on doing about it, nothing. I have a pretty spectacular fiancé who I happen to love very much. Levi's an attractive guy, but he's not you. I'd be foolish to risk losing you, Noah. Honestly, babe, I'm still trying to handle you," she smiled, attempting to diffuse the situation.

Noah looked at her, jumped out of the car and walked a short distance away. Marlena waited a moment before getting out and going over to stand beside him. She took him in her arms and held him. She reached up and played with the back of his hair, hoping to tease him out of his peculiar mood. He eventually glanced down at her and smiled. She traced the outline of his mouth with her finger. He captured her hand and kissed it.

"Do you want to talk about it, babe?" she asked gently.

Her use of the endearment melted his icy demeanor. He knew he owed her an explanation. He probably should have told her sooner. "Let's go home, Marly. We'll talk about it there," he said, sounding more like his usual self.

In mutual silence, they headed back to the car and drove to her apartment.

Marlena watched as Noah walked across the room and sat in the armchair near the sofa. She hesitated, and then sat on the sofa alone. This was the first time she'd ever known him to not sit on the sofa with her. He was being distant, as though he was in the room alone. She grabbed a pillow from beside her and hugged it, waiting for him to say or do something. She wanted to comfort him, but wasn't quite sure how.

Noah drifted back in time, remembering memories that he thought were dead and buried. He began to speak as if reliving a dream. He started from the beginning, the time of his and Colleen's marriage. He had been idealistic. He'd come to his marriage bed a virgin and she had not. He had accepted her explanation because he loved her. Everyone made mistakes and he had chalked hers up to being young and inexperienced. Time passed and he began to notice that she liked receiving attention from men. It didn't matter that she was married. He'd tried everything- gifts, romantic dates, weekend getaways, but to no avail. Eventually, she began to flirt. It even reached the point where she was doing it in front of him. When he confronted her, she'd laughed him off as being jealous. Finally, Jacob was born and Noah had prayed that having a family would settle her down. For a while, she was absorbed with being a new mommy and he had thought it to be the end of her flirtations, but the newness of being a mother wore off and she went back to the old ways.

Enter Levi Jamison, attractive and single; although, Noah found out later that he'd fathered a child out of wedlock. "At first I thought nothing of her flirting with him. He was like the countless other men, but then, she started buying seductive undergarments. I thought they were for my benefit; however, when she began dressing in a manner that she knew I didn't approve of, my suspicions were aroused. Instinct kept telling me there was someone else, but how could it be when our own intimacy level had increased. The signs were there, but my pride wouldn't allow me to see what was so obvious. I'd call home and she'd be gone on some phony errand or shopping trip. I wanted to believe her. She was the mother of my son, my wife. This went on for a month or so until Hal saw the two of them leaving a hotel. He circled around the block and watched as they shared a very intimate kiss in her car. He came to me and we prayed together. He wouldn't let me leave until he was sure that I wouldn't do anything stupid. I went home that evening filled with a strange sense of peace. I began packing my clothes. She pleaded with me to stay and confessed everything. Things I hadn't known. Events, places, times, everything, she had even taken Jacob over to his home to have a play date with his son. I was on my way out of the door when she told me that she was pregnant with Adam. I was floored. She, as though it would somehow make her and Levi null-and-void, informed me that she'd made him use protection at all times. I know, it sounds like a 'Lifetime' movie special and believe me, that's what it felt like. I didn't believe her, of course. How could I? She'd already proven herself to me. I took a two week leave of absence and went to stay with an old professor friend of mind. It was the most difficult two weeks of my life. I hardly slept or ate. I stayed before God. I wanted out of the marriage, but I knew Jacob and the baby (if it were mine) would suffer. I didn't make the decision to stay until Adam was born and a DNA test was performed to determine paternity. He turned out to be mine. From the time of his birth, she was very aloof with him. She resented the fact that my love for God and our sons was the deciding factor which saved our marriage. She actually wanted me to say that it was my overwhelming love for her that caused me to stay. Colleen understood, from that point on, I would not tolerate any more flirtatious behavior or any more indiscretions. It was a very long time before I could stand to touch her, and it took even longer for us to reach some semblance of normalcy in our marriage. I felt as though she had raped me. I know traditionally that term is used to apply to women and in a physical sense, but she took something from me that I never gave her permission to take. She stole my sense of self-worth, peace, and dignity. She even took what was promised solely to me, her body; and, against my will, gave it to another man."

Noah stared at Marlena, his eyes revealing the nakedness of his pain. "How could you do that to someone you promised to love?" He paused and then spoke quietly, "Now you know the sordid history of Levi Jamison and Pastor Noah's wife. I've no claim to perfection, but I was never unfaithful to my marriage. I often regret the fact that my sons never had the opportunity to see a healthy vibrant marriage and I learned the hard way what to look for in a future spouse. I've also become stronger in the sense that there are certain things that I just won't tolerate in a woman. I try not to bring any baggage into our relationship, but seeing you with Levi today, caused memories to resurface. I know that you're not Colleen, but he is still the same old Levi. I think that you can understand the hurt and the shame I felt, because Shawn put you through it."

She sat aghast, not knowing how to respond.

Noah continued, "You're the only person who knows the story in its entirety. Neither Jacob, nor Adam, is aware of what happened between their mother and me."

That didn't make Marlena feel any better. She was tongue tied due to the fact that she had found a man, who had helped to cause Noah so much pain, attractive. Marlena was deeply ashamed. She had put her pride over their relationship. It was wrong for her to have allowed flattery to trump commitment. Why hadn't he said something earlier? She now understood how he had felt when he'd seen her talking to Levi. That's why Hal had told her to go and find Noah.

"What were you and Hal talking about?" she asked.

"You, he advised me to tell you about Levi. What do you think of me now Browneyes?" he questioned, watching her closely.

Was he serious? "I think that I want you to come over here," she stated shyly.

"Why?" Noah asked unhesitatingly.

She blushed and admitted, "Because, I miss you."

"How can you miss me, if I'm sitting right here?" he answered.

She rolled her eyes, "You know what I mean."

"If you really want me, come and get me," he challenged.

She stood to her feet, walked to the chair, grabbed his hand, and tried to pull him towards her. Instead, he gave a tug and she fell onto his lap.

"Still want to be Mrs. Phillips now that you know all of my ghosts?"

With a teasing smile, she asked him if he'd just made up that story to get rid of her. Noah rewarded her with an amused chuckle and a warm embrace.

What an unbelievable day Marly recalled as she slipped beneath the soft cotton sheets. She had known about Colleen's unfaithfulness, but not to the extent that Noah had confided. She'd thought her marriage was rough, but he'd had it just as bad, if not worse. No wonder it had taken him so long to express an interest in a relationship. She understood that too. The shame of feeling inadequate could do years of damage that only God's Word could heal. No wonder she and Noah were kindred spirits. They'd both experienced the same kind of profound pain caused by the betrayal of faithless spouses. Adultery had a way of severing the spiritual and physical bond which God used to bind husband and wife together. It left emotional scars so deep that it sometimes took years for them to heal properly. She could still visualize the agony in Noah's face as he had told his story. It was her story, too.

"Please Lord. Don't allow me to hurt him any more than he's already been hurt. Let me be the kind of wife he needs, the kind of wife he can depend on and trust". It was long time before sleep claimed her restless mind.

Observing Levi talking to Marly had brought back memories from the past that were best forgotten. Marly was not Colleen and he needed to keep the two separated. He loved Marly, not in the same physical way he'd fallen for Colleen. This was completely different. He was older, more mature. He fully comprehended that love was a decision, a choice, an irreversible covenant established by God. It wasn't an emotion that could be turned on and off. He was hers and she was his by mutual agreement. Yes, there were feelings that each admitted about the other, but neither one of them were entering into the sacred covenant of marriage without the explicit understanding that it would only be broken by death. He knew that God had established marriage as a way of uniting one man with one woman, thereby, preserving the family as a whole. He had spent almost four years alone, in complete celibacy, allowing God to heal and preserve him for such a time as this. He had learned the hard way to trust God's judgment rather than his own. He'd never lacked the opportunity to be with women, but he had freely given God the right to select his next wife. He'd known that Marly was God's gift to him. He would love, cherish, honor and respect her in a way that garnished him her respect and faithfulness. He had chosen to overcome past fears and disappointments, and to make her his partner, denying all others in the process. He smiled as he remembered the salty lemonade and chasing her. He hadn't felt so alive in years. He knew exactly what Jim Wade had been referring to concerning Marly. Noah would forever have to chase her. He'd have to continually study and learn about her as one constantly studies and learns about God's Word. She would always keep him on his toes, ready to do battle. She wasn't the typical woman who would be content to just look pretty. She wanted to be there, on the battlefield with her husband. She had missed him simply because he hadn't sat near her. He'd pretended not to understand her, but that simple statement had spoken volumes to him. She had felt his distance and hadn't liked it. It had disturbed her. Marly was completely his. He wondered if she knew that she had unconsciously used an endearment when talking to him. It was the first time she'd called him something other than Noah. He closed his eyes and allowed sleep to claim him.

Chapter Twenty-two

Marlena frowned as Tina fussed and chastised her for not being on the ball concerning the wedding. She hadn't even started looking at dresses because, to be honest, the wedding seemed so far away, while Thanksgiving was next week and Christmas right on its heels. At this particular moment, she was more concerned with how many people were going to be at Noah's house for dinner, than selecting a wedding dress. There were so many things happening at one time. She and Noah had practically driven or flown, almost every weekend to attend one of Kaod's football games, including some of the away ones. In addition, Noah had finally tracked down the agent for the log cabin home and they were going to view the inside this Saturday. She didn't want to deal with planning a wedding until after the holidays. Of course, she knew better than to say that aloud to her best friend. Maybe, what she needed was one of those wedding planners. Marlena wondered how expensive they were. She didn't want a huge wedding, just friends and family. Whether or not Noah wanted to include his church family was something she hadn't quite thought about. This was becoming more complicated and that's exactly why she didn't want to think about it. She turned her focus back to Tina.

"What kind of dress do you recommend?"

"Think about Noah, what his taste is, and then compliment it with your dress. He's the one you really want to wow," Tina suggested.

Marlena smiled. "The dress should be simple, yet elegant. It should have a hint of sensuality, but meant for his eyes only."

Tina stared in amazement. "You've got that man pegged perfectly, haven't you? Noah is definitely a 'for his eyes only' kind of guy."

Marlena giggled, "What you really mean is he's possessive. At this stage in my life, I like possessive, but I prefer to say that he's guarded. He makes it very clear that he doesn't like sharing; but then again, neither do I."

"You two are an odd pair, to say the least. Think about it. He's a widower, you're a widow. Neither one of you have been with anyone else since, which kind of makes you both like virgins." She stopped and gazed intently at Marlena. "Have you talked to him about Shawn? You are ready to be his wife, in the intimate sense I mean?"

Marlena shrugged and looked away. "I've told him enough."

"What do you mean by enough? Does he know what Shawn did? How he treated you?" Tina asked with concern.

"I'm not sure that he needs to know everything about Shawn and me. Some things are better left in the past," Marlena explained with finality.

Tina respected her right to privacy, but hoped Marlena was truly ready to put the past behind. Her husband hadn't exactly been patient or kind. She doubted that Marlena truly understood how beautiful and loving physical intimacy between a husband and wife could be. She'd been a virgin when she'd married Shawn and extremely naïve. Shawn had been more into himself than into her. She was the prize that he'd won from other would-be suitors, and she'd had quite a few of them. She'd grown from a young, vibrant girl into a very reserved and serious woman. Tina could already see that Noah was good for Marlena. He seemed quite capable of handling her independent nature. He was the only man that Marlena had actually submitted to. She prayed a quick prayer for her friend.

✝

Noah watched Marlena's face as the agent opened up the front door and allowed them entry into the home. She could hardly contain her excitement. He grinned as she gripped his hand and pulled him behind her. Apparently, she felt he was moving too slowly. He had to admit, he was a bit excited too. This would be their residence, a place that they would make into a home to be shared. There would be no more her apartment or his place, but our home. They could finally come home to each other.

After they entered the front door, they had to walk through a foyer which led to the living room, with a formal dining area off to the side. The architect had built this room as the center piece for the rest of the home. It had a high arching wood-beamed ceiling with several strategically placed skylights directly overhead. This feature permitted you to gaze at the night sky within the comfort of your own home. To access the living room level, there were three steps on opposite sides of the beautifully constructed room. It was encompassed on all four sides by hand carved wooden walls with shelves built into them. The entire house had authentic oak wood floors that glistened as the light reflected upon them. Marlena noticed a spiral staircase which led to a second floor. It resembled a loft, but extended halfway around the upper level of the home. The agent informed them that there were three bedrooms and a full bathroom upstairs. On the main level, opposite the living room, was the kitchen which could be viewed through sliding shutter windows. It was large enough to have a traditional dining set and was equipped with all of the latest kitchen ware, complete with a stainless steel refrigerator, stove, sinks, microwave, etc... At each end of the room were storage shelves that reached from the ceiling to the floor. There were also storage areas directly below the counter space, underneath the shutter windows and on various sides of the appliances. The kitchen window presented a view of the stream and wooded area. There was back door which opened into the closed-in portion of the wrap-around porch.

The home boasted four bedrooms, including the master bedroom. Noah requested to see it first. It was the only one located on the lower level, and had its own private bath with twin sinks and an oversized tub and shower. It was luxurious with his and her walk-in closets and a sizable sitting room off to the side. Noah glanced at Marly with a knowing gleam in his eye. The agent smiled and discreetly left. Marly felt her face flaming as he advanced across the room.

"What do you think sweetheart? I can imagine a ..."

Marlena quickly cut him off, "I like the house so far, but we probably should see the rest of it."

He chuckled and grabbed her around the waist as she attempted to skirt around him. "I hope you won't be in such a hurry to leave our bedroom when we're married, Cinderella."

She tried to pull away, but he held firm.

"So, what size bed do you think we'll need? Are you an all over the place sleeper or are you going to snuggle next to me all night?"

Tina's words began to reverberate in Marlena's mind. This was for real, for keeps. In a few short months, she would be sharing this room and a bed with this man. She hadn't been living in some sort of fantasy, but being in this room brought it all to the forefront. She looked at him carefully. He was teasing her, but there was also a realistic aspect to his question. They would need to purchase a bed. She really couldn't answer him concerning the size. She hadn't shared a room, let alone a bed, with Shawn in years. She couldn't recall whether or not she'd ever snuggled up to Shawn. She did know that earlier in their marriage she'd always wanted him to hold her, but he'd smile, kiss her on the cheek, and then get up and smoke a cigarette. Usually, by the time he'd return, she'd be asleep.

She peered at Noah and answered truthfully, "I'm not sure. What are you?" she asked bashfully.

"Sleeping by myself, I'm an all over. With you, I think I'll become a sleep close to you kind of guy. Having said that, I suggest we do the twin sized bed," he advised seductively.

Marlena laughed nervously.

"Why does the idea of us sharing a marriage bed make you so nervous? If we decide to buy, this will be our bedroom. We are on the same page, right?" he asked, watching her intently.

"Can we have this discussion somewhere other than in this room?" she asked irritated.

"Why are you on edge, Marly? What's the problem?" he wanted to know.

"For goodness sake, I just said I don't want to talk about it now, so let's get out of this room and finish viewing the rest of the house," she snapped. She failed to notice the warning glint in his eyes as she flounced into the hall. That ought to teach him she thought annoyed.

Noah was right on her heels, but he made no effort to continue the conversation. He walked right past her and towards the agent. He extended his hand in thanks. Marlena listened stupefied as he explained that his fiancée hadn't particularly cared for the master bedroom, so there was no need for them to see the rest of the house. The surprised woman looked at Marlena and asked what part of the master suite wasn't suitable to her liking. Marlena fought back the urge to scream; instead, she managed to ask, in a reasonably steady voice, if she and Noah could view the bedroom again. The young woman nodded, pleased that Marlena might have a change of heart. Noah smiled a smile that didn't quite reach his eyes, and followed Marly back into the bedroom where he calmly closed the door and leaned against it.

He spoke in a deceptively mild tone, "Marlena, don't ever talk to me like that again. I'm not one of your schoolchildren, so don't take the teacher tone with me. I am a man, and as such, the head of our family and you will treat me with respect. You can either walk beside me or in back, take your pick; but, you will never walk ahead of me. I am in my rightful place with God, now, kindly get in yours. Furthermore, if you don't want to talk about whatever little hang up you have concerning bedrooms, then that is your prerogative. Either way Browneyes, we will always share the same bed, in the same bedroom, from our wedding night until one of us dies. Do we understand each other?"

Marlena stared at him. In her mind, she could hear Tina saying, "Oh snap". Now, it was her turn to feel like an adolescent being chastised. She shook her head, yes. How come she couldn't think of a single suitable reply back? The key word being suitable, she was biting back the urge to reply with a smart retort. She wanted to say a lot of things, but instinctively knew that he wasn't about to let her get away with it. Besides, she was wrong. He hadn't done a thing to deserve the way she'd spoken to him. Noah, still with edged hardness in his voice, asked if she wanted to talk about things later or not. Once again, she simply nodded yes. He moved aside from the door and opened it.

"After you," was all he said, allowing her to go first.

Brushing past him in rebellion, she marched out of the room and down the hall, but stopped when she realized he hadn't followed. She turned to see what was keeping him. He stood watching her with a purposefully blank expression on his face. Marlena knew she could keep walking, or she could submit to his headship. She absolutely hated his "Noahtudes". Couldn't he, for once, allow her to win the battle of the wills? From the expression on his face, the answer was no. She whirled around and marched back towards him and waited for him to escort her.

✠

Noah sat next to Marly on her sofa discussing their potential purchase of the home. They had gone on to view the rest of the house. There was a study and another room directly across from the master bedroom. On the same floor, but at the opposite end of the house was a family room, complete with a fireplace, a laundry room, a half bathroom, which was strategically located close to the living room, and a storage room that connected the two car garage to the house. The house, although spacious, wasn't overly large, but could adequately lodge their collective family if need be. Noah would arrange to have several of his friends inspect the house thoroughly for needed repairs and discrepancies. Based on the outcome of the inspection, they would decide whether or not to make an offer.

He stood and stretched before walking towards the kitchen. He was determined that he would not ask her what that little episode at the house was all about. She was being a brat concerning it and he was not about to give in to her. It was no small wonder that Drew hadn't made it past first base. She was as headstrong as they came. Give Marly an inch and she'd take a mile. If he wasn't careful, he'd find himself being led around by her. He heard her get up and follow him into the kitchen. Pretending to busy himself, he ignored her presence until she asked if he wanted to talk.

"Are you ready to talk openly, or am I going to have to plead with you to tell me what really happened in your marriage?" he asked bluntly.

"Will you promise me that you won't throw it back up at me later?" she demanded softly.

"What do you mean by that statement?" He wanted her to clarify herself before he would make such a promise.

"I want you to promise that you won't use anything that I say to make me feel badly later on," she repeated sincerely.

"You're serious aren't you?" he asked incredulously. "If you knew me at all, you'd never need to extract that kind of promise from me," he sighed.

Marlena turned her head and focused on a spot next to the table. "Shawn could be hurtful sometimes during sex," she blurted out.

Noah froze and then asked softly if Shawn had forced himself on her.

She wouldn't look at him, but answered yes. "It wasn't like that at first, but as time went on, I became less interested in being intimate with him."

"Why?" Noah wanted to know.

She cleared her throat and whispered, "It hurt. It was very painful. I tried very hard not to complain or make him feel as though I didn't love him, but he demanded sex more and more even though he knew it was painful for me. Eventually, I began to shut down, that's when the insults began. Something that was supposed to bring us closer together, instead it destroyed us. I'd hear other women talking about the pleasure they received. I never experienced anything like that, even initially," she explained truthfully. "We had no emotional connection. We didn't talk much. I arranged for counseling, but he wouldn't go. He said it was my problem and maybe it was, but I needed his support. I needed him to be an anchor. The situation had become so horrible, that I almost committed adultery. Frankly, I had been having an emotional affair for months. This friend had wanted me to leave Shawn and marry him."

"What stopped you?" Noah asked.

Marlena finally looked at him and gave a rueful smile. "I'd like to tell you that it was my great faith in God, but I'd be lying. It was more like God's supreme faithfulness and love towards me. I found out that I was pregnant with Kaod. When Shawn found out that I was carrying his child, his attitude changed. He was less argumentative, and during my pregnancy, he was very supportive. We started sleeping in separate rooms and it kind of stayed that way. I stopped confiding in my friend and started telling God about our problems, something I should have been doing all along. Shawn began going out more and more. I'd hear occasional rumors about this woman or that woman, but he never brought it to the house, and he always made sure that we were taken care of financially. Despite everything, I loved my husband and I believe he loved me. Only God knows why things happened the way they did. Out of the negative, God blessed us with a son. God loved me so much that He stopped me from doing something I would have regretted the rest of my life."

Noah walked over and stood directly in front of her. He pulled her close. "I could try to explain away your fears or Shawn's callousness, but it would be futile. You are going to have to trust that it will be different between us. Trust what God says about the marriage bed. I have no doubt that things will work themselves out."

She reached up and toyed with his curly hair. He smiled and grabbed her hands.

"You can play with my hair all you want after we're married, but right now, I'm a little short on willpower." Noah looked thoughtfully at her, "Marly, are you afraid to be with me?"

She glanced away, "Just a little. I'm really more afraid of disappointing you than anything else."

He kissed her on the forehead and pulled her close. "You already please me very much."

✠

Noah glanced at Marlena. She was watching and periodically laughing at the antics of the actor on TV. It was one of those silly romantic comedies she loved so much. She was, as usual, practically glued to his side. He had to admit that he rather enjoyed her habit of having to have some part of her body touching his. He knew that she wasn't even aware of doing it. It wasn't meant to be seductive in the least. Putting the pieces together, he guessed that she was bonding with him in a way that she had never been able to accomplish with Shawn.

He'd learned that in order for a woman to have a satisfying intimate relationship, it would be necessary for her to bond emotionally. Women were talkers and emotional thinkers and the key to their physical satisfaction was linked directly to their emotional security. Marly needed to know, beyond the shadow of a doubt, that he loved her and that she was the most important person in his life. He was pretty sure that Shawn probably had not met any of those needs, and as a result, Marly had been unable to respond physically, which in turn, had probably left him feeling angry and frustrated. That, however, in no way justified his use of force. In Noah's eyes, Shawn had raped his own wife. It was very evident to Noah that she wasn't frigid or that she didn't exhibit an adversity to touch, since she was constantly playing with his hair or touching him in some form or fashion. To be completely truthful, he had taken to grabbing her hands because his control was being tested by her continuous touching. He recognized that in a lot of ways, she was still very naïve about physical intimacy. She had been untouched when she'd married Shawn and he had stunted her growth in that area by his harshness. He now fully grasped why she was so bashful about intimacy, but he knew that sooner or later she'd become aware of the control that she held over his physical reactions to her. He groaned inwardly. At the rate she was going, that probably wouldn't be until after their wedding night. He wrapped his arms around her and pulled her close. She smiled at him in satisfaction, snuggled deeper, and contentedly watched the show.

Chapter Twenty-three

Thanksgiving arrived, and she and Noah celebrated it with friends and family. Jacob, Kara and little Collin, along with Adam and Kaod all came home. Marlena watched in awe as Noah assumed the headship of their newly forming multi-cultural family. He had somehow persuaded the entire family, his and hers, to come home for the holiday, and then to attend Kaod's game the following Saturday. Marlena rather suspected that the latter hadn't been so hard to do. The big surprise of the season had been when Noah had warned her in advanced that Kaod was bringing a young lady with him. When had her son started sharing information with Noah that he hadn't shared with her first? She didn't know whether to be happy or irritated. She was actually experiencing some resentment. Kaod was her son, and as such, he should have told her firsthand about this young lady. She shouldn't have to learn about it through Noah. It wasn't the girl; it was not being told about her existence. She and Kaod had always been extremely close. What was going on? She truly wanted Noah and her son to be close, but she still wanted her relationship with Kaod also. She looked around. All the family was there except Kaod and they were still expecting Hal and Valerie, as well as the McGhee's who Marlena still had not met.

The doorbell rang and Adam rushed to answer the door. He smiled a greeting as Hal and Valerie entered. Noah watched as his youngest practically bowled him over to help Marly. He'd never witnessed him assist his mother in that way. Adam had definitely bonded with Marly. One down, one more to go he prayed silently. Jacob hadn't been overly friendly. He'd questioned where all the pictures of Colleen were. Noah had kept their family portrait on display, but the others he'd boxed up. It was time to put the past behind. He was going to give Jacob and Adam the opportunity to select the photos they desired; however, the rest he'd decided to put in storage. Even after four years, Jacob still felt as though this was his mother's home. Noah understood and appreciated his son's feelings. This was his childhood home, the place where loving memories of his mother had been captured. He didn't want to take that away from Jacob. He only wanted what was best for his son. He didn't know how to present his new life to his son without putting away some of the old. Despite Jacob's attitude, Noah was proud of the effort he was displaying towards Marly. He prayed that God would reveal, in him and in Jacob, their wrong in order to make it right. He knew things would come to a head sooner or later, but the cleanup always followed a storm, and God, in his infinite wisdom, would cast off all that did not belong.

Marly had done a phenomenal job with preparing the dinner and the decorations. She'd incorporated food from both cultures. Some of which he was not willing to try, especially the chitterlings, which in his opinion, smelled so awful, at the first, that he'd thought they were spoiled or something. There was no way on God's green earth that he was going to sample those things. Noah heard another car pull up and glanced out of the window. It was the McGhee's. He couldn't wait to see Marly's expression when she met them. They'd come as a personal favor to him. Noah waited for them to ring the bell and Adam to answer the door before going to greet them. He retrieved Marly from the kitchen and introduced her to Layman and Marcella.

Marlena smiled with pleasure as she shook hands with the two of them and they both asked her if those were chitterlings they smelled. When Layman rubbed his hands together and asked what time dinner was being served, Marlena felt completely at home. Marcella linked her arm through Marlena's and asked where the kitchen was. The two women disappeared while Layman grinned in approval at Noah.

Marcella didn't ask if Marly needed help, she simply washed her hands and busied herself with whatever needed to be done. Soon the women were easily chatting away.

"Girl, you know that you've got it smelling good in here. How did you manage to get all of this done?" Marcella asked in wonder.

"I started cooking most of it yesterday. It's how my mom used to do it," Marlena admitted.

"I take it your mom is no longer alive," Marcella sympathized.

"She died almost two years ago. It's funny. You don't ever seem to get use to the lost. You just go on," Marlena reminisced.

Marcella nodded in understanding and after several minutes asked, "So tell me how you and Noah met."

Marlena laughed and launched into details. By the time she'd finished, Marcella was shaking her head in disbelief.

"You mean to tell me that man tried to ask you out wearing his old wedding ring on his finger?"

Marlena laughed aloud at Marcella's dramatic tone. It reminded her so much of Tina.

"What's wrong with that man?" she continued dramatically.

Noah walked in at precisely that moment. The two women looked at him and began laughing in unison.

He grinned and said to Marly, "Whatever Marcella's been telling you, don't believe it."

Marcella replied saucily, "No, what I can't believe is that you'd attempt to ask a woman out with your old wedding ring on."

Noah grinned at Marly, "She does that to me."

"Really, Noah, I have that effect on you?"

He nodded yes, pretending to be serious.

"Then, you'll try some chitterlings for me?"

Noah wrinkled his nose, "Sorry sweetheart, not on your pretty little life."

Marcella laughed uproariously. Before Marlena could respond, the doorbell rang.

"That must be Kaod and Nina," Noah said.

Marlena gave him a "so you know her name, too" look. Noah scooted out of the room before she could give him a tongue-lashing. Marlena sat down in a chair and invited Marcella to join her. She explained the circumstances to Marcella.

"Handle your business, girl. That boy has lost his mind," Marcella advised.

Kaod had finally garnered enough courage to stick his head around the corner and greet his mother. Marlena did not smile, nor did she say a word to Kaod.

"Hi, Mom, it sure smells good in here," he complimented, giving her a hug.

She introduced him to Marcella. Noah came into the kitchen and excused Marly and himself. He pulled her behind him into his study and shut the door.

"What in the world are you doing, Noah? Have you lost your mind?"

"No, Marly, I haven't lost my mind, but you just might lose yours when you get a good look at Nina."

"Why, what's wrong with her?"

"She appears to be a lot older than Kaod"

"Define a lot older."

He shrugged his shoulders, "I'd say at least twenty years. Marly, she's not his type and I don't think she's professing Christianity. Promise me you won't embarrass him."

"I will not promise you that. If he's brought a 'hoochie' up in here, he's through."

Noah looked at her strangely. "Do you know that's the first time I've ever heard you speak slang?"

Without batting an eyelash she said, "It might not be the only thing you'll hear that will shock you tonight. Let me go and see this woman."

Noah grabbed her hand and opened the door. He pulled her close to him and casually walked back towards the living room.

Adam glanced at Marlena and doubled over with laughter at the expression on her face. This set off a chain reaction throughout the room. Noah fought hard to control himself while he kept a firm grip on Marly's hand.

Marly pinned Adam with a direct stare, he intuitively knew what she was asking. He barely managed to point at the kitchen before doubling over again. Marlena felt a sense of dread as she determinedly walked into the kitchen. Marcella, bless her soul had started preparing the table, while Kaod was standing beside his guest looking every inch the village idiot. She took one look at Nina and immediately hit the ceiling. Older was the understatement of the year. She closed her eyes and then opened them. Maybe she was having an out-of-body experience. When Kaod smiled and warmly introduced his friend, she concluded, that her son must be using mind altering drugs.

Before she could say a word, Noah pulled her back into the study. She was sure she'd glimpsed Adam, Jacob, and Kara heading into bedrooms with tears of laughter rolling down their cheeks. For the life of her, she couldn't figure out what the heck was so funny. This was a desperate situation. She glanced at Noah, who also seemed to be struggling to control his laughter.

"Will you please tell me what in heaven's name is so funny? Am I the only one in this family who doesn't get what's so humorous? My son is stuck on stupid and all you can do is laugh?"

By now, Noah was doubled over and laughing so hard that she could only stare.

"If you won't help me Noah Phillips, then I'll take care of the problem myself."

Before she could open the door, he grabbed her hand and pulled her to him. He reached around her and opened the door. Adam, Kara, Jacob, and Kaod were all standing there laughing. It took Marlena a minute or two before she realized that the entire family had played a huge joke on her. She turned to confront Noah who was still shaking with laughter. Marlena vowed revenge on the whole lot of them. Noah hugged her to him and kissed her cheek.

"This is payback for that little lemonade incident at the picnic."

She smiled in obvious relief as Kaod and Adam teased her mercilessly. She asked Kaod who Nina really was. He laughingly explained that she was a member of the Ohio State Alumni. His car had unexpectedly stopped running, and since she lives in Canton, she had volunteered to bring him home.

"That woman must think I'm a nut," Marlena blurted out suddenly.

"I hate to tell you this sweetheart, but she agreed to be part of the joke. As a matter of fact, everyone except Marcella, who I knew would rat me out, was aware of my very clever prank," Noah proudly exclaimed.

Marlena stuck her tongue out at him and headed toward the kitchen where she promptly introduced herself to and thanked Nina. Marcella clucked her tongue in amusement at Noah's joke as they finished setting the table.

✣

Noah stood at the head of the table and waited for everyone to settle down. Marly was seated at his right and Jacob, the left. He pulled Marly up next to him and began explaining why the present Thanksgiving was so special to him. After allowing others to express what they were thankful for, he pronounced the blessing over the food and everyone dug in.

Kaod watched as Adam sampled a small portion of chitterlings.

"Do you know what you're eating?" he asked out of curiosity.

"No, but they're not half bad," Adam acknowledged in between bites.

Kaod grinned in secret delight as he caught the McGhee's knowing smiles. Barely containing his laughter, he glanced around the table and saw Mr. Linstrum and Kara, both, heartily enjoying their share of chitterlings. Kara, he noticed had even sprinkled them with the traditional hot sauce. Kaod wondered where she'd learned that from. Maybe some of her people were black. He glanced at Noah and his mom. She appeared to be attempting to persuade him to try them, but he wouldn't budge. Kaod tapped Adam on the shoulder.

"I'll bet you that twenty you've got in your pocket that my mom can convince your dad to sample some chitterlings."

Adam grinned cockily, "That, baby brother is a sucker's bet. There is no way that Dad is going to try them. Marly's been trying to convince him all day long and he hasn't budged, but I'm willing to take another twenty bucks away from you my soon-to-be rich kid brother."

Adam took out the same twenty dollar bill that he'd won from Kaod earlier that summer. They began to watch, with interest, the happenings at the head of the table.

"Marly, for the last time, I will not try those awful smelling things," Noah said firmly.

"Not even for me?" Marlena asked, pouting prettily.

"That's not going to work. You can pout from now until doomsday."

Marly leaned over and kissed him on the cheek. He remained unaffected. By now, the entire table watched to see if he would give in to her. Noah stood up and cleared his place at the table as though signaling the end of the conversation.

When he sat down again, he told Marly in a teasing tone, "Not only will I not try them, but if you eat too many, I might not kiss you ever again."

That comment brought considerable laughter from everyone.

"Really," Marly replied as she ate another forkful. "I'm finished anyway."

He grinned, "Good."

Marlena ignored Adam's shout of triumph. She slowly wiped her mouth and leaned over and whispered something in his ear. Instantly, the room quieted. Noah's eyebrows lifted in surprise, and then he smiled, before leaning over and whispering something back. She smiled shyly and nodded yes.

He stood to his feet, grabbed an empty plate, and said, "I guess I will try some of those chitterlings after all."

Adam's groan of defeat was met with gleeful chuckles from all, including Kaod, who quickly snatched up his earnings.

Jacob looked from his dad to Marly. His resentment was growing by the minute. This was his mom's house. He seemed to be the only one who remembered that little fact. He'd never witnessed his dad flirt around with his mom that way. It was too much. He excused himself from the table with the pretense of checking on his son.

✞

Hal and Layman gazed at Noah and shook their heads.

"That woman has you wrapped around her pretty little finger," Layman mused.

Noah informed them that she did and he was thoroughly enjoying every minute of it. Hal grinned and Layman pretended to be disappointed until Noah threatened to have a little talk with Marcella. Not wanting to leave Hal out of the fun, Noah asked Hal if he'd reached first base with Valerie.

"That depends on what you mean by first base," he said trying to avoid the answer.

Layman looked at Noah, "If he don't know what first base is, then he ain't been there yet."

Noah and Layman grinned at each other. Hal explained that he wanted her to be sure, so he was giving her time.

"In other words, you haven't kissed the woman yet, and you've been going out for almost two months. In two months, man, I had a ring on Cella's finger. I was not about to take the chance of losing her. If I'm not mistaken I stole me a kiss on the second date. What about you Noah?"

"Kiss on the third date, engaged in two and a half months, rounding third and on my way home. By the way, I stole second. I don't have time to wait."

All three men roared with laughter.

"Sometimes Noah, I'd swear you've got some black in you," Layman said as he shook his head in amazement.

Hal studied Layman and Noah. "Did you two really kiss them that soon?"

"Shoot, man, I would have kissed her the minute I saw her if I didn't think she'd have slapped me," Layman uttered in a completely serious tone.

Noah explained to Hal what he'd done the first day he'd met Marly. Hal was amazed. It was time for him to do a little base running.

Kara and Valerie were putting the dishes away as Marcella and Marlena washed and dried. Kara couldn't resist asking Marly what she had said to Noah to get him to try the chitterlings. Marcella eyed Marlena and winked in understanding. Marly pretended not to notice and gave Kara a vague reply.

Valerie giggled, "In other words, none of our business."

"Whatever she told him, made him jump up and get that plate," Marcella pointed out with amusement.

"How's the planning for the wedding coming?" Valerie asked.

"I don't know. I haven't started yet," Marlena confessed.

Three faces stared at her in utter dismay.

"What are you waiting on? You're wedding is six months away. May, will be here before you know it. Does Noah realize you haven't started planning?" Valerie demanded to know in her secretary voice.

Marly frowned and replied, "I haven't had the time. In between moving, Kaod's games, holidays, and Noah's ministry, I'm too tired to think about anything else. Oh yeah, let's not forget about teaching. What I really need is a wedding planner."

"At your service," Marcella answered.

"You're a wedding planner?"

"Yes ma'am, I am. That man of yours must love you something awful. I'm willing to bet he figured we'd get to talking about the wedding and he also knew you'd be needing help."

Marlena glanced at Valerie who nodded in agreement. Marlena smiled at the group of women.

"In that case, you're hired. When can you start?"

✝

Noah opened the door to the apartment and ushered Marly in. He tossed his keys onto a nearby end table and wrapped her in his arms.

"Thank you for the best Thanksgiving I've had in a very long time. It really meant the world to me that you put such effort into it, and thanks for being a good sport about Nina," he spoke sincerely.

"Thank you, for taking such good care of me," she said in return.

He raised his eyebrows questioningly.

"You knew I needed help planning our wedding. You sent Marcella. You're my Prince Charming and my knight in shining armor."

She said it so earnestly that Noah blushed from embarrassment. She played with his hair. He smiled and lowered his head.

She whispered, "What about the chitterlings?"

He whispered back, "I ate them too, remember?"

She suddenly recalled what she'd whispered into his ear earlier. She blushed and looked away. Noah did something he'd never done before. He nuzzled her neck. She gazed at him, not out of fear, but in surprise.

"You're not going to renege on our deal are you, Cinderella?" he whispered huskily, nuzzling her neck again.

"What?" she whispered back.

"The deal we made during dinner. You're not going to back out of it are you?" he asked again, lifting his head slightly.

Her eyes had darkened and she was looking at him strangely. Marlena had heard his question, but for some reason it wasn't registering. Her mind had gone blank. Well, that wasn't exactly the truth. It had been centered on Noah and her neck. She laid her head against his chest as a preventive measure. It didn't work. He lowered his head and nuzzled the other side of her neck. His arms tightened around her, not allowing her to escape.

"Stop it, Noah," she begged softly.

He loosened his grip slightly and held her gaze and repeated his earlier question. She blushed at the look in his eyes, but knew better than to turn her head.

"I'll keep our deal," she promised huskily.

"In May, one week before the wedding," he clarified.

She promised him she would. He released her and picked up his keys. She followed him to the door and laughingly pushed him into the hallway when he gave her one of his silly wet kisses on the forehead.

Noah pulled into the garage. His body was tired, but his mind was going over the events of the day. He had developed a habit of talking the day over with God before he went to sleep. Instinctively, he knew Jacob would be waiting up for him. He prayed for God to give him patience and wisdom. He didn't want to break his son's spirit, yet he couldn't allow him to hold on to the past. Jacob needed a life beyond his mother. Noah asked God to forgive Jacob for any harsh words that might come out of his mouth tonight. He recalled the Jacob in the Bible, and knew that his son was also following in his mother's footsteps. Noah also acknowledged that he had been as weak a father as Isaac and he was probably more to blame for Jacob's faults than his mother.

"Help me Lord," he prayed as he got out of the car and walked into the house.

As predicted, Jacob was in the kitchen waiting for his father. He looked every inch the hurt little boy. Noah grabbed a bottle of water from the refrigerator and sat down across from Jacob.

"Where are Adam and Kaod?" Noah asked.

"I'm not sure. They said they'd be back in an hour or so," Jacob said, shrugging his shoulders.

"So what do you think of Kaod?" Noah asked Jacob.

Once again, he shrugged, "He seems friendly enough. He and Adam are like two peas in a pod."

Noah smiled at the thought of Adam and Kaod together. There was no telling what those two were up to. He picked up his cell phone and pushed Kaod's number. After the second ring, Kaod picked up. Noah gave him the typical fatherly lecture. He reminded him that he was a Christian and to behave accordingly. He repeated the process with Adam, but was more firm since he was the older of the two. He replaced his cell phone. He needed Jacob to understand that he now considered Kaod his son also. Noah could see the anger in Jacob's eyes. If they were going to have it out, now was the perfect time.

"How can you treat him as though he's really your son? Where's his father at? In jail, on drugs, or did he simply walk out on him like they all do? He and Marly are black, Dad. They don't fit into our world. What is it going to take for you to understand that? You're dividing your own church. Did you know that some members of your congregation are threatening to leave if you actually marry her? What about Mom? You actually act like she never existed, as though you love Marly more than Mom," Jacob spit out angrily.

Noah listened calmly to his son rant and rave.

Finally, he spoke, "Is that what you think about blacks? What you've seen on TV shows or talk about in the corner with people who think just like you. Where is Christ in that? You are living in some kind of fantasy world, son. If someone doesn't have the same color skin, then they're beneath you. There is no need for me to defend Kaod or his mother. Their lives are a testimony to the God they serve, which, by the way, happens to be the same God I serve. If you hate them, then you hate me also. Are you asking me to explain the division in the church? First of all, it's not my church. It's God's. Secondly, Christ, himself, has explained that he came to divide not unite. Those that are for Him, against those that despise Him. Which side are you on? If you can hate those that love Christ, you are not one of his; therefore, you must be against Him. As far as your mother is concerned, I loved her as much as any man could have loved his wife. Don't attempt to make Marly a part of that."

"Do you deny that you love her more than you loved Mom?" Jacob pushed.

Noah sat silent before he recalled words spoken to him by Kaod, "Will you love my mother more than your sons and congregation?" Noah discerned immediately that he was at a crossroad.

Those words, spoken by Kaod, had a deeper, more significant meaning than even he understood. It was as if Jesus himself was asking, "Will you forsake all and follow me?" Marlena was a woman of God, while Colleen had been a woman of the world. Noah had a choice to make, choose to please God or choose to please the world. He knew there was no way his son could understand the spiritual implications of what he was about to say.

He held Jacob's gaze and boldly stated, "I cannot deny that I love the wife God is giving me, more than I loved the wife I chose."

"How can you love that nigger and her son more than you love Mom and me?" Jacob exclaimed with raw fury.

When his father remained silent, he whirled around to leave and found himself standing face to face with Kaod, and by the dark thunderous expression on Kaod's face, there was no mistaking the fact that he had heard Jacob's highly inflammatory remarks.

Instinctively choosing the same course of action, Noah and Adam grabbed Kaod just as he was abruptly lunging towards Jacob in anger.

"What did you call my mother?" Kaod demanded, struggling to free himself from Noah and Adam's hold.

He had managed to grab Jacob by the throat, pinning Noah and Adam in between them. Jacob, at least, had the God-given sense and grace to remain quiet. When Jacob didn't respond, Kaod looked from Noah to Adam. He let go of Jacob and angrily pushed free of them. He spoke in a deadly serious tone, "The wedding is off, and I don't want to see any of you near my mother again!" He turned and slammed out front door.

Adam started after him, but Noah restrained his son, explaining that Kaod needed some time to sort through his angry thoughts.

Adam turned and glared furiously at his older brother, "You're just like Mom, a self-righteous racist. You'd better apologize to Kaod and Marly!"

"How can you be on their side? Dad's behaving as though Mom never existed. She was your mom, too." Jacob exclaimed harshly.

Adam brushed past Jacob and down to his old room. He returned with a stack of letters, "Dad, I'm sorry, I didn't want to tell you this way, but it's about time that Jacob stopped living in his dream world. I found these after Mom died, but I'd known about her secret for years before that."

He handed some of the letters to his father and the rest to Jacob. "Mom was never the saint you thought her to be. Dad stayed with her because of us. You want a real life hero. Try taking a good look at Dad for once."

Adam went back to his room. Jacob was puzzled. He sat down at the table and began reading the letters. It was evident that they were addressed to his mother. He forced himself to read letter after letter. Tears began rolling down his face as he realized that his mother had been having an affair with some guy whose initials were L.J. After reading them all, Jacob stood and apologized to his father.

"Go to bed, son," Noah ordered, without looking in his direction.

Noah walked into the living room and dropped down tiredly onto the sofa. He'd deal with Colleen's mess later. He tossed the unread letters on the end table. Right now, there were three things he was more concerned about: Kaod's last statement, Marly's reaction to tonight's events, and why his oldest son was jealous of his relationship with Kaod. He desperately wanted to talk to Kaod and Marly tonight, but he realized that Kaod was not in the frame of mind to rationally hear anything he'd have to say. Who could blame him? Hadn't he already warned Jacob that he wouldn't be able to take those words back if he said them? He, himself, had wanted to tear into Jacob. He couldn't even begin to feel what Kaod was experiencing at the moment. There was no worse word for Jacob to use, than the one he'd chosen. Thank God, Kaod hadn't physically beaten the stuffing out of him. He and Adam would not have been able to restrain him if he had truly wanted to hurt Jacob. He'd dragged them both until he'd reached Jacob. That kid was nothing but strength and muscle. What a great big mess. Only God could sort this out. Noah thought about Marly. She was probably expecting his usual goodnight call. What would her reaction be? Trust the Lord, he reminded himself. He lowered his head in prayer and asked the Lord to move on his behalf. Reaching for the phone, he slowly dialed her number.

Marly heard Kaod come in with a bang. What is wrong with that boy she thought? She padded out of her bedroom and down the hall. Kaod was sitting in the living room staring at the picture of her and Noah. Right away, she knew something was wrong.

"Ka', honey, what's wrong?"

"I should have kicked his white ass from here, to the Hood and back," he spit out vehemently.

"Kaod, you know better than to use that kind of language!" she admonished.

"Well, he should know better than to call you a nigger!" he shot back angrily.

"What happened? Who are you talking about? Who called me that name, Kaod?"

Before he could answer, she heard her cell phone ringing in the bedroom. She ignored it and asked Kaod once again who'd called her that name. Kaod reigned in his anger and explained to his mom everything that had happened.

When he had finished his explanation, Marlena calmly said, "Well, it seems like we have two huge problems. Noah's son definitely has racial issues and my son has he-thinks-he's-my-father issues. You just took it upon yourself to call our wedding off. Look at me, Ka'! Did Noah do or say anything that gave you the impression that he's prejudiced?"

Kaod replayed the incident in his mind and concluded that neither Noah, nor Adam, had exhibited any prejudicial behavior. He'd gotten angry with all of them because of Jacob's comment. Kaod had to admit, that only Jacob had used the racial slur. She sighed and leaned over and ruffled his hair.

He glanced at her in amazement, "You don't seem the least bit upset that Jacob called you that name."

"People have called Jesus much more. Besides, I already knew that Jacob was struggling with his dad loving another woman. To be honest, I don't think it really matters whether I'm black or white. He's using color to justify his anger at his dad for desiring to marry again, and to push me away from Noah. He's going to have to come to grips with his bigotry. I refuse to become like him or anyone else who's struggling with the sin of racism. That's between them and God. Instead of being angry at him, I truly feel sorry for him. Unless he get's over this, he will forever be in bondage and how can he be a true believer if he hates some of God's children? Jacob is going to be held accountable for the example he puts before his wife and child. He needs to come to Christ. Now, what about you Kaod? What he said about me was wrong, but are you going to hate because someone hates you? Doesn't that place you into the same category? It's a trick of the enemy. You've got to be wiser than him, okay, sweetheart?"

He nodded in understanding. Rising from the couch, he hugged his mom tightly. "I love you, Mom. Thanks for being so wise."

She squeezed him back and said, "you are not out of the woods yet, Ka'. You broke off my engagement and it's up to you to get me reengaged."

"You still want to marry that guy?" he teased.

"Absolutely, he's the only one for me," she added honestly.

Kaod looked as though he'd just remembered something. "I thought that you might be interested in knowing the reason Jacob called you that name in the first place. Noah admitted that he loves you more than he loved his first wife."

Marlena didn't move. She was absolutely, positively stunned. She stood, walked over to Kaod, and lovingly shoved him back onto the couch. "That's for calling the wedding off."

He was still laughing as she walked back to her bedroom.

Noah listened as the phone rang. After the fourth ring, her voicemail kicked in. He closed his eyes and leaned back against the plush pillow. She must be pretty upset. He felt frustration beginning to form. He wondered if he should go up to her apartment. He decided to wait and call her back in thirty minutes or so. He picked up the letters and started reading.

As she was reaching for her phone, it began ringing. She smiled when Noah's name appeared. Marlena answered the phone on the second ring. Noah sounded a little worried. He asked if Kaod had calmed down and if she was aware of what had happened. He apologized for Jacob's behavior and was concerned about how it might have affected her.

"I'm okay. I'd feel a lot better if you were here," she flirted.

He was relieved to learn she wasn't angry with him. They talked for a little while and then made arrangements to meet in the morning.

Noah relaxed on his sofa and thanked God that he and Marly had not succumbed to the deception of racism. There were many professing Christians who still believed interracial marriages were wrong. The Bible only commands believers of the faith not to be unevenly yoked in regards to unbelievers. In other words, Christians should marry other Christians. God did not want his children entering into marriage covenants with Moslems, Jews, Hindus, Catholics, etc..., He knew that being unevenly yoked would cause His children to compromise His Word and eventually be led astray. People have held onto falsehoods because it gave them control over others and it has kept the different cultures separate. Noah grimaced, "Besides, there was money to be made if you could keep people hating each other." He knew there were hundreds of agencies, organizations, and lawyers who profited from the countless claims of racism. Thousands of individuals would be out of jobs and millions of dollars forfeited if prejudiced was eliminated. The sin of prejudiced, like most other sins, is in direct contrast to God's commandment to love your neighbor as yourself. How can we move closer to God when we hate the very beings He has created? Noah thought about Christ's imminent return; when He calls for his church, all believers regardless of their ethnicity, will be caught up in the Rapture. There will be no separate but equal policies. All will be of one body, on one accord, and serving one God. Noah prayed for Jacob's heart to be cleansed and for Kaod to be strong enough to forgive.

✝

Noah arrived a little after nine the following morning. He embraced Marlena and gave her his usual kiss on the forehead. Looking over her shoulder, he asked where Kaod was.

"He's hiding out in his bedroom. I think he's a little shame-faced."

"You've got to be kidding. He has nothing to feel badly about. I know how much he restrained himself. He carried himself a lot better than I would have, at that age; especially, if someone had called my mom a derogatory name like that. You do know that Adam and I couldn't have stopped him if he'd truly wanted to hurt Jacob? Kaod had wanted to get his point across, and he did. I hope you didn't make him feel ashamed about defending your honor. He didn't cross the line; he simply walked up to it. I'm proud of him," Noah declared candidly.

"Men are strange. Kaod should have just walked away and ignored Jacob," she corrected.

"Honey, there are times when you should ignore things, and then, there are the other times. Last night, was one of those other times. I can guarantee that Jacob will remember to think before he allows something like that to come out of his mouth again. Imagine how at liberty he'd feel to use that word if Kaod hadn't gone after him. I don't even want to think about what would happen to him if he decided to use that word towards someone like Malcolm or one of his buddies. It was far better for him to learn that lesson from Kaod than from a stranger."

Marlena pondered his words for a moment before saying, "Maybe you're right. I just hope Kaod knows when to walk away."

Noah grinned, "He knew when to walk away last night. According to your son, the wedding is off and I'd better not come near you again."

She eased her arms around his neck and flirted, "Then you'd better hurry up and kiss me before he comes out of that room."

He grabbed her hands and pulled them from around his neck. "Sorry, no can do. There will be no more kissing until the wedding is on again."

She pouted.

He laughed and winked at Kaod who had come out of his room and was smiling smugly. "Isn't that right, Kaod?"

Marlena turned to see her son leaning against the wall. "How long have you been standing there?" she wondered.

"Long enough to see you flirting with Noah; I guess I have no choice but to call the wedding on again," Kaod said mockingly.

Noah commented that he'd only take her back if it was a package deal. Kaod nodded his agreement. Noah embraced Kaod and apologized for Jacob's behavior. The two of them talked a little longer before Kaod left to go meet Adam.

Noah turned to Marly and said, "I'm ready for that kiss now."

She stuck her tongue out at him and shrugged, "No thanks, I'm engaged again, the excitement has worn off."

He tugged her into his arms and smiled when she slid her arms around his neck.

Marlena sat on the couch, sipping a cup of hot tea. God was so amazing. He was bringing two families with very different backgrounds and cultures together. It was evident that Kaod and Adam were inseparable. They had bounced back from the incident with Jacob as though it had never happened. She and Adam had developed a bond and so had Noah and Kaod. God had supplied, in Noah and her, a surrogate parent to ease the loss of the one each child had lost. Jacob had yet to accept her, but that was okay. It was still his choice. She thought about Christmas presents, and what to get all of the guys in her life. Finally, her mind turned to the wedding. Thank God for Marcella. That woman was on the ball. She'd already made an appointment for she and Tina to look at gowns. She was to stop by next week in order for she and Noah to pick out invitations, flowers, color schemes and the time and place of the wedding. Marcella had relieved her of the added stress. Marlena was so thankful to God for his continued presence in their lives. Without Him, there could be no them.

Noah sat in his study. He listened to little Collin crying and Kara trying to calm him. Jacob had apparently gone to fetch a bottle. It brought back pleasant memories of when Jacob was a baby. He loved his children and prayed that they would have blessed marriages the first time around. His mind went to Adam. He'd known about Colleen's indiscretion and hadn't said a word. No wonder he hadn't wanted to be around his mother. Now, he could understand Adam's desire not to get married. He was also concerned about the effect the letters would have on Jacob. He hadn't said another word about his mother since he'd read them. He hoped Jacob shared his problems with Kara. She loved him and would be able to help him overcome his disappointment.

His mind drifted to Kaod. Noah considered him to be his youngest son now. That kid was wise beyond his years. Noah had taken to calling him daily. They'd talk about everything under the sun, but his favorite two topics were his mom and football. Noah had been shocked when Kaod had questioned him about whether he and Marly had been intimate or not. Kaod had seemed relieved to know that they were waiting until marriage. He often told Noah things he remembered about his father. Sometimes they were good, sometimes bad, but every time he talked about his mother, it was always good. Marly, according to Kaod, had plenty of would-be suitors, but refused to give them the time of day. She always claimed to be waiting for him to finish school. Kaod was crazy about his mother. Noah pitied the poor girl he'd eventually marry. She'd have a high bar to reach.

Marly was full of surprises. He'd worried that she'd be upset about Jacob, yet she had been extremely levelheaded. She challenged him to be better on all levels. He knew that she was also becoming more physically aware of him. He'd caught her watching him several times with a strange expression on her face. If he asked her about it, she'd blush and turn away. It was a good thing. God was healing her and awakening something in her that she'd have to figure out. He didn't mind because he had purposed in his heart that there would be no intimacy until marriage and she had never intentionally crossed the line and was still too shy to even try. He thanked God for strengthening him and for blessing him. He prayed to do the will of God rather than his own. Thanking God for the atoning death of His son, he picked up his Bible and began reading.

Chapter Twenty-four

Marlena sat absorbed in her own thoughts while the blinking lights of the Christmas tree cast colorful dancing shadows along the wall. Noah had brought her an envelope that someone had placed in the mailbox of her old home. She had a weird feeling about it, as though she was standing on the edge of a precipice. She almost wanted to throw the letter away, but Noah had encouraged her to open it. She waited for him to return from the kitchen. For some unexplainable reason, she wanted him beside her.

"Sweetheart, you've got to open it up sooner or later," he commented, startling her out of her wanderings.

"You open it and read it first," she pleaded, sounding apprehensive.

Noah glanced at her and smiled encouragingly. He could relate to what she was feeling. Hadn't he felt the same way before reading the letters Levi Jamison had written to Colleen? It was as if the past was going to come back and destroy the future. You had no clue as to how it would affect the here and now. Apparently, Levi had wanted Colleen to leave Noah and be with him. Good old Colleen, even though she'd vowed to love Levi until the day she died, had evidently preferred being a pastor's wife to being the wife of the construction worker she supposedly loved. Noah had felt pity for Levi and a newfound disgust for Colleen. She had been as manipulative as Satan.

He tore open the letter and began reading, "Dear Mrs. Porter, Brother Shawn gave me this letter, along with instructions. He said to give it to you when his son finished college or when you decided to remarry, whichever one happened first."

Inside the large envelope was another smaller one. It was tightly sealed with tape and had the name Lena written on it. Marlena's heart began thumping wildly. No one but Shawn had ever called her that. Tears formed in her eyes and she began to shake uncontrollably. Noah pulled her into his arms.

"What is it Marly? What's wrong?"

Marlena's mind revisited time; she was being escorted down the corridor of the hospital. The sheriff's deputy kept glancing at her oddly, asking if she was okay. Each time, she nodded yes. The door opened into a colder dimly lit room. On a metal table was a body draped by a crisp white hospital sheet. The deputy was instructing another person to only uncover what was needed for identification. The man pulled an arm from beneath the sheet. Tattooed on the arm was the name "Lena". She couldn't properly identify the body because she hadn't been aware of the fact that Shawn had put her name on his body. They had to reluctantly pull the sheet off of his face. For the first time in her life, she had fainted. How could anyone do that to another human being? She had known the body was Shawn's and to her relief the coroner had indicated that he had died instantly from a gunshot wound to the chest. The other injuries had come after his death. Marlena heard a voice forcing her back to the present.

"Marly, are you alright?"

She looked at Noah and forced herself to smile weakly.

"I'm okay. This letter is definitely from Kaod's dad. It's his handwriting, and he's the only one to ever call me, 'Lena'."

"Do you want to read the letter in private?" he asked.

"No, you read it to me," she spoke softly.

He tore open the letter and waited until she had finished situating herself close to him.

He hesitated a moment and then began reading, "Lena, If you are reading this letter, then I'm no longer around and you are either remarrying or Ka' is graduating from college. Honestly, Baby, I hope it's because you have finally decided to move on. I know that I was not a good husband to you or even a good father, but know that you are the only woman I have loved. Please forgive me for all the times I hurt you, the times I forced you against your will. I hated myself afterward. I don't know why I behaved that way except that I did not truly know who Jesus was. Lena, I was living a life that you knew nothing about, a life that I'd kept hidden from you. You made me ashamed of that life, and so I tried to stay away. I'm so sorry, Lena. I could only seem to watch you from a distance. How could you be so happy with our son when I'd forced him on you?"

Noah stopped reading and gasped in complete shock. He held her tightly as though that would somehow take away the pain of the truth. "Oh, Marly, I'm sorry." He saw that she had her eyes tightly shut.

She opened them and said, "Don't feel sorry for me, Noah. Kaod was a blessing from God. He was never a mistake. God knew all along that Kaod would be the instrument to prevent me from doing wrong. He gave me something to take my mind off of me."

Noah kissed the top of her head and with an effort, continued to read where he'd left off.

"How could you still love me? I knew that I had never truly believed and that it had all been a lie to win you over. I'd been around enough church people to know exactly what to say and how to act. I did whatever it took to make you my wife. I played the role until it caught up with me. When I saw how much you loved God and read His Word, I became jealous. I wanted you to love me like that. I knew then that I could never have your heart. Something was preventing me from that secret part of you. Instead of truly turning to God, I began to mistreat you, trying to break you down, but you just got stronger in God. That caused me to take a deeper look at Christ and me. You had something that I needed. Lena, it took me awhile, but I finally gave my life to Jesus. I knew that there were so many things that I needed to bring to the foot of the cross. I started taking them one at a time. My intentions were to make amends with you and to beg a new start. You, me, and our son, but the past has a way of catching up with you. I couldn't get out of that old life. Christ had forgiven me, but people wouldn't. The only way I could escape was through death which meant life through Christ. I was no longer willing to be a part of my old crowd. I was fully aware of the terms and conditions when I joined and now I must reap what I have sown (Gal.6:7). I waited to have this delivered to you for safety reasons and because you would have made me out to be something more than what I was, a lousy husband. I want you to marry again- to a good man. Find yourself a pastor or something (they glanced at each other in surprise). I think you'd be a credit to him, as much as you like to keep your nose in that Bible. Make sure he will be a good father to our son. I'll be waiting for you in heaven. I'm so sorry for everything I did to you and I hope you can find it in your heart to forgive me. Thank you, for raising Ka' in Christ. I know I'll see him in heaven one day. I love you, baby, more than you could know. Thanks, for leading me to His saving grace. Love, Shawn. P.S. I left a key in Ka's box of firsts. It goes to a safe deposit box at our bank. I think you'll know then how much I love you."

Noah folded up the letter and handed it to Marly. They sat in quiet for a time before he spoke.

"Please tell me this letter will not affect us."

Marlena could not look at him, nor did she reply. Her mind was reeling. Memories were flooding her brain.

He shifted, in order to look into her eyes.

"What's the deal Marly? Does this change what you feel about me… us?"

Noah found himself in an unusual place. He was jealous of a dead man, a ghost. How could he compete with this new image she'd undoubtedly formed in her mind? The guy now sounded like a regular super saint. He didn't doubt that Shawn was telling the truth, he just didn't want Marly to drift down "what if" lane. Noah already knew as much, if not more than she did about Shawn's death. He'd asked John about it and had been told that Shawn had been killed by a professional, but they didn't know by whom or why. He decided to take a different approach.

"What do you think is in that safe deposit box?" he questioned.

"I don't know. Do you want to go with me and find out?" she asked, trying to conceal her excitement.

"Not really," he thought to himself, but aloud he responded with, "Sure, sweetheart, if you want me to."

She jumped off the couch and grabbed their coats. "We have to stop by the storage facility first. The key is in Ka's childhood box."

Noah prayed to God, "Please let me do this in the right spirit, or not at all." He loved Marly enough to help her bring some closure to the past, but he hoped this didn't backfire in his face.

After stopping by the storage facility, they drove straight to the bank. Marly hadn't known that Shawn had a safe deposit box. Apparently, someone had been paying the fee. She had no idea who. She gripped Noah's hand tightly as she presented the proper identification and was taken down to a lower level. Marly's hand shook as she took the box from the attendant. She peered at the box, and then at Noah. He gently took the key from her hand and unlocked the container. There were three large thick yellow envelopes. Lena was written on the front of two of them and Kaod, written on the other. Once again Marlena glanced at Noah in a silent plea, but this time he commanded her to open them. She reached for the envelope closest to her and pulled back the fastener. Out tumbled numerous pictures. There were mostly pictures of Kaod's athletic events from the age of five until his completion of high school. When had these been taken she wondered? Some of them had been taken after Shawn's death. She glanced at Noah and laughed delightedly. He grinned back and, picking up the pictures, began glancing through them. He chuckled when he saw a toothless Kaod holding a smiling Marlena's hand. Picture after picture brought laughter from the both of them.

"You've hardly changed," Noah commented in awe.

"I'm about twenty-five pounds heavier," she pointed out, blushing profusely.

"You are still gorgeous and you know it," he complimented huskily as he pulled her into his arms. He captured her lips before she had time to protest. She matched the tone of his kiss helplessly. He didn't ease up until she'd clasped her arms around his neck. Slowly he eased his lips into a gentle, less potent kiss. As he lifted his mouth from hers, she appeared dazed. He thought she looked like he felt. He grinned foolishly. She smiled back. They were back to normal. He was glad that he was here, sharing this special time with her. They viewed each picture. She looked at Noah when she and Shawn appeared together in several pictures. He studied them and then turned and handed the pictures back to her.

"I'm a little jealous," he confessed.

"Only a little," she teased.

"Okay, a whole lot," he admitted with a laugh.

"Good, I feel that way every time I glimpse that family portrait sitting in your living room," she said candidly.

He nodded his understanding.

"I wonder where he got these photos. I've never seen any of them."

She flipped them over and realized that there was something written on the back of every single photo except for those that had been taken after his death.

"He either took these, himself, or cared enough to have someone else take them. I think he really did love you, Marly," Noah said, feeling his jealousy dissipating.

"I'm just so happy that Shawn is in heaven. You can't imagine the feelings of guilt I carried thinking that I was somehow responsible for him not going to heaven. I know that everyone is responsible for their choices, but I kept thinking maybe, I could have done a little more,"

She looked at him in sudden understanding. "I was given to Shawn so that he would have no excuses and I believe it was the same for Colleen. She experienced Christ through you and she will have to answer for not accepting Him if she didn't. We all have burdens in life. Some just appear to be easier than others. Some have happy endings and others don't. You and I have done all that God knew we were capable of. It's time to let go and move on. What do you say about that Phillips?"

"I say you're a wise woman. Now open that other envelope so we can get out of here," he said, placing the pictures back where they belonged.

She unsealed the other envelope and gasped aloud. Clearly, there were thousands of dollars there, along with pay stubs. A hand written note was attached to the stubs, "This belongs to you, Lena. It's legitimate money from my job. I put most of that money away for you and some for Ka'. I guess my investment in life was you. You deserve it and more. Love always, S."

"What should I do with this?" she asked him, holding some of the money up.

Noah shrugged and said humorously, "Buy a new dress."

She rolled her eyes at him and put the money back into the envelopes.

"Marly, it's your money. He worked hard for it. That's what those stubs are proving. Whatever you do with it is your choice, but he wanted you and Kaod to reap the benefits of his labor."

She grabbed all three envelopes, "I guess I'd better deposit this money into my and Ka's accounts."

"That sounds like a good plan to me," Noah said as he escorted her up the stairs.

Chapter Twenty-five

Noah sat with his chin resting on Marly's head and his arms encircling her. In a couple of hours, it would officially be Christmas, the day that believers around the world celebrated the birth of their Savior. She and Kaod had received early presents from Shawn: Marly, twenty-five thousand dollars and Kaod, ten thousand dollars. Noah observed that Kaod had been awfully quiet since opening the letter from his dad. He was in a struggle, but with what? He couldn't help unless Kaod asked. Marly, on the other hand, seemed to be at peace. She was more carefree and flirty with him, as though a load had been lifted from her shoulders, freeing her to love again.

He became aware of Kaod's bedroom door opening, and footsteps coming down the hall. He looked up and watched as Kaod took in the scene. Noah was sitting on the sofa with Marly resting against him. Her feet were curled beneath her and her head was resting against his chin. They were in an almost identical posture as that of the picture sitting on the mantel. The Christmas lights had lulled them into a peaceful state of tranquility that was hard to resist. Kaod eased his muscular frame into the plush armchair. He stared at the tree for a time, before asking Noah if they could talk.

"Sure, in private, or is right here okay?" Noah wondered.

"We can talk in front of Mom, if that's what you're asking," Kaod clarified, "It involves Mom anyway. I just want your opinion on something. I already know what Mom seems to think."

Noah rubbed Marly's hand tenderly. "I take it that you don't agree with whatever opinion your mom has."

Kaod paused, as though weighing his words, "I guess I don't understand her opinion. That's why I'd like to hear yours."

"I'm all ears, son" Noah said, giving him his full attention.

Kaod confided that he couldn't comprehend why his mom seemed to be so understanding of all that had transpired. He felt like his father had the opportunity to be supportive, but chose not to be. He also was angry that his father had been living a lie, that he married his mom under false pretense. He had placed them in jeopardy and saying I'm sorry was not enough for Kaod. He went on to explain that the money meant nothing to him. He didn't really want it. He'd have preferred to have had a real father. Noah had listened quietly and had stayed Marly's response with a subtle squeeze on the hand.

"Are you blowing off some steam or would you like to have a serious discussion?" Noah questioned carefully.

"I'd like to discuss it," Kaod replied without hesitation.

"Okay, well then, I think there isn't a right or wrong answer here. You are entitled to feel one way and your mother another. The question becomes whether or not you are at peace with your choice and does that choice line up with the will of God. You seem a bit upset, so my guess would be that you are not at peace with your decision," Noah observed casually.

By the expression on his face, Kaod was taking in everything that Noah had said.

"You know, son," Noah said, "Maybe your dad wasn't there for you, especially, not in the physical sense that you desired and needed. You have a right to be angry, but don't let it turn into bitterness. God has His reasons for allowing things to happen. Ultimately, the answer to your question has to come from God. Remember that your life was determined by Him before you were even born, not by man. Your father made choices that God already knew he'd make. Those choices have helped to mold you into the mature Christian young man that you are today. Perhaps, if your dad had been stronger in your life, you might be leading the kind of life he led; the kind of life that eventually led to his untimely death. I think that maybe your dad knew this and took the only course of action available. He stayed away and allowed Christ to be the greatest influence in your life. According to your mom, you never lacked for anything, so he definitely understood that he was responsible for you."

At this point in the conversation, Marlena stood and walked over to the tree. She picked up an oddly wrapped present and handed it to her son.

"Generally, we wait until Christmas morning to open presents, but I think we can make an exception this one time. I hope this will help you to better understand." She bent down and kissed him on the cheek and then returned back to her spot beside Noah.

They watched as Kaod opened the gift and gazed in wonder at the newly created scrapbook. He flipped through page after page of pictures.

"Where did these pictures come from?" he asked.

"Your father either took them or had someone else take them. There are photos from every single one of your games, all of which I never knew existed. There are even photos taken after you father's death. That doesn't sound like a dad who didn't care about his child to me," Marlena pointed out. "He even took the time to write something on the back of each picture."

Kaod grinned as he looked at the picture of his very first game. "If you guys don't mind, I think I'll take this to my room and look through it." He collected the wrapping paper and the scrapbook and headed back to his room.

Noah looked at Marly and said sincerely, "You've got a great kid."

"We've got a great kid," she corrected softly.

Noah felt honored. He comprehended that she was bestowing fatherhood rights upon him. It was one of the best presents he'd ever received.

The clock on the wall showed twelve midnight. Noah was surprised to see Marly still awake. He nuzzled her neck and laughed softly when she begged him to stop. "It's time for me to leave, sweetheart." He waited for her to stand before coming to his feet. "Walk me to the door," he commanded softly as he put his arm around her waist.

Grabbing his coat from the rack, he slipped it on and fished his car keys out of the pocket. "I'll be here around eight tomorrow morning. Let's open up the presents here. I'll bring Adam with me, okay?"

She nodded in agreement.

"Merry Christmas," he whispered, as he gently kissed her goodbye.

☦

Marlena was dressed and ready to open presents by the time Noah arrived. He was always prompt which bugged her to no end, since she seemed to always be running late. He hated to wait on her and made it clear that he didn't like it when he had to. She had gotten into the habit of being early, whenever they were doing something together, so that she didn't have to hear his mouth.

Kaod looked at her teasingly, "Noah must be on his way. I've noticed he doesn't like to be kept waiting or late for anything. He's sure changed your habit of being late."

She wrinkled up her nose, "Just wait until you catch one of his 'Noahtudes'. He's something else, Mr.-Have-it-his-way-or-else."

Kaod stared at his mom. He'd never known her to do anything she didn't want to, yet he'd noticed how she submitted to Noah's authority. She wasn't one of those weak or helpless females. She was one of the strongest women he'd ever known, but she was changing. It wasn't in a bad way. She seemed more free, as though she'd found the answer to life. The way she was with Noah, he'd never witnessed her so comfortable around anyone else, even his dad. Then again, the way his dad had treated her, it still made him angry. He remembered hearing her muffled moans of pain and his dad calling her the vilest of names. If only he had been older, he could have stopped him, but instead, he had hid his head under the covers and prayed that God would take his father. He felt no guilt for that prayer, even when it had been answered. He dismissed his thoughts and smiled at his mom.

"Why do you put up with him, if he's so bossy?" he asked gently.

She thought for a moment before replying.

"He makes me a better Christian. I feel that I can drop my guard around him and he'll do the protecting. When I look at him, I see a reflection of Christ. Does that make any sense to you?"

Kaod went to his mom and hugged her.

"It makes perfect sense. I hope my future wife sees those same qualities in me."

"Oh, honey, I know that she will. She'll be the one getting the prize, and she'll know it."

Kaod hugged his mother tightly. He hoped his wife would have many of the same qualities that his mom had.

The doorbell intruded upon their thoughts. Kaod winked at his mom, and walked over to answer the door.

Noah, followed by Adam, entered carrying presents.

"Hey, Mom, 'Mr. Have-it-his-way' and his pesky son are here," Kaod called out.

"Has she been complaining about always being late again?" Noah questioned laughingly.

"Hey, baby brother, I know Marly didn't call me pesky. She's already told me that I'm the favorite son. You, on the other hand, are bullheaded and the least favorite of the three," Adam said, sauntering into the room.

He bent down and kissed Marly's cheek.

"Hi, Mom, you're looking ravishing this morning," he said casually.

Kaod, not wanting to be outdone, addressed Noah.

"What's up, Pops? You're the man. Way to handle your business," he said, indicating that Marly was the business.

Noah was the first to speak, "What are you two up to?"

Adam and Kaod smiled and remained silent. He continued to eye them suspiciously, before walking over to Marly and greeting her with a kiss on the forehead.

He held her hand and said, "Before we get started, let's offer up prayer to our Lord and Savior, Jesus Christ."

He led them in prayer thanking God for the gift of His son, His grace and mercy, and for His long-suffering. He also gave thanks to God for merging their families together and he prayed for continued strength and guidance as the soon to be head of the new family.

Noah sighed contentedly as he watched Adam and Kaod teasing Marly while she washed the breakfast dishes. He'd known, by observing Adam's demeanor this morning that Adam hadn't been joking when he'd called Marly "Mom". Marly was becoming a mother figure to his youngest son. That didn't surprise Noah. She was very easy to love. There was no superficiality to her. She was a no frills kind of woman. She wore very little makeup and didn't seem to be obsessed with how she looked. She enjoyed being a woman and that made him feel good. There was no competition for who was bigger, better, or stronger. She had chosen to show her strength by allowing him to become the head of their family and by allowing him to become father to her son. He'd met so many women who'd bought into the modern day philosophy of what feminists said a woman should be: the tough woman that could do it all. There was no need for man. If they wanted a child, they could simply go to a sperm bank. The problem was that no one had asked the men of the world what appealed to them. These women often came off as more aggressive and together, but in his opinion, they were less attractive. What man wanted to be with someone who was tougher than he or showed him all the goods without him asking to see them? He smiled as she giggled at some silly joke Adam had told.

Noah reached in his pocket and felt the long slender gift box which held the present he had yet to give her. She hadn't even batted an eye when he'd given her several inexpensive presents. She had actually gone crazy over the Hebrew and Greek translation/dictionaries and a set of romance movies on DVD. She was so easy to please that it made him want to do more. She'd been much more extravagant in her purchases for others. She had gotten him a suit which she'd said matched his eyes perfectly. That had drawn wise cracks from Kaod and Adam until they'd been presented with suits that matched their eyes. Kaod had grinned in delight, but Adam had been shocked. He couldn't say a word and that had left him wide open to be the brunt of Kaod's humor. Fortunately, for him, he'd bounced back, and soon the two of them were again teasing each other. All three suits had somehow fit perfectly. Marly had gotten him several other presents, but the one he liked the best was his golden key chain. It had an inscription on the back that read "To my Prince Charming, love Cinderella".

✠

"Dinner was great, Mom," Kaod said as he rubbed his stomach.

"It sure was," Adam echoed.

Noah remained silent and pretended not to see her watching him expectantly. When he still didn't say anything, she reached over and thumped him on the back of the head.

He grinned and said, "Dinner was okay." He avoided another thump by grabbing her hands and saying, "Dinner was excellent, sweetheart. Why don't you go and watch one of your movies. I'll be there once I've finished the dishes." He gave her a gentle push towards the living room.

Noah had finished drying and putting away the dishes when Kaod motioned that Marly had fallen fast asleep. Noah grinned and quietly crept into the living room. He pulled the box out of his pocket and opened it. He took out the diamond bracelet and gently put it around a sleeping Marly's wrist then he noisily plopped down beside her. She stirred and asked if he were finished in the kitchen.

"Good," she mumbled and promptly snuggled up to him and fell back to sleep.

Adam and Kaod began to snicker wildly. Noah chuckled despite himself. Kaod came up with another way to wake her and took out his cell phone and dialed his mom's number. Marlena awoke with a start.

"Is that my phone ringing?" she asked.

No one said a word. She jumped up and went into her room to retrieve the phone. Immediately, they heard a screech followed by "Oh my goodness, it's beautiful, Noah."

Noah grinned and braced himself for contact. She didn't let him down. She was out of her room and into his arms in no time flat. Her lips met his in a spontaneous kiss.

She flashed him a special smile and said breathlessly, "It's the most beautiful gift I've ever received."

"For the most beautiful woman I've ever known," Noah responded.

"I love you, Noah" she said softly.

He grinned and whispered in her ear, "Don't forget about your sons sitting behind you."

She blushed and moved back, but not before she'd felt his hands briefly tighten, holding her against him.

Kaod couldn't resist the opportunity to tease his mom, "I thought you said that I gave you the most beautiful gift. Remember, in kindergarten, I painted my hands on paper and gave it to you as a Mother's Day present?"

Marlena laughed and said, "You're right, Kaod. I guess you're picture does sort of put this bracelet to shame. Let me try it again. This is the second most beautiful gift I've ever seen," she said as she kissed Noah on the cheek.

Noah laughed as he caught her eye. The little minx was flirting with him.

"Remind me of that on Valentine's Day. I'll paint my hands on some paper and give it to you," he joked.

✝

Noah watched as Marly leafed through the books he'd gotten her for Christmas. Kaod had gone back to Ohio State and Adam was out covering some New Year's Eve story. The New Year would be here in less than four hours. She had kept her nose in those translations and had not given him a moments rest from questions. She was restudying the book of John. Noah had to admit to himself that she knew more than most Christian men, and they were supposed to be the heads of their families. She wasn't the norm, of that, he was sure. He decided to pick her head a little bit. He asked her different questions about Christ and the resurrection. She answered, in detailed accuracy, every question. He looked deeply at her. Not only had she answered, but her voice had been so full of passion and authority, that there was no doubting that she believed what the Bible taught.

"How come you've never belonged to a church?" he asked her.

She looked down and answered that she had her reasons. Noah believed he knew the reason why.

"You don't have much faith in 'organized religion' do you?"

She shook her head no.

"Will you explain to me why?" he entreated.

She closed her book and sighed, "I don't want to get into some huge debate with you."

"Marly, it's not about a debate or who's right or wrong. I just want to know your reasons because I want to know all about you. What makes you who you are, you know, those deep questions. In five months, you'll be my wife and I'd like to know how and why you think the way you do about certain things and I want you to feel free to ask me anything. Nothing is off-limits to you."

Noah could see that last little bit had caught her attention.

She sat back and began her explanation, "I did belong to a church when I first became a believer. I attended Sunday services and the Wednesday Bible studies, but I began to have a lot of questions that no one took the time to answer. When I did get an answer, it was so vague and distorted that it left me feeling dissatisfied. I tried asking the older women in the church, but they had their own little clicks going on, and the men were off limits. You should understand why. I prayed to the Lord to open my understanding of His Word. I understood the Word to say that the Holy Spirit could teach me. I began by reading the Bible all the way through, starting with the New Testament. Most of it I didn't understand, but I continued reading until I'd finished the whole thing. Then, I found this ministry that takes you through the Bible in five years and so I jumped in, after carefully checking its credibility. That's where I learned how to fellowship with Christ."

Noah glanced thoughtfully at her. "That explains your knowledge, but it still doesn't explain why you're not a member of a church," he pointed out.

She stood to her feet and exclaimed that she was thirsty. He followed her to the kitchen and grimaced in annoyance when she waited for him to open up the refrigerator and ask her what she'd like. After all this time, she'd still knock and call out before entering, and she wouldn't touch a thing without asking. She was quirky like that. Come to think of it, so was Kaod.

"For goodness sake, woman, would you just open up the refrigerator and grab whatever you want out. You're driving me nuts," he complained.

"She ignored him and said, "You don't have too far to go, and I'd like a Coke."

He stared at her, "I must be getting to you tonight if you're drinking the hard stuff."

Once again, she ignored him and said, "Just hand me the Coke, okay."

"Get it yourself," he shot back. When she just stood there, he reached in, grabbed the Coke and thrust it at her. "For heaven sakes, there are no good manners police waiting to ticket you at doors or refrigerators."

Marly gazed at him with raised eyebrows. "Maybe you should have this Coke instead of me," she said as she popped open the can and looked for a straw.

"I suppose you won't drink it if you can't find a straw? And one more thing, you'd better not have to use the bathroom, because if you ask me 'May I use your bathroom' one more time, I am going to deny you permission and then what?" he asked in exasperation.

She giggled and replied, "You'll just have a puddle to clean up. Here, you can have this Coke. I can't find a straw, and besides, you seem to need it more than I do." She folded her arms and grinned at him.

He looked around the kitchen, spotted the straws, and plopped one into her can.

She took a long exaggerated sip. "To calm my nerves, before I explain why I'm not a member of a church," she joked. "I told you that I almost had an affair. Well, he was a member of the church I belonged to. We had begun talking one evening after Bible study. Initially, it pertained to the study material. We decided to meet an hour or two before the class to discuss what we'd read. That led to talking about things other than the subject matter. Eventually, he started dropping little hints about Shawn's indiscretions and how he'd never treat me that way. I'd never told him anything about Shawn, but he knew that I was lonely. It was pretty obvious because by that time, Shawn had stopped attending church. He had complained that the people were hypocrites. Anyway, this guy started calling me more and more and sympathetically listened to all my problems. I decided that maybe things would be different with him, but before I could act on it, I found out that I was pregnant with Kaod. That woke me up. I realized that this man could not be of God. God clearly commanded against what he wanted me to do. He would call and I'd ask him questions concerning the Word and he couldn't answer them. He'd try to keep the conversation on me and him. I told him that I was pregnant, but he claimed he'd take me, baby and all. I stopped going to the Bible study and started studying on my own. Whenever he'd call, I'd start to talk about the Word and he never had any idea what I was talking about. I began to get the impression that this man was a false believer. He was there to prey upon foolish and unsuspecting women. After that, I realized that the reason the members of the church couldn't answer any of my questions was that they truly didn't know the answers themselves. It was as though the blind were leading the blind. I tried other churches and it was the same. Most of them had replaced God's word with their doctrinal beliefs and traditions. They weren't dealing with the heart issues, only the external. There were pastors and wives having affairs, members divorcing for unscriptural reasons, sexual perversion and promiscuity, and all manner of sin that was openly known. It genuinely scared me, so I stayed away and when Kaod was born, I taught him myself."

Noah understood exactly what she was saying, because he'd seen all the same things. As a matter of fact, God had him constantly teaching on the heart issues. God kept reminding him of the sin in the church. Marlena was surprised when he didn't say anything so she asked a question of her own.

"Why doesn't your church have any black members?"

He gave her the customary answer, "Because people tend to go to church in the community where they live."

She rolled her eyes at his answer. "Okay, let me rephrase my question. Why don't blacks live in your community?"

He looked at her and said truthfully, "Because people don't want blacks living here and I suppose that blacks are aware of those feelings."

"And you're okay with that?" she questioned tersely.

"I didn't say I was okay with it. I simply answered your question," he corrected.

"So why did you want me to move here?" she wanted to know.

"I wanted you near me and I didn't care what others thought. Marly, I can't change their thought processes, but I can state mine clearly," he reminded her gently.

"What did you say to the apartment manager? It was pretty clear that he didn't want to rent to me," she asked out of curiosity.

"I told him that God was watching and that I had a son who happened to be a reporter," he smiled boyishly at her surprised expression.

"You do know that there are members of your church who do not like the fact that we are together?" she asked.

"Of course, I know. I'm sure there's a deacon or two that doesn't like it either. There was this expectation that I'd select a wife from the single women in my congregation, but the problem was that I'd given God the right to choose my wife, or to even decide if I'd ever marry again. So they're going to have to argue their case with God," Noah stated in a matter-of-fact voice.

"Had you ever thought about marrying a black woman?" she wondered aloud.

"I'd have to say no, but I'd never been against it, not like you were," he reminded her.

She blushed and looked away.

"That's a little different. People have preferences for mates. You know, like preferring tall guys over short, or a certain color hair over another. I don't look at other cultures and think that mine is superior, or have unreasonable fears because of skin color," she defended.

Noah pulled her into his arms and asked, "What type are you attracted to now?"

She smiled and pulled away. "Do you want to know the name of the man that I almost committed adultery with?"

He looked at her strangely.

Marly stared at him. "Come on, Noah, you can ask me anything. He's probably one of your friends."

"Okay, Browneyes, you're dying to tell me anyway. Who is he?" he asked.

"Don't call me Browneyes. I'm being very serious, because I thought you wanted to know the reason I'm not a member of a church."

Noah saw the flash of hurt and quickly apologized, "I'm sorry. I shouldn't have made light of something so important to you. I would like to know the name of the man, please."

She held his gaze as if daring him to doubt her, "Pastor, or should I say, Bishop De'fleur."

He looked at her in stunned silence. That man was the unofficial voice for the black community; however, Noah had never fully trusted him for various reasons. Her lack of trust now made complete sense to him.

"I believe he's had several affairs since then and I'm wondering if his knowledge of the word has increased any. Somehow, I doubt it has. All you have to do is look halfway decent, be a charismatic speaker, spout a few Bible verses, and people will believe anything. It kind of reminds me of the cursed fig tree. You know, the tree that looks good from a distance, but once you get really close to it, there's nothing on it. Do you really think I wanted Kaod in that kind of environment?" she finished.

He continued to stare at her. Finally, he asked, "Why are you with me, Marly?" He needed to know the answer.

Without hesitating she answered, "Because you've captured my heart. You've taken the time to really know me, to always be respectful, even when you're angry. I've never seen you look at another woman as though you're comparing me to her in your mind, but most of all, I can recognize Christ in you and I can't help but love and respect Him. You take care of me in a way that, for me, mirrors how Christ protects the church. You've restored my hope in organized churches," she informed him in a matter of fact voice.

Noah wrapped her in his arms and said quietly, "You inspire me to be the best man I can be."

"Even when I'm late?" she teased.

"Especially, when you're late," he laughed.

✟

Noah lay in his bed wide awake. It was a new year and he had brought it in with Marly. He kept replaying the conversation with her over and over in his head. Why had God brought her into his life? He wasn't complaining, but he knew that there was a bigger picture. He loved her from the depth of his soul, quirkiness and all. He knew that she loved him too. She'd asked him some pretty tough questions about the members of his church. He was very much aware that some of them had serious problems with their upcoming marriage. He'd heard the stories circulating about petitioning the board and having him removed from pastor if he married her. He hadn't told Marly about it because she'd want to fix the problem by breaking off the engagement. God had a reason for selecting her to be his wife and he had to trust Him explicitly. Marly would become his wife and the district board would, no doubt, attempt to remove him as pastor. They were not ready to accept his marriage to a black woman. He'd already privately spoken to Hal, Layman McGhee, and Jim Wade about the potential backlash of his marriage to Marly and they were praying for them daily. He also perceived that those sitting on the board would bring charges accusing something else in order to cover up their own prejudices. He'd already, without prior notice, been hauled before the board and questioned when they'd learned of his engagement. It was just a matter of time until they took action against him.

His mind switched back to Marly. Noah recalled her comments relating to sin in the church. He couldn't pretend that his church wasn't just as guilty as the churches she had attended. He'd intentionally overlooked, during his earlier years, blatant sin, and had also lost members because of it. After Colleen's death, he'd made a vow before the Lord to hold himself and his congregation to God's standards. That alone had caused quite an up-roar. People didn't like to hear that they were sinners. Since he'd stopped preaching feel-good sermons, weekly complaints were now common place.

He finally closed his eyes and prayed, "God, please keep my steps according to thy will. Let me boldly proclaim your word. Give Marly the strength of faith and wisdom. Allow us to find peace and solace in each other and in your Word."

Marlena tossed and turned. Sleep continued to evade her. Noah had revealed that he knew about some of his members not approving of their engagement. She hoped that there wouldn't be a serious backlash because of her. He was a great pastor and an asset to the church. He loved his members and most of them loved him. She didn't want to be the cause of any potential rift that may develop due to her. She'd rather break off the engagement than to have him torn between his congregation and her. What was wrong with Christians? There was no way that believers should be having the same problems as nonbelievers. How could a sincere believer hate another fellow believer simply because of the color of their skin? Where was the love of Christ in that? Marlena had long since thought that there should be one central church where everyone came to worship. All cultures, all believers worshipping God, at the same time, in the same place. She knew that would only be accomplished when Christ, alone, reigned. She thought about Christ and the pain and hurt he must be suffering again as he watched the different denominations and cultures, separate and apart, not only from each other, but from God also.

"Forgive us Jesus," she prayed. "We suffer from continuous sin because we do not know your Word and we lack the faith to believe in your power and authority." It was a long while until she slept.

Chapter Twenty-six

Marlena smiled as she unlocked the front door to Noah's home. Calling out before entering, she stepped inside and was met by an ecstatic Beauty. The dog jumped around happily, wildly wagging her tail as Marlena rubbed her ears and head.

"Did you miss me, little baby?" she crooned softly.

The huge beast dropped to the floor and rolled to her back, indicating that she wanted her tummy rubbed as well. Marlena laughingly obliged. She reached for the dog's leash, and giggled as the big dog jumped to her feet. She snapped it onto the collar and headed back out the door. Beauty seemed to know exactly where they were headed. Marlena allowed the dog to have a little lead. It was April and the spring break was here. Flowers had begun to peep up from the ground and tiny green buds were appearing on trees and bushes everywhere. Wild birds were chirping happily as they searched for twigs, string, and anything else deemed useful to build a nest. She checked her watch. She, Tina, and Marcella were meeting for the final fitting of her wedding dress in about one hour. Tina's dress was already finished and waiting to be picked up. Marcella was a miracle worker. She had taken care of all the arrangements. The only thing Marlena had had to do was give her approval on selected items. That had freed her to concentrate on the log cabin home that Noah and she had purchased.

Noah had masterfully handled that transaction and they'd gotten a great deal, at a below value price, and with a low interest rate. She smiled as she recalled the day he'd told her the house was theirs. She had been so excited that she could hardly talk and Noah had laughed tirelessly at her. The house was now almost completely cleaned and furnished. The only item Noah had insisted on picking out was a king- sized bed for the master bedroom. They were going to select the bed this afternoon. That thought, although she knew it was silly, still caused her no endless amount of embarrassment. She checked her watch again and turned Beauty back toward the house.

✟

Tina and Marcella gazed at Marlena and smiled. The wedding gown was beyond description. Beautiful could not adequately describe it. The dress was uniquely divine. It accentuated her skin tone and presented a look of elegance and sophistication, with a touch of modest sensuality which would definitely appeal to Noah, and probably every other male there. When Marlena had initially told her that she'd chosen navy blue as her colors, Tina had rolled her eyes. She'd thought the colors to be too dark for a wedding, but, after seeing Marlena in the dress, she had to admit that those colors were perfect. Marlena looked every inch a queen. The dress was floor length and slightly formfitting with a small train. It was made completely of shimmering navy blue satin and had full billowy sheer sleeves, with a modestly tapered bodice and waistline. The view from the sides gave the appearance of royalty, as though you'd expect to see a king's guard escorting her to whatever event she'd be attending. From the front however, there was a subtle hint of sensuality every time she stepped. Noah would be treated to fleeting glimpses of shapely calves. Embroidered around the bottom of the dress were tiny grey tassels which were used to offset the navy blue color. The dress was modest, yet alluring. It was a dress to turn heads, but said, "Hands off, I am part of royalty." To put it plainly, Tina thought, it screamed, "I belong to Noah!"

"What do you think?" Marlena asked.

Both women could only stare.

Finally Marcella confessed, "Honey, I've seen dozens of dresses and brides to match, but you put them all to shame. That dress on you is absolutely stunning."

Tina was nodding her head vigorously in agreement. Marcella left the room, but quickly returned with Noah's suit, shirt, and tie. She held it up beside Marlena and screamed in delight.

"Girl, when everyone sees you and Noah, they are going to want to copy your style. What made you choose those colors?"

Marlena explained what happened the first time she'd gone to church with Noah and how they had, inadvertently, both worn navy blue. She even divulged how he'd become irritated with her when she'd felt embarrassed because they'd looked like a couple. Since then, navy blue had become her favorite color.

Tina then asked, "Why grey?"

Marlena smiled a girlish smile and said, "It's the color of his eyes."

Noah glanced at the clock on the kitchen wall and absentmindedly rubbed Beauty's ears. Marly must have been here. He noticed that both the food and water bowls were full. He had planned on cooking for the two of them, but decided instead to wait. He reached into his pocket and pulled out the handwritten note. He smiled as he read it again. She had started slipping little notes where she knew he'd find them. Sometimes the notes were silly, sometimes serious, but they always made him smile. On today's note, she had simply written Marlena Renee' Porter loves Noah Stephen Phillips. He'd begun to know this mood of hers very well. Whenever he was scheduled to go out of town, she'd start missing him a day or so before he left. That's when he'd get most of the love notes. It was as though she understood how much he wanted to bring her along, but couldn't. He used to enjoy traveling to different conferences, Marly had changed that. He hated leaving her alone for two or three days at a time. Who was he kidding? He hated not being with her. They would talk on the phone for hours, but it wasn't the same. In a couple of months, she would be his wife, and as such, able to join him on some of those trips. "That's if you're still the pastor," he reminded himself. Noah stood to his feet and waited when he heard a key at the front door. He shook his head in annoyance when he heard her call out before entering. Placing the note back in his pocket, he made up his mind that quirky was, at times, very lovable.

He pulled Marly behind him as they (you might as well say he) looked for the perfect king sized bed. He'd tried to get her to participate in the selection of the bed, but all she kept saying was, "You choose". Noah glanced at her out of the corner of his eye. She kept her eyes averted.

"Marly, it's only a piece of furniture. Which design do you think would best suit the bedroom? If you're not going to help me, then don't get upset if I select a style you don't like."

That got her attention. If nothing else, she definitely liked decorating. Everything in their new home was beautifully coordinated. From the curtains, to the floor coverings, everything had to match the room for which it had been selected. She turned and began looking at the different designs. He pointed out the suite he liked best, and she smiled in approval. Noah spoke with the sales representative and made the necessary arrangements for home delivery.

✝

Noah sat beside Marly in the booth at the popular Italian restaurant. He had observed her behavior at the furniture store and wasn't quite sure what the nature of the problem was since they'd already discussed that aspect of her marriage to Shawn.

He studied her for a moment before saying, "Marly, intimacy is a normal part of God's plan for a man and his wife. There is nothing dirty or vile about it. I don't want you to be embarrassed or ashamed of a part of marriage that God himself created. I understand that the world has a distorted view of intimacy, but it's not that way with God. There is no one else in this world that will know me, or you, in the way that we will know each other. You won't ever have to share me, nor I you. My body will be your private domain, to study, to touch, to learn and vice versa. Christ has established that the marriage bed is holy and undefiled before Him and it is ultimately the way we become one."

She fumbled with her napkin and tried to shyly explain, "I know what the Bible says about it, but I have no experience to base it on. I've only experienced the worldly aspect of marriage and it was pretty defiled. Even now, I feel embarrassed just thinking about the humiliation I endured, not being able to respond. You can't imagine how it feels, unable to please your mate. Knowing that he may have another image in his mind, thinking of another woman or something worse, as he's making love to you; it makes you feel as though you want to cover up or hide. You are unable to respond. You don't want to respond. I think I know how God feels when we claim to follow him, but instead, we give our attention to the things of the world. It's almost unbearable."

He reached over and grabbed her hand and brought it to his mouth. Kissing it gently, he smiled at her and said tenderly, "Sweetheart, it won't be that way between us. You are all that I desire, God's gift to me. You alone, excite my senses. Jesus commands me to love you as he loves the church. He's faithful to her alone. Would he ever hurt you? Hasn't he always loved you tenderly and protected you from harm? He has commanded that I do the same and I promise you, sweetheart, I will honor that commandment. We will take our time and learn about each other, okay?"

She gazed at him deeply, and for the first time, he saw in her eyes the fear of intimacy fade to be replaced by trust. She no longer resembled a frightened girl, but a woman displaying an unconcealed desire to experience the type of intimacy of which he spoke. He knew, at that moment, beyond a shadow of doubt, that God had just freed her from the gripping bondage of fear, and that knowledge penetrated the very core of his being.

He grinned and said, "I found this note on my car this morning. Some woman is crazy in love with me. I hope you're not jealous, but I have to tell you that she's gorgeous."

Marlena pretended to be upset, "Do I have reason to be jealous?"

"With this one, yes, she's the 'real deal'," he teased.

"What can I do?" she asked.

"Well, it takes a lot of daring, but if you were to kiss me, that might make me forget all about her," he whispered conspiratorially.

Marlena, without the slightest hesitation, kissed him laughingly.

When she sat back, he had a funny expression on his face. She intrigued him and he'd, at last, figured out why. He'd known her now for nearly a year, but he'd never once gotten bored. He enjoyed and looked forward to their many conversations. She stimulated him intellectually as well as spiritually. She kept him on his toes with her constant barrage of Biblical questions and he was very aware of her expectations of him. She didn't have him on a pedestal, and she definitely kept his ego squarely planted on solid ground. Everything he said or did, and even her own thoughts and actions, were constantly measured against the Bible. He found her thoroughly adorable and, he had to be honest with himself, intoxicatingly sensual. Her eyes, her mouth, her mocha-colored skin, all fascinated him. It seemed to him, during this past week, there had been a shift in their relationship. He was more aware of her now, than the entire time he'd known her. He didn't know whether she was as aware of him or not. It wasn't lust. He had experienced that with Colleen. It was a yearning from his soul to become united with his other half, to share the last remaining part of himself with her. He knew intuitively, that only she could complete him. He would finally be whole after years of emptiness.

✙

"I'm going to miss you," Marly told him as they drove home.

"You always miss me," he laughed.

"I know, but this is different. We are on spring break, so I won't have anything else occupying my time," she complained.

"Forget it, Marly. You are not coming with me," he stated firmly.

"Well, since you brought it up, why can't I come? I'm on break and we'd only be gone three days," she cajoled.

"You're not coming because we are not married and it's not appropriate," he answered firmly.

"I went to Atlanta with you and we weren't married. What's the difference?" she countered.

"The difference is you were going to meet Jacob and, Adam came along," he explained impatiently.

"We'd be in separate rooms, Noah," she pouted.

"The answer is still, no! Stop being so naïve, Marly. We have less than two months before we are married. It's not getting easier for me to keep my hands to myself, it's becoming harder. Are you deliberately trying to drive me insane?" Noah questioned.

Marly rolled her eyes and refused to answer.

"Did you hear what I said?" he questioned again.

"Of course, I heard you. You were practically yelling it," she said, sounding irritated.

"Good," he replied.

Marly knew when he said "good" in that manner, that was the end of the subject. It was one of those "Noahtudes" she disliked so much. He had a habit of tying up the loose ends on conversations too. It effectively prevented a person from establishing a loophole to be used later on. It must be all those counseling courses and sessions he had over the years. She knew he was right, but she wasn't ready to admit it. He was the most levelheaded person she'd ever met. It was as though he thought every little detail through before answering and it bugged her to no end. She wondered if he'd ever lost an argument in his entire controlled life. He certainly was batting a hundred with her. She could usually talk circles around most men and they never knew whether they were coming or going, but with him, he seemed to always be right. She suddenly became aware of the negative direction her thoughts were heading. God was advising her to take a long look at herself. The point of being a couple was to become one. His role as the man, as her husband, was to ensure they stayed on the right path, to be obedient to God. Noah had always done that. Isn't that what had drawn her to him in the first place. She was behaving in an immature and selfish manner. They had come so far and now she wanted to place them in a position of extreme temptation. Hadn't he been honest concerning his physical limitations? She needed to support, rather than hinder him. She reached over and grabbed his free hand.

"I'm sorry, Noah. I was being selfish. You are right and I need to be more considerate of the situation. Will you forgive me?"

He nodded yes and gave her hand a gentle squeeze.

Noah smiled at her puzzled look as he drove past their usual exit.

"I thought we'd pay John and Teresa a visit," he explained casually.

"Are their grandkids going to be there?" she asked with a laugh.

The two of them chuckled as they remembered their last visit. John's youngest grandson had come up to Marlena and looked her over. Abruptly, he'd turned back to his grandfather and had casually remarked that his grandfather was wrong. Marly wasn't black, she was brown. John and Teresa had both turned a deep red, while Noah and Marly had laughed heartily.

He and Marly had played several different games with the children, and by the time they were preparing to leave, all three grandsons were calling her Aunt Marly. It didn't matter where they went. Kids seemed to gravitate towards her. They didn't care or have any hang-ups about color. He remembered young Stephen from the picnic. He had boldly told Noah that he'd take care of Marly because he was going to marry her one day. Noah wished that adults would learn to judge by character rather than color.

✟

John looked at the couple sitting across from him. He loved his younger brother and could tell that Noah was deeply in love with Marly. He could also tell that she felt the same way. Her eyes would follow him no matter where he went. If he left the room, they would brighten when he returned. Those two were in for a heck of a battle with the District Board, Noah's church, and some of the leadership within the black community. At first, John had been resentful of Marly because he'd thought she was coming between Noah and his church. Later on, after talking with Noah, he'd understood that she was the instrument being used by God to expose deeply imbedded racism in the church, and not just in the white community, but in the black as well. It was becoming evident that they were drawing notoriety when even he had overheard his own officers, black and white, discussing their impending marriage. People were also talking about the fact that Noah and she had established a street ministry of sorts at what everyone now called "Chandra's House". Even through the winter months, they had ministered from her old home and had invited the local community to fellowship with them anytime. It had started off with just kids and teens, but soon young and old could be seen going in and out. John had been told that they (Noah and Marlena) had secretly been helping people out financially also. They had established a program whereby if someone received help, then they in turn had to help out a fellow neighbor in need. John had received reports that crime in that particular neighborhood had gone down significantly. He'd even been told by his officers that they'd seen teenagers out shoveling the walks of the elderly.

He had called Bishop De'fleur, the self-appointed spokesman for the black community, and advised him to duplicate Noah and Marly's efforts, but all he'd done was talk about a white man using a black woman to further his own agenda. It had appeared to John that the good Bishop was desirous of, not only Noah's success, but of his fiancée as well. Bishop De'fleur, from what John had seen, loved his title and status more than God and the people of his community.

John hoped that he could get in a private word with Noah because he didn't want him to get caught off guard by the latest developments. Maybe he'd use his wife to lure Marly away.

✝

John shook his head at the lovesick expression on his brother's face as Marly and Teresa left the room. "Noah, she's not leaving the planet, she's only going into the kitchen. You've got it bad baby brother," John teased. Noah grinned and shrugged his shoulders nonchalantly. John glanced guiltily at the kitchen door and quickly filled him in on Bishop De'fleur and the talk around town. He watched as a range of emotions played across Noah's face.

Finally, Noah spoke, "I'm familiar with the good Bishop and I'm sure he doesn't like the idea of me marrying Marly. I wish that I could tell you why, but I can't break that confidence. I can tell you this though, when God begins to shake up things, He leaves no stone unturned," Noah declared.

"Why couldn't you have picked a white woman to fall in love with? You are aware that the two of you are the talk of the town? A year ago, nobody cared about Pastor Noah or Marlena the teacher. Now, I've even got my officers, black and white, talking about it," John complained laughingly.

"I keep telling you, Johnny, that God picked her. I just concurred, whole- heartedly with his choice," Noah corrected.

John, again, glanced at the closed kitchen door.

"Do me a favor, Noah. When you leave on Wednesday, keep Marly away from Chandra's House for those three days that you're gone. I'm not saying she's in danger, but some of those fellas are getting a little worked up over you and her. It's better to be safe than sorry," John said soberly.

"What are you saying? Has someone made a threat against her? Do you know something more than what you're letting on?" Noah demanded with steel in his eyes.

"Calm down Stevey Boy," John said, using Noah's childhood nickname. "No threats have been made, but De'fleur is using a lot of 'master, housewench' terminology, and we both know his intent is to stir up anger and hatred. I'd hate to see her get caught up in his rhetoric."

Noah pent his brother with a direct stare trying to determine if that was the extent of what John knew. Satisfied with what he saw, Noah agreed to keep Marly away from Chandra's. Noah knew he was in for the battle of a lifetime when he broached the subject with Marly. She loved their little ministry. As a matter of fact, she had come up with the concept of neighbors helping neighbors, and had actually donated the twenty-five thousand dollars that Shawn had left her to Chandra's House. Noah looked at John and frowned. How was he supposed to keep her away? She had already agreed to never be there alone, but if he wasn't there, Hal usually was; however, Marly was his responsibility, not Hal's. It hit him like a ton of bricks. The truth, he'd simply tell her the truth. She was levelheaded enough, after she calmed down, that she'd listen to reason.

✣

"What?" Marly thundered. "First you say I can't go with you and I understood that. Now, I can't go to Chandra's because you won't be there. You're being bossy, Noah and I'm only going to take so much. Give me a break," she added storming from the living room to her bedroom.

"Arm or leg?" he thought just before he heard the door slam with a bang. Browneyes was back with a vengeance he noted. He took a deep breath and headed towards the combat zone. He tapped on the door and announced his entry. She was sitting on the bed with angry sparks igniting her eyes.

"What are you doing in my bedroom? Don't you know that you are being highly inappropriate?" she asked sarcastically.

When he didn't respond she threatened him. "If you don't get out of my room, I'm going to undress in front of you and where would that leave your self control?" she challenged.

Noah decided to call her bluff. He put his hands in his pockets and leaned against the wall. Who was she kidding? She was the only woman he knew who still buttoned her shirt all the way up. The only button that was ever left undone was the very top. He was surprised that she could still breathe let alone issue that silly threat. This could take awhile he thought humorously. She stood and unbuttoned the top button, then the next. Still he stood there, but admitted to himself that he was a little less sure that she wouldn't do it. When her fingers went to the next button, he could feel himself starting to sweat. He decided to go for all or nothing.

"If you want me to see what I'm getting before our wedding night, then that's your business, but we are going to finish our conversation before I leave here tonight," he stated firmly.

She stopped at the third button and quickly redid her blouse.

"You little chicken," he teased, secretly happy that she was so modest. Most women routinely wore their shirts as low, and in some cases a lot lower than where she'd left off.

Still seething, she brushed passed him and back to the living room where she plopped down in the armchair.

Marlena listened grudgingly to what Noah said. He told her everything that John had confided to him. When he got to the part concerning De'fleur, she stared at him accusingly. "Did you tell your brother the things we talked about?"

"Marly, don't ask ridiculous questions. If you're trying to pick a fight, it's not going to work. I need you to think logically, okay. I guess I've been a little naïve here. I had no clue that our marriage would become such a big deal. I knew that it would be a big deal with my church family, but to have others involved, kind of puts a new perspective on it. You need to remember that Chandra's House is not your ministry or mine, it's God's and for some reason, He's chosen you and me to lead it. We are a team, Marly, and I'm asking you not to go there without me," he said softly.

"Are you asking me or telling me?" she questioned stubbornly.

"I'm asking you, sweetheart," he responded humbly.

"In that case, I won't visit Chandra's until you come back," she promised.

"Good. Now you can button your top correctly."

He chuckled with amusement as she looked down and blushed. She'd inadvertently skipped a button in her rush to escape out of the bedroom.

✟

Marlena closed the Bible and meditated over the words she'd read. Jesus had taught his disciples to obey his commandments if they claimed to love him. Marlena knew that she hadn't completely done that today. Noah wasn't perfect, but he had been dead on today. She had been in rebellion against his headship. She knew that submitting to his authority was going to be difficult, but she also knew Noah. He'd hold his ground, and depending on her, it would be lovingly, like tonight, or firmly, as he'd done when they'd first gone to view the inside of the log cabin house. She understood that he loved her and it was his job to protect her. She bowed her head and confessed to God her sin of rebellion. She asked for His forgiveness and prayed for the strength of meekness and obedience. She prayed for a hedge of protection around Noah and their family. She also prayed for the different communities and Chandra's House. She thanked God for the sacrificial offering of His son and for Jesus being the perfect example of obedience by his choice to submit to the will of His father.

Noah picked up his pencil and began writing in the journal that Marly had bought him for Christmas. His thoughts flowed freely across the paper. He paused and allowed his mind to roam. God was using them as the catalyst to ignite both communities. The black community seemed to base everything on race. Words like "plantation," "housewench," and "Uncle Tom," were thrown around as a means, in his opinion, to control those they deemed to be traitors. He'd asked Layman and Marly about those terms and had been surprised at their answers. The black culture still seemed to view themselves as at the mercy of the white man, who is in essence the plantation owner. They could do nothing unless he allowed them to. This, in their minds explained the disparity of wealth across the land. Noah didn't doubt that whites had used, and still use some very questionable methods to obtain wealth and prosperity. He also knew, first hand, what some whites thought about, not just blacks, but other cultures as well. What puzzled him the most was the lack of authority and power this way of thinking attributed to God. It was as though God didn't exist. He had no dominion over man. No wonder the black communities were seeing their families and neighborhoods self-destruct. They had given authority over their lives to something other than God. They were in bondage, not to the white man, but to their own thoughts and beliefs. It was God who ultimately determined a person's position and status. He allowed both the just and the unjust to become affluent, but through it all,

God remained solely in control. Noah thought about De'fleur's comment pertaining to Marly being Noah's housewench (a female slave who stayed in the comfort of the master's house, purely for the master's selfish and lewd desires). The Bishop was willing to degrade her, a black woman, in an overt attempt to bend her to his will. Had it ever occurred to him that God's will reigns supreme to the pathetic personal desires of men? His community was no different. Irrational fear and hatred, as well as the consuming desire to stay on the top of the social ladder, enslaved them. They had no real use for God. They enjoyed religion, but it was separate and apart from God. What a mess. Only God could harmonize communities that were hell-bent on singing different tunes.

Quite naturally, his thoughts strayed back to Marly and her little striptease. He chuckled aloud as he recalled her crookedly buttoned shirt. She'd become embarrassed when he'd pointed it out. It served her right. She was spoiled rotten from all those years of submitting only to Christ. To Noah's knowledge, she'd never had a man exercise godly stewardship over her. That was a direct result of never having belonged to a church. She hadn't experienced any type of manly headship. God had allowed her free reign under Christ's supervision. He imagined God saying, "Here she is, Noah. She'll make you a great wife. She loves me with all her heart and I love her. She's my precious daughter, so take good care of her. I'll be watching your every move. Oh yeah, you'll find out that she's a little on the spoiled side." He smiled and admitted that he wouldn't have her any other way. Noah put down his pencil and slid to his knees. There was so much to pray for. He started with himself, and by asking for forgiveness for his sins.

Chapter Twenty-seven

Noah hid a smile from Mrs. Dreussi, his new dance instructor. She was chastising him for waiting so long before coming. He'd tried explaining to her that this was all on the spur of the moment and all he needed was a refresher course, but she apparently thought he'd need more. This grand scheme was all Kaod's doing. He'd called during Noah's trip and had explained that he'd wanted to surprise his mom on the day of the wedding by dancing with her. He went on to explain to Noah about Marly's favorite song in the world and asked Noah if he would dance with his mom to that song. Noah had agreed, hence the visit to Mrs. Dreussi. She wasted no time in pointing out that she had been Kaod and Marly's dance instructor. Mrs. Dreussi had proudly informed him that Marly had insisted on a young Kaod learning formal dance, and to persuade her son, she had taken the lessons with him. She hoped Noah would be up to the task of dancing with Marly. He had smiled politely and allowed her to show him the proper way to hold his dance partner. Marly had better appreciate this he thought to himself. He was confident that if he didn't behave, he'd get his knuckles rapped or worse yet, be made to stand in the corner. She'd already made it clear that she would not tolerate any misbehaving.

Marly looked at the clock on the wall. Hal was due to leave in a couple of minutes and Noah didn't want her to be here alone, at Chandra's. Hal poked his head into the kitchen and asked if she needed him to stay.

"Thanks, but I'm only going to be here a few more minutes."

She glanced out the back door and saw Malcolm with a couple of his buddies. "Malcolm's out back. He can help me if need be."

Hal gave her a friendly wave goodbye and headed off. Marlena decided to start cleaning the kitchen. Noah had wisely returned some of the more necessary items from storage and she was sure she could have the refrigerator cleaned in no time. She'd just started looking around for cleaning supplies when she heard the front door open. Assuming it was Noah, she spoke without looking, "You're just in time to help me."

"I didn't realize you were expecting me, but I'm all yours," a deep masculine voice replied.

Marlena whirled around to face, none other than, Bishop Reginald De'fleur. She stood rooted to the spot.

"Aren't you going to say hello or does that cat have your tongue? You always were a shy little thing," he challenged with a grin.

"Hello, Reggie," she greeted stiffly, intentionally leaving the title off of his name.

"You're still the only woman I've ever allowed to call me Reggie. What's this I hear about you marrying some white-boy pastor?"

When she still didn't reply, he continued in his most seductive voice, "You know, I should have chased you down and married you when I had the chance."

Marlena ignored his statement and asked, "What do you want Reggie?"

He moved closer towards her, putting one hand on either side of her and effectively stopped her from escaping. "Marlena still looked good," he thought as he allowed his eyes to wander the entire length of her body. "What do you want to give me? I came to talk to the head of Chandra's House, but since he's …."

"Standing right here, you can move away from my fiancée," a low menacing voice commanded.

De'fleur, unmoved by Noah's sudden appearance, winked at Marlena and moved away in a deliberately slow manner. She knew instantly that he was purposefully goading Noah.

"Malcolm!" Noah commanded.

When Malcolm appeared at the backdoor, Noah, without taking his eyes off of De'fleur, instructed him in a calm voice to please escort Marly to his car and to keep her there.

"Noah, don't…" Marly pleaded putting her hand on his arm.

"Malcolm, escort my wife out to the car please!" Noah repeated his command, while ignoring her and still looking directly at De'fleur.

Malcolm firmly grabbed Marly by the wrist, and pulled her out the back door and straight to Noah's car.

No sooner had the back door close, when Noah closed the distance between himself and the arrogant bishop.

With his face inches away from De'fleur's, he asked in a steel laced voice, "What would you do to a man who deliberately insulted the most valuable gift that God had given you?"

"I never touched her," De'fleur replied.

"Oh, but you insulted Marlena by calling her a housewench to others, implying what exactly?" Noah asked.

"Loosen up, Pastor Noah. It was meant to be a 'black' joke, but then again, you wouldn't understand that," he mocked.

"Really, a joke about her being a slave to my sexual whims, somehow I don't find that very funny and I don't think God does either. So, we can either handle this man to man, right here, right now, or you can apologize to her. Which will it be Reggie?" Noah asked, not backing down.

Reggie could sense that Noah was deadly serious. He decided that is was in his best interest to appear contrite. "If it's that big a deal I'll apologize. You do know that Marlena and I go back a long ways. I met her when she and Shawn were having problems."

Noah relaxed his stance, fighting the urge to drop the cocky bishop on the spot.

De'fleur stood to his full height, backed away, and smiled, displaying perfectly aligned teeth.

"I used to counsel her quite a bit. Of course, I wasn't a bishop then."

Noah knew what he was implying, but chose to ignore him.

"I thought about dating her myself, but there was too much baggage. You know what I mean, 'the bitter black woman thing'."

Noah could feel his ire rising. This man was an embarrassment to whatever church he belonged to.

"Sorry Bishop, I don't know what you mean. Generally, when you have a bitter woman, there's a man who caused it, and that stands true for every culture, not just black women."

Noah wondered how this man could say he represented his culture when he was so degrading to the women. Bishop De'fleur continued talking as though he hadn't heard Noah.

"So how did you and Marlena meet? There have been plenty of men trying to tap that, but word is she's as cold as ice. One brother told me she was in deep- freeze. Is that true?" he deliberately goaded.

"What are you here for Bishop? Surely, not to discuss my personal business, which is none of your business," Noah asserted.

"I've done a little checking around and from what I hear, the powers that be in your little world, don't like the fact that you're dating a sister. I hear your pastor days may be over if you marry her. Are you sure that you're willing to trade God in for Marlena?" De'fleur chuckled slyly. "You two seem pretty cozy. I'm sure you could have your cake and eat it too. Why go through all the trouble of marrying her?"

"I'm sure that you didn't come here to talk about my marital status either. What do you want Bishop?" Noah asked in a voiced laced with obvious impatience.

Reggie looked at Noah with disdain. Who did this white boy think he was dealing with? "Why don't you leave the Hood to those of us who live here? Stop pretending that you're all sympathetic to what's going on, 'cause you ain't. You come in here like some kind of savior, but at night you're tucked away in your safe all-white neighborhood. You don't have a clue."

Noah shook his head in disgust and said, "Is that why you came here, on some kind of power trip? I thought we pastors all wanted the same thing, to bring souls into the Kingdom of Heaven. That's the only way this, or any other neighborhood is going to change. This ministry isn't about you, me, or even Marlena; it's about glorifying God. This neighborhood and everything in it belongs to Him, not you and definitely not me. Now, if you'll excuse me, I have other matters that I need to attend to."

Noah turned to walk away, but De'fleur stopped him with his vile words.

"You really think you're the 'man' just 'cause you got a black woman. That don't mean crap to me. They come a dime a dozen over here. Let me give you a little tip about Marlena, she ain't worth you risking losing your church. Hit it if you need to, but according to her dead husband, she can't get the job done in bed. She's a…."

De'fleur barely had time to spit the words out before Noah's fist slammed into his nose cutting off the rest of his words. The force of Noah's right hook sent De'fleur slamming into the storm door causing the latch to groan and break free, allowing the bishop's helpless body to tumble in a sprawling heap onto the back patio. Noah stared without compassion at the dazed bishop and fought the compelling desire to finish what he'd started.

Marlena was in a panic outside, "Malcolm, please go in there and see what's going on."

Malcolm dismissed Marlena's request and asked in a calm tone that mirrored Noah's, "Why? Pastor Noah can handle himself. Besides, if Bishop De'fleur had come on to my girl like that, I'd have already beat him down, and had my boys come and take the trash out, but I don't expect you to understand that a man's got to step up to the line every once in a while, even if he is a Christian."

"Malcolm, if you don't go and check on Noah, I'm going to step up to the line with you," she asserted, abruptly stopping when she heard a loud bang come from the rear of the house.

She quickly hopped out of the car and followed a sprinting Malcolm around the back. There, lying on his back and holding his bloodied nose, was the bishop.

Malcolm grinned at a scowling Noah and said, "All you had to do was ask, and I'd have taken the trash out for you."

Noah walked back into the kitchen, grabbed a wet towel and threw it to De'fleur. He looked at Marlena and waited with arms folded as she stepped into the kitchen.

"I thought I told you to stay in the car," he pointed out.

"No, you told Malcolm to keep me in the car. And don't take that tone with me. I was worried," she attempted to explain.

"About what, me getting hurt, or me hurting him?" Noah questioned in a chilling tone.

"I told her that you could handle yourself," Malcolm interjected.

"She prefers me to be a sissy. After all, aren't all Christian men wimps, especially the white ones?" Noah commented, looking directly at Marly.

She blushed and looked away, knowing she had thought precisely that.

"By the way Marlena, what were you doing here, alone?" Noah asked.

She opened her mouth to speak, but realized she was in the wrong in that aspect as well.

"Exactly my thoughts," he said as he and Malcolm walked out the back door to help the beleaguered bishop to his feet.

Marlena knew that she had broken their agreement and had not only betrayed his trust in her, but had hurt his feelings as well. She had acted independently, and then hadn't really trusted that he could handle the situation that her lack of good judgment had gotten him into. She'd assumed that he'd get hurt. She'd wanted to protect him instead of trusting that he was quite capable of protecting them both. Noah wouldn't put himself in a situation in which he was out of his league. He had called her his wife to signify that she was under his mantle, and to insult her meant that he'd hold that person accountable. It was like Christ's warning to the world concerning the sensitivity of the Holy Spirit, but on a much lower level of course. She stared out the back door and watched as he chatted easily with Malcolm. She had inadvertently stumbled into men's territory. Their actions and reactions were of a foreign nature to most women, including her. He'd tried to explain it to her when Kaod and Jacob had gotten into it. She should have listened more carefully, instead she'd hurt his feelings by throwing him into the category of "weak Christian men" who were afraid of confrontation. Worse yet, she had stereotyped him, even when she hated being stereotyped herself. She was a hypocrite and should have allowed him to handle it. There were some things in life that men handled differently than women. She didn't have to understand it, but she should have trusted him. Noah had saved her life when she had behaved in a reckless manner. His judgment had been extremely perceptive. He was not in need of her protection, but she, his. Marlena, at long last, came to grips that he was her covering. Without him, she was left open and vulnerable to the exploits of any man. By agreeing to become his wife and eventually assuming his name, she became his responsibility, to love, to honor, and to protect. Anything less from Noah, would take away his manhood.

Noah could feel Marly's gaze, but he continued to ignore her. He was still fuming inside. Why was she so hardheaded and stubborn and what was it about this woman that caused men to want to possess her? She didn't seem to have the foggiest notion concerning her effect on the opposite sex. She honestly thought that dismissing them with that nonchalant tone of hers would solve the problem. How many times had he explained to her that men considered that a challenge? De'fleur was blessed that he'd only gotten a tap on the nose and even more blessed that he hadn't laid so much as a finger on her. Noah had encountered many so called believers exactly like him. They were cowards who used their positions and titles to hide their misdeeds. They were the reason many people stayed away from God and the organized church. Marly's life could be considered a direct result of this type of hypocritical behavior. She, however, had been fortunate to be blessed by a desire to truly understand the Word of God and had benefited greatly from her self-imposed exile. The vast majority of people who duplicated her choice, usually ended up by the wayside; never growing into mature believers, if they became believers at all.

Noah spent some time explaining the Word to Malcolm. He had become a fellow believer some months ago. Noah and he had begun to forge a solid relationship built on mutual love and respect. As a result, Noah had given him the responsibility of checking on the house daily and he was one of the few people who had twenty-four hour access to Noah's personal cell phone. He'd called and informed Noah of Bishop De'fleur's arrival and the fact that Marly was there alone. Noah was exceptionally proud of him. He was rough and rugged around the edges, but more dedicated than most. Malcolm had taken it upon himself to keep Noah informed about the various activities happening in the neighborhood. Malcolm would, in Noah's opinion, make a great pastor some day.

"What happened in there with Bishop De'fleur?" Malcolm asked excitedly.

"I stepped to the line and handled my business," Noah informed him with a slight grin.

Malcolm laughed at Noah's use of slang and gave him a hand check. "Why'd you hit him?" Malcolm wondered aloud.

Noah sat down and began talking, "He crossed the line, even when I'd made it clear. Marly can't defend herself against men like him. His attempt to defile our covenant before God was deliberate. That kind of behavior from a believer of his stature is unacceptable. Malcolm, I don't want to give you the impression that this is the norm or how conflicts should be handled, but I also don't want you to think that Christian men are supposed to allow everyone to walk all over them. Marly is my responsibility, and she needs to know that I'll defend her with my life. Understand that I can only do that if I am in my rightful place with God. I couldn't defend her if she and I had already been intimate. That's the first lesson that I want you to understand. The second is this, my brother always taught me that if there's a potential for a battle, always make sure that the odds are in your favor. Never challenge a man in front of anyone else, unless it's absolutely unavoidable. You do everything you can to walk away or make it one on one. This makes it easier for them, or you to back out and still save face. It also gives you the opportunity to size up your opponent and determine if he's willing to take the chance of a confrontation. Most men would rather avoid that, unless you embarrass them in front of others. Even the worst coward would fight under those circumstances. I used that tactic with our friend. I gave him the opportunity to make amends, and he continued his verbal assault on Marly. He called my bluff, and I answered."

Malcolm smiled in understanding and asked, "Have you ever had to do that with others around?"

Noah chuckled, "Come to think of it, only one time and it, too, was over Marly."

✠

Noah followed Marly back to the apartment and waited for her to park her car and climb in with him. He could tell that she was anxious for them to resume their normal status. She kept sneaking glances at him to determine his mood as he drove to the local park. Without looking in her direction, he got out of the car and walked to the nearest bench and took a seat. He wanted her to experience being without his mantle.

She sat in the car stunned. He hadn't even bothered to open her car door. Nervously, she exited the car and walked to where he sat. Eventually, she slid down next to him.

"Are you still angry with me?" she asked softly.

"Very," Noah said curtly.

She sat silently, waiting for him to speak. A million thoughts were flying through her mind. Should she apologize? Had she really blown it?

"I'm really sorry, Noah. Will you please forgive me?" she pleaded, holding on to his arm.

"Marlena, are you ready to get married? I need to know, because you seem hell-bent on having things your way," he asked earnestly.

She looked away, unable to look him in the eye, but very much aware of the fact that he'd called her Marlena. She sensed the seriousness of the situation and said, "I truly want to marry you Noah."

"That's not what I asked you. I want to know if you're ready to be married. You've been on your own for so long, I'm wondering if you're prepared to trade your independence for submission. Is having my name worth that independent streak of yours?" he questioned.

"Are you trying to break up with me?" she asked quietly, choking back tears.

Noah resisted the urge to comfort her. Now was not the time. He needed her to fully understand the consequences of her actions. This time he'd been there to step in. He cringed at the thought of what could have happened. He didn't think De'fleur would have gotten forceful, but why take the chance. She shouldn't have been there. They'd made an agreement and she had violated it. She hadn't honored her word to him. He could not afford to take this lightly. He took a deep breath and made himself say the words he knew would hurt her.

"I'd be lying to you if I said that thought isn't present in my mind."

Her mind went blank. Her heart seemed to stop beating. She tried to think of something to say. Trust was part of the crucial foundation of every relationship and she had given him reason to believe she couldn't be trusted.

"I'm sorry. I put what I wanted to do before what was best for us. I'm sorry that I didn't trust that you could handle Reggie. I'm sorry that I'm making you doubt us," she whispered miserably.

It was ridiculous, but she felt bereft, even with him sitting beside her. Doubt had lodged itself between them.

"I am who I am, Noah, but I promise you that I'll make you happy and content if you can just be patient with me. I was wrong today, and it could have turned out a lot worse than it did. I'm not perfect. I'm going to disappoint you at times, but don't throw us away because... because I would give my life for you," she finished quietly.

Noah contemplated where to go from there. "We are six weeks away from the most important step in our lives. I have to be sure that you are not going to be a stumbling block to me. There is no doubt in my mind that you love me and I love you as well, but will you have the strength to allow me to lead, to trust that I am capable of protecting you, to let me be the man. I want a bold woman who is not afraid that others will think less of her because she submits to her husband," Noah explained solemnly. "Will I be able to count on you?" he asked again.

Marlena closed her eyes and sighed. "I could say yes, and would that make you believe me? If you don't know the answer in your heart, then nothing I say will make a difference."

He closed his eyes in prayer and confessed to God the sin of doubt. How could this relationship work? There was so much against them. The church, the community, his oldest son, their racial backgrounds, the opposition seemed endless. He opened his eyes and became aware of the fact that she had walked back to the car.

Marlena sat in the car as the tears flowed freely from her eyes. Noah had doubts about their relationship and she knew it. Why had she trusted him? It had all been a fairytale, a dream, a fantasy. She began a slow shutdown of her feelings. Her body knew the drill well. If you don't feel, you can't hurt. She would not allow any emotion to affect her. The walls that Noah had systematically knocked down, her mind commanded to be rebuilt. No one, save God and Kaod, would ever gain access to her heart again. She had been a fool. Black and white was not meant to be together and true love between a man and woman was just a dream. She sat stiffly without saying a word as he returned to the car.

Noah slid into the driver's seat and started the engine. He reversed the car and drove in the direction of her apartment. Neither of them said a word. Both were drowning in their own thoughts when they arrived at the apartment complex.

Marlena silently found her car keys. With shaking fingers, she pulled her engagement ring off and handed it back to him.

"You keep it. It's yours," he said, his voice sounding strained.

Marlena cringed at the thought of keeping something that would only bring more pain.

"No, thank you, it never really belonged to me," she said, reaching over and dropping it into the ashtray.

"Marly, don't say that," Noah commanded softly.

"My name is Marlena," she corrected before she climbed out of the car, calmly shut the door, and walked steadily towards her car.

He watched as the Jaguar disappeared from sight. This was for the best, he reminded himself. Better now, than later.

Noah traced the outline of the ring. The two hearts interlaced had held a special meaning to him. It represented the marriage covenant. The coming together of two souls, separate but unified; he and Marly becoming husband and wife. The ringing of his cell phone was a welcome interruption. It was Malcolm notifying him that Marly was at Chandra's House alone. Now what was she up to he wondered as he put the ring into his pocket, summoned Beauty, and picked up his car keys. He was well on his way before he realized that she was officially none of his business anymore. Who was he kidding? She'd always be his business.

It was dark by the time he reached Chandra's. He didn't see her car so he assumed she'd parked it in the garage. He decided to use the rear entrance and smiled as Beauty loped ahead, eager to go into the backyard.

Noah quietly eased the door shut and suddenly stopped. He heard a noise coming from the front room. He identified it as weeping, and it tore at his heart. It reminded him of a small wounded animal desperately trying to escape a trap. He rounded the corner and there, huddled on the floor sat Marlena. Her arms were wrapped around her knees, her head tucked. She was simultaneously weeping, moaning, and praying all at the same time. She was asking God to take the pain away and explaining that it was too much and then the weeping would begin again. He stood frozen by the image. It would be permanently etched in his mind. After promising that he'd never hurt her, he'd reduced her to this. Tears filled his eyes as he walked across the room, gathered her to him, and held her. He began rocking her, as a parent tenderly rocks a child. Whispering over and over again how sorry he was and how much he loved her until she finally quieted in his arms. Noah hugged her to him, afraid to let go. He could still feel her mouth moving against his chest in silent prayer. Her vulnerability stirred him in a way that nothing else, other than God's love, ever had. This woman was the bone of his bone, flesh of his flesh, and he suffered her hurt just as surely as if it were his. He began praying for forgiveness. He was guilty of the sin of disbelief. He hadn't truly believed that the Lord was mightier than all the forces that opposed their union. He'd demanded that she make a believer of him instead of exercising faith and standing on what God had already declared to him. Every individual was responsible for their own faith. He had allowed himself to fall victim to doubt and she had paid the price. His tears fell anew on top of her head. He shifted and buried his face in the side of her neck. She was so still that he thought her to be asleep.

He whispered hoarsely, "I'm sorry, Marly."

"Me too," she whispered back.

"Can you ever forgive me?" he pleaded.

"I already have. I love you so much Noah. I didn't mean to hurt your feelings," she sobbed as the tears began afresh.

"Please don't cry. I was wrong. I doubted God and I doubted us. Please Marly, don't cry," he begged as his eyes filled with tears.

He shifted once more and brought his mouth down to hers. He kissed her tenderly and tasted the saltiness of their mingled tears. Her arms slowly crept around his neck as she gently returned his kiss. Noah lifted his mouth and caressed her face.

"Let's go home," he said, getting to his feet and pulling her up behind him.

They rode in silence, having opted to leave her car behind. She didn't say a word when Noah headed towards their log cabin house. He parked in the garage and the two of them walked into the house, fingers entwined. Noah pulled her behind him into the kitchen. He started making sandwiches and smiled to himself when she opened the refrigerator to retrieve the beverages. Dinner was accomplished with very little conversation. They were both tired and in need of some sleep. Noah cleared the dishes and led her down the hall to the master bedroom.

"Do you trust me, Marly?" he asked softly.

She nodded yes, shyly.

He smiled and kicked off his shoes and then invited her to do the same. Pulling her into his arms, he prayed, kissed her on the forehead, and wished her goodnight.

Noah listened as her breathing changed, indicating that she had fallen asleep. He held her tightly in his arms. He needed this closeness. It wasn't lustful or shameful. After what he'd done to her, he wanted her to know that she could trust him. He wanted her to feel safe in his arms and he needed to know that she felt safe. He'd almost made the biggest mistake of his life tonight. He thanked God for giving him a second chance. The image of Marly huddled on the floor in such emotional pain was more than he could bear. He'd done that to her. She'd opened herself to him and he'd pretty much told her it wasn't enough. He asked God to forgive him and to teach him to be a better man. He reached in his pocket and found her ring. Gently, so as not to disturb her, he slid it back on her finger. This was her ring. It could belong to no other. He fell asleep thanking God for His kindness and enduring mercy.

Chapter Twenty-eight

The week of the wedding dawned and Marlena awoke feeling refreshed and excited. She'd thought that she'd be nervous, but she wasn't. Maybe that would come later. She said her morning prayers as she lay there and was soon lost in thought. She and Noah had spent every waking moment together since their short breakup.

Marlena laughed aloud as she recalled Reggie laying flat on his back, holding his nose. Noah and Malcolm had given him a wet cloth and helped him to his feet. She had watched in total amazement as the two men shook hands and Reggie had left. Men were a breed unto themselves. For as long as she would live, she'd never understand them. She relived how angry Noah had been with her. He'd hardly said anything to her until they'd reached the park. She'd known that she'd agreed not to be there without Noah, but she'd gone anyway. One thing had lead to another and they'd split up. She'd gone back to her old home seeking the familiar, but everything had changed. It was no longer her home. She no longer wanted to be there. Her only desire was to be where Noah was, to be his wife and helper. She'd never felt so all alone as then. She remembered praying to God and asking him to help her. Then the tears had started flowing uncontrollably. Somehow, Noah was there, and incredibly, he was the one apologizing. They both had been wrong. They'd gone back to their home and he held her all night. She'd felt cherished, loved, and safe. God had restored them. The next day, they'd prepared the Sunday sermon together. Noah had preached on the failure to believe. He had based it almost completely on the book of John and had taught with such passion and authority that people had been stunned. Many had chosen to rededicate their lives, while others stepped forward to become believers for the first time. No one knew that his sermon was a direct result of what he and Marlena had gone through.

Marlena stretched and rolled out of bed. She had to admit, she was feeling timid about today. Today was the day she had to keep her promise to Noah. He hadn't allowed her to forget it either. He'd awakened her early this morning reminding her of their Thanksgiving covenant. He'd teased her for a full five minutes, laughing huskily, before he'd finally hung up the phone. She glanced at the bedroom clock. Hopefully, Kaod wasn't in the shower. Noah was due there in one hour. She'd definitely be happy to get out of this apartment. She grabbed her things and headed to the bathroom. It looked as though Kaod had already gotten up and was gone. He had a lot on his plate these days. This was his last year of college, and speculation said that he would most likely be selected as a first round draft choice. He had his heart set on playing for the Browns, but he had to get through this last year first.

Noah unlocked the door and was pleasantly surprised to see Marly sitting on the sofa slipping her shoes on. She smiled hello and stood to greet him. She'd worn his favorite pair of jeans (of course she didn't know that). They framed her full hips perfectly, not to tight, but not overly baggy.

"Thank you, God. Saturday was only five days away," he thought as she turned to fetch her purse.

"Focus on something else," he attempted to command his eyes. When she turned and faced him, he grimaced and shook his head. She was wearing his favorite top too. He frowned and forced himself to walk into the kitchen. He opened the refrigerator, pulled out a can of Coke, opened it, and drank it down in seconds.

"What's wrong Phillips? You're acting rather strange, even for you," she teased.

He grabbed her hand and pulled her out of the apartment.

"What happened to my kiss, hello?" she asked pouting.

He stopped, kissed her on the forehead, and said, "Can we leave now?"

She smiled prettily as she realized what the problem was. They'd been together for over a year now, and she'd become familiar with his little moods.

"Are you sure you want to do this today, right now?" she questioned with a knowing smile.

Noah felt his face go warm.

"Noah Stephen Phillips, you're blushing," she stated in complete amazement.

She couldn't recall ever seeing him bashful about anything.

"Oh Yeah, let's go on our little mission. I think that I'm going to enjoy myself a lot more than you will," she said confidently.

"Want to bet," he thought mischievously, watching her walk ahead of him wearing his favorite pair of jeans.

✞

After stopping for breakfast, Noah drove to the Wedding Boutique. Marly looked at him with a question in her eyes. He got out of the car and walked around to her side, opened the door, and helped her out. He put his arm around her waist and escorted her into the exact place where she'd purchased her wedding dress. Immediately, the store manager came to greet them with a genuinely warm smile on her face.

Glancing directly at Noah, she stated in a pleased voice, "The items you requested to view are all over here. I've arranged for the two of you to view them privately."

Now it was Marlena's time to feel her face heat up as Alicia, the boutique manager, led them into a private room. Waiting for them to be seated, she brought out several different styles of nightgowns. Marlena gazed at each gown. They were exquisite. Leave it to Noah to break the mold of the typical male. She had expected the world's version of seduction. The garters, thongs, or something equally provocative, but he hadn't fallen into that trap. Everything that she saw spoke of beauty and sensuality. These were nightgowns that a woman wore for the husband who adored her. Something not meant to simply provoke an arousal, but to establish an intimacy beyond the sex act. These gowns symbolized elegance, loveliness and sensuality verses sex, seduction, and pornography. They were chosen for and worn by the women men loved. She didn't say a word as Noah looked at her, then at each gown. At last, he chose two, one a navy blue for sentimental reasons, and one a rich creamy brown to offset the color of her skin. The navy blue gown was almost floor length with two thigh high slits on each side. It had spaghetti straps and a deep cut bodice. The creamy brown was designed to stop just above the knee. There were small pearl buttons up the sides as well as on the straps. The bodice was modest, but the buttons definitely appeal to the mind of the male. Both gowns were made of a combination of silk and satin and were absolutely beautiful.

Marlena asked Alicia if they had men's nightwear. When she left the room to fetch them, Noah, for the first time, looked at Marly with blatant desire in his eyes. She blushed, but held his gaze.

He said huskily, "Sweetheart, I don't wear pajamas, I sleep in my underwear."

Holding his gaze, she surprised even herself when she asked breathlessly, "Boxers or briefs?"

He leaned in and stopped just short of her lips.

"Which do you prefer?" he whispered.

She swallowed and answered softly, "On you, it doesn't matter."

Before he could kiss her, Alicia came loudly back into the room carrying men's sleep attire. Noah smiled a secret smile with Marly and selected a pair of navy blue lounge pajamas.

Noah grinned as he seated Marly and placed the packages in the trunk of the car. Sliding in the driver's seat he turned to face her and spoke, "Still curious?"

She blushed, and avoided his gaze.

"Okay then, I won't tell you," he teased.

He knew he'd wetted her appetite and she was dying to know. This was going to be the toughest week yet, but he'd decided if he had to suffer, then so should she. The kid gloves were coming off and the flirting would begin. She had five days to learn how to counter. By Saturday, she'd hopefully be a little less bashful with him.

"Guess which gown I'd like you to wear on our wedding night," he said happily.

"Stop teasing me, Noah."

"I'm not," he stated, "I'm being serious. It is my choice, right? Isn't that the promise? If I tried your chitterlings, I could pick out what you'd wear on our wedding night. So guess which gown I'd like you to wear. Really, wear is not a good choice of words. You'll probably only be in it for a couple of minutes, maybe one, two at the max."

"Noah," she gasped.

"Marly," he echoed, amused at her response. "I'm surprised you didn't say, 'Pastor Noah'," he teased mercilessly. "You do remember our little talk about not seeing me as your pastor, don't you?"

"How could I forget?" she mumbled as she listened to him explain it again.

Again, her face felt warm, but this time for different reasons. Her mind began to envision their wedding night. She tried to change the direction of her thoughts, but he seemed to go on and on.

Finally, feeling frustrated, she asked him, "Briefs or boxers?"

Noah imitated her earlier tone, "Sister Marly, stop it."

She reached over and hit him on the arm.

"Ouch! What was that for?" he yelped, pretending that it hurt.

"Boxers or briefs?" she repeated.

✞

The day had come and gone and he still hadn't answered her question. Noah unlocked her apartment door and ushered her in. Kaod was off somewhere with Adam. He'd better give them a call later to check on them. He watched as Marly turned on the lights and put the packages in her room. He glanced at his watch. He was meeting with Jim, Layman, and Hal this evening and he didn't want to be late. He still had plenty of time. He observed her come out of her room and fiddle-faddle around. He frowned and remembered their first date. She'd behaved the exact same way then, but this time he knew she was conscious of her own response. He waited for her to make the first move. He'd long since stopped staying late, it had become too much temptation, but he never left without kissing her goodnight. She walked up to him and laid her head on his chest. He smiled. She often did that for no reason. He liked it. He grabbed her hands and held them firmly. She knew that meant he was going to kiss her, and not on the forehead either. She met his lips halfway. He kissed her arduously and she responded. This time when he nuzzled her neck, she didn't ask him to stop.

He pulled back and whispered, "Both."

It took her a full minute to comprehend that he was answering her question concerning boxers or briefs. Her brown eyes darkened as she looked at him.

"Marly Renee' Porter, get your mind out of the gutter," he teased and roared with laughter when she hid her face in his chest.

He'd guessed her thoughts correctly. She'd been wondering which one he was actually wearing. He hugged her to him, still amused by her embarrassment.

✞

Noah met his three friends at Chandra's House. They were there to discuss the latest charges the District Board intended to question him about. Jim Wade opened up in prayer and soon they were in a lively discussion concerning the board. Layman, although pastoring an independent church, seemed to grasp the totality of the situation.

"Noah, let's face the facts here. They're going to say that you are neglecting the needs of your flock since they've even gone so far as to ask your secretary about your office hours," he stated in a matter of fact voice.

Noah agreed with a nod of his head.

"I'm not worried about that or anything else they could bring up. God is in charge and He'll determine the outcome of all of this." He held up his hands to hold off what he knew his friends would say. "Nevertheless, I am prepared to mount a defense. Valerie has been keeping a strict record of all my work time and whereabouts. This includes street and jail ministries, home and hospital visits, fundraisers, time set apart for preparation of sermons, etc..."

They all began to chuckle. They knew that the average pastor spent way more time ministering than even the board realized. His day was endless. There was always someone in need or some event to attend. People tended to look at their pastor as their own private counselor. They should be able to call on him day or night. The men chatted on, everyone adding valuable insight to the situation.

Hal glanced at Noah and asked candidly, "Have you told Marly what's going on?"

Noah shook his head, no.

Jim glanced at Noah in what was akin to disbelief.

"You still haven't told her? What are you waiting for?"

Layman snorted, "That's a simple question to answer. He's waiting till after the honeymoon." Laughter filled the house. Layman added to the amusement by further declaring, "What man in his right mind waits a whole year for a woman, and just before the getting gets good, tells her something like this? Noah knows Marlena. She'd probably want to do something crazy, like break off the engagement for the good of his career. Women think all crazy like that."

That sent the men into another round of laughter.

Hal looked at the others and said earnestly, "But don't you think she should know beforehand? Give her the choice."

The three looked at him as though he'd lost his mind.

Layman glanced at Noah and Jim and shook his head, "Once again, I say what man in his right mind, emphasis on right, would stop just short of home plate?"

Noah couldn't resist the urge to jump in on the teasing, "Maybe one who hasn't made it to first base yet."

That caused Layman and Jim to double over with laughter. Hal's face turned a bright red. Layman decided to explain to poor Hal why.

"Do you recall the story of Abraham and Sarah? Remember how Sarah came up with that silly idea of Abraham getting with Hagar to produce a son? That emotional little plan backfired on all of us. We are still suffering from that today. Noah knows that God has a bigger plan, but Marly won't be able to see it because the only thing she'll see is her little teddy bear Noah being hurt. She'll naturally think it's because of her and will want to fix the problem. Right, Noah?"

Noah stared at Layman and smiled. He felt extremely relieved that someone else understood. Layman nodded in understanding and turned back to Hal.

"Now let's talk about you and first base."

Noah and Jim howled with laughter as Hal became adamant that he'd reached first base.

Marlena giggled on the phone as Tina retold a humorous story about Josh and church. Josh had actually turned out to be a pretty decent guy, once he'd given up the notion of chasing Marlena. He and Noah would often chat about different things whenever they'd see each other. He had started attending their church and had even been one of those who'd come forward to accept Christ after Noah's passionate sermon on the sin of not believing. He was now suffering from the curse of overzealous females in the church. He'd told Tina that they were as bad as worldly women. Marlena shook her head. There ought to be a difference, but unfortunately there didn't seem to be. They talked for a couple more minutes before hanging up.

Marlena's thoughts went back to Noah. She was experiencing a physical awareness of him that was putting her thoughts into overdrive. He had flirted with her nonstop and that was a first. She had to admit that it was fun. She couldn't recall being this free with Shawn. Kaod had commented on several occasions how different she seemed. They'd always been close, but now, they shared jokes and he'd tell her about the different things that were going on in college. He'd even shared with her that he'd thought about getting back with Mia. Marlena sincerely prayed not, although she'd never tell him that. Mia had been his first real crush. She was light brown with long dark hair and very pretty. She'd seemed to care for Ka', but when he hadn't attempted to sleep with her, she'd kicked him to the curb for Cue. Quasar, or Cue as he was called, had been on the fast track in basketball. He was one of the best players in the state. He was also a "player" with the girls. He'd chased Mia until she'd given in. The result was a baby girl. Cue had gone on to college and eventually the fast life offered more than Mia and their daughter. She'd heard some time ago that he was going to marry some girl he'd met in college. Chandra had been Mia's younger sister and had always vowed to marry Ka'. She'd been a pretty little thing. Marlena smiled as she remembered how Chandra would follow Ka' around and he'd call her his little wife. Mia hadn't had the time for Kaod then and had even made fun of the idea of waiting to get married before being intimate. That had crushed a younger Kaod and he hadn't really shown an interest in any girl since. She prayed that Ka' wouldn't fall for her twice and she prayed for the strength to mind her own business.

Chapter Twenty-nine

Marlena looked at her image in the mirror. Marcella had done an incredible job. The woman looking back at her was beautiful. Her brown eyes looked exotic and full of life. She had the look of a beautiful queen. She glanced over her shoulder at Tina and Marcella. They had the same stunned expression.

"It is you," they laughed.

"What have you done to me?" she smiled.

Marcella looked at her with a quizzical expression on her face. Did she really not know how beautiful she was? All she'd done was to add a little make up here and there. "Honey, it's all you. No amount of makeup could make a woman beautiful if she wasn't already."

Tina smiled before nodding in agreement and saying, "It's almost time to start. Are you ready?"

Marlena nodded a little shakily as Marcella placed a wreath-like crown on her head of shimmering black curls.

Noah took a deep breath, looked in the mirror, opened the door and walked to his place in front of the officiating pastor, who happened to be Layman. He was followed by Hal, the best man. Noah was strikingly handsome as he stood at the altar waiting for his bride. His navy blue suit fit him perfectly while the grey in his shirt and tie beautifully reflected his charcoal grey eyes. His jet black curly hair hung enticingly low around his collar. He'd intentionally left it longer for Marly. He laughed at a joke Layman told and appeared to be completely relaxed, but his eyes remained fixed on the spot where his bride would appear.

Kaod knocked lightly on the door, signaling that it was time. Marcella opened the door and Tina, framed in a navy blue dress, walked gracefully to the entrance of the sanctuary. Kaod's eyes widened as he caught the first glimpse of his mother. She was stunning, he could only stare.

"Mom, you look incredibly beautiful," he said.

She smiled and took his arm.

"Are you ready?" Kaod asked as he led her towards the sanctuary.

She nodded her head.

Kaod grinned, "Here we go then."

Noah watched as Tina walked down the aisle and took her place. The music sounded and Marlena appeared. She was absolutely breathtaking. He had to force himself to wait. They were walking way to slow and she looked ready to bolt. He caught her eyes and willed her to only look at him. He smiled a smile meant only for her and waited.

Marlena heard the music and took a step into the sanctuary. There was a collective hush as all eyes focused on her. Suddenly, she was nervous. Her eyes dropped to the floor and she focused on walking. She hated being the focal point. Kaod must have sensed it as well because he whispered for her to look at Noah. She lifted her eyes and gazed intently at Noah. He was smiling at her. She smiled back and concentrated on him.

He had her complete attention and winked his approval. He knew she was blushing and he couldn't help but grin. She was gorgeous beyond words. Finally, she stood before him and he heard Layman asking who was giving this woman in marriage. Noah vaguely heard Kaod say something or other. He put his arm around her waist and pulled her beside him. Layman, as well as everyone else, laughed as Noah practically cut Kaod off with his instinctive reaction towards Marlena. Kaod grinned, shook his head, and sat down.

Noah didn't take his eyes off of her the entire ceremony. He repeated the vows and listened as she said hers. He slipped the ring on her finger and waited as she slipped his ring on. Finally, he looked at Layman who seemed to be deliberately taking his time in pronouncing them man and wife. Layman grinned at Noah who narrowed his eyes threateningly.

Layman ever so slowly closed his Bible and said the words Noah wanted to hear, "I now pronounce you husband and wife. You may kiss your bride."

Noah pulled her towards him. He knew she was expecting a brief chaste kiss from him, but when his mouth met hers, he changed his mind.

He claimed her mouth in a kiss that had her arms sliding up and around his neck and into his hair. It slowly registered that the guests were clapping and cheering as he reluctantly pulled back. Marly looked dazed, Layman grinned, and Noah appeared relieved as he pulled her to his side and waited for the guests to settle down.

Layman stepped forward and patted Noah on the back. The guests began to laugh and clap again.

Finally, Layman said in a loud clear voice, "Ladies and gentlemen, I present to you, Mr. and Mrs. Noah Stephen Phillips."

The guests stood and applauded as Noah led his bride back down the aisle and waited to greet the guests as they departed the sanctuary.

Noah waited until all the guests had left the sanctuary before he turned to the wedding party and family members and asked if he could have a moment alone with his wife. After the door had shut behind the last person, he faced Marly. They were alone at last. He reached for her hand and brought it to his mouth.

"Your beauty takes my breath away," he said softly.

She smiled and reached up to gently touch his hair at the nape of his neck.

"You are so handsome," she whispered as she played with his hair.

He slowly pulled her close. He touched her shoulders freely before his hands came to rest on her back. He closed his eyes and enjoyed the feel of her fingers in his hair. With a soft moan he kissed her sweetly, savoring the closeness and the touch of his wife's mouth against his. When at last he'd released her mouth, both of their pulses were racing.

"I guess we'd better let them back in," he said ruefully.

She reached up to wipe the evidence of her lipstick away as he grinned and said, "Trust me. They're all well aware of why I wanted some privacy."

He was absolutely right. The moment they returned, the wisecracks and the jokes began. Layman led the charge and soon everyone was enjoying teasing them.

✝

Marly glanced at Noah from beneath her long lashes. He was talking to Kaod. Dinner was ending and she was tiring of the endless picture taking. To her surprise, Mrs. Druessi was at the wedding as well as the reception. Ka' must have invited her. She was glad to see her. Noah walked up behind her and wrapped his long arms around her. He kissed her on the side of the neck and laughed huskily when she chastised him softly. Suddenly, the music stopped and Kaod asked for everyone's attention. He explained that it was tradition that the bride dance with her father, but that tonight he wanted the honor of dancing with his mother. Everyone began clapping. He walked over to Marly and asked Noah for the permission to dance with his wife. Noah smiled and released Marly. Kaod led her to the center of the floor, however, before the music could begin, Jacob, looking dashing in his blue suit, interrupted.

"Sorry, baby brother. As the oldest son, I get to dance with my new stepmother first." He nodded for the music to begin and then took Marly in his arms and began dancing.

Noah could only stare as the guests began clapping in response to Jacob's chivalry.

Marly was as surprised as Noah, but she smiled at Jacob. He didn't say a word, but his actions spoke louder than any words could.

Eventually, he even grinned at her and said, "You even dance well. Is there anything you can't do?"

Marly looked him in the eyes and said with a smile, "I can't swim very well, and your father wouldn't have married me if he'd heard me sing."

He threw back his head and laughed with glee, before kissing her on the cheek and handing her over to Adam. Adam proved to be a very capable dancer. He teased her endlessly about various things then asked in a calm voice if she minded him calling her, Mom.

She smiled and kissed him on the cheek. "You are going to make me cry," she said giving him permission.

The song was over by the time he'd danced her over to Kaod. "Sorry, little brother," he apologized with a grin.

Kaod took his mom's hand and led her to the center of the floor once more. He winked at his mom and waited for their favorite song to come on. Marly hugged her son and laughed when she heard the first notes playing. A husky male voice began singing about the power of love. She used to hum that song to him when he was small or whenever he faced a challenge. She had constantly explained that he needed to believe that the power of God's love, and love for each other could overcome any obstacles that were put in their way. Kaod was reminding her that she and Noah could face any challenge if they remembered that they had love which is the greatest power of them all. They danced so gracefully together that the guests began clapping along with the song. Mrs. Druessi smiled her approval. As the song was ending Kaod hugged his mother for the longest. He knew she was beginning another chapter with Noah; and he, with his career, but they'd always have each other. Still, he was reluctant to let her go. He squeezed her hand and it reminded him of the first day of kindergarten, something new, something frightening. Kaod couldn't explain this sudden fear and sadness that seemed to hold him captive. He slowly slid his hand from hers and placed it in Noah's as he approached the two of them.

Marly went to walk off of the floor, but Noah stopped her. "You have one more partner left. Dance with me, Mrs. Phillips?"

She nodded at Noah through tears. She was leaving her son behind. She was all he had.

"You're not losing him, sweetheart. He'll always be your son. Will you dance with me, Cinderella?"

She nodded and went into his arms. When she heard the music, Marly's eyes opened wide and she glanced at Kaod who smiled through his own tears and blew her a kiss. This was her most favorite song in the world. She'd always told Kaod that she'd only dance to it with a man who truly believed its meaning. She wanted to comfort her son. She needed him to know that she wasn't abandoning him, but Noah held her firm. He pulled her close and began dancing.

"Look at me Marly," he commanded gently as the tears flowed down her face. "Those words describe exactly how I feel."

The song spoke of a man vowing to love only his partner and being faithful to her alone. She smiled and began following his lead. They made a dazzling couple, a king dancing with his new queen. No one doubted their love. It could clearly be seen by all.

"Keep up with me, Mrs. Phillips," he whispered as the chorus approached.

She laughed delightedly as he spun her around and then brought her back close to him. He slid his hands up her arms, and then guided her arms around his neck. He placed his hands on her waist and instructed her with his hands to keep rhythm with him. When he dipped, she dipped along with him. All the while, their eyes never left each other. They were oblivious to the onlookers. This song was now their song. The words were now his words. They moved as one, as though they'd danced all their lives together. Wives began looking at their husbands, while the husbands pretended not to notice. Their song slowly ended to the loud applause of the guests. Noah lovingly escorted her off the floor and held tightly to her hand. He'd spotted Kaod heading outdoors. He knew his youngest son was crying and probably didn't want his mother to see him in that state. God was severing one bond while solidifying another. No longer would people say Marlena and Kaod, but Noah and Marly. He watched as she tried to locate her son. For years, those two only had each other, but today that had changed and neither one of them had really been prepared. Noah caught Tina's eye and motioned for her.

"Keep company with Tina, Marly. I'll be right back," he commanded gently as he headed outdoors after Kaod.

Noah found him under a tree. Tears were flowing down his cheeks. The big strong football player now appeared a fragile boy.

"How's it going son?" Noah asked gently.

Kaod attempted to wipe his tears away, but they kept flowing.

Noah tried to reassure him, "I promise to love only your mother for the rest of my life and to take care of her always. Our home is now your home. She'll always be your mother."

Kaod looked away and spoke, "I guess I wasn't as prepared as I thought I was. It's always been Mom and me against the world. I tried to stay away so that we'd get used to it not being just me and her. I know that I probably look like a big punk, but she's what I care about most, why I've worked so hard. She gave up so much for me. I know it's your job to take care of her now, but it's still something I want to do."

"You're the last guy I'd call a punk. I understand how you feel. My mom and dad were taken from me way too soon. Our bond was severed in an instant. I never had the chance to take care of them or to have them see me as an adult. I've always wondered if they would be proud of me. You know, I've never really stopped missing them. Kaod, staying away from your mom, I think it had the opposite effect. She missed you and you've missed her and the both of you are making me think I'm going to have to invite you on our honeymoon," he joked.

Kaod laughed in response. "I'm going to miss her. We talk every day," Kaod informed him.

"The fact that she's now my wife isn't going to change that. You can still call her every day."

Kaod smiled, "I think I'd better wait until you get off your honeymoon."

Noah chuckled, "Come back in and talk to your mom. I think she needs you as much as you need her right now."

Tina was doing her best to convince Marly that everything was going to be alright. She hoped Noah hadn't underestimated the bond Marly had with her son. She knew her friend well enough to know that Marly couldn't take it if she thought that Kaod was feeling abandoned. Tina smiled gratefully when Noah returned with Kaod in tow.

Marly hugged her son to her. Kaod grinned feeling reassured that he hadn't lost his mom. Noah and Tina walked away to give them some privacy.

"I'm going to miss you Ka'. It's always been you and me for so long. You do know that you have a room at the house and a key waiting on you?" she declared.

He suddenly felt happy again.

"You fixed me up a room?"

"Of course, where else are you going to stay? That apartment was only temporary for us. Our house is all ready. Noah and I fixed up your room. We figured that you'd stay at the apartment only until we returned from the honeymoon. You are planning on staying with us right?"

Kaod hid his relief.

"Sure Mom," he replied as he hugged her tightly.

✣

Noah held Marly's hand as they cut the cake and shared their piece. He'd been watching her like a hawk. She and Kaod seemed to have overcome their separation anxiety. He was behaving more like the mature football player. He wondered if that's how Adam and Jacob had felt when their mother had died. He could see now that both of them were still in need of a mother figure. Jacob had approached Marly several times with a sincere smile on his face, while Adam had hardly left her side. Kaod, he noticed, watched over his mother from a distance. He pretended not to be paying attention, but he was aware of everything. Noah looked around and sure enough, Kaod was talking to Layman, but was observing his mother at the same time. Once again, Noah felt sorry for the girl who aspired to become Mrs. Kaod Porter. She'd have to be a Marly clone.

At last it was time for Marly and him to depart. Marcella called the guests together and cheered happily as her single daughter caught the bride's bouquet. Noah stood beside his wife and waited while friends and family wished them well.

He laughed aloud when Layman stated, "That's right Noah. You do all that fancy smancy dancing and then leave us simple men here with wives who expect us to duplicate it. That's all we men folk are going to hear all night long is how come you don't dance like Noah. Boy, I'll tell anybody if they ask that you got some black in you somewhere. I ain't never seen a for real white boy dance like that. No wonder she agreed to marry you, you ain't really white…"

They could still hear Layman fussing as he walked back into the banquet hall. Noah couldn't stop laughing as he and Marly hugged their sons and Kara goodbye.

At long last, they were finally alone, save the limo driver who discreetly rolled up the darkly shaded partition window. The sleek black limo drove slowly toward their home. Noah pulled his wife close. He tilted her head back and looked deep into her eyes. Finally, he kissed her. He took his time and explored her mouth with his. He wanted no shame between them. Slowly, he reluctantly lifted his mouth from hers.

"I've been waiting to do that for hours," he confessed honestly.

She smiled shyly, thinking about the night ahead. Her body was responding to him in an unfamiliar fashion, yet she was still apprehensive about what was to come. Noah saw the uncertainty in her eyes and silently prayed for God to be with them.

☦

Noah dropped the keys on the kitchen table and glanced at Marly. She looked nervous. He laced his fingers through hers and walked towards the master bedroom. Stopping at the door, he began to pray with her. He asked God to be with them and to bless them as they consummated their marriage. He prayed for God to put a protective hedge around their marriage bed which would allow them to have pleasure in each other and to keep their marriage bed pure and undefiled from the world. He thanked God for giving them the strength to abstain until their wedding night and then opened up the door and gave her a gentle push inside.

"I'm going upstairs to shower and change. You can have the bathroom all to yourself tonight."

Marly felt a rush of relief as he turned and walked down the hallway. She walked into the bathroom and couldn't believe her eyes. There were flowers everywhere. The blue nightgown was hanging on the door and a note was taped to the mirror. It read, "Trust God. I love you, your husband". She smiled and turned on the shower.

Noah was in and out of the shower in no time. He felt calm. He was trusting God to work things out. He reminded himself to take it slow with her. She was, in his mind, still a virgin. He was sure that she hadn't ever known a woman's pleasure. "Please God, let her respond to me. I don't want to receive pleasure unless we experience it together."

He slipped on his new lounging pants and walked with sure steps to their bedroom. He eased the door open and walked in. He didn't hear the shower going so he assumed she was almost through. He dimmed the lights and waited with anticipation for his bride to appear.

Marly fingered the silky nightgown. It made her feel beautifully loved.

"Dear God, please allow me to be pleasing to him. I'm not a child, I know what takes place between a husband and wife, but I am nervous about it. Be with us tonight, Lord," she prayed.

Taking a deep breath, she turned off the bathroom light and stepped into their bedroom. She walked slowly towards her husband.

Noah sucked in his breath at the sight of her. He stood to his feet and watched as she walked to stand before him.

"You are so beautiful Marly"

She blushed and said, "You're wearing pajamas."

"Only for my shy wife," he admitted as he ran his hands up and down her bare arms.

She reached out and shyly touched his chest. She laid her hand where his heart beat and smiled when she felt it racing as fast as hers.

He somehow knew her fear. "You already please me so much Cinderella," he said, holding her hand against his chest.

His use of that particular nickname broke through all remaining barriers. She stepped into his arms and felt them tighten around her...

Hours later, Noah thanked God as he watched his wife sleeping contentedly in his arms. He fingered the chain with the tiny golden key faithfully around her neck. He knew she never took it off. She was so beautiful and intoxicatingly sensual. This must be what the original Adam felt like with his Eve. She completed him and made him happy. He'd never experienced such pleasure in all his fifty years. She was so responsive to him that it left him utterly speechless. God had graciously answered his prayers and then some. They'd made exquisite love throughout the night. Each time, he'd discovered something new about her, a secret spot that had sent her over the edge with him quickly following. He couldn't get over the feel of her soft creamy brown skin. It was so smooth and silky to his touch. She was soft where he was hard muscle. He loved the way she softly called out his name and the feel of her hands in his hair. She was all woman and all his. He knew it was foolish, but he wanted to wake her up just to tell her how much he loved her. He smiled with delight as he remembered the expression of wonder on her face the first time she'd experienced pleasure. Afterwards she'd smiled with such joy that he couldn't help but smile right back. They had giggled like children discovering a secret that only the two of them knew about. She was his treasure and he was hers. He yawned and glanced at the clock. They had a couple hours before sunrise. He reached down and pulled the comforter around them. He kissed the top of her head and pulled her tight against him. God is so good was his last thought as he finally drifted off to sleep.

Marly awakened slowly. Her head lay nestled on Noah's muscular chest. She looked down at her hand where the simple golden band now proclaimed to the world her marital status. She was now Marlena Phillips. She blushed when she recalled last night's events. Noah had been so tender and loving. She felt her face go even warmer when she remembered the pleasure he had given her. She smiled and had to force back a girlish giggle. She'd never known anything like it. He'd made love with her until she'd fallen asleep exhausted. She wanted to stretch, but she was afraid she'd awaken him. Slowly, she lifted her head and blushed when she realized he was already awake.

"Good morning sleepyhead," he whispered huskily. "I thought I was going to have to wait all day for you to wake up."

"Good morning," she whispered back shyly.

Noah shifted her to where her face was eyelevel with his. He ran his hands up and down her back and asked, "What would you like to do today?"

She tried to keep her mind off his hands rubbing her bare back. "What do you mean?" she squeaked out breathlessly.

Noah grinned impishly. He knew what she was thinking. He quickly reversed their positions and gazed down at her. "I mean what would you like to do, after we make love?"

"Oh," was all she could manage just before his lips claimed hers.

Chapter Thirty

One full week had passed since their marriage and Noah and Marly still hadn't left their home. They had opted to honeymoon at the log cabin, and hadn't revealed to anyone where they were. They'd just enjoyed a picnic lunch under the willow tree in their backyard. Noah sat with his back resting against the tree. He had his arms wrapped lovingly around Marly's waist and his chin resting on her head as she sat comfortably in front of him. He closed his eyes and smiled at recent memories. She was insatiable and he was enjoying every minute of it. It was difficult for him to remember her as the woman who was afraid of intimacy, who doubted her own ability to please him. He's never been so pleased in all his life. She was still as quirky as ever though. He couldn't understand how she could make love with him without inhibitions, but then turn around and ask him to close his eyes so he wouldn't see her naked. He'd tried explaining that he'd seen every inch of her body; however, all she'd say blushingly was, "but that's different". He was determined to break that quirky habit and in a hurry.

Noah kissed the top of her forehead and asked, "Would you like to venture out this evening? I thought we'd go to Sophia's."

"Sure, why not. I think you could use a break," she giggled.

Noah smiled and said, "I'm not the one who falls asleep immediately afterwards, but that's not why I want to take you out. I have a surprise for you."

Marly giggled again.

Noah knew exactly what she was thinking. "Not that kind of surprise you little tease. A gift, you know the kind you open."

He could tell that she was now curious as she tilted her head back to look at him.

"What is it?" she questioned.

He chuckled softly, "Now, it wouldn't be a surprise if I told you, would it?"

"Will you give me a hint?" she begged.

"No," he laughed.

"Noah Phillips, you just want me to wonder about this the whole day. Why tell me? You could have waited until we were at Sophia's," she protested.

He changed the subject.

"When are you going to call Kaod?"

She glanced at him and asked timidly, "You don't mind if I call him?"

"No, I'm pretty worn out. It'll at least give me a couple minutes rest," he teased laughingly. He took out his cell phone and handed it to her as she kissed him on the cheek.

Marly quickly dialed Kaod's number. Noah sat back and closed his eyes. He figured Kaod wouldn't have a moments rest until he heard from his mom, and although she hadn't said a word, he understood that this was the first time that either one of them had gone this long without some form of communication. He smiled as she explained that everything was fine. Eventually, he asked to speak with Noah and she passed the phone to him. He talked with Kaod for several minutes before hanging up.

Noah gently turned Marly to face him and asked curiously, "Was Kaod aware of things between Shawn and you?"

"What do you mean?" she wondered.

"I mean, he sounded pretty relieved to know that you were okay. What did he think was going to happen?" Noah questioned.

She shrugged her shoulders. "To my knowledge, he doesn't know any of the details," she answered.

Noah was beginning to think that kid knew more than he let on. That would explain why he was so protective of his mom. He'd thanked Noah because his mom was okay? That didn't add up. Noah recalled his statement about Marly having cried enough tears over his father. He was going to have a talk with Kaod the next time he saw him. He tried to recall Kaod's face at the wedding. Had that been fear? He was definitely going to find out. He looked at Marly, who was looking at him strangely.

"Is there something wrong?" she asked.

He bent down and kissed her on the cheek, "Everything is perfect."

✠

Marly sat in the booth across from him looking beautiful. They hadn't dressed up, but she had a radiance to her that couldn't be denied. Dinner had been fantastic as usual and he knew that she was waiting to open the gift that he had deliberately placed on the seat next to her purse.

"Are you going to open your gift or not?" he asked with a smile.

She tore open the package and looked at him curiously.

"It's a children's book," she exclaimed with a puzzled expression on her face.

Noah grinned, "Maybe you should open it up and read it."

She began reading, "This is a story about a little African-American boy named Doak. Doak's daddy had died and he was very sad. Then one day, his mommy fell in love with a man, but the man didn't look like them."

Marly stopped and looked at the cover of the book and then at the dedication on the inside. The dedication read, "To my lovely new bride and my new stepson".

Her big eyes widened in surprised delight as she hugged the book close and gasped, "Doak is Kaod spelled backwards. You're Noah Flood!"

Noah nodded yes, and grinned sheepishly as he moved to her side of the booth.

Completely overcome with emotion, she threw her arms around his neck and kissed him thoroughly, oblivious to all. When she finally pulled back she whispered, with shimmering eyes, "I have every book you've ever written. I've read them to my babies at school. This is the best present I've ever received!"

He chuckled softly, "Better than the painted hands and the diamond bracelet?"

"Way better," she cried softly, as she clutched the book to her.

"You're the only one, besides my attorney, who knows that I'm Noah Flood," he informed her.

"What made you start writing children's books and why do you use a pen name?" she questioned.

"I use a pen name because I don't want to be known. I enjoy my privacy."

He sat back and explained how he'd felt after Colleen's death. The need to express himself came out in the form of children's books. He felt like children could understand far better than the adults. He told her about how the children would all come up to him and ask him if he was sad or give him a picture they'd drawn to make him feel better. One little girl in his congregation had explained that she'd told her mommy that Pastor Noah didn't need another wife, he just needed to know that Jesus still loved him. Things like that caused him to go back and look at the way Jesus had responded to the children. He'd put them first and even declared that the kingdom of heaven was made up of those who came to him as children. Not childish, but open to believe that He was who He'd declared himself to be. He wants us to come to him with an open mind, as a child believes what his or her parents say, ready to accept His Word and believe.

"That's why I began writing for children. If we could give them an understanding of Christ at a young age, then maybe they'd be less likely to fall for worldly teachings that dismiss Christianity as made up fables when they're older," Noah spoke earnestly.

Marly hugged him to her.

"I'm so proud of you, Noah. I couldn't be blessed anymore than I am right now. You're incredible. Do you know that?"

He smiled at her compliment and returned her hug.

✟

The Phillipses arrived at their church early as usual. Today was officially the last day of their honeymoon, but it also marked the day of the annual contest with Jim Wade's church. Noah knew that his Assistant Pastor would be preaching today so he would be able to sit with his wife during the service. He'd been told in advance that several families had left because of his marriage to Marly. He also was aware of the fact that a petition had been circulated by those families in an attempt to remove him as pastor. He looked around the parking lot and smiled when he saw Kaod's car. Adam had probably ridden with him. He'd arranged, ahead of time, to have a family dinner after church. He wanted to inform them, himself, of the events that were taking place. Noah needed them to understand everything that could occur in the future. He didn't want his family to be caught blindsided by the mean-spiritedness of others. He had already prepared himself for Marly's reaction. She was sure to blame herself. He reminded himself that God was in control and he prayed that eventually she'd remember that. He took his wife's hand and led her towards the entrance of the sanctuary.

Just before entering he turned and brushed a quick kiss on her forehead and asked, "Have I told you how much I love you, today?"

She smiled and straightened his tie, "Yes, you have, but you can tell me again if you like."

"How about I show you later?" he flirted as he opened the door and escorted her in.

Instantly, they were greeted by Adam and Kaod and by the look on their faces, they'd already discovered something was wrong. Kaod began hovering protectively around his mother as though she were in mortal danger. Noah looked around at the congregation. For the most part, they all seemed very happy to see them. He glanced at his deacons. With the exception of two, all were present and nodding their allegiance. He acknowledged them with nods of his own. "Ten out twelve wasn't bad," he thought as he and Marly, along with their two sons headed towards the front row.

The message was appropriate and fit their circumstances. Assistant Pastor Grady Peterson spoke on loving your neighbor as yourself. He told how it was the second greatest commandment Jesus had given and of how each one of them should be ashamed that Jesus had to give it as a commandment. He explained how God knew what was in the hearts of every person there. He asked everyone to look around the sanctuary and if they saw a fellow believer that they couldn't love then sin, instead of love, filled their hearts.

Marly was conscious of Noah's hand tightening around her shoulders. She looked up at him and saw reflected in his eyes a love for his congregation. She knew that it didn't matter to him that some may dislike the fact that he was white and she was black and they were now husband and wife. That wouldn't stop him from loving them. They were his sheep and he their shepherd, and he would do his best to teach and guide them. He would continue to show them love just as Christ had been unending in His love for him. She knew God's love, in the form of Christ, was the greatest gift that He had given the world. It wasn't just love for a spouse or child, but an all-consuming love for his children. Her spirit discerned that her husband understood that his congregation needed to be shown this type of love and he was willing for God to demonstrate it through him. His eyes were asking her if she would be his helpmate even to those who did not love her. She reached for her pen and wrote the word "always".

Marly saw the moisture that clouded his eyes and understood that her simple word, written in the margin of her Bible, had significantly lightened the tremendous burden that he'd been carrying on his shoulders during the past years. Noah now had someone with whom to share it. He was no longer a solo traveler on a lonely road. He had her to walk along beside him, to share the ups and downs of life's challenges. She reached for his hand, proud that he had chosen her to be his wife.

✚

Noah settled the restaurant bill and looked at each member of his family. Marly, by now had caught on that something was wrong. He began explaining what was happening and why. He further detailed events he felt were sure to follow.

Marly was the first to speak, "Noah, are you telling me that some of your members want to remove you because you married me?"

He grabbed her hand and held it tightly. "Sweetheart, you already knew that there were those that opposed us. Does it surprise you that those same people would want me removed?"

Kaod stared at his mother and then turned to Noah and asked, "What are you planning to do?"

Noah was well aware of what Kaod was asking. He wanted to know what was more important, his mother or Noah's congregation. Noah kissed his wife's hand.

"It's not my church, it belongs to Christ. It's His responsibility to take care of it. My responsibility is to love the wife he gave me as He loves the church which is to someday be his bride. What do you think that Jesus would do Kaod?" Noah asked affectionately.

For the first time that day, Kaod smiled and then answered, "He would love his bride."

Noah grinned, "That's precisely what I intend to do. Our honeymoon was way too short anyway."

They all laughed as Marly blushed and shushed her husband.

"So Dad, are you and Marly going to participate in the games this afternoon?" Adam asked with a grin.

Noah looked at Marly and said emphatically, "Wild horses couldn't keep us away."

✚

Marly looked around the crowded gym and glanced at Noah. "There seems to be more people here than last year," she observed.

"Getting a little nervous Phillips? Don't worry, I'll be by your side if you need me," he teased.

She sat down beside him and groaned to herself. Levi Jamison was here and it looked as though he was playing on the other side. She wondered

255

if he was any good. She spotted Caroline talking to Pastor Wade and his wife. Suddenly the crowd seemed to come alive. She smiled when she realized why. Kaod and Adam had walked through the door. Marlena watched as the young ladies vied for their attention. Adam introduced him to several male friends, and all but ignored the females much to their disappointment.

Noah kissed her on the cheek and headed down to speak with Jim Wade.

"Great, leave me with the wolves, why don't you," she mumbled to herself.

She watched as he greeted Jim with great affection. Jim must have asked where she was because Noah turned and waved. She smiled and waved back.

"I hope you're playing today," a friendly voice said from just behind her.

Marly shifted and looked. Levi Jamison sat smiling engagingly at her. She couldn't help but smile back. He wasn't flirting with her. She had become very mindful of giving Noah any reason to relive past hurts. She shifted back and looked straight into the eyes of her husband and he looked furious.

"Darn, darn, triple darn," she murmured to herself. How could he be angry? He'd left her up here alone. So he could just turn that burning gaze back on himself. What did he expect her to do? Be impolite and not speak. That was positively asinine. She had nothing to do with that little episode between him, Colleen, and Levi.

"So are you playing today?" Levi persisted, interrupting her train of thought.

Marly pretended not to hear. Was this guy stupid? Could he not see the blazing wildfire in Noah's eyes? Was he a glutton for her punishment? She could still feel the heat. She peeped from under her lashes and sure enough, Noah, without a word was unmistakably, not asking, but commanding her to come here and his gaze had not left her face.

"Darn, darn, darn," she thought again as she stood and grabbed her bag. "Sorry, no fraternizing with the enemy," she threw over her shoulder at Levi as she made her way towards Noah.

That caused Levi to let out a hoot of laughter which in return made Noah even more incensed.

"Great, Marlena, why didn't you keep your big mouth shut?" she chastised herself as she watched Noah's eyes narrow even further.

It was mean, but she wished Reggie was there so Noah could take it out on him by giving him another punch in the nose. A silly giggle escaped out of her mouth at the mental image that formed in her mind. Noah, she could tell by the glint in his eyes, evidently didn't find anything amusing about what he thought he'd just witnessed.

Noah gritted his teeth to keep from saying anything. Hadn't he told her not to be too friendly with Levi and why? He'd turned his back for a hot second and what was she doing, cavorting with prettyboy. He'd only left her up there just in case Jim had wanted to speak privately with him. He forced himself to remember rule number one. She'd better be praying that he'd calmed down by the time they reached home. He glanced at her face as she made her way toward him. He'd heard that little giggle. What was so funny? He guided her down to their side of the bleachers and up a couple of rows. He smiled politely as people continued to congratulate them on their marriage. He hoped she remembered that she was now a Phillips not a Porter. He could sense her attempting to judge his mood. She wanted to know his mood. He turned and looked directly at her. He was riled up. He felt somewhat satisfied when she quickly glanced away.

✟

Noah, Marly, and Kaod cheered Adam's team on to victory. As with last year, Pastor Wade's younger team was unable to compete and lost handily. Marly gave Adam a victory hug and smiled as Kaod teased him about his lack of game. Those two actually behaved like biological brothers she thought. She chanced another glance at Noah who was looking at her. He wasn't smiling, but he wasn't scowling either. She took a chance and smiled hesitantly at him.

He leaned over and whispered in her ear, "You and I, Mrs. Phillips, are going to have a little chat when we get home."

To everyone present, it appeared as though Noah was being intimate, but Marly could tell by his tone that he was not feeling the least bit romantic.

✟

Noah looked over his players. He had five strong players this year, but so did the opposing team. This was going to be a difficult match. He watched Marly warm up and admitted to himself that his anger was due to jealousy. This was so unlike him. Typically, it had been the other way around. Colleen had not taken well to other females. She'd barely tolerated him speaking, let alone holding a conversation with other women. He hadn't minded because it kept the drama away. "Trust you wife," he said to himself.

He looked up in the stands and smiled as little five-year-old Stephen called out her name. She turned and walked towards him smiling. Noah shook his head, laughing in disbelief as Stephen kissed her on the cheek. What was it with this woman? Even little boys were falling for her. He caught her attention and smiled, letting her know that he was no longer upset. She returned his smile happily.

✟

Noah observed Marly's face. She wore a blank expression, but her stance indicated that she was now in the zone. The referee had called three serves in bounds, for the other team, that had been clearly out of bounds. He listened to his congregation boo their disapproval. He'd thought about calling a timeout, but it was the first game and they were down by only three points. Besides, she didn't seem in the least bit rattled. He hoped the referee was actually blind, not prejudiced. He saw Kaod smile and immediately knew that Marly was on her game. She had put her bright pink shoe on the line, clearly indicating to the referee where the line was. Noah smiled too. She was banking on Caroline serving it to the wide open space she'd created to cover the line. He heard the whistle blow and saw the ball fly over the net. Marly had played her cards perfectly. He grinned as she slid and dug the ball high and to the front. His grin broadened when he heard a loud voice yell, "Way to go, Mom." He knew that voice and it wasn't Kaod's, it was Adam's.

The game continued and soon Noah's team was up by two with Hal serving the game point. He wasn't quite sure what happened, but the next thing he saw was Marly on the ground holding her knee. Levi was bending over her and Caroline was smirking. Noah rushed to her side and demanded to know what happened. Levi stared at Caroline while Marly explained that she and Caroline had collided at the net. Noah wasn't buying it for one second. From the look on Caroline's face, this was no accident. He carefully examined Marly's leg.

"Noah, I'm fine. It's just a stinger. Stop making a fuss," she exclaimed blushing.

"I need to make sure you're okay," he said flirtatiously. "Come on, sweetheart. Let me enjoy myself for a moment. It's not every day a man can get away with feeling his wife's leg in public," he admitted, enjoying her blush.

Marly felt her face grow warmer as players from each side began to chuckle. He grabbed her by the hand and effortlessly pulled her to her feet, to the applause of everyone. Noah walked her over to the bench and motioned for her to take a seat. He waited for the explosion, but it never came. She sat down without saying a word. He was proud of her. Noah was certain he saw Caroline's smug smile as he returned to his side.

Noah rotated an extra player off the bench and stated, "All right guys, let's play volleyball."

Hal glanced sharply at Noah. He knew what that tone meant. He gave Noah a half smile and set his stance.

From that point on, Noah took over the game. Hal would set and Noah would slam it home. He was making a statement to everyone concerning his wife. She was not to be trifled with. After scoring eight straight unanswered points, Noah called time to rotate players. Marly had been enjoying watching him play when she heard him call for Phillips to come in the game. She suddenly realized that he was referring to her. She stood to her feet and made her way to their side of the net. He'd called her that on purpose and she knew it. Once again he was placing his mantle around her.

"Show off," she whispered as she walked past him to take her position on the floor.

He grinned and said, "Only for you."

Fifteen minutes later, the match was over and once again, Pastor Wade's team would have to host the end of the summer picnic.

With his arm protectively around his wife, Noah watched as Levi Jamison approached them. Levi complimented Marly on how well she played and then asked to speak with Noah in private. Noah smiled as Kaod appeared at his mother's side.

"That kid doesn't miss a beat," he thought as he walked away with Levi.

Noah listened with humbleness, as Levi apologized and asked for forgiveness for having an adulterous relationship with Colleen. He offered no excuses, and Noah could respect him for that at least. Noah understood that he had two choices. He could either keep Levi in the bondage of guilt and shame, or he could forgive him and set him free. Funny, how the thought of him and Colleen didn't bother him anymore. God had given him a new life with Marly. He was a new man. He had been set free from the shackles of bitterness and unforgiveness. The least he could do was to return the favor to Levi. He stared at Levi and then with a sincere smile, grasped his hand and forgave him. Pastor Noah knew it was God's will when Levi Jamison thanked him with tears streaming down his face. Noah hoped it was sincere, but that was between Levi and God. He'd done his part and his conscience was clear.

Marly glanced in the mirror at her reflection. She hadn't exactly been honest with Noah concerning her and Caroline's collision at the net. Caroline had deliberately kicked her in the knee. That woman had some serious issues. She said a quick prayer for patience, but it was getting harder. She sincerely hoped Caroline wasn't some kind of serial basket case. She giggled as she imagined Caroline squatting behind bushes with a ski mask on. Marly walked out of the bathroom and headed across the gym floor to grab her sports bag. She noticed a folded up piece of paper with her name on. She looked around wondering who placed it there. Curiously, she unfolded the paper and began reading. She sighed in exasperation and crumbled the paper in her hand.

"A note from a secret admirer," Noah teased from behind her.

"Hardly," she said, handing the note to him.

He uncrumbled it and began reading. He frowned and stuck the note in his pocket. "Let's go," he said, taking her bag and escorting her outside.

Noah started the car up and shifted in his seat to look at Marly. "You don't believe that do you sweetheart? You can't think that you're the reason some people are leaving."

"Let's not pretend that it's not true. I am the reason why the church is losing members. We've only been married for two weeks, and your ministry is already starting to suffer. It's not too late, we could get an annulment," she suggested in a flat voice.

He dismissed what she'd said without commenting and calmly drove out of the parking lot in the direction of their home. She couldn't be serious, he thought. That was exactly why he hadn't said a word to her concerning the board's actions. He'd known she'd become emotional about it. "Lord, please give me something to say to her; something that will give her a sense of peace," he pleaded silently as he drove along.

Twenty minutes later, he pulled into their spacious two-car garage. He opened her door and grabbed the bags out of the trunk.

Marly unlocked the door and headed to their bedroom where she sat tiredly on the bed.

Noah walked past her and into the bathroom. He sat on the side of the tub and started her bathwater. "How's your knee?" he called out.

"My knee is fine. Did you hear what I said in the car? We can still get an annulment," she repeated.

Again he chose not to answer. "Lord, help me here. I don't know what to say to her. Give me the words," he prayed fervently. He hoped the Lord would give him a word soon because she was beginning to irritate him with her emotional nonsense.

"Marly, whoever wrote that note was trying very hard to make trouble between us. Clearly, you can see that, right?" he asked as he poured bubble bath into the water. When she didn't respond, he walked out, sat on the bed beside her, and placed his hand over hers. "Those who have left our congregation have done so because of their own prejudices, not because of you. We have to have faith in God and believe that he has brought us together for a reason. It's not our job to work out solutions that may, ultimately, interfere with God's plan. We have to keep in mind that when they reject the church, they are rejecting Christ, not you or me. They'll eventually have to settle up with Christ, not us," he explained gently.

She was lying on the bed with her eyes closed. "Who would want to destroy us so badly that they'd write something like that?" She paused for a moment and then said, "I love you, Noah and I'm sorry for making that ridiculous comment about an annulment. I guess I'd rather be hurt than to be the cause of you getting hurt."

"That's noble of you, Marly, but I do the protecting in this marriage, okay? Now come on before you fall asleep. Your bath is probably ready," he informed her as he pulled her up and off the bed.

"You're the best husband in the world," she proclaimed sleepily.

"Don't forget that when I leave the toilet seat up," he chuckled merrily.

Chapter Thirty-one

It wasn't easy to shock Layman McGhee, but Noah was sure he had just accomplished the impossible. Layman was staring at him in such a stupefied manner that Noah couldn't help but grin.

"You think what?" Layman asked, not sure that he'd heard Noah correctly.

"I said, 'I think Marly is carrying our child'," Noah reiterated slowly.

Layman repeated, more to himself than Noah, what he thought he'd heard his friend say, "You think that your wife is pregnant."

"Yes, that's what I said," Noah confirmed with a laugh.

Layman sat down to overcome the shock. He started laughing. It began as a low rumble, but soon filled the room. "You sure don't waste any time, do you? Y'all been married what, a little over two months, and you think she's having a baby?"

Noah sat down also. He was still trying to absorb this information himself. He remembered from his sons' births, the changes that occurred in a woman's body, and Marly's body was definitely changing. He was sure that she was pregnant; although, it might not have registered with her yet. This was the surprise of the century. He was fifty years old and she'd just turned forty-four and they were having a baby. He was absolutely thrilled and feeling a bit puffed up. He was fifty, and going to be a new father. He wondered how she'd feel about being pregnant so late in life, and how their sons would take the news.

He peered at Layman who was still smiling and probed, "What do you think?"

Layman laughed, "I think you and Marly are going to make terrific parents. You're still young enough to enjoy being a father, but old enough to know how to be one. Remember Abraham was one hundred and Sarah was ninety when they had Isaac. That makes you guys youngsters compared to them."

Layman stopped and pondered his thoughts for a moment before saying, "Have you given any thought that this may be God's way of unifying your family? Jacob and Adam will now have a blood brother or sister that is half black and vice versa for Kaod. This baby could be what truly brings your family closer together."

"Sister," Noah absentmindedly corrected.

"What?" Layman asked.

"Sister, this baby is going to be a girl," Noah stated firmly.

Layman chuckled and declared, "I don't doubt it for a second."

✝

Marly could not figure out why she'd been so tired and queasy lately. She hadn't done anything strenuous or overly taxing and she wasn't getting up any earlier than usual. She picked up the phone and dialed her physician's office.

✝

Marly pulled into the vacant spot beside Noah's car. He was expecting her for lunch, but she now had a doctor's appointment. She'd decided to stop in on the way there to tell him in person.

Noah watched as Marly walked into the building. He glanced at the clock. She was thirty minutes early. He stood and greeted her at the door with a little longer than usual kiss. She blushed in surprise and looked at Valerie who was pretending not to notice. Noah couldn't help himself. He was supremely happy with the possibility of her carrying his child.

"What brings you here so early?" he questioned, pulling her into his office and sliding his arms around her waist.

"You're on your own for lunch today. I have an appointment with my physician in twenty-five minutes," she explained, looking at her watch.

"Why are you going to the doctor? Aren't you feeling well?" he asked, being careful to keep a blank expression on his face.

She explained the problem and told him not to be concerned. "I probably have a minor bug or something," she rationalized.

Noah grabbed his car keys, instructed Valerie on where he'd be, and escorted Marly out the door.

"You don't have to go with me," she protested.

"It's okay. I want to come. Besides, I don't have anything scheduled for this afternoon," he said as he ushered her into the car. He was absolutely positively sure that she was pregnant now and he wanted to be there when she got the news.

✠

Marly sat in the examination room waiting for the results of the specimen she'd given. When Dr. Thompson came in, she looked at Marly strangely and asked if her husband had accompanied her.

"Yes, he's out in the waiting room. Is there something wrong?" Marly asked with obvious concern in her voice.

"No, I'd just prefer to have him present in this instance," she replied, exiting the room.

Marly could hear her instructing the nurse to have Mr. Phillips come to his wife's examination room.

Noah tapped on the door lightly and entered. "Hey sweetheart, they told me that your physician wanted to see me. Are you okay?" He noticed that she looked extremely worried. He reached over and pulled her in his arms. "Did the doctor say anything?"

Marly shook her head and said, "She simply said that she wanted you in here."

He eased her on to a chair and then sat down beside her.

There was a light rap on the door followed by Dr. Thompson's entry. She included both of them in her gaze as she spoke.

"Marlena's test results indicate that she does not have the flu or any other virus; however, the test has come back positive for pregnancy," she concluded smiling.

Marly stared at Dr. Thompson in complete shock. "Pregnant, me, I can't be! I haven't had a menstrual cycle in at least five months and I'm forty-four years old. I thought I was premenopausal." She looked from Noah to Dr. Thompson. "Are you sure that you didn't mix up my test with someone else's?"

Dr. Thompson shook her head in amusement and said, "I double checked myself and I'm positive that you're pregnant. Congratulations, Mr. Phillips."

Noah stood and smiled at the doctor with barely concealed excitement. He shook her hand and thanked her warmly. Marly still looked to be in shock, but remembered her manners in time to thank the doctor before she departed.

✢

Marly was solemnly quiet as he drove back to the church. He was concerned about her reaction towards what he considered to be a blessing from God. Truthfully, she had seemed ready to break into tears. Was she disappointed that she was carrying his child? He tried not to think that way, but what other reason could there be? He walked her over to her car and kissed her on her forehead. "I'll see you in a little while. Do you need me to pick up anything on my way home?"

She shook her head no and surprised him by laying her head on his chest. He wrapped his arms around her waist and they stayed that way for a long moment before she lifted her head and kissed him. Again he was surprised, but said nothing. This strange mood of hers was perplexing.

"We're having a baby. I'm having your child," she whispered, her voice full of wonder. "Are you pleased Noah?"

He was taken aback by her question, but he finally understood her. She was waiting for his reaction. He reached down and scooped her up in his arms and began to twirl her around until she laughed uncontrollably.

Grinning, he placed her back on her feet and said, "Does that answer your question?"

She laughed and nodded yes.

"What about you, Marly? How do you feel about being pregnant?" he wanted to know.

"I'm still in shock, but I'm happy," she admitted somewhat cautiously.

Noah looked deeply into her eyes. He loved this woman beyond life itself and now, a tiny life, his child was growing within her. He wanted to shout it to the world. There was no greater gift, other than herself, that she could have given him. He was truly a blessed man. He helped her into the car and stood watching as she drove off. God was indeed an awesome God.

✢

Two weeks had gone by and they still hadn't revealed to anyone, other than Layman, that she was pregnant. Noah had wanted to tell all three sons at one time. Both Adam and Kaod lived at home, so that meant they were waiting for Jacob who had arrived for a week's vacation yesterday evening. Noah had gathered their clan together for a picnic at the beach, and before the fun began, had informed them that he and Marly had something to say. He pulled Marly to his side and stared at the four, five including little Collin's, faces looking expectantly at them. He grimaced as he attempted to wiggle his fingers which felt numb from Marly's death grip on them.

Adam, always the jokester, stared at his father before saying humorously, "Dad, whatever it is you have to say just spit it out. You two are acting like you're having a baby or something."

That sent everyone into rounds of laughter, everyone except Noah and Marly, who both felt themselves flushing. Kaod noticed their expressions first and let out a shout of glee before rushing to his mother and enveloping her in a bear hug. Adam and Jacob still hadn't caught on, but Kara had. She gazed, wide-eyed, before laughing and elbowing her still clueless husband. Slowly Jacob and Adam's laughter subsided to be replaced by dawning disbelief. Jacob, being the oldest, assumed the right to express himself first.

"Dad, please tell me you're not having a baby."

Now that was funny Noah thought.

"Okay, I'm not having a baby, but Marly is."

Both Marly and Kara stifled the desire to giggle as Jacob looked in complete astonishment at his father.

"How could this happen?" Jacob demanded to know.

That did cause a giggle to escape from his wife's mouth. He glared at her before turning and confronting his dad again.

"Didn't you use protection?"

All eyes abruptly fixed on Marly and Noah, clearly reversing roles as though they were naughty children being scolded by stern parents who couldn't understand how such a thing might happen. Marly felt her face flaming while Noah chuckled and acknowledged to himself that the last thing on his mind during his wedding night was birth control.

He pulled Marly in front of him and said tongue-in-cheek, "It's all her fault. She's been flirting with me for a whole year and I finally succumbed to her wanton ways."

Marly, blushing profusely, but deciding to follow Noah's lead, strongly denied it was her fault. She cast the blame back at Noah saying, "He seduced me. I couldn't resist. What was I to do?" she asked helplessly. "After all," she added, "he is my husband."

Jacob reluctantly acquiesced. "All right, all right, I get it. I'll mind my own business, but Collin's going to have an uncle younger than he is," he emphasized, letting them hear his disapproval.

Adam grinned broadly at his father. "I would chest bump you or call you the man, but I guess Marly had a little to do with it."

Noah grinned proudly, "Very little, I do all the umph…" he was stopped short by a well placed jab to his middle. "Okay, okay, if not for her, we wouldn't be in this mess." He laughingly dodged another blow.

Kaod asked excitedly, "So when is my little sister going to be born? It is a girl you know."

Kara smiled and added, "Collin will have a playmate no matter if it's a boy or a girl."

Kaod adamantly declared again, "It's a girl. I'm going to have a little sister."

"What makes you so sure it's going to be a girl?" Adam questioned. "And, by the way, she'll be our sister too, not just yours, baby brother."

Kaod frowned and looked at Noah as though he'd forgotten that he'd anything to do with it. Suddenly, Kaod began to laugh uproariously. He glanced from Noah to his mom and then to Jacob. Marly intuitively knew what Kaod was thinking and fought to control her mirth. She quickly interjected that the baby was due in February of next year. All, but Noah and Kaod, were unaware of her diversionary tactic. Noah looked at her with eyebrows raised.

"I'll tell you about it later," she promised quietly, hoping he wouldn't pursue the issue at the present moment.

✟

Marly reclined on her blanket, opting not to go into the water. She preferred dry land to water any day. She observed Noah playing with Collin in the water. He was going to make a great father to their child.

He must have sensed her watching him because his gaze met hers as he handed his grandson back to Jacob and strode casually towards her. He had the unique ability to cause her heart to beat faster. He always made her feel as if she were the only woman in the world. Paying no attention to the appreciative glances cast in his direction, his eyes never left hers as he made his way up the beach to where she was reclining in the shade.

"Hi gorgeous," he greeted easily.

"Back at you," she smiled.

"Do you want to take a walk along the beach with me, Mrs. Phillips?"

"I'd love to."

He helped her to her feet and gently pulled her along beside him. He rolled his eyes when he noticed her gym-shoed feet. He'd barely convinced her to put on a swimsuit. It was probably asking way too much for her to walk barefooted. He spotted Kaod. He hadn't been in the water either. He'd immediately walked toward the nets and had begun playing volleyball.

"Kaod doesn't swim either?" he wondered aloud.

"He swims. He's just found something else that's caught his interest," she smiled.

Noah glanced in Kaod's direction. "Which girl is he showing an interest in?"

"The darker-toned black girl that's dressed very modestly."

"How do you know he's interested in her? He doesn't seem to be paying her any attention."

"That's how I know. The other girls are all over him, and he's still sticking around. Normally, he'd have left already. She's got his interest all right."

Noah shook his head in wonder. "You two watch each other like hawks."

"You have to remember, Noah, that for so long, we've only had each other," she reminded him.

He hoped that eventually, they'd come to understand that they were part of a larger family now. It wasn't them against the world anymore. He prayed that Kaod would one day accept him as his father.

✠

"So Mrs. Phillips, will you go into the water with me?" he asked her sometime later as they sat enjoying each other's company.

"I knew you were going to ask me that eventually. I hate beach water. It's full of slimy, slithery things," she pouted prettily.

"That's not what I asked you. I asked if you'd come into the water with me?" Noah persisted.

She looked at him, and then peered at the waves creeping up the sand.

"I promise not to let anything happen to you and if anything slimy comes near you, we'll get right out, okay?"

"I'll go in only for a couple of minutes," she agreed.

She kicked her shoes off and gingerly followed him into the water. She stopped as soon as the water became knee deep. He grinned and clasped her hand firmly as he led her further away from the shore. She was waist deep when he let go. She stood there, trying to figure out exactly what was so fun about being in the water when a splash of it covered her entire body. She squealed in surprised anger and quickly wiped the offensive beach water from her face. Glaring at a guilty Noah, she turned and headed back towards the shore only to be hit with another splash of water. Furiously, she whirled around to confront him, but he had disappeared from sight. She turned in every direction trying to locate him. A momentary fear captured her before realizing that he was playing cat and mouse with her. She decided that she was not about to play this silly game and determinedly stood still. Arms folded across her breast and her bared foot tapping the underwater sand in annoyance, she waited impatiently for him to reappear. She was still startled when he suddenly surfaced directly in front of her. She opened her mouth to give him a tongue lashing and was hit with another spray of water. She was beyond furious now. She was positively livid. She wiped the water from her eyes and her now dripping hair.

Noah watched his wife wipe the water from her face. He could tell from her expression that she was furious with him. He knew that he had ambushed her, but he'd been hoping that she'd leave her serious nature behind for a little while. She looked adorable. He decided to get a little closer in order for her to splash him back. Maybe that would loosen her up a bit. He stepped toward her smiling boyishly.

Marly stood with her arms folded and waited for him to come closer.

"Truce," he called out just before a splash of water hit him.

He grinned and wiped his face. Another splash, then another hit him. Anger melted away replaced with humor. She laughed cheerfully when he just stood there and allowed her to take her revenge. She watched him sink below the surface of the water and screamed when his arms wrapped around her waist. She found herself gazing into laughing grey eyes.

"Hold your breath," he called out, a second before he plunged them both under water.

They came back up for air with Marly's arms wound tightly around his neck. She was actually starting to enjoy being in the water with him.

Noah instructed her to hold on as he began easing out into deeper waters.

"Can you tread water?" he asked.

She still had her arms locked around his neck, but nodded yes. He ventured out to where the water reached his chin.

"Okay sweetheart, let me see you tread water," he commanded gently.

She slowly released her grip and pushed away where she began treading.

She started off awkwardly, but soon her motions became more fluid. He took several minutes determining how well she swam, floated, and held her breath. Satisfied with what he saw, he pulled her into his arms and told her to hold on. He inched out to where the water was now over his head. He maneuvered onto his back to support her. He knew that in order for her to come this far out, she had to trust him with her life. He looked back towards the shore and saw Kaod, as well as Adam watching.

Kaod shielded his eyes against the glare of sun and focused on the dim shapes of Noah and his mother. He asked Adam in a serious tone, "How well can your dad swim?"

Adam could tell that Kaod was not in the mood for jokes as he watched the two figures in the distance.

"Don't worry. Dad is a master swimmer. He could have made the Olympic team, but he turned them down and went to seminary instead. You gotta know that Dad wouldn't take her out there if he couldn't protect her."

"My Mom has never in her life been in beach water, let alone, so far out. I'm nervous just thinking about it. Seriously, she doesn't even like getting her face wet."

Adam acknowledged Kaod's feelings with an observation of his own. "Well, you want to know something? I've never seen Dad behave this way, ever. Not even with my mom and we came to the beach all the time. It's kind of weird. I look at them and wish I could be that little baby growing inside Marly. That way I'd experience having a mom and a dad that not only love God, but are in love because of God." He glanced sideways at Kaod. "Do you know what I mean?"

Kaod looked at him strangely as though Adam had read his heart's desire.

"Noah is probably one of the godliest men I've ever met."

Adam picked up a stone and threw it wistfully into the water.

"My dad was never the problem."

Kaod nodded in understanding.

"Neither was my mom."

Suddenly, they reached the same conclusion, but neither one dared to speak it aloud. God had answered a prayer that each had tucked away in the deepest corners of their hearts, a prayer that almost seemed impossible even for God. Kaod and Adam both knew that God had not forgotten them. It had taken years, but he had supplied Kaod the father he'd prayed for, and Adam, the mother he'd yearned after. Without saying a word, their focus had shifted. Kaod confidently watched his father while Adam was on pins and needles as he waited to catch glimpses of his mother.

Noah grinned and explained to Marly that he was going to go below the surface and take her with him, but they weren't going to stay for very long. He gave her enough time to prepare herself, and then dipped beneath the water, taking her along with him. Seconds later, they resurfaced. Again and again they went under and reappeared. Each time they stayed a little longer under water. Finally, Noah turned and headed towards the more shallow water. Reaching the point where his feet touched the bottom, he stood and pulled her close as she wrapped her arms around his neck. Without a word, their lips met in the tenderest of kisses. His lips thanked her for the trust she had bestowed upon him, while hers reciprocated in gratitude for his patience and understanding of her fears. They had moved as one through the water. He had lovingly urged her to face and conquer yet another fear, another barrier that had stood firm for years. She was learning to trust a man, this man with her very life even through uncertainty and darkness. Never had any male earned this high honor. They gazed into each other's eyes discerning that something deeper, something more profound had transpired between their spirits. He reached down and touched her stomach, aware of the tiny mound that had begun to take shape.

"I love you," he said softly as his mouth gently found hers again.

✟

Marly glanced at Noah as they emerged from the water. Their fingers were interlaced and she could sense the curiosity of others as she and Noah made their way toward the blanket. They toweled off and slipped on t-shirts over their suits. He collapsed on the blanket and pulled her down beside him. Reaching for another towel, he began to dry her hair. She blushed profusely and closed her eyes to avoid the stares.

"Do you want me to stop?" he asked hesitatingly.

"No," she managed to choke out. It felt so relaxing that she leaned back against his broad chest.

He fished through their things and found her comb. With gentle hands, he combed through the tangles not caring in the least what others thought. This was his wife. She was his, to have and to hold, to love and to cherish for however much time God granted them. He wanted her to feel his love for her. He needed her to know his single-minded devotion to her. This was the intimacy he had longed for from the very essence of his soul as Christ longs for intimacy with his church. Noah sighed with pleasure as she relaxed against him.

Jacob watched as his father combed through Marly's hair. Anger bubbled to the surface. His love for his mother held him captive, a prisoner with no hope of escape. He had no valid reason to dislike Marly, except that his father loved her in a way that he'd never loved his mother. Everyone could see that. In fact, he was blatant with it. Maybe if his dad had loved his mom in that way, she wouldn't have had an affair. Jacob remembered the vow that he'd made to his mother? He wished that he could go back in time and undo his promise, but he couldn't. He turned away from the intimate image of his father combing Marly's hair, but not before resentment filled his heart.

✠

Marly listened to the different sounds of nature drifting in through their bedroom window. Noah was on his side propped up on an elbow watching her while his free hand softly caressed the swelling mound of her tummy. Today had been a day of growth for her. She hadn't wanted to go into the water, but she'd known it was important to him. He loved the water and anything that was important to him, was now important to her. She'd never been a great swimmer or even liked being in the water much, but she had enjoyed it today; although, it had nothing to do with the water, and everything to do with being with Noah. She remembered the sensation of being under the water with her eyes closed and holding her breath. In the past, that had always frightened her, but holding on to him and knowing he was with her had given her the courage she had previously lacked. She recalled the Bible verse that tells how Jesus said he'd never leave or forsake us. During the darkest hours of her life, when she had felt so alone, God had never left her. She'd known as long as she'd kept a hold of Him, she'd make it through. Today, she'd relied on Noah's strength and skill to keep her safe. She looked at her husband. Every night, before she'd fall asleep, he'd tell her how much he loved her and since her pregnancy, he'd caress her tummy as well. She loved him in a way that she'd never loved anyone else, and it was because he first demonstrated his love for her. She'd been acutely aware of the seductive looks that women had cast in his direction today. He never acknowledged them. He always gave her the impression that he belonged solely and completely to her. That had given her the strength and desire to come under his headship. She couldn't believe how liberating submitting to her husband was. It was hard to explain to other women, but she now had the freedom from so many responsibilities that had kept her feeling bogged down. Her only job now, was to please her husband and that was such a pleasure that it really couldn't be considered a job. Why hadn't anyone ever explained what a true Christian marriage felt like? She realized that they'd have trials and tribulations, but having a God-centered marriage allowed her the freedom of knowing He was in charge.

Noah was thinking about an earlier conversation he'd had with Kaod and Adam. Today was the first time Kaod had ever seen his mother in the water at a beach, but he'd seemed okay with it. Adam, however, had behaved like a basket- case. He'd gone on and on about her not being able to swim that well. Noah had gotten his fill and finally had to explain to his irate son that she was his wife and that he wouldn't do anything to put her life in jeopardy. Adam had stared him in the eye, said "good", and walked away. Noah had been completely astonished because his son had actually had the gumption to chastise him about Marly and her fear of the water. Noah had known that Marly didn't like swimming, but he hadn't known about her fear. She'd allowed him to take her out there without so much as a word. She'd trusted him with her life. He was in awe of her trust in him. He looked at Marly and knew that she would give birth to the daughter he'd always longed for. God's Word says that he'll give you the desires of your heart. Noah had always understood that those desires had to line up with His will for your life. He'd never bought into the "name it and claim it" belief that had so permeated the minds of some Christians. It gave the impression that God was like a glorified Santa who sat waiting to grant your every wish. This erroneous understanding of scripture had caused many to turn from the faith when their wish list of prayers or miraculous healings hadn't taken place. Believers needed to understand the necessity of being in God's will, which in turn would give you the earnest desire to understand his will for your life. That alone, should shape your prayer life. If Christians would begin to pray for those things that would glorify God, then prayers would be answered in abundance. He gazed lovingly at his wife. God had yet to reveal His ultimate reason for bringing her into his life. He prayed that he would be obedient to God's will.

Chapter Thirty-two

Noah reached for his and Marly's wedding picture. Her big brown eyes always seemed to follow him wherever he went. He smiled and replaced the picture and picked up the letter. He had read the letter twice. The District Board had ordered a hearing to determine whether or not a recommendation for removal was warranted. Two accusations had been charged, dereliction of duty and sexual harassment. He wasn't at all shocked at the charges or at the person bringing the harassment charge. It was none other than Caroline J. Rivers. Her accusation didn't bother him, but the note she'd written to Marly did. It was one thing to initiate a false accusation against him, but to try and destroy Marly in the process was unacceptable. He'd thought he'd made that clear to Caroline on at least three separate occasions. Noah unlocked his desk and pulled out a file. In it was every love letter or note Caroline had written to him. Some of them were sexually suggestive. "At least I'd had the presence of mind to keep these," he said to himself. He compared the handwriting on the note written to Marly with the handwriting on the notes written to him. It was identical. He read aloud what she'd written to Marly. "You are the reason people are leaving Noah's church. Go back to where you belong, with your people".

He closed his eyes and asked the Lord to give him the strength to forgive Caroline. He'd accepted responsibility for his part. His weakness and failure to rely solely on God to assist him through that first year after Colleen's death had contributed to Caroline being able to bring accusations, although false, against him. He asked God to forgive his past foolishness and to spare Marly from reaping the whirlwind that he discerned was yet to come. He remembered that old saying, "Hell hath no fury like a woman scorned". His mistakes were of bad judgment. He shivered when he thought of how much worse they could have been. This was definitely a subject he would bring up with his sons. Hopefully, they'd be wise enough to steer clear and not make the same mistake. He always, within limits, tried to use his life as an example to his sons of what not to do.

Noah never could understand parents who always pretended that they'd never done anything wrong. God put so many examples in the Bible of what not to do in an attempt to help us avoid the same traps and snares. Yet, many adults willingly allowed their own children to fall into the same pits due to the fear of not wanting to appear in a bad light before them. If sharing his mistakes would keep his children from making them, then he was willing to do it. He glanced at the letter again. He knew it was time to share this with Marly. Trust in God he reminded himself.

Marly's face lit up as she watched Noah swing open the classroom door. He had insisted on driving her to school today in order to be with her for the baby's ultrasound. She thought of the first time her class had met him. Not one of the children had remarked about the difference in their ethnicity. They had been more interested in the fact that he was a pastor than anything else. Why couldn't adults be more like kids? She stood and began gathering her things together. She looked around at the expressions on the faces of the children. Her students seemed just as excited as they were about her appointment. Noah grabbed her satchel and waited while she gave the children instructions. He smiled as he watched them hug her goodbye. They left to the chorus of, "Bye, Mrs. Phillips."

Noah was in awe as the baby's heart beat echoed loud and rhythmic through the machine. The technician glanced at Noah as she pointed out the different distinct features of his tiny child growing inside Marly. When she'd finished her thorough examination, she asked if they wanted to know the gender of their child.

Without hesitation, they both answered, "Yes."

He waited breathlessly and nearly leaped out of his chair in joy when they were informed that it was a girl. He bent down and kissed Marly excitedly and said a brief prayer of thanks to God. God had, once again, granted him the desire of his heart. He would unashamedly teach his daughter the Word so that her life would bring glory to God.

Noah whistled a tune of praise as they walked hand and hand out of the hospital into the warm October sun. He heard God's message to him. He would trust and believe God rather than the things of the world. His heart was light. Who would believe that at fifty years of age, he'd be having the daughter he'd always wanted?

✝

Noah glanced at his wife. "We're going to make a stop at the house before going to Chandra's."

"Did you leave something behind?" she wondered.

He reached over and grabbed her hand. "No. I just...We need to talk."

"About what?" she asked with a frown.

He squeezed her hand lightly. "Can we wait, please?"

She nodded, leaned back, and closed her eyes.

She looked tired he thought. He wished she'd take a leave of absence from the school, but she was being stubborn about it. He knew she was going to throw a fit, but in a month or two, he was going to insist that she request a significant amount of time off. She was going to need the rest, not just for her sake, but for the baby's also. Noah hadn't brought it up yet, but they were going to have a long talk about their responsibility to their child after she's born. He refused to have their child anywhere, but with her mother or father, especially during the early years. He had no idea how she'd take the notion of being a stay-at-home mom. As far as he was concerned, there were no other options and no one else was responsible for raising their child. This touchy subject was going to be their first real test and he was not looking forward to it.

His mind switched gears as he began to wonder what their daughter was going to look like. He briefly thought about Jacob's possible reaction to having a black sister. That was what Kaod had found so amusing, the fact that Adam and Jacob hadn't given any thought to the color of their baby sister. He knew that it hadn't occurred to Adam because he didn't care about color, but Jacob had made that comment about Marly. Noah wondered how Jacob would feel if someone would call his sister that. Nevertheless, Noah hoped his daughter would resemble her mother. He thought Marly's complexion to be beautiful. He chuckled softly as he thought about having two Marlys in the house. Maybe, he was biting off more than he could chew. He carefully maneuvered the car into the garage and turned to study his sleeping wife. He'd take a dozen daughters if they'd all turn out like her.

✞

Marly plopped wearily on the bed. Whatever he wanted to talk about must be pretty important if he wanted to discuss it in the privacy of their home. She sincerely hoped that he wasn't going to ask her to stop teaching. He knew how much her students meant to her. Besides, she didn't want to leave without at least a month's notice. She reached in her satchel and pulled out the ultrasound photos. They were having a girl. Marly decided that he should name their daughter. She hoped the baby had grey eyes like her father. She prayed that their daughter would have a lot of his qualities. Noah was a godly man and he would definitely raise their daughter in Christ. She rubbed her stomach. She was just beginning to show. Her stomach hadn't gotten very big when she'd been pregnant with Ka'. She'd carried him mostly in her hips. The way things were going, it looked as though she was carrying this baby the same way. Her mind shifted to Noah. He was a great husband and the best thing that had ever happened to her. She couldn't imagine life without him. He was definitely her better half. She smiled as she heard his footsteps approaching their bedroom.

"What are you smiling about?" he said as he strode into the room.

Marly held up the pictures.

"She's beautiful, isn't she? She's going to look exactly like her mommy. Have you thought about any names?" he asked as he looked at the ultrasound photos.

"No, I haven't. I'd like her father to have that honor," she said as she stood up and laid her head against his chest.

He laughed softly. "Why do you rest your head against my chest? I like it, but I'm curious as to why you do it."

"I'm listening to your heartbeat. It's well… comforting. It may sound silly to you, but your heartbeat makes me feel safe. I know it's weird, but that's why I do it," she explained softly, without bothering to move from her position.

He pulled her closer and whispered, "It's not weird at all. I liked it before, but now that I understand why, I love it."

They stood that way for sometime before she asked quietly, "What is it that you want to talk about?"

She heard him sigh before he asked her to sit down. Noah took out the letter from the District Board and handed it to her. He sat quietly watching her every expression as she read the letter.

"I don't understand. What does this mean?" she asked, her eyebrows arching in concern.

He explained in detail what was happening. He knew within his heart that she was blaming herself. She handed the letter back to him and looked away.

"Marly, look at me!" he commanded. "Tell me how this is your fault. They're telling me that I haven't been doing my job and that I've behaved inappropriately. How is that your fault?"

He watched as her bottom lip quivered and knew that she was trying hard not to cry.

"They're accusing you of those things because you married me, because I'm black," she said, her voice breaking.

He knew she was dead-on, but he couldn't allow her to assume responsibility for the prejudices of others.

"That part may be true, but I was the one who exercised bad judgment concerning Caroline, and that was way before you were a part of my life. So if you want to blame someone, blame me," he stated firmly.

"I can't blame you," she replied.

"But you can blame yourself? It's just a part of life's trials and tribulations. We've both been through it before and we'll get through it again. We can handle anything they throw at us as long as we trust God, and as long as we have each other," he said pulling her into his arms.

"Can I count on you to be strong for me?" he asked nuzzling her neck.

She slid her arms around his neck and sighed.

"I love you, Noah," she whispered earnestly.

He moaned when her fingers began playing with his hair. "Stop it, Marly or we'll never make it to Chandra's," he teased.

"What time are we supposed to be there?" she asked huskily, continuing the movement of her fingers.

He glanced at his watch and whispered, "We have plenty of time." Noah turned his attention back to her neck. "Now Mrs. Phillips, where were we? Oh yeah, now I remember," he said softly as her fingers drifted through his hair.

✠

Noah opened the car door for Marly and waited for her reaction as she stepped out of the car. She glanced at Chandra's House and threw herself into his arms in thanks. There, in the middle of the front yard, was an official sign declaring "Chandra's House" a non-profit organization. Noah's attorney had handled all the necessary paperwork. Noah had even established a board to oversee operations. The board's first order of business was to recruit a badly needed volunteer staff. The volunteers stood on the porch clapping and cheering. Malcolm, who was a part of that staff, was grinning from ear to ear as he watched Marly hug Noah. Noah slid his arm around her waist as he introduced each member of the staff to her. Some, she was acquainted with, others, she was not.

Hal's familiar F150 pulled into the driveway followed by Layman's dark colored Ford 500. Noah grinned when Layman helped Marcella out of the vehicle and arched his eyebrows in surprise as Hal assisted Valerie out of the truck. The newly engaged couple was beaming. He observed Marly as she greeted both couples with warm hugs. Marcella glanced at Marly's stomach, and then whispered something to her husband who gave a barely perceptible nod.

Marcella stared at Marly's gently protruding belly and asked in a no nonsense tone, "When, exactly where you all planning on telling everyone the news? When's the due date?"

Hal looked confused, while Layman appeared smug.

"What news?" Hal asked.

Layman shook his head at Hal and turned his attention back to Noah. "I was wondering the same thing myself. When are you going to announce it?"

Hal looked around at everyone. "What news?" he repeated.

Layman pinned Valerie with a look of exaggerated sympathy. "I sure hope he'll know if it happens to you."

Valerie blushed while everyone, except Hal, laughed. He still had no clue what Layman was going on about.

Layman took one look at Hal, shook his head in total exasperation, and then stated, "Darn it, man, Noah and Marly are expecting a baby."

Hal's mouth dropped wide open. "How, when?" Hal stammered.

"Well son, let me explain a little theory called the birds and the bees. You see, when a man falls in love with a woman a whole lot, they get married. Now on their honeymoon what happens is that they…. Didn't your momma ever tell you about them birds and bees?" Layman could be heard saying as he led Hal into the house.

✠

Marly tried to control her yawns as she fought hard against the sleep beckoning to her. She was much too comfortable she realized. Her head was resting against Noah's chest. The steady beating of his heart was lulling her to sleep.

She felt Noah's breath against her ear and then heard him whisper, "Remind me to never make love with you before we go out."

She came instantly awake and felt her face go warm. She took a cursory look around the room to see if anyone else had been privy to his comment. She could hear the amusement in his voice, and knew he was referencing the fact that she always fell asleep after they were intimate. Marly quickly stood up and stretched, ignoring Noah's amused chuckle. She turned and glanced over her shoulder at him and smiled.

Noah sensed instantly that she was flirting with him. That wasn't just her normal smile. She was beginning to comprehend her effect on him. He watched as she walked across the room and into the kitchen. She returned a few minutes later with two bottles of water. She offered him one as she sat down beside him. He continued to watch her as she drank from the bottle. He knew that she was very much aware of his eyes on her and she was enjoying it.

Setting the water aside, she moved closer and whispered in his ear, "If I were a betting woman, I'd bet that this evening you have on briefs."

It was his turn to glance around the room before he whispered back, "What are you willing to bet?"

She blushed and was saved from answering when Jim walked into the room.

✟

Noah could feel Marly's gaze as Jim Wade explained what was happening at the District Board. Jim's demeanor was very serious which in turn caused everyone to sit up and pay closer attention to what he was saying. Apparently, there was a possibility of civil and criminal charges being filed if the sexual harassment allegations were found to have merit.

"The board is probably going to initiate a vote to sit you down, even without good evidence, to be perfectly honest, with little or no evidence. I think all of us here are aware of their true motives, but they're hoping you will not make a big fuss and simply resign," Jim informed them, looking directly at Noah and Marly.

"How many people have actually signed the petition?" Hal wanted to know.

Jim shook his head in humor and declared, "Right now, thirteen."

The entire room, except for Marly, laughed. In her mind, that was thirteen too many. She was still attempting to grasp the idea of Noah not being able to preach. Were these people serious? They would strip him of his pastoral position because he married a black woman? This was truly unbelievable. A situation like this was not supposed to happen anymore, not in this country, not in the age of so called "cultural awareness". Especially, since these individuals were considered believers. She didn't regret, not for one single moment, having not belonged to a church; although, she was now officially a member of Noah's. The hypocrisy was mind shattering. They all claimed to have the love of Christ, yet on one hand, you had the black community throwing slavery terminology at one of their own in a bid for control, while on the other hand, you had pompous, want-to-live-in-Mayberry-forever whites, doing all they could to keep one of their churches from becoming tainted by a pastor whose only crime was marrying a black woman. This was the height of stupidity. She looked around the room. Was she the only one who couldn't believe genuine Christian pastors actually went along with this nonsense? It all seemed a bit Pharisaical to her. She looked at Layman who was staring intently at her. If that was the case, what ridiculous notions did they have concerning her? She turned her attention to Noah. He was barking up the wrong tree, if he thought for one minute that she'd allow her daughter to be raised in such a bigoted environment. Suddenly, she was angry at Noah who seemed to be going along with whatever the "District Board" dictated. If the District Board said, "Jump off a cliff", would he follow those ridiculous orders, too?

Marly stubbornly ignored Layman's, and now Marcella's silent appeal for her to hold her tongue and stood to her feet saying, "Please excuse me, I need some fresh air. I'm feeling a little sick."

In truth she was sick, but not from her baby. She was sick of the complete and utter hypocrisy the "District Board" was openly displaying. She hurried to the back door afraid that Noah would try to stop her. She'd barely made it outside when Noah, followed by Layman and Marcella, reached for her hand.

"What's wrong? Is it the baby?" he asked, concern evident in his voice.

Marly swung around to face him, but before she could say a word Marcella grabbed her arm and pulled her down the steps and purposefully away from Noah.

Noah stared at Marly and Marcella in complete bewilderment. He was abruptly stopped from following them by Layman's hand on his arm.

"Let her go, Noah. She's going to have to sort through this dilemma herself."

"What dilemma? I thought she was feeling sick. Tell me what I'm missing here," Noah pleaded.

"Let's go back inside so the others won't be concerned. When the meeting is over, I'll do my best to explain it to you, okay?"

Noah's eyes followed Marly as she and Marcella walked down the driveway. Satisfied that she appeared okay, he turned and preceded Layman back into the house.

Marcella could feel the tension in Marly as they walked. She understood what Marly was thinking because she had experienced similar feelings in the past. As a pastor's wife, there were times when the callousness of others went beyond understanding. Marly was in a very difficult position, especially now that she was carrying Noah's child, a child that would have to identify with two cultures, but would be expected to choose one or the other. Marcella had sensed the exact moment that Marly had come face to face with "religion". Marcella knew that it was difficult for her to understand why Noah had chosen to submit to the rulings of a board that had clearly shown itself to be flawed.

"Marly, who are you angry with? Is it Noah or those sitting on the District Board," Marcella questioned, "or are you angry with yourself?"

Marly looked straight ahead and replied, "D, all of the above."

"Why? What's got you so angry?" Marcella dared to ask.

Marly placed her hands in a subconsciously protective manner over her stomach. "I don't understand this concept of having to do whatever the board says. It seems wrong. This whole episode is like a dream happening in slow motion while everything around you is at normal speed. If Noah and Jim know that the charges are trumped up, then why stay a part of the organized problem? It's as though we've all agreed that it's wrong, but since they're the ruling body there's nothing we can do about it. I will not raise my daughter in that kind of hypocrisy. If Noah wins this battle, then what's next? Will they have a problem with my biracial child?"

Marcella stopped and clutched Marly by the hand. "First off, that baby you're carrying belongs to Noah as well. It would do you good to remember that. Do you really believe that he would permit anyone to harm his child? Secondly, you chose to marry a white man, and now you have to learn to deal with all the extra baggage that comes along with it. There's no doubt in my mind that you and Noah can work through all those issues. You two were made for each other and God's not going to give you more than you can handle. Lastly, submission to the authority in your life is not necessarily always bad. I hope you submit to your husband, even if you don't agree with him. Being without a church home has made you much more of an independent thinker than most. You're going to have to begin to think in terms of we, rather than I. You can't always run from the problem. You've got to take a stand somewhere, and that can only happen when you've learned to work as a team, within the body."

She began explaining to Marly about order in the church. She told how Christ, Himself, submitted to the will of God and allowed the Jews to capture him and then later on, allowed the Romans to scourge and in the end, crucify Him. He understood that He had the power to resist, but He didn't. He understood the greater mission even though He appeared weak to others. He taught His disciples what they needed to know in order for them to take up their cross and follow Him. Jesus also understood that whatever was going to happen could only happen by the will of God. He was submitting, not to man, but to the complete and total authority of His Father.

Marly comprehended that Noah was voluntarily submitting to the board. He had already told her that no matter the outcome, God was in charge. In essence, he was submitting to God, not to the board. Noah trusted that God always knew the end result. He was her husband; therefore, she should trust his judgment. Marly listened intently to what Marcella had to say. She heard the ring of truth in her words. She recalled Noah's words to her earlier, "Can I count on you to be strong for me?" The last thing he needed was for her to add an extra burden to the heavy weight he was now carrying. Her job was to be there for him in a way that no one else could. She smiled gratefully at Marcella and thanked her for stepping in and preventing her from saying things to Noah that she would have regretted later.

"Don't mention it. You should have been around me when Layman and I first married. I gave that man fits. Honestly, I don't know how he put up with me," Marcella admitted. She turned and faced Marly. "You do realize how hard this is for Noah? That man loves you more than anything. You should try hard to never put him in the position of having to choose between you and his ministry. That's something you need to be mindful of."

Marly nodded in understanding and silently thanked the Lord for sending wisdom, in the form of Marcella, to help in her hour of need. She also sought the Lord's help in the area of patience. She had wanted Noah to take action in her time, not when God instructed him.

"Forgive me Lord," she whispered as they headed back toward Chandra's House.

✝

Noah forced himself to concentrate on what was being said. He was worried about Marly. What was wrong with her? He hoped she understood that he wasn't the least bit worried about the board's decision. If God wanted him to continue being a pastor, then He would clear the path. If not, he had a beautiful wife, three sons, and a soon to be born baby girl with whom he would be more than content to spend the rest of his days. God was quite capable of choosing another pastor to take his place. He was not that important in the grand scheme of things, nor was he vain enough to think the church would fall apart without him.

Jim had finally finished speaking. Noah thanked him for the information and made a beeline for the backdoor. He met Marly and Marcella halfway down the driveway.

Marcella gave Marly's hand a reassuring squeeze and left them to rejoin her husband. Noah looked at her questioningly, waiting for some type of explanation.

She shifted nervously before saying, "I didn't understand why the board could get away with treating you so badly and I wondered how they'd treat my daughter."

"Oh, is that all? You couldn't have waited to ask me those questions at home? What else Marly? Marcella had to practically drag you off of the porch to keep that temper of yours from flaming," Noah commented wryly.

Marly kept her eyes averted, refusing to look at him. She could tell that he was not happy with her actions. She touched her stomach, hoping that would draw his attention and assuage his growing anger.

Noah wasn't buying her demure act. He'd been quietly going out of his mind and for what? Questions she could have asked him in the privacy of their home. To add insult to injury, she kept on referring to their daughter as though the baby was hers alone. She was making him crazy. One minute, she was so trusting to the point that she had allowed him to take her into water that was considerably deeper than she ever experienced. While the next, she didn't trust that he could satisfactorily handle matters pertaining to the church. He wasn't angry, simply irritated, and rubbing her stomach was not going to sidetrack him from the issues at hand.

Marly had no valid excuse except that this was all so new to her. She blurted out what was in her mind, "Give me a break Phillips. This is all new to me. I haven't even had time to get my feet wet, and you're already in trouble."

He was taken aback for a moment, but then a slow grin spread over his face. She did have a point. The concept of being accountable to a governing board was completely foreign to her. She'd never in her life experienced belonging to an organized church or being married to a pastor. Nevertheless, they were going to have a long talk not only about accountability, but about their unborn child as well.

"I'm not in trouble, but you will be if you don't learn how to control your feelings," he warned sternly.

Marly bit her tongue to keep from replying. His grin became broader as he watched her fight to keep quiet. His big fat grin was the final straw.

"I think I control my feelings rather well. You can't imagine the things I'm feeling right now, but not only am I keeping them to myself, I'm also planning on not talking about them later," she retorted smugly.

Noah was prevented from replying when he saw Layman and Marcella approaching. He gave Marly a will-see-about-that look before turning to face Layman.

"You two lovebirds want to go and get a bite to eat?" Layman asked casually.

"Way too casually," Marly thought as she watched Noah turn to face her.

"I'll leave that decision up to my lovely wife."

She glanced from Marcella to Layman and smiled.

"Sure, why not? We haven't eaten dinner, now that you mention it," she said, taking hold of Noah's arm and waited for his lead.

Noah led Marly to the car and helped her in. He glanced at her as he waited for Layman to back out of the driveway.

Marly really didn't feel much like eating, but she did not want to hear one of his "Noah knows best" lectures either. She closed her eyes and relaxed. All too soon, they were pulling up in front of the restaurant.

Noah cast a quick look in Marly's direction. He could see that she was running on fumes. He should have just taken a raincheck on dinner and took her straight home. He was encountering that stubborn streak Kaod had talked about. She was definitely a handful. He placed his hand around her waist and followed Layman and Marcella. The place was pretty packed, but it was evident that Layman and his wife were well known there. In no time at all, the foursome was escorted to a table.

Noah, the minute they entered the establishment, could sense some very hostile stares mainly directed at him. He stood as Marly and Marcella excused themselves to the ladies room.

Layman looked at Noah and said in serious tone, "Welcome to her world."

Noah immediately understood the point Layman was making. He knew that the hostile stares were from people, mostly black men, who disliked the fact that he was with a very attractive black woman. This type of attitude seemed like an obvious double standard since he'd seen a lot of interracial couples which consisted of black men with women whose cultures were something other than African-American.

"I'm convinced that God gave you your wife," Layman said, interrupting Noah's observation of his surroundings.

"What makes you say that?" Noah responded.

"She's a thinker, like you. I'm willing to bet you that she is wondering why a 'church board' isn't more concerned with the spiritual lives of the thirteen people who signed that petition than with whom the pastor married. After all, that's thirteen souls which may be lost. That is a much larger problem than black or white and she's got a valid point. Shouldn't the church be more concerned about converting people into true believers rather than someone's ethnic background? Remember the Pharisees, they weren't excited about the fact that Jesus had healed a man's withered hand and restored his life to him. They didn't care one bit about that man. Instead, they were upset that Jesus had healed on the Sabbath. Their knowledge of the law and standing in the community had become more important than the vitality of God's people. That was the height of hypocrisy. Isn't that the very reason you said your wife had refused to be a part of the organized church? Maybe that's why God gave her to you. Not simply to shed light on prejudice, but a much deeper, more profound reason, to bring to light spiritual corruption in our so called organized churches."

Noah sat back and took in all that Layman had spoken. He'd brushed off Marly's reactions as emotional, but it kept coming back to the same conclusion, hypocrisy. He reflected on Reggie, Colleen, Jacob, and even Shawn's reasons for not going to church. Hypocrisy was the common ground. Either they were a part of it, or their life was a result of it. He wondered how many people actually stayed away from church because of fraudulent believers. He'd lost members in the past because of that very reason. Maybe this whole thing wasn't only about his and Marly's skin color. If that were the case, he should start paying closer attention to what his wife was "feeling".

Marcella glanced at Marly through the reflection of the mirror. She wondered if Marly had noticed the hostile glances of others as they were escorted to their table.

Marly saw the questioning look in her friend's eyes and gave a nonchalant shrug of her shoulders.

"I've gotten used to it. It doesn't bother me anymore. It doesn't seem to have ever bothered Noah," Marly said casually.

"How'd you know what I was thinking?" Marcella asked.

Marly's eyes twinkled, "Because I used to wonder the exact same thing; especially, if it was a sister and a white guy."

Marly leaned against the counter and began telling how, initially, she'd been uncomfortable being in an interracial relationship with Noah. Over time, she'd realized that the biggest obstacles weren't others, but her own personal prejudices. God had helped her come to terms with herself and as a result, had blessed her with a strong Christian husband. The color of Noah's skin no longer mattered to her, nor did it matter what others thought.

"Girl, it wouldn't matter to me either if I could find a white man as fine as your husband," a voice quipped in from across the room.

Marly laughed and thanked the stranger for her obvious compliment.

✠

Noah pondered what Layman had said at the restaurant. He lay there waiting for her to finish procrastinating about coming to bed. He could sense that she did not want to discuss anything tonight. He knew that she wasn't up to it and neither was he. He closed his eyes and listened as she fiddled around in the bathroom. At last, he heard the familiar sound of the light as it clicked off and the movement of the mattress as she climbed into bed. He waited for her to situate her head on his chest as usual. When she didn't move, he reached over and pulled her close to him and began his nightly ritual of caressing her stomach. "I love you, Marly," he said softly.

"I love you too," She responded quietly. She closed her eyes as he began to pray.

After praying, Noah lay there with various thoughts flowing through his mind.

"Noah, are you still awake?" she whispered.

"Have I kissed you goodnight, yet?" he asked warmly.

"No," she replied with a giggle.

"Then I'm still awake."

She giggled again which indicated how tired she really was.

"What is it Marly?" he asked, amused at her silliness.

"Have you thought of a name for our daughter?" she wondered.

"I thought we'd call her Orphra or Bilhah or one of those equally challenging names from the Bible."

That threw Marly into a fit of delirious laughter which caused him to add silly name after silly name until she begged him to stop.

"You'll be the first to know when God gives me her name," he informed her.

Noah reached to kiss her goodnight, but she pulled him closer. What should have been a brief kiss became lingering. He pulled back in surprise.

"Marly, you're too tired," he protested half-heartedly.

Not listening to a word he said, she continued to persuade him otherwise.

Chapter Thirty-three

Noah was experiencing the peace of God as he sat before the District Board answering their many questions. The board consisted of nine members, each from a particular district located within the state. Right away Noah discerned, by the type of questions asked, that at least three of the members were not happy with his decision to marry Marly.

"Just wait until they learn of her pregnancy," he thought, fighting back the urge to laugh.

One member, Bishop Benson, sat with a continuous snarl on his face. He seemed unable to control the contempt he felt for Noah. Noah sensed the rage behind each question, but remained unaffected. They would have to answer to God for whatever decisions were made. He was going to count it all joy as the Bible instructed him.

When questions concerning the charge of sexual harassment began, Noah knew immediately there was no case. Not one board member, not even the angry Bishop Benson, could find grounds for those charges. Caroline had not produced a shred of reliable evidence to support her claim, nor did the board have any eyewitness accounts of Noah ever making any inappropriate comments or suggestions towards her or any other female. Noah had been made aware of the fact that they had questioned Valerie, as well as several of the more attractive women of his congregation, about his conduct towards her or them. They hadn't found anything which gave credence to Caroline's harassment accusations. He had answered each question openly and honestly. The majority of the Bishops had either very little or no questions at all. He thanked God silently as he watched the men debate amongst each other concerning the validity of the sexual harassment charges.

Marly watched as the energetic children ran and played. Under normal circumstances, she would participate in their play time. Today, however, her mind was on Noah. She glanced at her watch. He was probably appearing before the District Board at that very moment. They had prayed over the entire situation and both were now comforted by the knowledge that God, not man, was in control. They had placed the eventual outcome into His hands. She would be there for Noah no matter the end result. It warmed her heart, as she recalled his words from this morning. He had told her that she, next to God, was the most important thing in his life. He had emphasized that he could live without being a pastor, however, he never wanted to live without her. Yet, she was still saddened and even a little angry at the fact that he had to suffer because of the prejudices of others. Suddenly, Marly remembered Philippians 4:10 which spoke of knowing Christ through the power of his resurrection and the fellowship of his suffering. God was drawing them closer to Him through this whole crazy process. This was to be a time of joy knowing that He was proving Noah and she belonged to Him. She couldn't wait to see Noah to tell him about this revelation. He was going to be so proud of her. That thought surprised even herself. She could now admit that she needed him to be pleased with her. In much the same manner, that she wanted to please Christ. A Christian husband, she'd come to realize, should represent Jesus through the eyes of his wife. Noah had accomplished that, and as a result, he'd become her best friend. She couldn't recall when it had happened, but he had supplanted Tina. She still loved Tina and their friendship hadn't changed, but she trusted Noah with knowledge that she'd never dared to tell anyone else, and she couldn't imagine being without him. She was startled out of her musings about Noah when the baby moved for the first time. She smiled and quickly called the children over.

✝

Noah fished his phone out of his pocket and pushed his wife's number. He wasn't surprised when she answered on the first ring. "Hey, Cinderella," he teased.

"Hi, Prince Charming," Marly teased back. "Are you still at the ball?" she quipped.

"Yep, I'm still dancing. How's my baby doing?" he asked, changing the subject.

"I'm fine, thanks for asking," she replied saucily.

Noah chuckled huskily, "You little flirt. I meant our daughter."

"As a matter of fact, she moved for the first time. The children were so excited," she said happily.

"She's moving already? She's only a week or so over five months. Isn't it a little early?" he wondered.

"I don't know what the norm is, but Kaod moved at four and a half months. He only did it once and it kind of reminded me of riding on a rollercoaster. I guess she doesn't want to be outdone," she laughed.

"Just out of curiosity, did Kaod do everything early?" Noah asked.

"How'd you guess? He walked at ten months, was potty trained at eighteen months, wrote his name at about twenty-nine months... Shall I continue on?"

"No, no, that's quite enough. I wonder if she'll be the same way. Hey, wait a minute. How was Kaod with the girls?" he laughed.

Marly laughed too. "With girls, he moved very slowly."

"Phew! You were beginning to scare me," he admitted with a chuckle.

She was quiet for a moment then asked in a serious tone, "How's the hearing going, Noah?"

He knew she'd eventually get around to it.

"Actually, it seems to be going really well. As a matter of fact, better than I expected. Sorry, honey. I see them motioning for me. I've gotta get going. Remember what we talked about, okay. I love you, sweetheart and I'll see you in a little while."

He waited for her to respond back, hung up the phone, and calmly walked back into the hearing.

☦

"We see here that your secretary has provided times and hours in reference to your work schedule," one of the friendlier Bishops declared. "Everything seems to be in order. In fact, you appear to consistently work many hours beyond the required amount. It is also duly noted that you and your wife have begun an inner-city ministry which has been officially documented as having helped to reduce crime in that particular neighborhood. Have you had any converts?"

Noah gazed at the Bishop before he carefully spoke.

"I personally know of several, but the fact that crime has gone down should testify that the Lord is at work." He was not about to allow this church organization to lay claim to the accomplishments of God.

"How is this ministry being financed? Has the church contributed any funds?"

Noah's eyes narrowed, "Several very large donations have been contributed by citizens who wish to remain anonymous and no, the church has not donated anything."

"May I ask why not?"

Noah's countenance remained sober as he spoke honestly.

"I think we all know the answer to that. It would simply create another opportunity for this board to bring accusation against me."

Several of the board members hid smiles, while others turned away in shame, but the scowling Bishop Benson was not affected by Noah's candor.

"So, Pastor Phillips, you feel we have no valid reason for calling you before this board."

Noah assumed a more casual posture. This was exactly the opportunity he'd been waiting for. "My feelings on this matter have been of no concern up unto this point. Why ask me now, unless this board is prepared to allow me to speak freely?"

Bishop Benson's face reddened to the point where Noah thought for sure it would explode.

"Speak what is in your heart Noah," a kindly silver haired man replied.

Noah recognized him as Bishop Teren. They had met several years ago at a conference retreat. Noah looked each member in the eye before speaking.

"I would like to know whether the color of my wife's skin bears any issue to my being here today."

The room became deathly silent. Noah sat calmly waiting for someone, anyone to reply. Finally, Bishop Benson spoke, attempting to censor his words.

"Since you've brought up your wife, I can be frank and say that several of your members have complained that they would not be able to uh, I'm trying to find the proper words, uh …relate to her. They felt there was no common ground. I hope you are not offended," he finished with a satisfied smile.

"I'm never offended by the truth Bishop. I'm sure we are all in agreement with the fact that it would be very difficult, if not impossible, for a true believer to find 'common ground' with those that are merely professing to be believers," Noah informed him in a dismissive voice.

Silence thundered once again and held the room captive. No one dared to utter a word as all eyes centered on Bishop Benson. The Bishop spoke through clenched teeth and with barely concealed malice.

"Are you implying that any member who dares to bring a complaint about your wife is an unbeliever?"

Noah leaned forward and addressed his answer to the Bishop alone.

"I dare to say that all believers should have at least one thing in common and that something should be none other than the Lord Jesus Christ. Furthermore, I must insist that in Christ there is no division. If someone has a problem, the answer can be found in His Word, not in a man, or in this case a woman. Which of you would want others to base their salvation on 'common ground' with you?" Noah finished in a sure tone.

Marly, he knew, would be on her feet giving him a standing ovation if she were there. Especially, since he'd just quoted her.

"So, Pastor Phillips, what do you suggest we do about your disgruntled members?" another of the Bishops asked.

"Please, word my mouth Lord," Noah prayed silently before answering. "I suggest that we do as I Corinthians 5:5 says, 'Deliver such a one unto Satan for the destruction of the flesh, that the spirit may be saved', and then let the church get on with the business of bringing the unsaved to the foot of the cross in order for them to be grafted into the family of believers," he said firmly.

"The purpose of this board is to assist our members with conflicts between them and their pastor, not to remove them from the church simply because they have a complaint about your wife," Bishop Benson inserted.

"I don't think that is what Pastor Phillips is implying," Bishop Teren interjected. "Those members that have departed have chosen to leave based on reasons that are clearly non-Biblical. We should pray for them, but we should not allow them to disrupt the church," Bishop Teren finished.

The majority of the board nodded their agreement, while Bishop Benson remained steadfast in his dislike of Noah. Noah was asked to once more step outside of the room in order for the board to discuss their decision.

✟

Noah picked up his briefcase and headed towards the exit. He gave God all the glory for the victory today. There was no other way to explain it. Not only were all complaints dismissed and his professional file cleared, he and Marly were to have dinner with Bishop Teren tonight to discuss their inner-city ministry with a huge possibility that they could be supervising the establishing of Chandra's Houses throughout the city. If all went well, eventually throughout the state. Bishop Teren had requested to personally meet Marly. Noah smiled and wondered if the Bishop was up to the task. The Board had also voted to send notice to Pastor Wade requiring Caroline to appear before the board to discuss her false allegations. Noah thought about Romans 12:19 which says that "Vengeance is mine; I will repay, saith the Lord". He had tried to warn Caroline on at least three separate occasions not to interfere with that which the Lord had put together (his and Marly's relationship). She had chosen not to heed those warnings. Now, she was going to have to deal with whatever the outcome was of her foolishness.

☦

Noah quietly opened the door of the empty classroom and smiled as he watched Marly studiously correcting lessons. She was frowning as though trying to figure out exactly what that particular child had attempted to write.

"I'm glad that's not my paper you're grading," he said quietly.

"Noah!" she gasped excitedly. "You're early," she noted, rising to eagerly go into his waiting arms.

She kissed him warmly before remembering where they were.

"Wow, now that's a greeting. Maybe, I should leave and come back again," he chuckled softly and held her firmly as she blushed and tried to ease away.

"Why are you blushing?" he asked. "There's no one else in this room, just you and me."

"What if someone comes in?" she whispered.

"For heaven's sake, you're my wife. If I want to kiss you while the whole world is watching, how is that wrong? It's not like we're…"

"Okay, okay, I get it," she said, cutting his words off before he could finish.

"Good," he responded, allowing her to escape.

Noah watched as she gathered her things. He found her satchel and helped her with her coat. He intentionally grabbed her hand and smiled as they walked past various staff and out the door. He shook his head in exasperation when he saw her blushing. She was behaving in that quirky manner of hers again.

✟

They'd been riding for a good ten minutes before she finally asked, "How'd the hearing go babe?"

Noah pretended not to hear her hoping that she'd repeat herself. She'd never called him anything but Noah, except for that one time at the park when she'd called him "Babe".

"Did you hear me, babe?" she repeated.

He'd heard her loud and clear.

He wanted to pull over to the side of the road and kiss her senseless, instead he glanced at her and calmly said, "It went extremely well."

"Is that all you have to say? What about the details?" she complained laughingly.

"Are we busy tonight?" he asked.

"No, why?" she inquired.

"Because sweetheart, you and I have a dinner date with Bishop Teren," Noah declared.

"Who's Bishop Teren?" Marly wondered aloud.

Noah went on to explain who the Bishop was as well as everything that had transpired during the hearing.

Marly was thankful, but stunned.

"Why does he want to meet me?"

"You'll have to ask him that. Are you afraid of meeting him?" he teased.

"No, I just don't want to embarrass you. I have no clue about the protocol for this type of thing," she replied.

"Just be yourself Marly and everything will be fine," he said as he maneuvered the car into their garage.

✟

"Be myself! That's easy for him to say," Marly mumbled to herself as she browsed through her wardrobe. "He keeps conveniently forgetting that this is all new to me. I don't even know what I should wear to meet a Bishop," she muttered to herself. Feeling frustrated, she went in search of Noah. "Babe," she called out as she entered the family room.

Two heads turned to face her as she entered.

Adam grinned and said, "I think she's referring to you, Dad."

Marly stuck her tongue out at Adam and perched on the arm of the sofa upon which Noah was sitting.

"What are you wearing tonight?" she asked.

"Why? Do you want to dress alike again?" he teased, reminding her of the first time he'd taken her to his church.

Adam looked on in curiosity.

"Noah, you know that I had no idea what you were wearing," she stated in self-defense.

"I don't know. Now that I think about it, I think you were staking a claim. You were telling the other women to steer clear because Pastor Noah belongs to Marly."

Adam laughed, enjoying this little exchange.

Marly rolled her eyes and said, "Really, weren't you the one that was so upset with me for complaining that we looked like a couple?"

He smiled impishly and claimed, "No, I just used it as an excuse to kiss you, and my diabolical plot worked."

Adam glanced at his dad and then at Marly.

"I wondered what that little exchange between the two of you at church was all about. So why'd you kiss her Dad? What happened?"

Before Noah could answer, Marly covered his mouth with her hand, but Noah grabbed her and pulled her onto his lap.

"Tell Adam who's your daddy!" he demanded.

"I will not," she laughed.

"Okay, I'm going to tell him our little secret," he warned.

"No," she blushed, attempting to cover his mouth.

He held her hands captive and demanded that she tell Adam what he wanted her to say. Adam laughed delightedly as Marly agreed to say the words that his dad had commanded.

"Who's your daddy Marly? Last chance or I'm going to spill the beans."

She blushed further and reluctantly exclaimed, "You are."

Noah grinned happily and released her. She was so flustered that she had no idea how to respond to his teasing. She recovered enough to stand and quickly make a beeline out of the room. Male laughter followed her down the hallway.

✝

Noah opened the car door and escorted his wife into the restaurant. She looked radiant in her light brown casual pantsuit. The suit enhanced the creamy brown texture of her skin. He resisted the urge to lift her shiny black curls from her neck and nuzzle that soft spot she loved so much. Instead, he placed his hand in the small of her back and guided her towards the hostess. The hostess smiled brightly and informed them that their table was ready.

Bishop Teren hadn't yet arrived so Noah occupied the time flirting with a somewhat bashful Marly. He leaned over and whispered in her ear how he loved it when she called him "babe".

She gazed at him with warmth that touched his soul and questioned softly, "Really?"

"Yes, really," he whispered just before he reached for her hand and brushed it gently with his mouth.

This woman was positively intoxicating to him. She was without pretense. God had given him a woman that didn't have the art of seduction practiced and perfected. She was like the scent of a fresh flower without the artificial fragrances, a flower that hadn't yet discovered how alluring it was to him. He smiled to himself when he thought of the mischief she'd be able to cause him when she began realizing the power she had over his senses. Noah watched her big brown eyes darken in response to his words and the simple touch of his mouth on her hand. If anyone would have told him it would be possible to find a woman like her, he would have been a scoffer. There was no doubt that God loved him. He glanced at Marly. She didn't have to say a word. He knew that she wanted him to kiss her and he would have happily obliged her, but Bishop Teren had chosen that moment to walk through the door.

He winked in understanding and said, "Sorry, sweetheart, but the Bishop just walked through the door. Still want that kiss?"

Her eyes widened in surprise and he could tell that she was wondering how he knew what she'd been thinking.

✠

Introductions had been made, dinner ordered, and Marly still hadn't said a word. Marly sensed Noah looking at her strangely. She didn't know what he expected of her. She wasn't sure how a pastor's wife should behave or what she should talk about. She opted to remain quiet and listen to the conversation. It wasn't her usual choice, but she was now representing Noah, and that made her more cautious, especially after that District Board nonsense.

She stood and excused herself to the ladies room.

Once inside, she looked in the mirror and said to no one in particular, "If Noah gives me one more of those strange looks, I'm going to scream."

Bishop Teren smiled at Noah. "Your wife is very beautiful, but is she always this quiet?"

"Thank you, and no. We usually engage in very lively discussions. I think it's your title. Try talking to her about the different theologies," Noah suggested. "That ought to perk up her conversation."

Bishop Teren nodded and waited for Marly to return.

She returned to find that Noah had excused himself to take a phone call.

"Great, what am I supposed to say to this man?" Marly thought.

Bishop Teren began espousing on some nonsensical doctrine from some absurd book that he'd read. Try as she might, she couldn't keep quiet when he asked her what she thought. By the time she had finished tearing that particular doctrine to shreds, the food had arrived and Noah had returned.

Noah observed the Bishop's expression and knew that Marly had said something that had completely shocked him.

"What did I miss? You two look as though you were enjoying the conversation."

"Your wife was just explaining the necessity of the blood atonement to me. We were just about to discuss divine forgiveness when the food arrived," he exclaimed with a knowing twinkle in his eye.

Noah deliberately kept a neutral expression on his face.

Bishop Teren blessed the food and then looked directly at Marly and said, "So tell me about divine forgiveness."

Noah averted his eyes and pretended to be preoccupied with his food. He smiled to himself as he listened to her explain divine forgiveness to the Bishop.

✠

The two men watched as Marly headed towards the ladies room for the third time that evening.

Bishop Teren glanced at Noah and laughed. "Are you sure she's never had any formal training? Her grasp of Bible theology is above average and she's quite passionate about her beliefs," he stated as he shook his head in wonder.

Noah chuckled knowingly, "Imagine my surprise when I found out that she was not a member of any church and that she'd studied on her own. I was completely floored, and that's putting it mildly."

"Well, I can now see why some have stated that they have no 'common ground' with your wife. Not many of our members have an understanding of scripture equal to hers," Bishop Teren admitted somewhat regretfully.

He then surprised Noah by asking when their child was due. If you looked at Marly, she hardly looked pregnant.

"How'd you know she was pregnant?" Noah wanted to know.

It was the Bishop's turn to smile. "She keeps touching her stomach which is something most pregnant women do, besides that, she has that glow that pregnant women get, and she's continually going to the restroom." Bishop Teren paused, and then added, "I'm going to level with you Noah. I didn't know what to expect. It had nothing to do with the color of your wife, but everything with whether or not she would be an asset to your ministry. I no longer have any doubts concerning that. She's a blessing to you and to our denomination. I will be sending a letter of strong recommendation to the District Board for you to head the establishment of community ministries starting locally, and God willing, advancing throughout the state."

Noah gripped the older man's hand in a firm handshake and thanked him for his kindness. Once again, God had shown him favor.

✞

Marly turned and reached for her husband, only to find an empty bed. She sleepily glanced at the clock on the nightstand. Where in the world could he be? She eased from beneath the thick comforter and found her slippers.

Noah sat in his study staring at the blank screen of his laptop. He waited for God to give him what to type. He closed his eyes and imagined a baby girl with shiny black curls. Her skin was a deep rich caramel and she had big brown eyes. His fingers began to type out the story that seemed to be whispered to his heart. A story about a little girl whose daddy was white, but her mommy was black. He was so thoroughly engrossed in the story that he was not aware of Marly's presence until he felt her arms slide around his waist.

"It's two in the morning. What are you doing typing?" she murmured against his back.

"I type when God tells me to type. You should be in bed," he suggested gently as he pulled her around to face him.

"I can't sleep without you," she complained.

"You say that now, just wait until the baby comes," he laughed softly, pulling her into his arms. He held her close, simply enjoying the privilege that marriage afforded him. He remembered the many lonely nights, before their marriage, when he had dreamed of being able to hold her like this. This simple pleasure caused him to close his eyes and give thanks to his Father in heaven.

She relished the security of his strong capable arms. Arms that were so full of strength and protection; yet, they always enfolded her gently; this was her husband, her shepherd, could there be any greater gift to a woman, other than the son of God and salvation? He was her mantle, her covering, provided by God himself.

"Thank you, God," she praised silently.

She was standing, listening to the melodic beating of his heart, with his arms wrapped around her.

"Come on," he whispered into her ear, leading her back to their bedroom.

He waited until she was in bed and beneath the covers before lying down and putting his arm around her and pulling her close. Noah listened to the sound of her breathing until he sensed that she was sound asleep. He gently removed himself from the bed and quietly crept back to his study. Once there, he began typing again. This story would be dedicated to his and Marly's daughter. She, he now fully understood, would be the thread used to help bind their family together. He prayed that it would cause people to wake up to the fact that prejudiced behavior was still alive and well in our society, but love could overcome it.

Chapter Thirty-four

Kaod gazed at his mother. She did look radiant. He was wondering if all pregnant women had that particular look about them. He watched Noah and wondered how he was feeling. It was senior night and the stadium was packed. He knew when his name was called to be escorted out onto the field by his mom and dad the fans were going to go wild. The noise would be deafening and to most, a little intimidating.

"Are you guys ready for this?" he asked, looking at Noah.

Noah shrugged and gazed at Marly. She was staring at the tens of thousands of fans situated in the "U".

"Where are you at in the lineup?" she asked Kaod.

"Since my last name starts with the letter 'p', I'm probably somewhere towards the end," he informed her.

She nodded and linked her arm through his.

Noah could sense the many curious stares of the other families surrounding them. He turned when he heard a familiar voice call out to his wife. Before she could respond, the owner of the voice had enveloped her in one of his bear hugs. Noah watched as Marly smiled warmly at Drew and returned his hug. He fought the sudden urge to pull her to his side in a rare show of possession. He realized that he had no reason to be jealous, but he couldn't shake the notion that Drew was in love with his wife. That, coupled with the fact that he was out of his element and now in Drew's. He was also very much aware that most of the people here had expected Drew and Marly to be the couple escorting "The Pittbull" onto the field for Senior Night. Noah forced a smile to his face as he shook hands with the popular coach. It was crazy, but he was experiencing the same uncertainty about himself as he had the first time he was to meet Kaod's infamous coach. He wondered if Kaod wished that it was his mother and Drew that were walking with him for Senior Night. Worse yet, did he still desire Drew to be his father. Suddenly, he became self-conscious about the color of his skin. Noah observed the three of them talking and laughing and acknowledged that they looked like a family.

Marly felt Noah's withdrawal and immediately turned to face him. His expression was deliberately blank which meant he didn't want her to know what he was thinking. Normally, she was a very private person, but she could sense that Noah needed her to openly display her love for him. She knew that people were staring at them, wondering how this unknown guy replaced Coach Drew in Kaod's life. This was nothing new to her, but Noah hadn't experienced this crazed sports crowd, where football was their god, and their god was football. A place where race didn't matter as much, but athletic ability did. She arched her brows and smiled at him before resting her head against his chest. Marly stayed in that position until she felt his arms come around her.

"I hate crowds," she confessed. "I always feel like I'll get lost or lose the one I love in them."

When he didn't respond, she took a deep breath and prayed for the Lord to give her strength. She was not a bold woman in the matters of the heart and the open display of affection, but she understood what Noah was feeling. His security and sense of peace were being threatened. His confidence in this situation depended upon her actions at the moment. She stood on the tip of her toes and pulled his head down until her lips met his in a kiss that could only be described as possessive.

Noah was amazed at her boldness, especially with so many others looking on; however, the minute her lips met his, he felt at liberty to possess as well as be possessed. Noah met her lips in a mutual claim of ownership, a message sent to all who witnessed. She pulled back and hid her face against his chest. He gazed down at her and wondered how in the world she could be bashful after she'd just kissed him in front of thousands of people. He chuckled at her quirkiness and glanced at Kaod and Drew who were standing there with their mouths wide open. Noah grinned at the two of them. She'd definitely left no doubt in the minds of others as to who she preferred. She hadn't said a word, but the message was loud and clear.

He spoke softly for her ears only, "Thank you, sweetheart, that took a lot of courage."

✣

Noah, Marly, and Kaod watched as, one by one, the seniors on the football team were announced. Proud parents escorted their children onto the field to the applause of the thousands of fans at the stadium. The noise was so loud that they had to shout just to be heard. Kaod shouted to his parents that they were next. Marly reached for her son's arm while Noah positioned himself on the other side of Kaod. Marly smiled at them and waited for the announcer to speak.

An unknown voice, filled with anticipation, informed the excited crowd of Kaod's educational major, his hobbies, and his seemingly endless list of football accomplishments before concluding in a dramatic voice, "Being escorted by his parents, Mr. and Mrs. Noah Phillips, our very own, Ohio grown, All-American, Kaod 'The Pittbull' Porter."

Applause and wild cheering erupted from within 'The Horseshoe'. Marly laughed and hugged her son to her. Kaod picked up his mom and twirled her around which caused the crowd to cheer even louder. They listened and watched as the fans came to their feet in a standing ovation and began chanting, "Pittbull" over and over again. The cheering went on and on until Kaod, mindful that there were other seniors awaiting their turn, motioned for the crowd to settle down. Marly and Noah were even more proud of their son as his consideration for others spoke even more volumes than the standing ovation. She watched as Kaod hugged Noah and said something to him. She couldn't make it out, but they both looked at her and grinned.

She stepped towards them and said, "What are you two smiling and whispering about?"

Noah pushed Kaod towards his mother and said, "You tell her."

Kaod shook his head no and turned back to stand behind Noah.

"You big chicken," Noah teased him.

Noah reached for Marly and pointed at the huge screens in the stadium. There, on the screen for the entire viewing audience to see was an up close shot of Noah and her kissing.

She couldn't believe her eyes. How did that get on television? That kiss was for Noah's sake, not for the whole world to see. She did a quick peek on each side of her and felt the hot embarrassing heat invade her cheeks. Everyone was smiling and clapping. Someone had reported their newlywed status and since anything involving "The Pittbull's" mother was newsworthy, there they were as big as you please, kissing on the big screen. Normally, she would have thought it romantic, but that was when it didn't involve her. Some of that wild clapping and whistling had been for her and Noah.

"Please tell me that kiss is not going over the airwaves," she pleaded with God.

Simultaneously, Noah's and her cell phones began vibrating. She pulled out her phone and recognized Tina's number.

"Great, if Tina's seen it, then the whole world has too," Marly groaned. "Yes, Tina," Marly answered reluctantly. After five whole minutes of wisecracks from her best friend, Marly disconnected and turned her phone off. She refused to look anywhere, but straight ahead. She knew from studying the Word that God has a sense of humor, but this was over the top she complained to Him. Somehow, she got the feeling that God didn't think so.

Noah had received phone calls from Layman, Hal, and his brother John over the past ten minutes, each one making some witty comment or joke. He glanced at Marly who determinedly kept her face averted. He knew she was embarrassed. She'd intended that kiss as a way to show him support. Well, she'd wanted everyone to know who she preferred. God had simply lent her a helping hand. He was just thanking God that they hadn't captured her hugging Drew. Noah eased Marly's hand into his and gave it a squeeze. He probably should tell her that they were already calling her kiss the "Under Armor Play of the Day".

"Remember when I told you that I didn't care if the whole world saw me kissing you? You didn't have to take me literally," he said humorously. He saw a reluctant smile tug at the corners of her mouth. "Would you like to try for an encore performance?" he suggested softly in her ear as he casually slid his arm around her waist.

✠

Thanking God that they were no longer down on the field, Marly watched as Ohio State kicked the ball off to Michigan. The crowd roared excitedly as the perfectly kicked ball landed into the end zone for a touchback. She said a quick prayer for her son as he ran onto the field for the first defensive series. All around her, chants of "Pittbull, Pittbull, Pittbull," filled the capacity packed stadium. By now, Marly knew the drill and she pitied the guy who took the first handoff. She watched as Kaod called out signals to his defense. She was always amazed at his ability to know where the football was going and to meet head on the unfortunate player carrying the ball. The whistle blew and ten seconds later, the offense had line up. She held her breath as the opposing team's quarterback called for the hike. Immediately, two linemen fired out towards Kaod who seemed to already know the play. He sidestepped the first and drove the second back into the hole where Michigan's running back assumed there would be running space. Kaod quickly bounced off the remaining lineman and with unbelievable speed and strength hit his intended target with such force that the running back's helmet dislodged and fell in a spinning heap onto the field. The sound of the impact could be heard throughout the "U" and caused a reflexive gasp, followed by the customary pandemonium.

Michigan's running back lay momentarily confused as he attempted to regain a state of awareness which "The Pittbull's" hit had knocked out of him. Once again the crowd chanted, "Pittbull, Pittbull, Pittbull," when an injury time-out was called to escort the dazed Michigan player off the field. Marly waited for Kaod to locate her section and point. She completed their tradition as she pointed back at him.

Noah shook his head in amazement. Since his and Marly's engagement, and subsequent marriage, they'd attended almost every one of Kaod's games, but the caliber of his stepson's athletic ability never ceased to astonish him. He smiled as Kaod pointed to his mother. He had learned that it was a tradition between the two of them, starting during his Midget League Football days. She had begun pointing at him during the games to let him know he was as good as any other kid out there. Then, as he'd become older, she'd started pointing to let him know it was his field and that he needed to initiate the first big hit to strike fear in the opposing players. Kaod had started pointing back as a way of thanking his mother.

Kaod loved football, but he had confessed to Noah that he had another goal in life. He wanted to become a law enforcement officer, but he didn't know how his mom would take it. He'd asked Noah to bring up the subject with her.

Noah faced Marly and asked, "Has Kaod talked to you about changing his major and the fact that he only wants to play professional football for five years?"

"No, he hasn't told me anything, but Adam spilled the beans," she answered.

"What do you think about it?" Noah questioned.

"I think it's no more dangerous than playing football. Being a police officer is an honorable profession. If Kaod wants to change his major, then he'd better get busy. Maybe your brother John could give him some advice," she surmised.

"I'll give John a call and maybe set up a meeting with Kaod. John's going to be thrilled to have someone follow in his footsteps," Noah laughed.

"Would you like to have someone follow in your footsteps?" she asked without looking away from the game.

Noah looked puzzled.

"Adam wants to go to Seminary. He's decided to stop running from God and become a pastor," she supplied with a smile. "I say we help him out. What do you think?"

He hugged her to him and shouted for joy.

Ohio State easily defeated Michigan by a twenty-four point margin. Kaod had his typical outstanding game. Reporters, agents, and women were all camped outside the locker room, vying for his attention. Noah pulled out his cell and pushed Ka's number. He picked up on the third ring and agreed to meet them back at the hotel in two hours. Noah clasped Marly's hand in his and proceeded to weave their way through the swarm of reporters. They were asked to provide several interviews after some in the media recognized Marly. Noah quickly declined and led his wife to their rental car. By the time they arrived back at their hotel, both were hungry and decided to dine in-house.

Quite naturally, all of the viewing screens were tuned to the sports channel. Marly thought to herself that she'd had enough football for today. She'd rather watch the news or something else. Noah was pulling her chair out for her when the "Under Armor Play of the Day" was announced. Thinking it had something to do with Kaod she paused and watched the screen. She couldn't believe her eyes or ears when the commentator joked about "The Pittbull's" parents having the play of the day.

She watched in total disbelief as the commentator drew those stupid little yellow circles around her face and proceeded to explain, "As you can see, the safety is coming in on a safety blitz, and just as the running back gets to the hole, boom! Look at that contact!"

He continued to rewind and play the kiss, over and over again, in slow motion before exclaiming, "Now, we all know who 'The Pitttbull' gets his moves from. That, football fans, is our 'Under Armor Play of the Day'."

Marly turned to face Noah. He was trying valiantly not to give into his humor. Before she could say a word, a young boy came over to the table and asked if he could have her autograph. Noah, unable to contain himself any longer, plopped onto the nearest chair in an unsuppressed fit of laughter. Marly ignored him, politely took the pen from the boy, and proceeded to autograph his football. Her young fan excitedly thanked her and ran back to his parents. Before the night was over, she and Noah had signed several more autographs. At least, she thought to herself, no one had interrupted them during their meal.

They had finished their meal and were heading up to their room when Kaod arrived. He greeted them as they were stepping into the elevator.

"Are you guys tired?" he asked. "Coach invited us over to his home. There are going to be some agents there and I'd kind of like you two to be there with me."

Noah spoke first, "If your mom is up for it, then we'll go. What do you say, sweetheart?"

Marly looked at her son and narrowed her eyes.

"Did you know that I was on the 'Play of the Day'?" she asked sweetly.

Kaod glanced at Noah who tried unsuccessfully to warn Kaod with his eyes.

"Why are you looking at Noah? Either you knew or you didn't know," she announced calmly.

Noah observed Kaod shift his feet and realizing that their son couldn't withstand the pressure, that he was caving, stepped forward and advised, "Don't admit anything. She has no proof. Be strong, man. Be strong."

Marly began to giggle as she realized Noah's guilt.

"You both are guilty," she accused laughingly as she watched them point at each other.

☦

Noah flipped open his wallet and placed another business card inside. That made the eighth person wanting to become Kaod's agent next year. He'd put a small cross on the three that impressed him. He'd have John run checks on them later. He shook his head in shock as he gazed around the room. So this was how the other half lived. He definitely hadn't missed a thing. This type of environment made him appreciate his simple way of life. The women were practically naked and seemed without shame. Why were they here in the first place? It came to him all at once. They were there as lures to snag Kaod into signing with one of their bosses. He thanked God for his modestly dressed wife. She stood out like a rose among thorns and thistles. Both mother and son carried themselves way above reproach. Kaod hadn't so much as talked to any of the, as the book of Proverbs called them, "strange women" that were gathered there.

Noah was making his way towards his wife when one of those women clasped his arm and seductively asked, "What's your name, handsome?"

Without missing a beat, he responded, "Happily Married," and firmly removed her hand from his arm as he walked away.

He searched the room looking for his wife and son. It was time to go.

✠

Marly was tired and ready to leave when Drew approached her with a smile.

"You look beautiful, Marlena. Kaod tells me that you and Noah are expecting."

She returned the smile and nodded yes.

"You do know that it should have been us escorting Ka' out onto the field today," he said with a wink.

Marly knew better than to go down that road.

"I'm with the man God wants me to be with," she answered.

Drew opened his mouth to speak, but thought better of it.

"Why do you have these women here tempting my son?" she questioned in her no-nonsense voice.

Drew frowned as he attempted to avoid his part in this gathering. "Come on, Marlena. You know the game. The agents bring these women along for the ride. I have nothing to do with that part of it," he said, attempting to defend himself.

She wasn't buying his excuses.

"This is your house, Drew. I would like to think you're man enough to decide who's invited and who's not. Furthermore, …"

"Marly!" a strong male voice interrupted.

Marly turned to see Noah in the doorway. Ka' was standing behind him.

"It's time for us to get going," Noah informed her. The tone of his voice softened as he pulled her to him. Drew came forth and hugged Kaod, but didn't attempt to hug Marly. He would have had to step around Noah and

308

he was pretty sure that Noah's actions had been deliberate. Noah handed his wife to Kaod and asked if he could have a moment alone with Drew.

Kaod glanced from Noah to Drew warily. He was hesitant until he saw the look in Noah's eyes. It wasn't a request, it was a command. This was the first time he had encountered the authoritative side of Noah. Kaod gripped his mother's arm and led her from the room.

Noah turned to face Drew. He wasn't, in the least bit, intimidated by the coach and Drew knew it.

"I want to thank you for all that you've done for Kaod. He needed you and you were there for him, but I hope you'll appreciate what I'm about to say. Kaod is doing all he can to abstain until he gets married. Parading all of these inappropriately dressed women in front of him is a hindrance to him and a huge disrespect to his mother. Even if you don't agree with their beliefs, the least I'd think you'd want to do would be to honor them, and since I'm pretty sure that you're still in love with my wife, I'd think that you'd respect her desires for her son. I know that you've known them a lot longer than I have, but they are both my responsibility now, and I take that responsibility very seriously. If you don't have Kaod's best interests at heart, I need to know that."

Drew suddenly felt ashamed of his part in tonight's gathering. He did love both Kaod and his mother, but he'd never really believed in that abstinence thing. It had caused him to lose Marlena and now the same thing was happening with her son. He'd realized that Noah had begun to replace him in Kaod's eyes. There was something that he was missing. What did this guy have that was causing the people Drew loved to turn to him? If he didn't understand anything else, he knew that he was wrong and he needed to be a man and admit it.

"I'm sorry. You're right. From this point on, I'll respect his beliefs and make sure I do my part to help him hold true to them."

Noah looked Drew in the eye and held his gaze.

"One more thing, don't hug my wife anymore. She may see it as being friendly, but I see it as touching something that belongs to me."

Noah didn't bother waiting for a response. As far as he was concerned, that was a done deal. He turned and headed in the direction of Kaod and Marly. He heard Drew following them as they walked towards the door.

Drew's gaze followed Noah's departure. It was difficult for him to dislike the man. Noah had been nothing but forthright with him from the very beginning. He hadn't even become angry with him when he'd overheard him ask Marly for a goodbye kiss. Drew wouldn't appreciate another man hugging his wife either, especially if they had been somewhat involved. He grimaced when one of the women came up and slid her arm around his waist in a possessive manner while scowling at Marlena. He glanced at the woman and then at Marlena. There was no comparison. "Marlena was the real deal," he thought bitterly.

Noah glanced at Marly who wasn't paying the woman a bit of attention. He knew that she was still simmering over the way he'd called her name. Well, he had a bone to pick with her too. She was behaving in a very naïve manner when it came to Drew. The man was obviously in love with her. Even Drew's lady friend had picked up on that. It was why she'd staked her claim in front of them and had glared warningly at Marly. Drew had been a fool to gamble Marly away, and from the look on his face, he knew it.

✠

Noah watched as mother and son said their goodbyes. Kaod promised to be home for the holidays. He also vowed to do everything he could to be there when his baby sister was to be born.

Soon Noah and Marly were on their way back to the hotel. She still hadn't said a word to him directly. Noah decided to break the silence.

"Why do you hug Drew?" he asked in a calm voice.

She seemed taken aback for a moment. "What are you talking about Noah? You couldn't possibly be jealous of Drew. I'm married to you and carrying your child."

He pretended not to hear her tirade and asked again, "Why do you hug Drew?"

Marly decided to simply ignore him and closed her eyes.

"Honey, I promise you that I'm not angry or jealous. I simply want to know why you hug Drew," he stated softly.

She kept her eyes closed, but answered, "I don't know, Noah; probably, because he initiates the hugs." She replied sounding a bit dismissive.

"Why do you think I began hugging you? Besides the fact that I found you extremely attractive," he added as an afterthought. He could tell that he had her interest now.

She opened her eyes and looked directly at him. "I'm not sure."

He remained serious as he began his explanation. He told her of the bonding process between men and women. She learned that he'd used simple touch to start them bonding with each other. That type of touch is crucial for the female because it allows her to connect with her mate emotionally and is an important ingredient in helping her feel secure.

310

Marly recalled the first time they'd held hands and how he'd always hugged her.

"So you set out to deliberately make me bond with you," she stated dryly.

"Why are you acting offended? You already know that love is a decision, not an emotion; although, I did experience some rather strong emotions in your presence. As I got to know you, I realized that you were the one that God had set apart for me. I prayed about you, and then I did everything I could, with the direction of God, to persuade you to trust me with your heart. Do you remember when I asked you if you and Drew had been intimate? I needed to know if you were tied to him in a way that would have made it difficult for me to win your complete love and dedication."

"What does any of this have to do with me returning Drew's hug?" she interjected.

"I don't think you should continue to bond with a man who still has romantic feelings for you. There can't be a purely platonic friendship as long as he thinks there's still a chance for something more. Are you following me?" he asked softly.

"I understand," she said blushing.

"One more thing," he said. "You were right in your observation about those women being stumbling blocks to Kaod, but please talk to me before you make a decision to chastise a man in his own home. I'll protect you with my life if I have to, but it's hard to defend someone if they are wrong."

"You just said I was right, so how could I be wrong at the same time?" she questioned.

He chuckled at her expression and explained, "You are the wife and I am the husband. You see the problems and then you bring them to me. We talk about the problems, decide what to do and who will do it. If it involves a man, then I will handle it which keeps you, my little angel, out of harm's way."

"Did you handle the problem with Drew?" she wondered.

Without taking his eyes from the road, he declared that he'd dealt with both problems. She knew he was also referencing Drew's hugs. She sat back and closed her eyes, but a smile was on her face.

☦

Marly snuggled deeper into her husband's arms. He was a very wise man and had taken care of the situation with Drew. Kaod had called and thanked Noah for his help. Apparently Drew had apologized for not taking Kaod's vow of abstinence seriously.

Noah had simply told Kaod, "That's what dads are for."

She realized that she had to learn how to be a wife all over again, to remember that her husband was the head of their family. It was as though her flesh still desired to be independent of God's edicts. Noah was, for the most part, very patient with her. He always told her how much he enjoyed her company and how she kept him on his toes. She wondered what would happen when the baby was born. Would they remain as close as they were now or would the baby change things? She suddenly had a thought. Who was going to watch the baby when she went back to work?

"Babe, are you awake?" she whispered.

"I am now," he replied sleepily.

"I just had a thought," she said.

"About what?" Noah asked.

"The baby, who's going to watch her when I go back to work?" she questioned.

Noah stiffened. "Can we talk about this tomorrow?" he asked, hoping that she wouldn't push the issue. He had a feeling that when the subject was broached, she was not going to like his answer. Thankfully, she agreed to wait until the next day, but Noah was now wide awake.

Chapter Thirty-five

Noah had remained awake for an hour or so after that, thinking about what was sure to turn into World War III. The drive home was uneventful and she never brought the subject up. As they pulled into the garage, he knew it was time to talk about their responsibility to their child. It was Sunday, but they were not going to make the service and no one was expecting them. He grabbed the bags from the trunk and followed Marly into the house. Adam was away on a weekend assignment and wasn't due back until tomorrow sometime. Noah headed towards their bedroom and dropped the bags at the foot of the bed. He took his shoes off and stretched across the mattress. He only meant to close his eyes for a couple of minutes, but fatigue claimed him.

Two hours later, he awoke to the smell of dinner cooking. He sat up and to his surprise the clock showed the time to be a little after two in the afternoon. He heard Marly coming down the hallway and stood to his feet. She poked her head into the room and smiled when she saw him awake.

"Dinner is ready. Are you hungry?" she inquired.

"Sure, sweetheart, I'll be there in a minute," he said as he went into the bathroom to freshen up.

He stared at his reflection in the mirror and asked God to word his mouth. He could discern that this would be the first real test of their marriage and he asked the Lord to go before him in battle. His wife's independent spirit would have to submit to the will of God and she wasn't going to like it one bit. He was at a crossroad with her. He didn't want to break her spirit, but she was going to have to accept her new role as wife and mother, at least for the next four to five years. No child of his was going to daycare. God had provided the financial security for Marly to be able to stay home, so this was purely going to be a matter of choice for her. He prayed that she'd choose to stay home with their daughter during those first vital years.

"Okay God, show me how to husband your daughter. She's going to resist my headship, and I'm going to rely on you to instruct me and guide me through this rough period. Grant me the same patience with her that you, Father, have continued to bestow upon me. Let me be obedient to your will. Amen."

✞

Noah wiped his mouth and complimented Marly on the meal. She smiled her appreciation and stood to clear the table. Noah observed her for a moment before standing to assist her. In no time at all, the kitchen was spotless.

He glanced at her and asked, "When are you planning on taking maternity leave?"

"In January, about a month before the baby is born. I feel okay, and I don't want to just sit at home doing nothing," she explained.

"What about your plans after the baby is born?" he continued.

"That's what we need to discuss. Who's going to watch her when I return to work? I thought we could hire someone to come here, Monday through Friday, to babysit. She could be sort of like a weekday nanny. The only other alternative would be daycare," she concluded hesitantly looking at Noah.

He read her mind like a book. She already knew his answer and that was why she hadn't brought the topic up again. She wasn't ready to rock this particular boat, and neither was she prepared to hear his decision. They had agreed that when it was all said and done, he had the final say.

Noah held her gaze and said, "There is one more alternative that we haven't discussed. You could choose to stay home with our daughter and that would solve the problem."

Marly had known all along that Noah would want her to stay at home with their child. He sounded very calm about his little suggestion, but she knew it wasn't really a suggestion. It was his final word. The only thing he hadn't added in there yet was "good". Well, she wasn't going down without a fight.

"I don't want to stay at home, I want to go back and teach. I should be able to make this decision since it affects my life the most. Lots of women work, and manage kids and homes at the same time."

He leaned back against the sink and folded his arms.

"You are not one of those women. You are my wife and I would think that you, of all people, would understand how crucial those first years are. Don't you deal with the repercussions of 'daycare' kids in your class? How often have you told me that little children are like sponges? They soak up the world around them. By the way, my life will change drastically also…"

"Really," she cut in. "You'll still go to work every day and do the same things you've always done. I'm the one that will be stuck here at home all day long. Her voice had risen in anger.

"Are we talking about what's best for you, or are we talking about what's best for our family?" Noah asked gently, trying to keep civility to the conversation.

"Both, if the both of us are happy, then the whole family unit is happy. Why can't she go to a Christian daycare, or better yet, let's hire a Christian in-home babysitter."

Noah suddenly struggled to stay calm. Was she truly self-centered or just spouting off?

"You make our daughter sound as though she's on the same level as Beauty. This is our daughter, not some animal. What did you do with Kaod? You never worked until he started kindergarten. He never even went to preschool. You taught him at home. How is our daughter any different? Does she deserve less because she's not being born into a dysfunctional family? She will be a priority in this home not a bothersome chore on the weekend."

"I was young back then and…"

It was his time to cut in.

"Young and wise enough to be afraid for your son, that he'd learn the wrong things. Well that same thought should be uppermost in your mind concerning our daughter. You think that just because something or someone claims Christianity that their beliefs mirror ours. Don't be foolish, Marly. It is our job to teach our daughter the faith and all the other godly attributes she'll need to learn. We will be preparing her to become some fortunate guy's wife and the mother of his children, and most importantly, a woman of God. You will either model that before her or you won't. Take your pick," he finished in a raised tone.

"Noah, I can do both. I love teaching. It fulfills me and those kids need me," she confessed.

"And our daughter won't? Her needs will come after yours and those of your students. Am I getting this right?" Now, he was angry.

"That's not what I mean. You're twisting my words," she contested angrily.

"I'm not twisting anything. You explain to me, in your words, exactly what you mean. I don't want there to be any misunderstanding between us," he spoke with thinly controlled anger.

Marly studied him before saying, "I've worked hard to establish my career and I don't see why I should have to give it up. In a year, I'll be eligible for principal, but that won't happen if I take four or five years off."

"I'm beginning to get the picture here, Marly. This is about you and success. This is about your pride, the right to have a career that others look up to. After all, nobody looks up to a stay-at-home mom except her husband and children, but that's not enough exultation for you, is it? Have you even bothered to pray about this? Somehow, I doubt it. All that matters is you. Do things your way, Marly. I'm finished with this discussion," he said as he pushed away from the counter and walked out of the room.

Marly watched him leave and realized that she had fell a notch or two in his opinion. She had hurt him, but he had hurt her too. The way he'd looked at her. It was as though she had suddenly become distasteful to him. She stood and went in search of him only to find the door to his study shut. She wasn't sure how to proceed. She cautiously opened the door. Noah was on his knees praying. Marly felt a shame so deep, that the need for instant repentance flowed through her. Without waiting to be asked, she knelt beside him, grabbed his hand, and began praying.

She told the Lord of his goodness and loving kindness. She prayed for forgiveness of her sins and confessed that she had been prideful and self-centered. She asked God to forgive her for hurting her husband and to restore their marriage. Marly thanked the Lord for sending His son to die for them and for blessing her with Noah who provided for her daily and protected her with his life. She thanked God for the gift of their daughter. She asked the Lord to help her make godly decisions and to teach her how to willingly submit to her husband's authority. She acknowledged Christ's sacrifice on the cross and reaffirmed her belief in the virgin birth, the crucifixion, resurrection, and the ascension of His son.

When they had finished praying, Noah stood to his feet and helped her up. He led her into the bedroom and sat on the bed.

"I'm not trying to rob you of a career or force you into some kind of boring nonexistence. You have been a wonderful mother to Kaod and I'd like our daughter to experience everything you gave him and more. I don't want her cheated of her right to have her mom at home with her. Furthermore, I desire so much for our boys, all three of them, to finally experience what it's like to have both parents in the home on the same sheet of music. Adam watches you like a hawk. He smiles when you smile. He loves teasing you and helping you. He's learning about women through your nurturing. He's never had that before. Jacob needs you also. I know they're grown, but they still ache for a mother's love. What more influential position can there be then that? You have it within your power to mold and shape the lives of not only your children, but that of your husband's as well. Why don't you allow us to be your students and teach us? I, we need you here at home with us."

Looking into Noah's grey eyes and hearing the passion in his words convinced Marly that her place was there in the home with her family. She slid closer to him and felt his arms come around her.

"Okay, Noah, I'll resign from my teaching position as soon as they can find a replacement."

She saw no need to hang around the school any longer than that. Noah sighed with relief and silently thanked God.

"You won't regret it, sweetheart," he whispered reassuringly.

✠

Three weeks had passed and the school had hired a replacement for Marly. Marly had liked the woman immediately. She had a warm personality and it was evident that she adored children. Mrs. Garner's husband had passed away recently and she had nothing but time on her hands. Marly and Mrs. Garner had spent the last week preparing the children for Marly's departure. Noah had arrived earlier than usual to pick her up.

Marly choked back tears as she hugged and kissed her students goodbye. Most of the children were openly crying as they watched her gather her things. As Marly stepped into the hallway, several staff members were gathered there to pray for her and to ask God's blessing upon her. By the time she was seated in the car, tears were flowing freely from her eyes.

Noah didn't say a word. He'd experienced this side of her before when she had moved into the apartment. This was the way she dealt with change. She would get a good cry out, and then she'd talk. He was determined to be there for her. He'd taken the next week off to help her prepare

Thanksgiving dinner. Ka' had finally invited a young lady and Marly was excited about that. They were going to paint the little sitting room in their bedroom and convert it into a nursery for the baby. There were so many things to keep her preoccupied, Christmas and New Years, just to name a few, but first they had to make it through today.

✝

Marly awoke to find her husband's arm still wrapped protectively around her. Her eyes felt swollen from crying. Why did it seem like she had to do all of the sacrificing. She remembered moving from her house to the apartment, and now, the baby and having to quit her job. It just seemed so unfair. She didn't ask to get pregnant. In truth, she'd thought her body was going through menopause and hadn't worried about becoming pregnant. A baby was the last thing she'd wanted to happen. Her thoughts strayed to the conversation in the church parking lot. She could tell that Noah was excited and when he'd asked her how she felt, she'd blatantly lied because she didn't want to steal his joy. She hadn't been happy. She'd been scared stiff because she'd known even then that he'd want her to stay home with their child. Why hadn't she simply told him the truth then? She didn't want to hold this secret inside, but how could she tell him that she resented the intrusion that this baby had caused in her life. Hadn't he told her how Colleen had resented Adam? She loved her baby, but she wished that she'd been conceived in her earlier years. She wanted so desperately to share everything with him, but she didn't know how to explain it without hurting their relationship.

Noah knew the precise moment she'd awakened. He'd decided to lie still and let her collect her thoughts. Hopefully, she'd want to share. If not, he would have to be patient and wait. He tried to put himself in her place to feel what she was feeling. She was bound to be resentful. He wasn't sure if that resentment would be directed towards him or the baby. He was pretty sure that she loved their daughter. There were times when he'd observed her rubbing her stomach and smiling, but it had to be very difficult to walk away from a job you loved. Lord, just let her open up and talk to me. We can make it through this; for in Christ, we are more than conquerors.

Marly eased Noah's arm from around her waist and gently slid off the bed and into the bathroom. She turned on the faucet and sat on the edge of the tub. She'd just relaxed in the tub when she heard her cell ringing. She blushed and slid lower as Noah came into the bathroom with her cell

318

phone in hand. "It's Tina," he said, chuckling as she attempted to hide beneath the bubbles. He handed her the phone and turned to walk out. He stopped abruptly, did an about face, knelt down, reached for her and pulled her to him. He bent his head and captured her lips in a kiss that rendered her speechless. She watched as he stood, winked at her, and disappeared out of the bathroom. Marly could hear him whistling in the bedroom. She'd completely forgotten about the phone until she heard Tina saying, "Hello, hello…"

✣

"Tina will be over in an hour or so, and she's bringing pizza," Marly told Noah as she joined him and Adam in the kitchen.

She glanced down at their feet and rolled her eyes. Noah laughed delightedly while Adam looked confused.

"What? I don't get it," he said.

"She hates to see a man wearing flip-flops and sandals. She thinks it makes him look like a sissy. You know that she won't even ride with me unless I change shoes first." Noah complained humorously.

Adam grinned and began swinging his feet back and forth.

Marly looked at Noah's feet and said, "I thought I threw yours in the garbage during the move."

"You did, but I retrieved them when you weren't looking," he confessed.

"That's kind of weird Marly. You're the only woman I know that feels that way," Adam grinned.

She arched her brows and calmly said, "How many women do you know?"

Noah roared with laughter at Adams blank look. "It's the flip-flops, son. She's insinuating that you'll never get a woman wearing them."

Adam turned red and exclaimed, "But Dad got you."

"Not wearing sissy shoes he didn't. He kept that little secret to himself. As a matter of fact, we're having marital problems because of it, and I'm on the verge of a nervous breakdown. I think we may need to call in a counselor," she said, keeping a straight face.

Noah approached her with his sissy shoes on and she grimaced and raced for the door. He wasn't quick enough to catch her.

She poked her head in and taunted, "It's the sissy shoes."

Noah turned and in a split second was out the kitchen door and close on her heels. He caught her just as she was about to enter their bedroom.

"Take it back," he commanded softly as he held her to him.

"I will not," she giggled.

He twirled her around to face him and heard Adam yell that the pizza was here.

"Saved by Tina," he told her in a husky voice as he released her.

"Saved from what?" she asked.

"The guy wearing the sissy shoes," he answered with a grin.

✝

They were munching on pizza when Adam asked Tina what she thought about a guy wearing flip-flops in public. Marly giggled. Anybody who knew Tina wouldn't have asked her that question.

Tina froze in the middle of taking a bite and said, "I'll give you one word that describes what I think, 'sissy'."

Adam reached down, took his flip-flops off, and tossed them in the trash. Everyone laughed as Tina told him that it was okay to wear them in the house.

✝

"Are you telling me that you don't want to have this baby?" Tina whispered. She was staring at Marly as though she didn't know her.

"No, that's not what I'm saying. I'm feeling a little resentful and I wish this was during another time in my life," Marly corrected.

Tina was still staring at her strangely.

"You'd rather have had this baby when you were married to Shawn and that would have made it okay?"

Again, Marly shook her head no. "I just assumed that it would be Noah and me and our three boys. I didn't think I could get pregnant or else I would have prevented it from happening."

"So, you don't really want this baby because she will interfere with your perfect little life. That sounds a bit self-centered, Marlena. That man, your husband, has gone to hell and back for you," Tina informed her.

"What are you talking about? Do you mean the board?" Marly asked.

Tina looked away, debating whether or not to say anything. "The fact that you don't know testifies of his love for you."

"Know what?" Marly asked innocently.

Tina gazed at Marly and said, "I don't understand why someone as learned in the Bible as you are can't understand why you should consider it a privilege to be able to stay home with your daughter. Do you realize how many women would love to be in your shoes? You have a husband who adores you and is financially secure enough for you to stay home with the baby. What more is there to life? Success in God's eyes is raising your children in the admonition of the Lord, not careers, vacations, and fancy homes in the suburbs. Those things will pass away, but the things of the Lord are eternal. I've stayed at home with my children and there is no more important job than that. Your responsibility and loyalty should be to your family first."

"I do love my family and I love my baby," Marly spoke firmly.

"Then do what God would have you to do, not what feels good to you," Tina advised lovingly.

Chapter Thirty-six

Noah handed Marly a list of words that he needed translated from the Greek and Hebrew into English. She was turning into the best assistant he'd ever had. She took every task he gave her seriously. She never handed him anything back unless she'd double checked it. He was preparing tomorrow's sermon with her help. He looked at his watch. It was almost noon. They'd been at it since 9 A.M. and he could hear Beauty whining at the door. It was time for her walk. He put down his notes and stretched.

"Let's take a break. Its lunch time and Beauty needs to be walked."

He disappeared and returned a minute later with their hats and coats.

Noah held Marly's hand and laughed at the antics of Beauty as she raced about and stopped to sniff the trails of various animals. She couldn't figure out which smell to follow. She'd start off in one direction and abruptly stop and head in the opposite direction. Suddenly, Beauty stopped and stood perfectly still. The hackles on the back of her neck were raised. She began a low menacing growl. Instinctively, Noah pulled Marly behind him and attempted to locate the object of her warning growls.

"Do you think it's a wild animal?" Marly asked, holding on to his hand tightly.

"Come on, let's head back," he commanded softly without bothering to answer her question.

"What about Beauty? We can't leave her," she protested as she tried to pull from his grasp.

He forcefully jerked her back around to face him and spoke in a strained voice, "I'll come back after her. I promise."

He pulled her behind him in a quick stride. He could hear Beauty snarling and snapping at something behind them, but didn't stop until they were safely inside the house. He ran into the study and grabbed a locked metal box. Marly stood transfixed as he shouted orders for her to lock the door, and not open it for anyone except him. She watched him run back out the kitchen door, unlocking the metal box at the same time, and disappear down the path before snapping out of her trance-like state and locking the door.

Marly kept glancing simultaneously from the clock to the path. It felt like an eternity before she spotted Noah coming from the woods. Limping slowly behind him was Beauty. Marly gasped and flew out the door when she spied the blood seeping from a deep gash in Beauty's side.

"Get back inside, Marly!" Noah ordered.

She stepped back inside at his command and watched as he coaxed the huge dog to follow him into the house. Noah shut and locked the door as soon as Beauty had managed to limp through it.

"What vet do you take her to?" Noah asked with concern evident in his voice. "Get them on the line and tell them we're bringing her in and that she has a large gash on the front left side!"

He hurried from the room to gather a blanket and some strips of cloth. Marly rested Beauty's large head on her lap as Noah bound the wound and wrapped the big dog in the blanket. He went out the back door, opened the garage, and backed his car out. Waiting for the garage door to completely close, he came back into the house and heaved Beauty into his arms. She had ceased whimpering and didn't make a sound which caused Marly to glance apprehensively at Noah. He wanted to reassure her that Beauty would be okay, but he wasn't certain of that.

They reached the vet in record speed and watched helplessly as the technicians hurriedly carried Beauty into the building. Noah pulled out his phone and sent a text to his brother and then he held Marly close to him.

"What do you think happened to Beauty?" Marly asked him.

"Maybe a wild animal," he responded absentmindedly.

She began biting her nails (something he'd never seen her do). "What if she dies?" she asked him softly.

"Oh, sweetheart, I don't know. Let's just pray that she pulls through this, okay," he responded, kissing her on the top of her head.

"She's a hero isn't she, Noah? She saved us," she whispered to him.

"Probably more than we know," he thought to himself.

The vet finally came out to greet them. He explained that Beauty had lost a lot of blood and had needed to be stabilized before any operation could be performed. He verified that permission had been given to proceed with any and all attempts to save Beauty's life. Dr. Samuelson gave them permission to see Beauty for a couple of minutes prior to surgery. After which, he advised them to go home and wait for his call. Everything else could be decided pending the outcome of the surgery. Marly rushed through the doors while Noah pulled the doctor off to the side.

"What do you think caused her injury?" he questioned.

Dr. Samuelson looked at Noah. "That type of injury is common among canine units of the Peace Corps. If I had to take a guess, I'd say that your dog tangled with a two legged animal, the human variety."

Noah nodded his appreciation and asked the vet to keep his thoughts to himself.

✞

Marly gingerly rubbed Beauty's head. The big dog seemed to be resting painlessly. "Please don't die," she pleaded in between her sobs.

She became aware of Noah when he slid his arms around her waist and began to pray for Beauty. When he had finished, he too, rubbed the "pony's" head. He thanked her for being a great dog and told her how much she meant to them. He then pulled a reluctant Marly out of the room.

✞

Noah pulled the curtain back and watched as his brother drove around the back. He looked in on a sleeping Marly and prayed that she'd stay that way until John left. He quickly walked to the kitchen door and opened it. His brother's expression confirmed his worst fears.

"Did they find anything?" Noah asked.

John frowned and sat down. "Boot prints and evidence which suggest that Beauty struggled with a person, a man more than likely; the local authorities recovered a hunting cap. They believe that it may have been a hunter who accidentally stumbled onto your property. It is feasible that it could have happened that way."

Noah nodded at John and sat down. He ran his fingers through his hair tiredly.

"She still doesn't know about all the letters and the threats. I don't want to have her afraid to live. I have to level with you John. I'm having a hard time believing that in this day and age people would still be this upset about our marriage. I don't believe that these letters are coming from people that are black. I'm confident that they're coming from residents of my old community."

John leaned back and considered all that Noah had said.

"People don't like change baby brother. I have to admit, I'd have preferred you to marry a white woman, but now that I know Marly, she's the best thing that's happened to you. She's crazy for you. That's for sure. You were a good man before, but I can see that she fulfills you and has made you stronger and happier. You are always smiling now, and the way you look at her reminds me of a love so innocent and pure. You two seem to have somehow evaded the contaminants of the world. I don't know why anyone would send threatening letters, but take them seriously. It's better to be safe than sorry. You do still have your gun don't you?"

Noah nodded yes. "I hate guns, but this last letter was fanatical enough to encourage me to keep it locked and loaded."

John sat up and gazed intently at Noah, "What did it say?"

Noah reached in his pocket and slid the folded up letter across to John and watched as he unfolded the paper and read it silently.

John let out an oath and stood to his feet. "So this crazy nut is threatening to kill Marly and the baby at the same time. Whoever wrote this letter is completely insane. He's the kind of nutbag that you shoot first and ask questions later. Does the sheriff know about this letter? This should have made a difference in how they handled what happened today."

Their conversation was cut off by the ringing of the home phone. The caller ID showed that it was Dr. Samuelson. Noah quickly picked it up. A grateful smile came to his face as the doctor explained that Beauty was out of surgery and that he was confident she'd be okay, but she'd need to stay there for the next week or so. Noah thanked the vet for all of his help and replaced the receiver.

Marly jumped at the sound of the ringing phone. It was Dr. Samuelson's number. She quickly headed to find Noah. She walked in the kitchen and was surprised to find John sitting there. She hugged him warmly and then turned to face Noah. When he winked at her, she threw herself into his arms. Noah laughed and told her everything that Dr. Samuelson had reported to him.

"So your dog is going to pull through, huh," John said smiling at the two of them.

Marly turned to face John. She blushed when Noah's arms encircled her waist, keeping her in front of him.

"That's great," John said, pretending not to notice her blush.

"I wonder what kind of wild animal did that to her? That was a pretty deep wound," Marly questioned.

Noah quickly spoke, "I guess the only thing that matters is that she's going to be okay."

The three continued to chat for some time before John took his leave.

✝

Noah read over the outline that he and Marly had just completed. Everything was in order and could be easily understood. He wasn't one of those pastors who taught from memory. He always used a detailed outline which required studying and note taking. Generally, he read over the outline two or three times before he went to bed. Tonight was no exception except that he read it aloud to Marly who listened appreciatively. He found it humorous when she would raise her hand to ask him a question; however, her questions were anything but funny. He had to dig much deeper than the material in his outline in order to adequately answer them. He loved this woman he thought to himself as they discussed the Word late into the evening. When he'd finally finished reading the outline, he knew that he was ready for tomorrow's sermon.

He stared at Marly until she blushed and said, "Why are you staring at me like that?"

He leaned back in his chair and said, "You fascinate me. I've never met a woman that could keep me on my toes in every aspect of a relationship."

"Did you go out on dates before me?" she asked shyly.

"I'll answer your questions after you answer mine. Why do you ask me things in a way that suggest you're not sure if it's your business or not?"

She shrugged and said, "People are extremely closed about their lives, especially their past."

"I'm not people," he said, "I'm your husband, but I do understand what you're saying. My life isn't closed to you though. If you want to know something, ask," he told her solemnly. "The answer to your question is yes, but for the most part, it was not intentional. There were people who'd invite me to a function, and low and behold, an unattached female would miraculously appear. Things like that."

"You never asked anyone out?" she asked.

"No, I didn't, but there were several that asked me out. I'm not one of those modern guys. I prefer to do the chasing, and the catching," he said, winking at her.

He laughed when, predictably, she blushed.

"Do you ever feel awkward about being with me?" she wondered aloud.

"Only once, and that was at Kaod's 'Senior Night'. You, Drew, and Kaod looked like the perfect family and I kind of felt out of place, you know, the white guy. I guess I wondered if Kaod still preferred Drew to me. Have you ever felt that way?" he asked her.

She nodded yes and said, "Sometimes I can sense the disapproval of others, but I'm getting used to it."

"Like who?" Noah questioned.

"Like your brother, the first time I met him. He didn't approve. I got the impression that he thought that I would ruin your ministry," Marly responded.

"You were right, but now he thinks you make me a better man, and he's right."

Noah paused for a minute before holding her gaze and asking, "Marly, how do you really feel about the baby?"

"Oh, Noah," she sighed, "I love the fact that I'm having your baby. I… I just wish it was at an earlier time in my life. I guess what I'm saying is that I wish I'd met you first so that you could have been the father of both my children. That way, we would be having this time in our lives to ourselves. Can you understand that?"

"Come here, Marly," he commanded softly.

She stood and walked over to him. He pulled her gently onto his lap and said, "I promise that you and I will always have time to ourselves. Our daughter will not come between us and you won't be raising her alone. Do you know how much I've always wanted a daughter? God waited until I married my soul mate before granting that blessing. You were chosen to carry my child at this particular time in our lives. God knows what He's doing and we're going to have to trust him. I love you more than you could possibly know," he said, hugging her close to him.

"I love you too, Noah," she replied laying her head on his shoulders.

✠

They were on their way to church when Noah's cell began to vibrate.

"Answer that for me sweetheart," he told her as he kept his eyes focused on the road ahead.

He'd seen many a husband and wife who guarded their cells from each other as though it were a national security issue. He didn't have anyone calling or texting him that required secrecy from his wife. If anything, he wanted her to be secure in her trust of him. He was still mulling about in his head the right time to inform her of the threatening letters that would periodically arrive at the church. He'd have to tell her soon, that was for sure. He listened to her as she answered the phone.

"Hello, Noah's phone."

He shook his head. She must have graduated from "polite school" with honors. It was as though she envisioned boundaries in her head and did everything within her power to never cross them.

He grimaced in frustration when she said, "It's for you."

"You must be having a 'moment', sweetheart. Who else would it be for? It's my phone. Will you ask who it is and tell them I'll call them right back?" He felt the arctic chill as soon his words were out.

Marly turned and gazed at Noah's profile. He'd accused her of having a "moment", whatever that was supposed to mean.

"I wasn't having a 'moment' then, but I'm having one now; therefore, no, I won't ask who it is or tell them you'll call back. You can call your secretary and ask her to do that. After all, that's her job, not mine."

Noah shot her a quick glance as he pulled over to the side of the road to take the call. He frowned as he listened to Hal's reason for calling.

"No, don't do anything about it. We are on our way there. Yes, I know. She's a Phillips. She'll be fine. Thanks, Hal."

Marly could tell that something had happened at the church and it had to do with her. She wondered what Noah meant by "she'll be fine".

She waited until he'd hung up the phone before asking, "Were you referencing me?"

Noah held his wife's gaze. He was trying to formulate exactly how to explain Hal's call. He wanted to shield his wife, but he was now positive that it was time to bring it all out in the open.

"Marly, someone painted some derogatory comments on my parking spot and Hal was calling to let us know in advance."

"What kind of comments?" When he hesitated, she became more persistent. "What does it say, Noah?"

"Actually, they're referencing me," he told her.

"So they're calling you a 'nigger lover'?" she guessed correctly.

Noah winced at the words, but then quickly turned towards his wife in shock. He could have sworn he heard her mumble something under her breath.

"What did you say?" he asked, wanting to be sure he'd understood her.

"What do you think you heard?" she countered.

He looked directly into her eyes.

"I thought I heard you say that they were a bunch of 'punk-asses', but I want to believe that my wife wouldn't use that kind of language, no matter how ticked off she'd become."

"I'm sorry, but I seem to be experiencing one of those 'moments' you accused me of having earlier. Don't worry about it. You'll get over the shock just like I'll have to eventually get over the shock of your congregation calling you a 'nigger lover'. It makes me wonder how you'll know which of us they'll be talking about when our daughter is born," she replied sarcastically.

"Marly, it's not the entire congregation. I'm not even sure it's anyone connected to the church. In any event, it's useless to get riled up about it. I'll address the problem today," he said in a matter of fact tone.

She continued to stare at him. "Are you implying that I shouldn't be angry? Worse yet, why aren't you angry?"

"Oh, sweetheart, you've no idea. To have someone call your wife those kinds of names and not be able to confront them is a form of torture. It's taken me a while, but I know that God will handle it. I just have to do my part," he admitted.

She closed her eyes and began to pray silently. She was very angry and she needed God's help. It was one thing to deal with Jacob, someone you knew, and something completely different when you were dealing with strangers. It could be anyone, even someone pretending to care about her. She thought about her promise to Noah, to be by his side and love their church family no matter what. "Please, God, help me to stand by my husband."

When she opened her eyes, he had taken off his seat belt and was smiling. "I need some encouragement," he said as he leaned over and unsnapped her seatbelt.

Marly reached up and hugged him to her. "I love you," she whispered softly into his ear.

✝

They arrived at the church a little later than usual. Noah avoided his regular parking spot and chose to park elsewhere. He helped her out of the car, put his arm around her waist, and casually walked towards his office. He knew that she was curious as to why they were going to his office instead of to the sanctuary. He unlocked the door and followed her in.

"Why are we in here?" she asked.

"You'll find out in a minute. Why don't you sit at my desk," he suggested.

"You must really, really love me if you're allowing me to sit behind your desk," she kidded. Marly eased into the chair with exaggerated motions.

Noah looked at his wife and hoped she'd remain upbeat after reading the letters. He walked over to her and turned the chair so that it faced the window. "I sat right here, the day of our engagement, gazing at the parking lot and praying I'd see a gold Jaguar pull into the lot."

He turned her back around to face him. "I knew that you were going to be my wife the first day that I saw you, it was confirmed when we met again at Chingo's." He unlocked a drawer in the desk and pulled out a file filled with letters. He handed her the letters and sat on the desk. His eyes were glued to her face trying to determine her reaction.

Marly read each letter, but the only one that gave her cause for concern was the letter which threatened to kill her and the baby. "Why would someone want to kill me, or our child?"

Noah had only one answer. "It's because of who you serve."

She went into his arms.

"Do you want me to take you home?" he asked.

She shook her head no and told him that she'd rather be with him.

"Good, because I'd rather have you near me," he confided.

Noah looked out into the congregation after the children had been dismissed. The sanctuary was nearly full. Instead of beginning his sermon, he explained that he was going to read various correspondences that had been delivered to the church directly after his marriage to Marly. He began reading every sentence of every letter that he had received. He ended by reading the last letter that spoke of the writer's intent to kill Marly and the baby. The sanctuary was silent. Members began scrutinizing each other and wondering who would write such things. Noah chastised his entire congregation and told them how ashamed he would be, if any of those letters were traced back to members of his church. He apologized to Marly and to any guests that were present there. He went so far as to advise those guests to find another church home until his church, if they hadn't already, could come to realize that hatred directed at others was wrong, especially when it was solely based on the color of their skin. He advised all those that were still harboring prejudice to immediately repent and confess it to the Lord in order to receive forgiveness. He prayed that God would reveal those that were responsible for the letters and that God would bring healing and a true love for all God's children to their church. The sanctuary was still completely silent as Noah finished his impromptu speech.

From the back of the sanctuary, a woman yelled, "We love you, Marly. Please, forgive us."

Soon other shouts of the same were heard throughout. Noah met his wife's eyes and determinedly looked back at his congregation. He told his church family that this wasn't simply about Marly; it was about genuinely welcoming all newcomers with open arms, not just as guests, but as future members. He reminded them that they were all God's children and as such, deserving of courtesy and respect. He had them all turn to the New Testament book of Matthew 22:37-40 where Jesus offered up the two greatest commandments: to love the Lord your God with all of your heart, with all of your soul, and with your entire mind, and to love your neighbor as yourself. In conclusion, he instructed them to go home and read Luke 10:30-37 in which Jesus gives a parable on neighbors.

Noah turned to his assistant, gave him several instructions, and headed off the stage and towards Marly. Together they walked down the center aisle and out of the sanctuary. He prayed that there would be sincere repentance.

Chapter Thirty-seven

Marly smiled at Noah as they watched Kaod help a young lady out of his car. She glanced at Noah and remarked that Ka's friend was the same girl that he'd taken an interest in when the family had gone to the beach. Noah noticed that he didn't touch her as they walked towards the house. He was willing to bet that Kaod was waiting to see what they, in particular, what his mom thought of his lady friend. This was a special Thanksgiving in more ways than one. It was their first Thanksgiving in their home, Kaod had brought home a girl, and Beauty had been released from the vet. God had been good to them. The entire Phillips clan was home and the house was full of joyful noises. Little Collin was now fourteen months old and full of energy. Marly giggled as she watched Jacob trying to settle his son down while Adam and Kara were in a heated debate over politics and religion. She wondered if Kaod had told Sasha about their blended family. The kitchen door opened and Marly smiled as Kaod immediately enveloped her in a warm hug and then turned to do the same with Noah and the rest of the family. Finally, he introduced the young lady at his side. Her name was Sasha Kendricks and she was definitely a dark-skinned beauty. She had long coal black hair with eyes to match. She was about Marly's height and of average build. She had a beautiful smile and was quite shy. Marly liked her immediately.

"I don't believe it," Noah said in amazement as he watched Kaod and Sasha exit the kitchen.

"You don't believe what?" Marly threw over her shoulder as she checked the turkey and dressing.

"He did it! Kaod actually went out and found a Marly clone," he informed her.

"What in the world are you talking about? Sasha and I look nothing alike," she answered.

"No, not physically," he admitted, "But she has your mannerisms. She's shy and sweet. She even dresses like you."

Marly stopped and stared at Noah and then shook her head in denial. Noah laughed and knew better. Sasha was a younger version of Marly and he had a gut feeling that they'd just met their future daughter-in-law.

✝

Marly set the table according to Noah's instructions. This year he was seated at the head with Marly at his right. Jacob was at the other end with Kara to his right and Collin to his left. Adam was seated to the right of Marly with Kaod and Sasha directly across from them. Marly watched as the food was brought to the table and everyone took their places. She smiled as Noah pulled her close to him and began their new family tradition by stating why he was thankful. Each member of the family followed his example. Everyone smiled as Sasha told why she was thankful. Marly observed Kaod's demeanor as Sasha spoke. His eyes never left her face and he smiled at her in encouragement. Marly knew instantly that her son was in love with this girl. She looked at Noah who was gauging her reaction. She squeezed his hand in silent acknowledgement. Kaod was heading into the unchartered territory of courtship. She had another reason to be thankful.

Adam looked at his dad and asked if he were going to try the chitterlings again this year.

Noah glanced at Marly and said, "That all depends on my wife. I simply could not resist last year's deal."

Marly knew she was blushing, but she refused to say a word.

Sasha asked Kaod in a soft voice, "What was last year's deal?"

Kaod chuckled heartily. "That's what we are all trying to find out." He purposefully stared at his mom who was busily placing dressing on her plate. "Well, Mom, are you and Dad going to tell us the deal or not?"

She raised her eyebrows at his use of the word "Dad". She knew that he was trying to persuade Noah to divulge their secret deal. "Would you like some dressing Sasha?" Marly asked sweetly, ignoring everyone's gaze.

Noah began laughing at her antics, especially when the entire family was trying their hardest to pressure her into telling.

Marly turned to face Noah and asked him in the sweetest voice imaginable, "Would you like to try some chitterlings again this year?"

Noah's eyes darkened as his wife captured all of his attention when she leaned toward him and whispered in his ear. He then turned and whispered into her ear. She smiled at him and nodded. Noah faced their captive audience and asked if someone would kindly pass him the chitterlings.

"Ahh… come on Dad. This makes two years in a row. When are you and Marly gonna stop this lovey-dovey stuff?" Adam asked as he handed Kaod the worn twenty dollar bill back.

He'd just gotten it back from Kaod earlier that week. Everyone laughed while Noah and Marly exchanged secret glances.

✝

Marly watched as Noah changed Collin's diaper. She had to admit that he was pretty efficient.

"Just wait, Mom. In a couple of months, that will be you and Noah changing my little sister," Kaod bragged.

Marly glanced at Noah who was placing a worn out Collin in his mother's arms. She didn't know what to say because she wasn't exactly looking forward to it.

"I'll let her father handle the diaper changing."

"Who are you kidding Mom? I remember all the things you did with me. You were the greatest mom.

She looked away. She wanted to say that she was no longer that woman, but instead she said nothing. What was wrong with her? Why couldn't she be happy? She knew that Noah was staring at her so she smiled and pretended.

Noah was concerned about her reaction. He'd thought they'd gotten over her resentment.

"Have you guys picked out any names for her yet?" Adam piped in.

Noah told them that he was waiting to see what she looked like before giving her a name. The conversation went on and on about the baby. No one, but Noah, noticed that Marly hardly said one word.

✝

"God, why would you give her a child she doesn't even want?" Noah asked as he sat alone in his study. He couldn't sleep and had decided to talk to God about Marly and the baby. He was trying desperately to understand what she was going through, but it all seemed so foreign. They loved each other and out of that love, a child was conceived. Why then was it so hard for her to accept their baby? He'd seen how she'd disconnected herself from the conversation earlier. It was as if she'd wanted to forget the fact that she was pregnant. He asked the Lord to show him what the problem was. Noah wondered if it had anything to do with her first marriage. He tried to remember what she had told him. She had said that after Kaod was born, she and Shawn had continued to sleep in separate rooms and that he really hadn't participated in Kaod's life. Had Shawn been active in her life prior to Kaod's birth? He closed his eyes seeking solace in God.

"Help me Father to know the next step. We've had to deal with adversity from the very beginning of our courtship and you guided us through it and I'm depending on you to guide us now." He heard her soft footsteps coming in search of him and smiled ruefully as she called out his name.

"What are you doing sitting here in the dark?" she asked sliding next to him.

"Talking to the Lord," he responded. His answer was met with silence. "You're not going to ask me about what?"

"I already know about what. I could feel you staring at me all night long when everyone kept talking about the baby," she said.

Noah changed the subject and asked, "Did you love Shawn?"

Marly sat up in surprise. "What? Where'd that come from?"

"Well, did you?" he questioned persistently.

"Of course, I did," she replied somewhat mystified by his sudden line of questioning.

"So why did Kaod's birth cause distance between the two of you and why didn't you ever use birth control?" he questioned bluntly.

"Is this about the baby Noah? If it is, I'm tired of talking about it," she dismissed him in that tone of voice he hated so much.

He knew that she was trying to provoke him in order to steer the topic away from her and Shawn's relationship.

"Just answer the question Marly. Why didn't you use birth control?"

"I… because he wanted a child and I thought that a baby would bring us closer together," she said quietly.

"But you never really wanted a child. You were only trying to fix your relationship," Noah concluded accurately. "Do you think this baby will fix our problems?" he questioned.

She looked at him strangely. "We don't have any problems Noah; unless, of course, you're leading a double life or something." She examined him carefully before saying, "You're psycho-analyzing me. It's instinctive isn't it? Every time I sit on this couch with you, the counselor in you takes over."

He chuckled and grabbed her when she tried to stand. He bent his head and began to nuzzle her neck. Marly sighed and relaxed. He whispered huskily into her ear.

"Now I'm trying to figure out why kissing your neck turns you into a cuddle bug."

"I've no clue," she whispered back as she pulled his head up for a kiss.

He obliged her by kissing her lingeringly, but he then returned to her neck.

"Guess what I'm trying to figure out now?" he asked a somewhat distracted Marly.

"What?" she crooned softly.

"I'm wondering where my demure wife got a word like 'punk-asses' from," he teased gently.

She began laughing. "I told you that I was having a 'moment'. I was reliving an incident with Ka'. He was about eight or nine years old. He'd come home from the neighbor's house sporting a bloody nose. I asked him how it happened and he explained that the two brothers had jumped him when his back was turned. He said that they were a bunch of 'punk...' I was shocked, just as you were, so I asked him where he'd gotten that word from and he said that his daddy used that word to describe the men that would look at my butt when his back was turned," she giggled.

Noah couldn't help but grin. "Did you suggest a few alternative words he could have used, coward, weakling, spineless, or chicken just to name a few?"

She frowned distastefully. "Those are sissy words. You can't use those words effectively in the Hood. You have to come hard with it. You have to look them in their face and say you're a 'punk...'"

"Marly!" he quickly cut in.

She fell back in a fit of laughter. "I wasn't going to say it."

He smiled infectiously at her. "How'd you get Kaod not to say it?"

"I told him to use better words like coward, chicken, or gutless."

"Did it work?"

"Of course it didn't. That kind of educational logic has never worked in the Hood. You have to come hard," she explained, "or become a Christian."

"So," he said, "if I saw someone checking out your bottom, I should come 'hard' with it?"

She giggled and said, "First of all, we don't call it a bottom, it's a butt and you don't have to worry about it. You've got a solid reputation in the Hood."

He looked at her. "Why is that?"

She reached up and played with his hair. "You have a reputation for being a true man of God."

He shook his head at her naïve words. Did she really believe that would stop guys from looking at her? He lowered his head and sealed her mouth with his. Noah took his time enjoying the kiss. When he pulled away, he commanded gently, "Tell me some more of your little theories." He was enjoying this time together. He could tell that she was actually talking freely without her usual inhibitions.

"You are an enigma, Noah," she said.

"Tell me why you think that," he smiled.

"You fit well in both cultures. I watch you with Layman and he loves you like a brother, but so do Jim and Hal. You do things that I wouldn't guess you could do and you can 'man up' at the drop of a dime," she explained.

Noah arched his brows at her use of slang.

"You think white men are pretty weak, don't you?" he declared, observing her expression. He watched as she blushed.

"That's why you brushed all of us off that first day of the seminar. I gave you my best, most flirtatious smile and you were so cold to me. Then I watched those other losers try and you were even worse to them. Why were you so hard on us?"

She giggled and hugged him. "I actually thought you were very handsome, but just trying to get your curiosity about black women satisfied."

Noah began to chuckle. "I was very curious about you, but I was also intrigued by you. You were comfortable in both worlds and you blushed. Women just don't blush anymore. If anything, some of them cause you to blush."

He looked down at her. She had the prettiest sultry brown eyes he'd ever seen. He touched her hair. It was always so soft. Not at all oily or hard like he had been led to believe. She wasn't anything like the stereotypical black woman. She was intelligent and sweet, not at all mouthy or aggressive. He realized that just as she had been told things about white men that were untrue, he'd been exposed to similar fallacies about black women. He had broken the mold for her and she had broken the mold for him. Several guys had asked him about his and Marly's relationship.

They hadn't been mean, simply curious. They'd brought up all the usual stereotypes, but none of them had fit her. He'd tried to remove the false images rooted in their minds. Unfortunately, most assumed that Marly was just different.

His thoughts traveled back to their daughter.

"What are you thinking now?" she whispered as she reached up to play with his hair.

"I'm wondering what our daughter will look like. I hope she looks like you. You are so beautiful to me," he declared earnestly.

Marly didn't quite know what to say. No man had ever made her feel as beautiful or as loved as he did. She wasn't used to hearing such pure and sincere compliments. All of her life she'd heard men make comments about her body parts or what they'd like to do to her. Their so called flattery was often very sexual in nature. Even Shawn had always described her using sexual terms. It had always embarrassed her and had done nothing to elicit a response from her.

"You make me feel so loved. You overwhelm me," she confessed shyly. "You have from the very beginning. Would it sound selfish of me if I told you that I'm not ready to share you with our daughter?"

He was stunned. So that was it. She wanted him all to herself. It was his turn to feel overwhelmed. She hadn't felt the need to have a child because she was perfectly content with him and their boys. She didn't really have to share his attention.

"That is the greatest compliment that anyone has ever given me. You do know that the relationship between a husband and a wife should reign supreme over that of a parent and a child? Other than God, you will always be first in my life," he assured her.

Now he understood her. Hadn't he been a little apprehensive about his position in her life when he'd observed how close she and Kaod were? He remembered how reserved she'd been whenever Kaod was around. A subtle battle had taken place to determine who would be number one in her life. Patience, love, and the Biblical mandate had slowly given him the victory and as excited as he was about their daughter, he needed to remember to cling to his wife. His daughter would take her place in their family, but she would never be put ahead of his wife.

Marly felt free as she'd finally confessed her inner thoughts to Noah. She watched his face for signs of disappointment, but there weren't any. He appeared to be as relieved as she was.

When she felt no condemnation from him, she spoke tentatively, "I hope she has your eyes," she told him.

It was his turn to be embarrassed. He looked thoughtful. "Is that possible? I've never seen a black person with anything but brown or black eyes."

She smiled and patiently explained that, although it wasn't commonplace, blacks have been born with the same eye colors as the other cultures. "My first serious crush was on a black boy with green eyes," she admitted.

"Tell me more about this boy with the green eyes. How old were you?" Noah said.

"His name was Isaac and I was sweet sixteen and had never been kissed," she supplied.

"So what happened with this Isaac character?" he questioned with interest.

"I'm not sure. He was a preacher's kid and they moved to South Carolina about two weeks before school was to start. I remember him holding my hand and telling me that they were moving. I'd been crushing on him for months so it was a bit of a letdown. The night before they were to move, he showed up at my house and we sat on the front porch not saying much of anything. Eventually, he got up enough nerve to kiss me. The last I'd heard, he was in seminary and doing very well. Who was your first real crush?" she asked.

Noah grinned, "Do you want to know about my first kiss, my first crush, or my first love?"

"They're not the same?" she quipped.

"No, they're not smarty pants. My first crush was Colleen. I realize now, that I was infatuated with her. My first kiss was in high school with a young lady, who shall remain nameless. I knew that she liked me, but she had a boyfriend. I was a swimmer and she was a cheerleader. Her boyfriend was a star on the football team. One day, after a swim meet, she met me as I was leaving to go home. One thing led to another and she kissed me. The next day, I saw her walking down the hall with her boyfriend. She behaved as though nothing had ever happened. I couldn't even look at the guy. I felt guilty every time I saw him."

"What happened with the girl?" she wanted to know.

"I did everything I could to avoid her, but even now, she still calls the church.

Marly sat up, her eyes narrowed accusingly.

Noah laughed uncontrollably as she spit out the name, "Suzette". He grabbed her hands to keep her from poking him.

"Settle down Ms. Jealous or I won't tell you about my first love," he warned teasingly, holding her hands above her head. "My first love came about when I was much, much older. She had me wrapped around her finger from the moment I saw her," he whispered against her neck. "She has the most sensuous brown eyes and a smile that can light up any room. I prayed to God for her and he graciously answered my prayers."

Noah kissed his way up her neck and to her lips where he showed her with his mouth what words could not convey. He released her mouth and heard her soft moan of protest.

"Who's my first and only love?" he asked huskily.

She said with joy, as she wrapped her arms around his neck, "I am."

Chapter Thirty-eight

Noah and Marly sat contentedly in their family room. A soothing fire was burning in the fireplace while holiday music drifted from the high-tech stereo system that Kaod had given them as a Christmas gift. It was New Year's Eve and they were finally all alone. Beauty lay on the floor fully healed and back to normal. Whatever she had encountered on the path hadn't stopped her from enjoying her daily walks. Noah was reclining longways on the sofa while Marly sat in front of him. He was massaging her now protruding belly. Her stomach seemed to have sprouted into a medium-sized pumpkin overnight. He laughed delightedly when their daughter began to move right on cue. Whenever Noah would rub his wife's stomach, the baby would begin to move in response. The two of them would play this little game until Marly would laughingly beg Noah to stop. He grabbed her hands in his and rubbed her tummy. Sure enough, the baby moved as though following their lead. Noah brushed the side of her neck with his mouth. She smiled and tilted her head to the side to give him better access.

He was pleasantly surprised at how well she was carrying their child. She very seldom complained of anything. He knew that it bothered her that she could no longer sleep with her head nestled on his chest and as a result, she tossed and turned quite a bit throughout the night. In a couple of months, she could revert to her normal sleep position. She was due towards the end of February which meant that she'd become pregnant sometime during their honeymoon. That hadn't surprised him in the least, especially since she had proven to be so responsive to him. They had however, since then, discussed birth control. She had never used it before and neither had he.

Colleen had decided to have her tubes tied after Adam's birth. She hadn't bothered to discuss it with him, she'd informed him that her surgery was scheduled and that had been the end of the discussion. Noah had found out during a later argument, that it had been her way of denying him the daughter he'd always wanted. He hadn't said a word. He'd simply picked up Adam and grabbed Jacob's hand and walked them to the park. Colleen had reacted in an angry frenzy when he'd returned with the boys. She had gone so far as to deny him access to their bedroom. He'd slept in Adam's room for the next week or so and he hadn't minded in the least.

Marly smiled tolerantly as Noah played his daily game with the baby. He was so thrilled with the idea of finally having a daughter that he'd painted her room, selected the pictures for the wall, picked out her crib, and various pieces of baby furniture and had even installed the latest monitor. She'd laughed so hard when he had insisted on going with her to pick out baby clothes. He went on and on about the appropriate type of clothes. Marly had to remind him that she didn't think that they sold seductive baby wear. His joy was contagious to the point that she'd become genuinely excited about the baby's arrival. She read to the baby and talked to her constantly. She jumped suddenly when the baby's movements became more powerful and watched in total amazement as the baby followed their interlocked hands. When their hands moved so did she. If their hands stopped so would she. Noah pulled their hands away and grinned as the baby began to push against her stomach. He positioned their hands back on her stomach and the baby immediately went to them. He did that for the next minute until their daughter became still. Marly laughed and told Noah that he had worn the baby out.

Noah smiled at Marly and asked, "How does that feel when she moves around inside of you like that? Does it hurt?"

She searched her mind trying to find the right words to describe the sensation. She explained that it didn't hurt, but that it almost mirrored a massage, only on the inside. He nodded in understanding and settled her back against him. They sat contentedly listening to a music CD that Kaod had made for them. Suddenly they both began to smile as their song came on.

"It's too bad we can't dance to it. That was really sweet of Ka' to put our wedding song on this CD," she sighed.

Noah motioned for her to stand up. "Let's see if we can make this work," he said. She slid into his arms and waited as he positioned his hands on her waist. "Follow me, Mrs. Phillips," he spoke softly as he began slow movements, shifting from side to side.

"Always," she answered, resting her head against his chest and wrapping her arms around him.

They were intertwined in each other's arms and swaying gently to the beat when the countdown began. The music had long since stopped and the New Year had arrived, but neither husband nor wife seemed to notice or care.

Adam and Kaod watched their parents from the doorway. They both prayed that God would bless them with the same type of happiness and contentment on display in front of them. Kaod hated to break up their moment, but Adam needed to deal with a problem that had been haunting him for years. Kaod nudged him forward.

Without opening his eyes or stopping their rhythm, Noah spoke, "If you gentlemen are coming in, then come on. If not, leave me to dance with my beautiful wife."

Once again, Kaod nudged Adam forward. Adam wouldn't even look his dad in the eye, nor did he seem capable of speaking. Noah shifted Marly around to his side. She took one look at Adam and knew that whatever the problem was, it was serious. She grabbed Adam's hand and pulled him over to the sofa. In her no nonsense tone she demanded to know what was wrong. Adam handed her two letters. One addressed to Colleen and the other addressed to L.J. Marly was so worried about Adam that she didn't bother to ask anyone's permission to read them. After she'd read the both of them, she smiled at Adam and said it's not true. She handed the letters to Noah who quickly scanned them. His face became an angry scowl as he hurriedly left the room. He was back in no time and handed his son an official looking document. Adam read the paternity report and went sobbing into his father's arms. Marly motioned for Kaod to follow her as they quietly left the room, knowing that father and son needed this time together.

Noah held his youngest son to him. He told him over and over again how much he loved him and how sorry he was that he'd had to carry the awful burden of not knowing alone. He emphasized to him that he could always come to him with his problems and concerns. Eventually Adam pulled away and smiled at his father. He told his dad about finding the letters and about his mom's P.O. Box. He revealed that Jacob had known about it and that their mom had even had him pick up the mail from there on occasion. Neither one of them had realized why she'd had the box in the first place. He told of how his mom had insinuated, time and time again, that he didn't really belong to Noah, but to someone else. That was one of the reasons he hadn't wanted to be in his mother's presence. Noah listened, angry at himself for not adequately protecting his sons. He should have known that Colleen's egotistical pride would not stop with her illness. She had wanted him to suffer even after her death. He recalled her taunts that her boys would never accept another woman in his life and that he would pay an awful price if he ever remarried. What kind of mother would use her children as pawns against their father? Colleen had not only wanted to destroy him, but had been more than willing to destroy her children in the process. Noah realized that it was time for Adam to learn the truth about his and Colleen's marriage. He waited until Adam was seated and started from the beginning.

Marly hugged her son and told him how proud she was of him for persuading Adam to tell his dad about the letters. They sat in her bedroom talking. Marly relaxed with her feet propped up on pillows while Kaod lay comfortably sprawled across the foot of the bed. It was a posture they'd frequently shared before her marriage to Noah.

"How's Sasha doing?" she inquired.

"I'm not sure. I guess she's doing okay. I haven't spoken to her in about a month or so," he revealed.

Marly exercised her mother's prerogative and inquired as to why not.

Kaod smiled and said, "She doesn't want to see me anymore. She's got this impression that I'm a player. Besides that, I had been sort of talking to Mia on and off."

Marly wanted to reach down and smack some sense into that son of hers. She probably would have too if she wasn't so pregnant. She did the next best thing and nudged him with her foot.

"Ouch, what was that for?" he laughed.

"If you want Sasha, you're going to have to chase her. That bit about not wanting to see you again was code word for 'if you want me, make me feel secure'," she interpreted.

Kaod sat up and looked at his mom. "She's probably got a dozen guys after her."

She rolled her eyes. "Ka', get real and stop being a punk..., a sissy. Are you afraid to man up? I don't care if there are fifty men chasing her, if she's the one you want, then go and get her. You are the best thing that could ever happen to that young lady and she knows it. That's why she's just as afraid as you are. She's thinking that you can have any woman you want, why do you want her. Come on Ka', you and I have talked about how some dark skinned black women feel."

They sat in silence for some time before Marly asked her son if he'd prayed to God concerning Sasha.

Kaod grinned at his mom before saying, "She's the one. I just needed to hear your approval. 'Sasha Porter', that's got a pretty good ring to it, don't you think so?" he asked, smiling at his mom.

Marly smiled back in agreement.

✠

"So you knew the guy that mom was having an affair with? How'd you deal with it, Dad? I would have gone nuts," Adam said with feeling.

Noah shrugged, "God has his own way of exacting vengeance on behalf of His children. I don't think either one of them had happiness in their lives during or after the affair. Besides, I chose her to be my wife and I got exactly what I wanted, a pretty face with no substance."

"Is it different with Marly? I mean, aren't there more problems that you have to deal with because of the color issue?" Adam asked hesitantly.

"We have less to deal with because we are God-centered. Color doesn't matter, but whether both people have accepted Christ as Lord and Savior does. Marly is my soul mate. I had to go through God to get to her. What everyone else thinks is irrelevant. God selected her for me and I trust Him more than I trust myself."

"I want to go to seminary Dad," Adam confessed. "I want to fellowship with God and allow Him to lead me in the direction he wants me to go. I want to marry the woman He selects for me. I'm ready to commit my life to Him."

Noah stared at his son. "It's not an easy walk, Adam. It requires you to lose yourself in him and to give up all rights to make decisions for yourself. You must rely solely on Him through prayer and righteous living. Know that the moment you decide to serve God, you will encounter all manner of temptations and trials. Are you prepared to deny yourself?" Noah asked sternly.

"Yes sir, I am," Adam declared firmly.

"Then Marly and I will do all we can to help you. I'm proud of you, son," He exclaimed as he and Adam embraced.

✠

"Did you get everything straightened out with Adam?" Marly asked as Noah reached over and turned the lamp off.

"I'm pretty sure that he's on the right path now. I'd no idea that he was shouldering such a heavy burden. Colleen had a spiteful streak in her, that's for sure. I can't grasp how she could take her anger and disappointment in me out on her children. I'm more than positive now that she ensnared Jacob with some kind of weird promise to her." He sighed and closed his eyes. "I don't want to talk about her anymore," he said, sliding close to her and resting his hand lightly on her stomach.

"Adam's going to seminary. He's going to check on enrolling locally. He's a chip off the old block," he said proudly.

"Great, another Pastor Phillips. I don't know if I can handle two of you," she giggled.

"You handle us pretty well if you ask me," he responded.

She smiled to herself and closed her eyes as he began to pray.

Chapter Thirty-nine

It was Sunday, February 11, three days before Valentine's Day. Pastor Jim Wade's church was filled to capacity. Noah smiled as he recognized half of the faces sitting in the pews. They were there in support of him and Marly. He spotted his brother John and his wife Teresa. They had yet to come to the Lord, but Noah knew that the both of them were very close to accepting Christ as their Savior. He glanced at Marly sitting beside Adam and chuckled to himself. She looked ready to explode. Suzette had decided to attend the services and all morning long had been casting sly looks in his direction. He'd ignored her of course, but Marly had caught her one time too many. He prayed that Marly wouldn't have a 'moment' and relive that little episode with Ka' and the neighbor boys. She must have read his mind because she suddenly caught his eye and winked. Noah narrowed his eyes in warning to her which caused her to smile knowingly. When she turned to speak with Adam, he continued to scan the pews. He recognized Levi Jamison sitting in the back, a couple of rows behind Hal and Valerie. Noah listened as Jim started the service with prayer. He knew that their choir would perform at least three songs, to be followed by a soloist and finally Jim would introduce him as the guest speaker.

Marly tried not to go to the restroom during prayer, but lately the baby had begun pushing on her bladder. She excused herself and quietly walked from the sanctuary in search of a restroom. She hoped they were conveniently located. She'd never been in this church before so she didn't have a clue where they were. As she exited the sanctuary, she spotted Levi walking towards her with a ready smile.

"Are you looking for the restrooms?" he asked with a chuckle.

347

"Does it show that much?" she smiled back.

"Not really," he said pointing to where the restrooms were located.

She thanked him gratefully and walked into the ladies room.

Noah opened his eyes and immediately glanced in his wife's direction. Where was she?

He looked at Adam who smiled and mouthed the word, "bathroom."

Noah nodded and leaned back. Lately, the baby had developed this habit of pushing on Marly's bladder. Only two more weeks to go and their daughter would be born. He listened as Jim introduced the choir and politely clapped his hands.

Marly walked out of the restroom to find Levi waiting for her. He stood and prevented her from returning into the sanctuary.

"What are you doing Levi?" she asked with a frown.

"Let's take a walk," he commanded softly, as he firmly grabbed her arm.

Marly attempted to pull from his grasp, but found him to be a lot stronger than he looked.

"Let go of my arm. I'm not going anywhere with you," she spoke in a calm voice. She hoped her fear wasn't showing.

Levi yanked her effortlessly towards him and declared in a threatening voice, "If you want this precious baby of yours to live, then you'll stop struggling."

Marly gasped as she was made aware of the gleaming edge of a hunting knife that Levi had in his possession.

Noah sent Adam out to check on Marly, but when he returned looking somewhat concerned Noah knew within his heart that something was wrong. He looked in the back row and immediately saw that Levi was gone also. A sudden chill ran up his spine as a blind panic hit him.

"Stay calm, Noah, you don't want to panic," he disciplined himself. He caught John's eye and with a quick, barely perceptive motion of his head, indicated to John to meet him outside. He watched his brother come to his feet and head out of the sanctuary. Noah whispered into Jim's ear to hold the fort down until he returned. He excused himself and quickly walked out of the sanctuary followed by an anxious Adam.

Marly was dragged roughly down the hall towards a side door exit. She was praying that Noah would come looking for her and spot her gold key and chain that she had deliberately dropped as Levi had dragged her down the hallway. She knew that she had to make a stand before Levi got her outdoors.

"Why are you doing this to me? What have I done to you?" she cried out.

He stopped abruptly and pulled her to him.

"You are a very pretty woman, but you don't compare to my Colleen. Noah knew how she felt about another woman, yet he married you anyway. I tried to warn him off, but he just had to have you."

She stalled for time. "Did you send those letters?"

The look on his face sent a cold chill through her body. She sensed that he was going to kill her.

Noah had already checked both restrooms and hadn't found a trace of Marly. He listened as John called in the local authorities. Noah decided to search every room in the building. He headed down the hallway, but soon stopped when he spotted the gold key and chain. He looked at John, who seeing the look of panic in his brother's face, raced outside to retrieve his weapon. John yelled over his shoulder that he would meet him at the side exit.

Noah and Adam made their way silently down the hall. They stopped when they heard voices. He could make out Marly pleading with a man. He assumed that man to be Levi. He looked at Adam.

"Son, I don't have time to explain, but play along with me." Noah casually strolled towards the voices. He could clearly make out Levi's profile.

Levi continued talking. "I even tried to make him jealous at the park. Although, I did find myself somewhat attracted to you despite your color; there's a certain something about you. I could see why he'd want to claim you." He snarled as a look of lust appeared on his face. Seconds passed before his train of thought returned and he continued talking. "When that didn't work, I persuaded poor little silly Caroline to file false charges and to circulate a petition against Noah. You do know that she hates you? She was furious when Noah married you. She actually thought he'd marry her. Naturally, I consoled her when she came crying to me. She's quite the little slut."

Before Marly could respond, Noah and Adam rounded the corner.

"So this is why you left the sanctuary, to meet Levi," Noah accused loudly.

Marly looked temporarily confused.

"No, he forced me to come with him."

"I don't believe you. Have you been having an affair?" Noah asked convincingly.

Levi loosed his grip on her arm, enjoying Noah's jealous reaction.

Noah turned to confront Levi. "Colleen wasn't enough? You had to have Marly too?"

Suddenly, the side door was yanked open and John appeared, weapon drawn. Noah reached for Marly and pulled her towards him as he saw the knife come down in a slashing movement. Marly grunted as she was slung towards Adam. She spun around and watched in silent terror as the two men battled. John held the weapon steady and waited for a clean shot.

Noah used his heavier body weight to slam Levi into the wall and force the air out of his lungs. Levi collapsed but was brought straight again by Noah's powerful right uppercut to his chin. Noah showed no mercy as he began pounding Levi's midsection endlessly. Even when the knife dropped haphazardly to the floor, Noah refused to stop until he heard Marly's soft cry of pain.

He turned as if in slow motion. He saw her dazed expression as she touched her side and then looked at her hand. It was covered in a red sticky substance.

He barely heard her soft words of shock, "Noah, he stabbed me, I'm bleeding," before rushing over to catch her collapsing body.

"Marly, sweetheart, it's just a little cut," he said trying to convince her as well as himself, but he knew better.

The wound was serious as evidenced by the pool of blood forming on the floor beside her. Noah looked over his shoulder and saw John with his weapon pointed at an unconscious Levi, yelling into the cell phone for an ambulance to get over here right away. Noah turned and asked Adam if he were wearing a t-shirt and felt a measure of relief when he quickly removed it and handed it to him. Noah wasn't ignorant. He knew that she was losing a lot of blood. He used Adam's shirt to apply pressure which would help to stem the flow of blood coming from her side. Tears began to pour from his eyes as she reached up to play with his hair.

"I love you, Noah," she kept repeating over and over again.

Noah sat down on the floor and pulled her onto his lap making sure he kept the pressure applied to her wound. "I love you too, Cinderella," he managed to say through his tears.

When she stopped talking, he begged her not to leave him. "Please, don't leave me, Marly," he whispered in her ear. "I can't live without you."

Adam watched in silent helplessness as his father begged Marly to stay with him. "This can't be happening," he thought. He listened as his Uncle John pleaded for his father to allow the medics to take her. He wanted to reach for her hand, but he seemed frozen to the spot. Marly was dying. Adam became blinded by his own tears.

"Noah, you gotta let go of her," John pleaded as the paramedics gathered.

Noah reluctantly allowed them to take her. He watched as they put her on the gurney. He relived the day of Chandra's death. "Please, God don't let her be dead," he begged.

"Who's her nearest relative?" a paramedic asked unfeelingly.

John grabbed Noah before he could react and said, "He's her husband, you idiot. Show her some respect."

The seasoned paramedic appeared contrite as he apologized and told Noah that her vital signs were dropping and that she had lost a lot of blood. They needed to get the baby out as soon as possible. Noah climbed into the waiting ambulance and grabbed Marly's limp hand. He closed his eyes and prayed the entire time it took to arrive at the hospital. He was acutely aware of the fact that the brain needed oxygen to survive, and that blood was how oxygen was transported throughout the body. The less blood a person had, the more likely they were to become brain-damaged. Marly had lost consciousness due to the lack of blood and oxygen circulating through her body.

Chapter Forty

Noah stood numb as they rushed his wife into the emergency room. He needed solitude with God, but he had to be strong for Kaod and Adam. He would wait until they both arrived and then he would find someplace to be alone with God. He reached in his pocket, pulled out his phone, and stepped outdoors. Kaod picked up on the first ring. Adam had already called him and given him the gist of what happened. He was on his way there. Someone had pulled some strings and they were flying him, via helicopter, right to the hospital. He would be there in thirty minutes.

Noah turned off his phone and headed back into the hospital. He sat in the corner and hoped no one would attempt to hold a conversation. How could this have happened? Why hadn't he paid closer attention to Levi? Why did he allow her to leave the sanctuary by herself? He'd promised Kaod that he'd protect her with his life. Maybe she would have been better off with Drew. For the first time in his life he genuinely hated someone, Colleen, but she was dead and there was nothing he could do to her.

Noah looked up as the doors opened. Adam and John came in followed by Jim and Hal. He was thankful that no one said a word as they found empty seats. The door opened once more and Layman followed by Marcella and Tina entered. Jim Wade stood and went over to the newcomers. He explained all that he knew and the four of them sat down to wait.

✠

Without warning, a flurry of activity started outside. Sirens were blaring as a helicopter approached the hospital. People watched in amazement as it landed on hospital property. The "Pittbull" had arrived. Adam ran outside to meet his stepbrother. Layman intuitively stood and took a seat closer to Noah. If no one else understood what could possibly take place, Layman did, Noah observed. The entire emergency room suddenly came alive as people began to recognize who was in the helicopter. Kaod and Adam stepped through the doors.

Kaod approached Noah and asked, "Have you heard anything yet?"

Noah stood and the two embraced. A collective sound of released breaths could be heard throughout the room as everyone relaxed. Noah and Layman were the only two who recognized the calm before the storm.

Two excruciatingly long hours had passed before a doctor came out and asked for Noah. Noah turned and motioned for Kaod and Adam to come along. They followed the doctor onto the elevator which stopped on the floor of the nursery. He led them down the hall and with a smile, pointed to Noah's tiny daughter. Kaod and Adam hugged each other as the doctor explained that the baby was healthy in every way. They were still waiting on a couple of test results, but they weren't anticipating any problems. Noah stared at the doctor.

"What about my wife?"

"I don't know Pastor. My job was to get your daughter out as quickly as possible in order for surgery to be performed on your wife."

He apologized for not being able to give him more detailed information. Noah knew in his heart that it was not looking favorably for Marly. He turned and looked at the tiny sleeping infant. She was beautiful, just like her mother. She had black curly hair like his. He'd never seen a baby born with so much hair. Her skin was a light caramel brown. He wondered what her eyes looked like. As if on cue, she opened them. He did a double take. Staring back at him were tiny versions of his eyes. He was amazed and his mind immediately went back to Marly. She'd wanted their baby to have his eyes. There was a tap on the window and one of the nurses asked if they'd like to hold her. Kaod and Adam nodded eagerly, but Noah walked away. He needed to get back downstairs, back to his wife.

Noah didn't say a word about the baby as he walked into the emergency room. He soon realized that he didn't have to. Adam had called John who had spread the word. He was relieved when the room cleared. Everyone wanted to see his and Marly's daughter. He closed his eyes. He just wanted his wife back.

Layman stared at his friend. He'd never ever seen Noah in such a state. He prayed that the Lord would have mercy on Noah and not allow Marly to die. She meant the world to Noah and Layman wasn't so sure that Noah could bounce back from her death.

Rumor had it that Levi was in this same hospital in the intensive care unit as a result of the beating that Noah had given him. People were already saying that though Levi had tried to take Marly's life, she had saved his when she had called out to Noah. He smiled at the memory of Noah telling him about this woman he had met. He had gone on and on about her for the longest. Finally, Noah had looked at him and said, "Did I tell you that she is black?" He'd thought that Noah was joking. He'd tried to talk him out of it, not due to color, but because of his position and where he pastored; however, Noah had been adamant that God had given Marly to him. Layman had known that they would have a hard time of it, but if any couple could make it work, Noah and Marly could. Those two loved each other, of that, there was no doubt.

Layman quickly wiped a tear from his eye and said, "You know that sooner or later Kaod is going to erupt don't you?"

Noah shook his head yes without bothering to open his eyes.

"How's your daughter?" Layman asked, trying to give him a reason not to shut down.

"She's beautiful, just like her mother," he repeated unemotionally. Still, he kept his eyes closed.

"Noah, why don't you go to the chapel? I promise to stay right here and tell the doctor where to find you."

Noah stood to his feet, embraced Layman, and headed for the chapel.

✠

Noah opened the door of the chapel and sighed with relief when he found it vacant. He stared at the empty cross. What right did he have to petition God for anything? God had already given him everything. He'd sent his only son to die for his sins. Noah knew what the world had done with God's gift had broken God's heart. He had watched from heaven as His son was beaten, humiliated, and crucified. He had listened as they called His son the vilest of names and spit upon Him. His son had done no wrong to anyone. He had healed the sick, fed the hungry, cast out demons, and raised the dead all in the name of His Father. Jesus had died an innocent man's death in order to become the bridge back to God and how has man thanked Him? He is still being spit upon, called names, kicked out of places, and crucified daily. The world still hates his goodness even today. All one has to do is take a look around. There isn't a second that goes by where sin isn't happening. He was now experiencing a little of God's pain because in some aspects Marly had been treated that way. She'd done nothing wrong, yet people had mistreated her and had called her hurtful names. Noah knew that God owed him nothing and he owed God everything, yet he knelt before the cross and cried. He cried for himself, but mostly he cried for her. She hadn't done a thing to Colleen or Levi, yet she had suffered. He unashamedly lay before the cross sharing his heart.

He told God of his love for Him and of His righteous judgment. He confessed his hatred for Colleen and even for Levi and asked for forgiveness. He prayed that Kaod would forgive him for what happened today and his failure to protect her. Noah confessed that maybe he loved Marly too much, because he didn't want to live without her. He told God that he never put her before Him, but he loved her more than he loved himself. He thanked God as the tears streamed down his face, for the wife that He had given him and for their time together. He thanked God for their children and friends. Most importantly, he thanked God for the gift of His son and for Jesus' obedience and willingness to die on the cross. Finally, he asked God for mercy on behalf of Marly and the strength to endure regardless of the outcome, and then Noah sat quietly, waiting for an answer.

Minutes later, he heard the door open and turned to face Marly's doctor.

"I'm sorry, Pastor Phillips, we've done all that we could. Your wife survived the surgery, but she's lost too much blood and as a result her brain is no longer viable."

Noah stared at the doctor. He willed himself not to show any emotion as the doctor explained that the knife had sliced into her uterus…He tuned out the rest of the doctor's explanation.

Noah stepped off the elevator and headed towards his wife's room. He sucked in his breath at the sight of her. There were so many tubes. He walked over to her and reached for her hand.

"I'm sorry, Cinderella," he said as he dropped onto the chair beside her bed. "I couldn't rescue you. Your Prince Charming let you down."

He brushed her hand with his lips and stared at her face. He reached for the hospital phone and called down to the emergency room. He gave Layman all the pertinent information.

"They're on the way up. Let's make this look good, Mrs. Phillips," he said gazing at Marly.

✝

Kaod pinched himself. This had to be a bad dream. Noah was explaining that his mother was never going to walk or talk again, that she couldn't even breathe on her own. His mind couldn't comprehend the she had no brain activity whatsoever. This had to be a huge mistake. She was fine. Hadn't he talked to her just this morning? He heard crying. He looked up and saw Adam and Ms. Tina wiping tears from their eyes. Everyone, except Noah seemed to be crying. He leaned over and grabbed his mom's hand. He squeezed it, hoping beyond hope that there would be some type of response, but nothing happened. It was as though the life had already gone out of her. He was suddenly afraid of the future and angry that his mother would not be there to face it with him. He felt like that lost little boy facing the first day of school, being away from his mommy for the first time in his life.

Noah recognized that wild frightened look in Kaod's eyes. He'd encountered it countless times during his many hospital visits. He quietly asked everyone, except Kaod, to leave. As soon as the door had closed he turned and faced his stepson.

Kaod flew across the room and grabbed Noah by his jacket. The jacket parted, revealing Noah's blood soaked shirt.

"You promised me that you'd protect her," he shouted as he stared at his mother's blood staining his stepfather's shirt.

Noah didn't say a word nor did he try to defend himself. Kaod slammed him against the locker but didn't let go. Noah gently put his arms around his son as Kaod began to sob loudly. His anguished cries tore at Noah's soul. He knew that the two of them had lost the most, and that nothing could ever repair the gaping hole in their hearts. Kaod stayed in that position for a long while before he had the emotional strength to pull himself away. He went into the bathroom and shut the door.

Noah walked over to the window and glanced out. What was going on down there? It looked as though a crowd was gathering. He turned and picked up the phone as it rang. It was John informing him that people were beginning to gather in an impromptu prayer vigil for Marly. John was excited. He told Noah that both blacks and whites were out there. Noah thanked God. Maybe, Marly's death would be used to bring unity to the community as a whole.

"Ka', come and look at this," he called out.

Chapter Forty-one

Alone at last, Noah cradled his daughter in his arms and thanked God for her health. Through her, he would always have a piece of Marly. He had gotten permission to bring his daughter to meet her mother. He placed the tiny infant in the crook of her mother's arm. They were beautiful. He took out his phone and snapped several pictures and then he simply gazed at the two most important females in his life. Tears flowed down his face as he watched Marly's partially lifeless body. He bent down and kissed her lips and placed her hand to his cheek. They hadn't had enough time together he whispered. He understood God's will, but right now he was in so much pain. He also knew that Marly would be going to heaven, but he was selfish enough to want her to stay with him. Looking at their tiny daughter did little to dull the ache in his heart. He wanted his wife back. He wanted that quirky, shy, stubborn, extremely lovable woman. Only she could occupy that special place in his heart. In truth, he wanted to lie on that bed with her, close his eyes, and never wake up. The sound of a small cry brought him back to reality. His daughter was hungry. He fiddled around in the little bag that the nurse had given him for a bottle. He picked up the baby and sat in the chair next to Marly. He had to push through this. God in his infinite wisdom had granted mercy to their child and she needed him. Noah looked down at the baby.

"Mercy," he spoke softly.

She would be christened Mercy Noel Phillips. It was an appropriate name for their daughter and Kaod would be thrilled since he'd suggested the name "Noel".

✞

Noah held his wife's hand. He had spent the night by her bedside. He hadn't slept a wink. He and Kaod had agreed to remove Marly from the life support machines at nine o'clock this morning. It was the most difficult decision that he'd ever had to make. He and Mercy had stayed with her the whole night. He knew that most would think it silly, but he had tried to explain to their infant daughter the decision to remove her mom from the life support equipment. He'd also recounted to her every single detail of their life together. He'd started with the seminar, their first kiss, the description of their wedding, and ended with today's events. He told her how much her mommy, daddy, and brothers loved her, and how her big brother Jacob was on his way. Noah stood and walked over to the window. It was cold outside, but the crowd had steadily increased. Why did it take a tragedy to get people to wake up? He spotted the TV cameras and reporters. He likened them to vultures, circling overhead and waiting for something to die. He shook his head in disgust. They were selling papers and getting higher ratings off the death of his wife. One reporter had even asked him how he felt about the fact that his wife and Levi were being treated in the same hospital. He'd ignored the woman and brushed past her.

He looked up as a defeated looking Kaod, followed by a somber Adam, walked slowly into the room. Kaod avoided looking in his mother's direction. Noah had been witness to the same type of reaction displayed by others in the past. It was obvious to him that Kaod didn't want to, or was unable to deal with the finality of his mother's prognosis. Noah had instructed Adam not to leave Kaod for any reason. Now was not the time for his youngest son to be alone. Marly had been Kaod's life. She'd always been his one stable factor, the person he counted on to be there. She'd pushed him to be the best he could be, never allowing him to quit. She was his drive for success. It was going to be a long, up-hill battle for Kaod to overcome the tragedy of his mother's death. Noah was genuinely afraid for Kaod and how he would cope under these circumstances. He prayed that Kaod would be able to forgive, in time. He made a vow to God that Kaod would never be without family. His marriage to Marly meant that Kaod was now his son. He would be there for Kaod as though he was his true father.

Noah thanked God for the support of his loyal friends. Layman, Hal, and Jim were all asked to be there. Tina, Marly's best friend, had declined. Noah understood why and could not blame her or anyone else if they opted not to be present. He could tell by his sons' faces that they had not slept at all either. He listened as Adam and Kaod talked about their baby sister. He had already called and asked one of the nurses to bring up more supplies for Mercy. The door opened and a haggard looking Jacob walked in. It was obvious that he'd come straight from the airport. He took one look at Marly and immediately broke down. He asked his dad and then Kaod to forgive him for the things he'd said and how he'd treated her and, for the thoughts he'd had concerning their marriage. He held her hand and tenderly kissed her cheek. He told her that she had already been a positive influence in his and Kara's lives. Noah listened and willed himself to stay strong for his children. No tears were present in his eyes. He would cry in private. He would cry alone.

✝

Noah looked at every person in the room. His three sons, his infant daughter, his brother John, Hal, Layman, and Jim Wade were all present. He bowed his head and began praying. He had always known that the Lord was in control, but in this, it seemed to hit home. He prayed for strength, endurance, and love. A faint smile creased the corner of his mouth when he heard Layman add, "...and a belief in miracles". He walked over, placed Mercy beside her mother, and took his wife's hand in his and began speaking in a tender tone.

"Marly, I couldn't have asked for a more perfect wife or mother. From the moment I saw you, I knew you were going to be my wife. You are my soul mate, my right hand, the true love of my life. Without you, I will forever be half a man. I promise that our daughter will grow up knowing her mother and the love we shared. I also promise you that I will watch over Kaod as though he were my very own. Thank you, for accepting my sons. I know that it wasn't easy, but you made it look that way. Forgive me for the times that I may have inadvertently hurt you, but when you reach heaven always remember that I have always and will always love you. Wait patiently for me Cinderella as I wait for God to call me home."

He looked at Kaod and waited for his approval to shut down the equipment. With tears streaming down his face, Kaod nodded. Noah turned towards the doctor and gave the okay. He watched as one by one each machine was clicked off. He appeared calm and controlled on the outside, but a voice on the inside screamed, "No!"

He fought against the urge to run back to each machine and turn them back on. He listened as the room became silent. The only thing heard was the melodic beep from the equipment that monitored Marly's heart rate. Noah observed the doctor with pen in hand ready to annotate the time and date of death. He bent down and nestled his head in between her shoulder and her neck, waiting, listening for the monitor to flat line.

Marly felt suspended in time. She was in a holding station. Waiting for something to happen, but she had no way of understanding what that something was. She looked around, but she was surrounded by voidness. Why was she here? What was she waiting on? Where was Noah, had he abandoned her? She was weightless and emotionless. Then, she became aware of His presence. Jesus was there, holding her hand.

One minute passed, and then two, and finally five, still her heartbeat continued. Noah placed his ear near her nose. It couldn't be. She was breathing unaided. Noah jerked a look towards the doctor. The physician couldn't disguise the look of confusion displayed all over his face. Suddenly, inexplicably Noah fell to his knees and began to worship God. He began to experience love, peace, joy, goodness, mercy, compassion, understanding, and a host of other godly attributes all at once. It overwhelmed him to the point that his only posture was that of bowing and his only words were those of praise. He couldn't move. He dared not move. Noah heard a voice from within declare, "Glorify my name!" As suddenly as it came, it was gone.

Marly felt His perfectness, the purity of His holiness. Nothing on earth could have prepared her for this. There was nothing in her limited mind that could compare to the sheer beauty of the peace and joy that was overwhelming her senses. "Don't look at me Lord!" her mortal mind screamed, but the spirit within her rejoiced.

"Return to your husband. You are my gift unto him," His voice declared.

Marly's spirit leaped in obedience, as though her flesh no longer existed. Her only desire was to do His will. Her mind seemed unable to communicate anything other than complete selflessness. She had somehow become one with His spirit. Marly smiled and opened her eyes.

Noah opened his eyes and looked around. The doctor had disappeared while John and Jacob looked confused as they, along with the others in the room, slowly climb to their feet with indefinable expressions on their faces.

Noah glanced at Marly. She was gazing at him smiling. He was afraid to speak or to let go of her hand. Was he dreaming? If so, he refused to move or in any way disturb this moment with her.

He heard Kaod call her questioningly, "Mom?", and then with confidence, "Mom!"

Noah closed his eyes and then opened them slowly, afraid that he'd find her gone. She was still there.

"Marly," Noah whispered hoarsely. "Talk to me sweetheart," he commanded gently.

"I love you, Noah," she said weakly.

The whole room, except John and Jacob, erupted in praise. Those two were still looking on in utter fright and confusion. Noah, overcome with thankfulness, buried his face in her neck and wept unashamedly.

☦

Everyone present watched as several doctors and technicians arrived. The physicians immediately began to examine her, while the technicians searched in vain for malfunctions in the equipment. Marly had fallen back asleep but new equipment brought in to replace the old, showed her vitals to be within the normal range. A medical team approached Noah and asked for, and received permission to conduct new tests on his wife.

Layman grinned at Noah and said in a loud voice, "I can tell them what happened. They don't need to run any more tests. The Great Physician was in here today, and He's the one that operated on her. He graduated, numeral uno, from the top medical college in the universe. The college of the mighty 'I AM'."

Noah gazed at a sleeping Marly and concurred. Dr. Jesus had performed a miracle today and all glory would be given to Him.

☦

With all the excitement over, Noah took the time to observe each person that was present during the miraculous events of his wife's recovery. The only two that hadn't seemed to understand what had taken place were John and Jacob. He could understand John since he wasn't a professing believer, but Jacob, had he ever truly dedicated his life to Christ? Had he fooled himself and everyone else? Was he pretending like his mother had done? That would explain his initial hatred of Marly and Kaod. He hoped that Jacob, after witnessing today's miracle, would dedicate his life to Christ and become a true believer. He would never be at peace any other way.

Noah heard the door open and turned to see a disheveled Tina quickly enter the room. She approached her best friend's bedside and stared at a sleeping Marly and then glanced hopefully at Noah who nodded yes. She hugged him happily and sat down near the bed.

"What happened?" she whispered. "Kaod called and told me that they removed her from life support and she just started breathing on her own. I don't understand. I thought her doctor said that her brain was not functioning."

Noah gazed at his wife and softly began telling Tina everything that had transpired. When he finished, Tina was speechless. She stared at Noah.

"Are you telling me that God performed some kind of miracle on Marlena?"

"That's exactly what I'm saying, whether you believe it, or not, is your choice."

"What are the doctors saying?" Tina wanted to know.

Noah grinned slightly, "They don't know what to say. They've been running the same test on her all morning. They've had technicians checking and rechecking her equipment. I think they're afraid that I may sue or go to the papers."

"Are you serious? They really have no clue what happened?" Tina questioned again.

Noah shook his head and smiled.

"Will she make a complete recovery? She'll be the same as before?" she inquired.

"Do you mean will she still be stubborn, hardheaded, and quirky? I certainly hope so," he laughed. He looked at Marly tenderly. "I don't know if I could have made it without her."

Tina gave his hand a squeeze and said, "God knew that, Noah. That's why he gave her back to you. You're a good husband and father. You do know that she's never responded to anyone the way that she responds to you. You are her soul mate."

Noah nodded and stood as Kaod came into the room holding his sister.

"Ms. Tina, have you met Mercy? Isn't she beautiful? I think she looks just like a combination of both Mom and Dad."

Tina glanced quickly at Noah who smiled proudly. She couldn't tell whether he was more proud of the baby or of the fact that Ka' had just called him Dad.

Tina held Mercy and laughed when she opened her eyes. They were charcoal grey, the same as her father's, as was her curly black hair. In all other aspects, she was the spitting image of her mother.

"I think you're right Ka'. She does look like both parents. Do you think she'll be as stubborn as your mom?"

Kaod laughed and said, "I think Dad is going to have his hands full, but I'm sure that he can handle it. If he can manage Mom, a daughter should be a piece of cake."

Noah looked at Kaod and chuckled, "Thanks for the vote of confidence, but I haven't even come close to managing your mother. That's an art that I have yet to master, but she's just very good at making me think I have."

✞

Noah and his sons stepped into the elevator. He pushed the number one and relaxed. He needed sleep, but the crowd was refusing to leave until he spoke to them, and they hadn't yet heard the good news. The doors opened and immediately they were surrounded by cameras and reporters. He listened as they offered up their condolences, but said nothing as he walked to greet the crowd of supporters. He spotted Sasha standing off to the side and motioned to Kaod. He chuckled softly as Kaod quickly masked his delight. Noah knew that Sasha had been giving Kaod a run for his money. He turned his attention back to the crowd as he approached them. The people grew quiet when they recognized the Phillips family. A microphone was thrust into Noah's hand as he began to address the crowd. He thanked them for their support and prayers and informed them that God had heard, despite what the media claimed. He, with a tired smile on his face, informed them of the miracle that had taken place. He did not go into details, but said that both his wife and brand new daughter were blessed by God. The crowd shouted praises to the Lord. After several minutes, he bowed his head and led them in prayer. Ignoring the press, he rode the elevator back to Marly's room where he intended to get some much needed rest.

✞

Noah lovingly watched his wife as she slept peacefully. The hospital staff had moved Marly into a larger, more private room. They had even rolled an extra bed in for his use. He noticed that the room had a bathtub/shower off to the side. He needed to go home and get his overnight bag, but he didn't want to leave her just yet. Maybe he'd send one of his sons

364

to fetch it later on. He took his shoes off and lay back on the bed. He was sound asleep in a matter of minutes.

The three brothers came into the room and abruptly stood still. Their dad was sleeping in a bed next to Marly. He finally looked at peace. If any of them had questions pertaining to the love their parents felt for each other, they were erased with the past days' events. Not a person who'd witnessed Noah's reactions to Marly's possible death could doubt the bond he had with her or the bond she had with him. Adam had told his brothers of Marly's and their dad's words to each other before she'd lapsed into unconsciousness. Adam shook his head and smiled.

"I guess I'd better go and get Dad's overnight bag. I doubt if he'll want to leave the hospital anytime soon."

"A team of wild horses couldn't drag him away from Mom," Kaod added.

Jacob looked from Adam to Kaod and asked, "What do you think happened with Marly this morning? Do you really think it had something to do with the equipment or misinterpretations of prior tests?"

Both Kaod and Adam stared at Jacob in disbelief.

"Are you serious, Jake?" Adam questioned, aghast at his brother's words.

"That was nothing but the hand of Jesus in that room. You couldn't feel the pure goodness? The only thing I could do was bow. I felt so filthy, so unclean. That was a personal touch from our Lord. There was nothing wrong with their equipment. That's a lie straight from the pit of hell," Kaod finished, almost daring Jacob to deny it.

"Yeah, yeah, I felt it too. I just wanted to make sure that I wasn't the only one," Jacob said, trying his best to sound convincing.

Kaod scrutinized Jacob's words. He said nothing, but he secretly doubted that Jacob was a true child of God.

Chapter Forty-two

Marly awoke to a baby's cry. She felt so weak and tired. She forced her eyes open and squinted. It took a few seconds, but her vision finally cleared. Where was she? Then she remembered Levi and the knife. She began to panic until familiar arms held her close to his chest. She listened to his heartbeat and it soothed her fears. She felt safe. Soon she was drifting back into a sound sleep, but she knew that Noah, her husband, was nearby to protect her.

Noah stayed close to his wife's side. She'd been drifting in and out of consciousness for a little over two days. Her primary care physician had explained to him that physically she was healing and should have no problems making a full recovery, but they had to wait and see what her psychological state would be. She'd just gone through a horrific ordeal, and that was playing a large role in her refusal to stay awake. In the doctor's opinion, she was dealing with it by remaining in an unconscious state.

Noah had witnessed the panic in her face on one of the few occasions that she'd awakened. He wasn't worried. He knew his wife, and she'd come back when she felt ready to confront her fears. Until then, he'd be right by her side.

☦

Marly eased her eyelids open. The fear had begun to dissipate. What was that laying beside her? It was her baby. She reached out her hand and gently touched her daughter. She was beautiful. Marly touched the shiny black curls and smiled.

"Welcome back Cinderella," a husky voice said.

She turned towards the voice and whispered, "She has your hair."

"She has my eyes too, only bigger," Noah added with a smile. His voice became serious when he asked her, "Are you staying with me this time, or are you going to drift off again?"

She fought the urge to close her eyes. "I'm staying. I love you, Noah."

Noah picked up their daughter and handed her to Kaod. He didn't care what anyone thought as he sat on the bed and pulled his wife into his arms.

"Don't you ever leave me again; I love you more than anything in this world. Do you understand that Mrs. Phillips?"

Marly blushed when she looked over his shoulder and saw the crowded room. She hid her face against his chest.

He whispered in her ear, "Say hello to Kaod. He's been missing you."

Her eyes found Kaod. He was holding his sister, but his gaze was on his mother's face. There were tears in his eyes and he looked slightly lost.

"I love you, Ka'," she spoke softly.

He gently handed his sister to Adam and rushed to his mom. Noah stood and stepped to the side as mother and son embraced. He thanked God for sparing her and their daughter. He watched as one by one, those present, hugged her and offered up thanks to God. There wasn't a dry eye in the room.

Chapter Forty-three

Noah held on to his wife's hand as the County Prosecutor questioned her concerning the events that had taken place. Marly answered the questions in a very clear and concise manner. Noah was extremely proud of her. He knew that she was still suffering from the emotional trauma of it all. He had been dead set against them conducting this interview, but John had explained the necessity of the authorities gathering facts while they were still fresh in Marly's mind. Judging from the amount of nightmares she continued to have, he didn't think she was in danger of forgetting what had happened to her. Noah had made it absolutely clear to everyone that there was to be no mention of the fact that Levi was still a patient in the hospital as well. He had also forbidden the press to come near her, and had turned down all requests for interviews. Members from both churches, Noah's as well as Pastor Wade's, had volunteered to stand guard outside Marly's room in order to keep the press at bay.

"If nothing else, Levi's actions had managed to pull people from all walks of life together," Noah thought as he glanced at what looked like hundreds of flowers, balloons, stuffed animals, and cards that had begun to overtake her hospital room. He'd even received a call from Valerie stating that dozens of cards and letters addressed to the Phillips family had been arriving daily at the church. Noah had instructed her to place them in a box until he could get over to his office to retrieve them. He was still very much reluctant to leave Marly alone. He wasn't the only one who felt that way. Kaod and Adam had hardly left the hospital. It had taken both Marly and Noah to convince Kaod to return to Ohio State. He'd already missed a week's worth of work that he'd have to make up, but all of his professors had rallied around Kaod and were allowing him to make up his assignments.

"Just one more thing to be thankful for," Noah realized. He glanced at his watch. They'd been questioning Marly for almost an hour and he could tell that she was exhausted.

"Can we finish this another time? My wife is exhausted and she needs to rest," Noah said, standing to his feet and making it clear that it really wasn't a request.

"Sure thing Pastor Phillips. There are still a few more details that we need to ask your wife, but we can postpone those for a later date," Attorney Carson said as he thanked Noah and Marly for their time. He handed Noah his business card on the way out and informed them that his office would be in touch. The two men shook hands as they stepped outside the room.

"Your wife's a pretty strong woman," Attorney Carson complimented.

"Yes, she is. I'm blessed that she agreed to marry me," Noah supplied in a matter-of-fact voice.

Attorney Carson hesitated for a moment and then stated, "I want you to know that I'll be handling this case personally, and that I'm going to do everything within my power to see that this guy doesn't see the outside of a prison wall for a very long time."

Noah nodded in appreciation. The thought of Levi walking around free as a bird was a thought he couldn't afford to entertain. "Trust God," he reminded himself as he watched Carson walk towards the elevator. He turned and walked back into the room. Marly's big brown eyes looked apprehensive. She didn't relax until he stretched his long frame onto the bed beside her and pulled her into his arms.

"Get some rest sweetheart, I'm not going anywhere."

Marly was soon sleeping peacefully. Noah glanced at Mercy, who was also sleeping soundly in her bed. He closed his eyes and thanked God, resting in the knowledge that God had put a protective hedge around them.

✠

Noah looked over at Marly as he pulled into the garage. She'd lost a lot of weight and was way too thin. She hadn't eaten very much during her month long stay at the hospital. She was still tender due to the surgery and that, coupled with thoughts of Levi had caused her to have difficulty sleeping. She'd refused to take anything but over-the-counter medicine. He hoped that being home would bring some peace of mind to her. He definitely intended to get her to eat more. He glanced in the back seat. Mercy, on the other hand, seemed to have no problem eating or sleeping. She wasn't a fussy baby in the least. She'd spent the entire month with them in the hospital. He reached over and grabbed Marly's hand. Together they offered up thanks to God and prayed for Him to lead them.

✞

Marly rested comfortably on the bed and watched Noah and Mercy on the monitor. He had given the baby a bath and was now preparing her for bed. She listened as he prayed for Mercy. Already he was teaching her the importance of prayer. Marly eased off the bed and stiffly headed into the bathroom. She was feeling better and she wanted to take a bath. She sat on the edge of the tub waiting for the water to reach the right level. Her mind drifted back in time to the church and Levi. She was so deep in thought that she didn't hear Noah's approach.

Noah stood in the doorway observing Marly. She was oblivious to his presence. She seemed in a trance. He watched as fear gripped her. He knew that she was reliving that day. She hadn't been the same since. She hardly ever smiled or laughed aloud. Getting her to eat was a task in and of itself. She was keeping everything locked up inside and he could only pray that she'd break and allow it to all come out. He observed the level of the water rising.

"Marly," he spoke softly, "turn the water off." He reached around her and turned the spigot off when she didn't respond.

Marly felt something brush against her and screamed. She could hear herself screaming over and over again, but she couldn't seem to stop. She felt his arms go around her and heard his gentle voice.

"Marly, Marly, it's okay. I'm here," he whispered into her ear, "He can't hurt you anymore. You're safe, sweetheart."

Slowly she relaxed against him. She raised her head and looked at Noah.

"I'm sorry. I don't know what's happening to me. I seem to be encased in some kind of fear. It haunts me," she blurted out tiredly.

Noah smiled at her. At least she'd begun to talk. He walked out of the bathroom and returned with the baby's monitor. He situated it on the counter and then began casually undressing, talking to her the entire time. When he had finished, he stepped into the tub and closed his eyes.

"Are you going to stand there and gawk or are you getting in?"

She was staring wide-eyed at him. She'd always bathed alone. He still had his eyes closed as she slowly stepped out of her clothing and into the tub. The bath tub was obviously built for two so there was plenty of room as she slid into the hot water beside him. He opened his eyes and looked at her. She began to giggle as she stared back at her husband covered in bubbles.

"You are going to smell like a woman," she laughed.

"If you keep laughing at me, I'm going to get out," he pointed out in mock sternness.

That sent her into a fit of laughter. He pretended as though he were going to get out.

"Okay, okay, I won't laugh anymore," she said, throwing herself across him.

Her feeble attempts to imprison him in the tub made him smile as he lay back. He glanced at her. She was trying hard to smother her laughter. He'd missed hearing her laugh and her accented voice.

"Tell me what's going on in that head of yours," he said casually.

He put his arm around her shoulders and pulled her close. She let it all out. She told him about Levi and about her experience in the holding tank (That's what she called it). She'd felt Jesus' presence and began describing it. Jesus was there and the next moment she was opening her eyes and looking at Noah. She turned and faced Noah.

"He spoke to my heart. Jesus said that He was sending me back as a gift to you, but I wanted to stay with Him," she confessed guiltily. "I'm sorry, Noah. I love you so much, but I feel guilty, as though I betrayed you. I watch how you take such good care of me and of Mercy," she apologized.

"Are you sorry for loving God more than you love me? Marly, you of all people should know the greatest commandment, and it certainly isn't to love me first. I wanted you back with me. I was selfish. I needed you, I still need you, but I need you to love God first. That's something you've always done. Why should it make you feel guilty now? I experienced His perfect goodness in your hospital room the day you were healed, and I too, would rather have that than anything the world has to offer me and that includes you, sweetheart."

She looked into his eyes. He meant it. She threw her arms around him and thanked him. Noah hugged her back and thanked God. His wife constantly amazed him. Most women demanded to be loved above any and every thing. His mind went back to Colleen. She'd been jealous of his time with God to the point of throwing temper tantrums. She hadn't wanted to learn the Word nor had she wanted him to. She had demanded that he be enamored of her and nothing else.

Noah smiled as Marly reached for her washcloth and began lathering it. She'd gotten comfortable.

"She glanced over her shoulder at him and exclaimed, "There's one more thing. I don't trust you white guys anymore. You're all nuts!"

It was his turn to stare before he exploded with laughter.

He was still laughing as they lay in bed and he pulled her close. After their nightly prayer, she slowly rolled onto her good side and nestled her head onto his chest. She sighed in pleasure when she was at last able to assume her favorite sleeping position without the nagging pain. He was gently massaging her injured side and thinking about her fear.

"Marly, you do understand that God saved you, not me. I did everything I possibly could, but in the end, I failed. I would give my life for yours any day, but God is your ultimate protector. You have no reason to be afraid." She nodded in understanding and closed her eyes. He truly hoped she did.

He listened to her breathing and knew she was sleeping. God was mystifying in many ways. Tonight for instance, it was the first time he'd ever bathed with his wife. There had been no sensuality to it. They had been as children enjoying each other's companionship. They had conversed about the events that led to her hospitalization, the bad dreams, and Levi's eventual trial. The bath had allowed her to relax and open up to him. She had been able to share her burdens in a way that had put her at ease and had brought them closer together. They had reached another pinnacle in their relationship, yet it had never occurred to him that he could bathe with his wife, but not see her nakedness. It was a mystery to him because he'd missed being intimate with her throughout the past months. God, he reasoned, had blinded him to his need in order to assist Marly with hers. He fell asleep thinking about God's mysterious ways.

Chapter Forty-four

It was difficult to believe that an entire year had passed. Where had the time gone? Already she and Noah were celebrating their first anniversary. Marly smiled to herself as Tina dropped her off at the house. She'd been planning this for the last couple of weeks. She'd even called Valerie ahead of time to see if she could arrange for Noah to tie up some loose ends at the office today. He'd hardly let Marly out of his sight since she'd come home from the hospital. Marly knew that Noah was scheduled to preach on Sunday for the first time since his leave of absence and that their entire family would be home on Saturday. She had to take advantage of the next three days. If this didn't work, she didn't know what would. He seemed afraid to touch her ever since she'd come home from the hospital. She'd tried everything, but to no avail.

Noah glanced at his watch. It was their first anniversary today and he wondered if Marly would want to go to Sophia's. "She seemed to be doing better," he thought as he left the church and headed home. He pulled into the garage and wondered where Marly could be. Her car was missing so he assumed that Tina had probably taken her somewhere. He unlocked the door and headed towards the bedroom where he decided to take a quick shower.

Noah jumped out of the shower, wrapped a towel around his waist and walked into the bedroom. He stopped dead in his tracks. There, standing in front of him, was a vision of absolute loveliness. His wife, with her hair done exactly the way it had been on their wedding day, was standing before him in the shimmering brown nightgown that he had purchased the week of their wedding, and that she had yet to wear. It reminded him of their wedding night, her blush and all. She'd remembered her Thanksgiving promise. He said the first thing that came to mind.

"Where's the baby?"

She smiled shyly, "She's at Tina's for the night."

"Oh sweetheart, that's not long enough," he said as he came across the room and gathered her into his arms. "Are you sure you're feeling up to this?" he asked huskily, in between kisses.

In response, her arms went up, around his neck, and found their way into his hair. She was positive.

He was deep in thought as he traced the permanent scars imprinted on his wife's side and abdomen. Whenever he saw them, it reminded him of how much this woman completed his life. God had blessed him by restoring her health. They'd been through so much in such a short time, yet they'd come so far, both in their relationship with God and in their relationship with each other. He'd learned so much. Intimacy wasn't about having the power to command a physical response from your mate, but the natural extension of your relationship with your mate. It required hard work and dedication not only to that person, but to God's authority. Marlena's response to him was directly linked to his response to God. He recalled their bath together and wondered how things would have turned out if he had sought physical satisfaction to her deeply emotional need. He'd allowed God to lead which had brought emotional healing to her. He smiled to himself. She'd rewarded his obedience to God with the giving of herself to him tonight. She'd not held back. Her response to him had been that of a woman desiring to please her husband. She had searched for and found out his pleasure. She had dedicated herself to understanding him and had pleased him beyond expectation. This was his woman in every conceivable sense of the word. His love for her knew no bounds. She was his and he was hers. She was given to him by God's edict and he had given himself to her by his freewill choice of obedience to God's command. He had chosen to love his wife as Christ loves the church.

Noah leaned forward and met his wife's lips in a tender kiss. "What are you thinking about?" he asked softly.

She smiled up at him. "I was thinking about the type of man that I'd like Mercy to marry."

"And what type of man is that?" he wondered as his lips began a slow exploration of her neck.

She turned and whispered in his ear, "The Noah type."

His eyes met hers and then he smiled and proclaimed lovingly, "And you, Cinderella, are exactly my type."